For Jennifer:
With me always

PROLOGUE
FROM HER PAST...

She enjoyed seeing those chains of pure silver wrapped around the vampire's scrawny arms like tattoos. He barely resembled the picture of the old parish priest the Cardinal sent them two weeks ago. His brown skin hung from his bones like an ill-fitting suit. His paunch bounced up and down as he struggled to get loose. It took longer to catch him, much longer than it should have, but all's well that ends well.

Alex Stone, call-sign *Dagger*, ran her fingers through her dark hair. Flakes of dried blood and sand fell as she pulled the dirty mess into a ponytail. Benjamin Palmer, Team Commander, snatched her wounded hand back down and tightened the field dressing as he griped at her about how dumb it was to try to catch the sharp end of a knife with her hand. She knew that . . . now.

"Who do you think you are," he said as he gave the knot one last yank, "Superman?" Ben checked her busted lip with a shake of his head. "That's gonna hurt like hell 'til morning."

Alex just nodded, taking the pills in her good hand and swallowing them with a quick sip of warm water from his canteen.

Under normal circumstances, Alex would be

pulled from the field, evaluated, and possibly scrubbed from the next assignment for that stunt. But time was running out and this wasn't normal, not even for the top vampire hunting team in the country.

"We are no longer taking orders from them," the vampire barked. "The Council has gone soft living among humans. My sire will not bow to their rule any longer!"

This rogue clan called themselves 'Hellclaw'. They broke the agreement and trashed an entire village, so the Council of Pure Blood Vampires asked for help rounding them up and delivering them for punishment. Only this guy wasn't going to the Council.

This guy belonged to the Catholic Church. In their eyes, his being turned was an attack on the Vatican. And because vampirism had no real cure, he would be executed to save his immortal soul. Alex remembered having met a few Cardinals or whatever and they were a lot scarier than any vampire she'd ever come across. So if they were asking the DOD to get involved in his capture, he must be pretty important; although she couldn't see why if he'd been stuck out here in the middle of nowhere Mexico.

From the pew at the back of the small church, Alex and Ben watched as Matthias "Matt" Wolfe and K.C Becker conducted the interrogation like Beavis and Butthead on sedatives. They liked to get up close and personal with the vamps they captured—try to piss them off as much as possible. But the slow waltz was getting boring and they promised to wrap this up quick.

"Oh please," Matt said as the vampire spat and growled. "Your *sire* is on the Council's shit list! You can't just go snacking on innocents and expect us or them to turn a blind eye. And you're a priest! You think the Catholics are gonna take that lying down? No, sir!"

Their prisoner continued to try his luck at the chains. "Humans, you're such simple creatures. My sire is not afraid of anyone, not even the Pontiff! You'll never catch him. My sire is very smart, very smart indeed." He laughed, and then snapped his teeth at them. "Now be a good little puppy dog and go pee on a hydrant or something. You're boring me. I bet the girl is much more entertaining."

"Don't worry about her," Matt replied with a low growl. "Teach him some manners, K.C., before I cut off something that won't grow back!"

K.C. pressed a large hand in the center of Matt's chest and pushed him back a few steps. "Hold up, partner." K.C. fancied himself a cowboy. "Don't call him simple, ok? He's sensitive."

You had to be kinda crazy to do what they did; scratch that, really crazy. So crazy you had to be open to the possibility that vampires and werewolves and stuff were real. Alex always thought the world was full of nut jobs, but this was a whole new ball game. Alex Stone had been in this game since she was thirteen years old. Of course, she wouldn't show up on anything official in Washington—the Department of Defense did have rules, you know. But just to be clear, Alex was not just a bench riding second stringer—she was the game changer.

Being tested and retested, poked and prodded and studied like a lab rat was old hat for her. She didn't care about the blood tests and psychological exams anymore. She didn't even care that the only friends she had were standing right here in this dilapidated building with her, questioning a vampire. She and her companions were special; so special, in fact, that their chemical makeup responded to the drug in a way that enhanced their physical strength, mental acuity, speed, healing, you name it. Anything a vampire could do, they could too. The fight was fair now and that's what pissed off Hellclaw to begin with. At first, she thought her father was kidding. She was getting along just fine without a bunch of G.I Joes getting in her way. But, like her father said, there was strength in numbers.

Alex didn't really subscribe to that logic. Being on her own for as long as she could remember, she hardly needed help. She was still alive, right? But she agreed only because he asked her to. It seemed like he wanted to get to know her better, having been sort of an absentee dad for so long. Only popping in when his work brought him to town or making the occasional phone call at holidays and stuff. Convincing herself he felt guilt for all those missed years, she jumped on a plane to D.C. and didn't look back. That's where she made her first mistake.

In most parent/child relationships, the parent offered guidance, protection, and support. The parent could show the child the right path because they'd walked it. But this was no average parent/child relationship. Dr. Johnathan Carlisle was a big time scientist and the head of the program. Alex may have been his daughter, but he made it very clear that would not get her any special favors in this outfit.

"You'll learn more here than you ever will on your own," he'd said from behind his old beat up desk. "Their numbers are growing and their interests are becoming much more global. They don't care about hunting cities anymore."

Alex felt claustrophobic in his cluttered and cramped office. It took every bit of focus she had just to keep from ripping the door off its hinges to escape. "I get it, daddy," she replied.

He cleared his throat as he eased back in his chair. "Good. You'll train with Commander Palmer for a few weeks, then we'll see how you do in the field."

That got her attention. Alex remembered the anger in the pit of her stomach when he told her she had to be confined to this place like she didn't know what she was doing. She also remembered thinking she should be teaching them, not the other way around.

"I gotta stay here and train? Why," she glared at her father.

"Because there are protocols and rules of engagement, Alex," he glared back. "You're not running the streets back home anymore killing anything that moves. You have a place on the team, and you will learn to work within that team or you'll be restricted from field work indefinitely. Do you understand me?"

Effectively swallowing her pride just enough to nod her agreement, Alex stood and gave her father a defiant salute. Leaning forward in his chair, he grinned and told her she could go. It took everything she had in her not to slam the door. Acting like a spoiled brat would get her nowhere with him. She decided in that moment to show her father and the entire team just how awesome a vampire killing machine she could be. That very night she became the *Dagger*.

Alex's team, collectively known as *Night Command*, was attached to the Department of Defense for now. Finding a renegade vampire named Tristan Ambrose brought them here, to a dusty little town in Mexico running down a lackey that may or may not lead them to him. Alex was thinking not.

She knew this vampire hadn't expected to be chained to an altar at the end of their fight though, that was for sure. When his jagged blade sliced through her palm, Alex felt a trail of spicy pain shake her body. Before the others caught up, she had spiked him to the floor.

Alex's five foot six frame of lean muscle didn't seem intimidating in the least. She might have the face of a child, but if he thought her age was a weakness, he was sorely mistaken. As she approached him, the vampire priest smiled sweetly in her direction. The bolts were secure; not even he could pull them loose in his weakened state.

"You're running out of time," he said, "and none of *them* will live forever."

"What's that supposed to mean?" Alex replied as she pulled her silver Zippo from her pocket. "No one lives forever, not even you."

She found his obvious confusion strange. Did he really think he was going to live forever? His eyes darted from Matt to K.C. to Ben and back to her when she stopped short of the front pew. Everybody was quiet. The vampire priest's laughter ping ponged around the small space.

"She doesn't know," he said as his gaze slid from person to person. "With all that drug does for you, you still can't tell the difference between you and her? My goodness, you are in for a surprise my child!" He laughed so loud, dust sprinkled down from the rafters.

As footfalls bounded up behind her, the shots echoed around them as bullets whizzed by her ear like flies. Alex jerked sideways and bumped the pew. The slugs entered the vampire's body with very little blood and no real effect on him. They travelled straight through and lodged in the bell behind him. A dull clanging chased the gunshot noise.

"Shut your mouth," Ben barked in his face then snatched the lighter from Alex's hand.

The vampire's bloodshot eyes widened and his long teeth dropped slowly. He pulled in a deep breath then slid his tongue across razor sharp fangs. "She smells so good! Just one taste before I die," he said with a jerk of the chains, "see if the rumors are true."

"What rumors?" Alex replied as she stepped closer.

"If you were smart, you'd take your own life," he growled. "It will be far less painful than what they're going to do to you."

Before she could get any closer, Ben pushed her backward then lit the rags of the vampire's sleeve. "Suicide's a sin father," he chuckled, "shame on you."

Alex lowered her gaze when she saw the first rays of sunrise touch his bare feet through a hole in the stained glass window. Apparently, he hadn't fed enough if the sun was having that effect on him. *So, maybe he wasn't the only monster snacking on the locals,* she thought. As he stamped and twitched to put the fire out, she felt Ben's grip on her shoulder. "You didn't do this alone, did you?" she asked as she tried not to take in the smell. Then his burning flesh ignited the frayed cuffs of his tattered pants. "Who's helping you?"

With the foul odor of simmering flesh caught in her nose, Alex waved her bloody hand in front of his face just to pull his attention back to her. He looked up from the flames and purred with excitement at the smell of her blood. She knew her scent would wrap around his senses and trigger his need to taste it.

Ben jerked her back and pushed her ahead of him. "Go! Father Tomas is waiting outside." They followed the others down the aisle toward the exit. Common sense told her not to look back, but she did it anyway. Through the smoke and flames his white teeth stood out like a beacon. Would that be the only thing she'd remember about tonight—how white his teeth were? Or would she be stuck with the smell of his burning flesh buried in her clothes and hair forever?

"Tell Tomas the devil is waiting," the vampire yelled after them. "And, a friendly warning to you all, Hellclaw's reign begins with the next century and yours will end in her blood!"

After they emerged from the church one by one, her companions bolted the doors shut. The other young priest, Father Tomas, said a prayer, and then turned to Alex as she began to speak.

"Take the ashes and scatter them in the cemetery then pour holy water over them. The damage to the sanctuary should be minimal."

"*Ha tenido que matarlo*," the young man whispered. "*Era un hombre un sola vez; un hombre de Dios.*" He crossed himself, kissed the rosary clutched in his dirty fist and repeated his question in English. "Did you have to kill him? He was a man once; a man of God."

"We didn't kill the man of God," Ben answered. "We killed the thing that has been feeding on your village for weeks. And believe me when I say, we were much kinder than he was to those he fed on."

"*Gracias*," he said with a bow of his head, "*Y que Dios se apiade de sus almas.* Thank you and may God have mercy on your souls."

Black smoke billowed from underneath the door bringing the vampire's stench outside. His screams announcing the beginning of a new day.

"Thank you, Father," Alex replied.

What would she confess if she could? She

9

didn't know anything that wasn't classified, even from God. Besides, no priest would be able to change anything that had happened since she joined the team and he certainly wouldn't be able to stop what was coming. Alex wasn't even sure they could either. How do you fight the invisible? All they had was a name; no description, no solid location. Tristan Ambrose just moved to the top of every known covert agency's 'Most Wanted' list overnight. And *Night Command* had drawn the assignment to find him and the book.

"The next century," Alex sighed as she climbed into the passenger side as Ben took the wheel of the Jeep. "Do you know what he was talking about?"

"Why would I know," Ben chuckled. "He was just trying to save his own ass anyway, Dagger. Relax. It's over. And by the way, scatter the ashes in the cemetery and holy water?"

"Come on, they love that superstitious crap! Just call me Bram Stoker," Alex laughed.

"Dagger sounds cooler," Ben replied as he slid his sunglasses on his tanned face. "Besides, after Sandbox, everything goes back to normal again. We get the book, they get the vamp and we go back to being regular grunts again, right?"

"Say 'duck' next time," Alex said with a punch to Ben's shoulder, then she pushed her sunglasses back up her nose. "I'd like to get home in once piece, it that's alright with you," she giggled.

"Home," Ben let out a loud fake laugh. "You mean the hole in the ground we live in! Yea, I can't wait to get back to cafeteria food, the bunkhouse and no real sunlight. I say we swing by Cancun on the way back. You in?"

Alex didn't really mind life at Area 51 as much as the others seemed to. That place had been home for the last five years. For her, it beat wasting away in regular school. By the time she was seventeen, she had an entire secret facility for a playground. What regular teenager could say that? The bottom five levels belonged to the team. Nobody else came down there unless it was to sneak a peek at the test subjects for bragging rights. But for *Night Command,* there was no place like home.

"What's the difference between you guys and me?" Alex asked as she turned in the seat to look at Ben. He still had dried blood in his hair and a long scratch down his neck that was healing.

"If I gotta tell you that, you need to go back to school kid," Ben laughed, then he shrugged her off. "Forget it. He was just trying to get into your head. They like to fuck with us as much as possible—you know that."

"Yea," Alex sighed again. "So, training for Sandbox? Whoopee."

Their rusty Army Jeep bounced down a dusty road toward the old hotel they had taken over two weeks ago and Alex felt really tired all of a sudden. She fiddled with the damp cloth on her hand, and could feel the blood flow slow down and begin to heal with spasms of pain.

"Don't act like you're not excited about going,"

11

she heard Ben laugh. "Dugway Proving Grounds ain't gonna get over us anytime soon!"

"I know we're getting the best survival training in the world, but we're still stuck in Utah for six weeks," Alex said. "And Army Rangers aside, vampires are growing stronger and becoming immune to daylight. We need an edge Ben, a good one."

"We are the edge, Dagger," Ben answered with a tug of her ponytail, "The best one in the world."

The ride back to Edwards Air Force Base in Nevada, as predicted, was bumpy and hot. Mexico wasn't all it was cracked up to be, unless you were on Spring Break. And even then, wake up on the wrong side of town and it might cost you more than a cab ride back to the resort. Still she had to admit, no other kid in the world would ever be able to say they'd hunted vampires. As she dropped her duffle next to the rest, she walked slowly toward the elevator that would take them 100 stories underground for debriefing, chow, and hopefully, sleep.

What wish would she make if she were free to dream?

First off . . . No more freaking vampires! At least not the kind that still saw humans as food. Damn! Wouldn't that be great? She could attempt to have a normal life; one that included friends and fun. Instead, she was in the ass-end of Hell with a vampire chained to an altar of all things. And, as always, her night ended with one less vampire in the world and a bumpy ride back to the States.

Alex crossed the threshold of her sleeping quarters and stripped down as she passed through to the small bathroom. Her tired body was covered in bruises, blood, and dirt as she stepped into the stall. Under the hot spray all her muscles began to relax as warm steam closed in around her. Her head lowered under the water and she let out a long exhale. Boom, boom, boom. That was the sound of water as it bounced off her skull in a soothing pattern. It stung her eyes when she opened them to see the bruises disappear and circle the drain at her feet mixed with blood and dirt. That was the coolest part. For the next few hours she would still feel the pain of a couple of bruised ribs and a sucker punch to her right jaw, but still, it was pretty cool to be able to heal overnight.

The longer she stayed hidden in the steam of the hot shower, the clearer her brain became. The action from today untangled as it replayed in her mind. One by one the questions began to form so fast she couldn't stop them: *What did he mean they wouldn't live forever? No one would, not even them. And, what were they keeping from her? And . . . Stop*, she barked inside her mind. *It doesn't matter now. He's dust and the mission is done.*

Wrapped in the scratchiest towel ever, Alex stood at the mirror and wiped it clean. She tried to relax her mind, but if she relaxed too much she'd hear everything. That was one of the not so cool things about being on the supplements. Everything was better: sight, hearing, strength, everything. The other downside? You had to suffer through the healing process. It may only take about a day, give or take, but it hurt like hell. There was nothing they could take that would really stop the pain. The Doc said it was because of the supplements. But ice would dull her bruised ribs enough for her to at least get some sleep. The others would drink until they passed out. She pressed the ice pack to her side, took a handful of aspirin and settled down to get some rest.

The flight home was hell. Ben hated Air Force transports. Everyone else had passed out before they left the tarmac—everyone but Alex. She never seemed to sleep. He would watch her eyes, heavy with fatigue, begin to close. Then, after about fifteen minutes, she was wide-awake again. Maybe that was what the doctor was looking for: strange behavior, side effects, or abilities that couldn't be explained. He wrote everything down in the small notebook, then stuffed it in his pack.

Back at Area 51, there would be clean sheets and hot food, but no matter how it was dressed up, it was still a cage. A high security cage buried deep underground. They only came out after the sun went down, living by the light of the moon.

The base bar was the only place they could unwind without much trouble. Once they were debriefed and examined, they would usually head there for drinks and pool, but not tonight. Tonight was a special occasion, after a little business was concluded, of course.

Ben slouched down in the uncomfortable office chair and closed his burning eyes. Every muscle was screaming for a hot shower and sleep. He was so tired, even his hair hurt. He could still smell the desert around him. When he scratched at the dark buzz cut peppered with sand and blood and ash he felt the mixture fall to his face. His long lashes met as he squeezed his eyes tighter. Explosions of color swirled around in the dark behind his eyes.

He rolled his head left then right to crack his spine back into place and ease his headache and the tightness in his shoulders. As his long legs stretched out in front of him, his arms reached high overhead. As he worked out the kinks in every muscle, his ears pricked and tingled when the noise around him focused to a sharp edge in his head.

All the sounds below him were mixed together in a whirlwind of confusion and chaos. Various conversations ranging from mission notes to ordering more toilet paper raced through his brain. Sometimes he hated those damn pills. He wasn't sure why his hearing was affected most by the drug. All of his ex-girlfriends had told him he was never a good listener. He bet his exes would be impressed with him now though. But old memories would have to wait. This was Alex's eighteenth birthday, and the others were getting the mess hall ready for the party.

The door swung open and Dr. Johnathan Carlisle walked in, clipboard under his right arm, cup of coffee in his hand. *This guy probably bleeds caffeine*, Ben thought as he stood. He'd never seen the man without a cup of coffee, ever.

"Transport was a little behind schedule, sorry," Ben said, shaking the doctor's free hand. "You know how those Air Force pilots can be." Dr. Carlisle's grip was firm, in direct contrast to the softness of his hands.

Wispy curls of dark hair, cut low, framed his face. He looked much younger than his forty years. Average height and a bulky build made him appear more like a blue collar Joe than one of the nation's top geneticists and bio-chemical engineers heading a secret project of super soldiers.

"Welcome home, Commander Palmer," he said as he motioned for Ben to sit. He removed his glasses in one smooth motion.

Dr. Carlisle placed his hands on the desk. He always had a look of perpetual thought—of something unknown simmering deep inside him.

Ben could only imagine what went on inside the mind of a man like him. A man who had created a pill that altered human DNA and changed the hunting game forever.

"Thanks, doc," Ben replied. "It's good to be home again."

"Well, we're happy to have the team back in one piece," Dr. Carlisle said. "Your report looks good. Any surprises?"

"Not really."

"Did they all perform well in the field?"

"Yea," Ben said as he fidgeted, "but, Dagger . . . she . . ."

"She what?" Dr. Carlisle asked as his posture straightened and he leaned forward in his desk chair just a bit.

"She doesn't sleep," Ben answered. "I mean not like the rest."

"I don't understand."

Ben took a deep breath. "She might close her eyes for a few minutes, but eight hours of sleep?" he shook his head. "I don't think she needs it, not really. Is that supposed to happen?"

Dr. Carlisle opened the brown folder in front of him. Flipping through the typed pages, he nodded as he scanned the Ops Report. "Maybe. Does it seem to affect her performance at all?"

"No. She's the first one out the door: ready and waiting before we've had breakfast."

Dr. Carlisle gave him a slight grin. "Then don't worry about it, Commander. I'm sure it's nothing. I'll take a look at her test results in the morning."

Ben relaxed back into the chair.

Dr. Carlisle cleared his throat, "How did she do against the priest?"

"Good," Ben answered. "She held her own. He seemed pretty damned surprised to get taken down by a little girl though. You should have seen his face!" He laughed then started to cough. All of a sudden beads of sweat rolled down his spine, icy and creepy feeling. It had been about six hours since his last dose. He'd be sure to take two pills tonight. It wouldn't be very cool to pass out without the help of alcohol at a party, would it?

"Do you think she's ready then?" Dr. Carlisle said. "We can't avoid it any longer."

"She's ready. She's even learning to keep her temper in check. Don't worry."

Dr. Carlisle's eyes narrowed and his usually serene expression turned hard.

"It's not her temper I'm worried about. If she gets seriously wounded or bitten this early, we'll have to scrap the entire project. If that happens, all my work goes to hell and me with it."

Ben raised his arms over his head and stretched long. He grinned as he laced his fingers together and rested his hands on top of his head. "No one can't tell she's dhampire, not even her. That's what we hoped for, right? That since it's been so long, no one would even remember what a female hybrid smelled like anymore. We're as close as we're ever gonna get, so it's now or never."

Dr. Carlisle didn't control the smile that pushed his mouth out on both ends. Ben knew what to say to alleviate the good doctor's fears and keep him from pulling her clearance for the assignment. Everything hinged on the target, the team, and the plan playing out exactly as it had been laid out.

"Smell is one thing," Dr. Carlisle said as he stood. "What if someone gets a taste . . .?"

"They won't," Ben interrupted. "Even if that does happen, they'll drink regular human blood and once the effects have worn off, they won't remember it. It's kinda perfect."

Dr. Carlisle pushed the papers on his desk around absently. He forced out a hard breath then looked up at Ben again. "I'm glad you're so confident, but from what I can tell, that only works on those who've been turned. What about those born vampire? We have yet to capture and test the effects on a pure blood. And we can't be sure what will happen in an environment we don't control."

"Sure we can," Ben sighed as he rose from the chair. "Your operative is ready to enter her life as a best friend, so don't worry. It's time for her to go out into the real world and see what happens. She's the real deal—first female human/vampire hybrid in 600 years! Right now we have the advantage. But one day, she will find out what she is, then we'll have to pay for what we did to her." Ben stared at the doctor without blinking. Dr. Carlisle didn't seem as scared about what would happen to all of them when Alex realized she wasn't on the drugs. Ben was scared shitless. "If that's all, I'd like to grab a shower and get downstairs. We have a celebration to get started."

Dr. Carlisle followed him to the door.

"Tell her 'happy birthday' for me, would you?" Dr. Carlisle asked as he shook Ben's hand.

"You're not joining us?" Ben asked.

Dr. Carlisle smiled and shook his head. A hard slap on Ben's shoulder was followed by a small push out the door. He locked it with a key and led him down the hall to the elevator. "No. I'm afraid I have too much work to do, but enjoy."

"Don't worry, we will," Ben said as he pressed the button to take him down 30 stories, "but, you should at least stop by for a few minutes. I mean, she'd want her father to . . ."

Ben stepped inside the elevator while Dr. Carlisle held the door open with his wing-tipped foot as Dr. Carlisle interrupted him.

"She'll understand if I don't," he replied. "She always has."

Ben narrowed his eyes and sighed, "Sure doc. I guess you know her better than we do."

"I do," Dr. Carlisle continued to grin. "Besides, I don't want to intrude, so let's not be hypocrites. She hates me and I'd like to keep it that way. Have a good time Commander Palmer."

Twenty Years Later...
Chapter 1

"Are you watching the news?" Ivy Rose huffed as she walked in without knocking, which she always did. "I can't believe you're not watching the news!"

Ivy turned on the flat screen attached to the far wall of the office. With a little trot, she returned to the desk, pushed the pencil cup out of the way and slid on top of it. Her dark brown hair hung half way down her back in huge bouncy curls. The natural light from the floor to ceiling windows across the room gave a warm glow to her slightly bronzed skin. Alex watched her back as Ivy sat on the edge of her desk with all of her attention on the screen.

"Good morning to you too," Alex said. Her business partner and best friend stayed focused on the news report, but Alex couldn't care less. Ivy seemed hypnotized by the action. "Don't mind me, I'm just working."

"Trust me, you wanna see this," Ivy answered, eyes still glued to the television screen.

The tap on her head was a little irritating and Alex was forced to redirect her thoughts and attention to the news report as Ivy pointed toward the television on the wall.

She shivered when the perky blonde newscaster stepped into the frame with a mic in her hand and a somber look on her shiny round face. The little logo in the corner of the screen read '*live from Las Vegas*'.

There was plenty of action behind the reporter. With the background looking like that of the latest crime drama, the reporter said something about a murder on the set of a movie. The man had been discovered around two in the morning in a dumpster. The details of his demise spilled from her lips with ease similar to giving directions to the nearest burger joint. Every blink of her blue eyes preceded a new detail, a new lie she had been instructed to read. Then the scene shifted to video of a witness—the makeup artist.

"He was just in the trailer," she sniffed with a quick wipe of her pointed nose. "I finished his makeup and he walked out headed to the set."

The shift back to the live scene felt deliberately abrupt. The reporter, with a tone of cold indifference, explained that the cause of death and the victim's identity would not be released until the next of kin had been notified. With that, Alex was suddenly uncomfortable in her perfect leather desk chair. She was uncomfortable with the stillness of the air around her too.

The blurred image of the body bag being wheeled away was something Alex had never gotten used to, no matter how many times she'd seen it before. The heavy plastic showed the slightest outline of a body; someone's son or father or brother was in that bag.

Someone was going to have to tell his family he was dead. And not just dead, but bled dry and dumped like trash. But that detail would never see the light of day, and no one would ever be told the real cause of death, not anyone in the real world anyway.

A slight chill made its way up her spine again as she thought how hard it must be to give notice to a family. Then she thought they also had to lie about *how* that person died. Who was going to believe in vampires anyway?

"That is so sad, right?"

As Alex took a seat next to Ivy on the edge of the desk, her mouth went dry and her heart began to race in her chest.

"Who would do that?" Ivy whispered.

"I can think of about dozen people off the top of my head," Alex answered, still focused on the news.

"Of course you can," Ivy replied with a soft elbow to Alex's side. "So, what do you make of that?"

"Nothing," Alex sighed under her breath when she spotted a familiar face in the crowd. "Like I'm watching a rerun of a bad movie."

"What?" Ivy asked.

"Nothing. Guy gets killed in Vegas. What am I supposed to think about it? I don't know him."

Back behind her desk, Alex let out a long breath. When she picked up the paperwork again, she hoped Ivy would just leave, but she didn't.

Ivy turned and dropped the remote on the paper in Alex's hand to get her attention.

"That doesn't bother you at all?"

"No," Alex laughed. "Just goes to show, you gotta be careful who you cross in this life."

"Cross," Ivy chirped. "You know what happened to this guy, don't you?"

"No," Alex replied. "Maybe he owed somebody some money and didn't pay."

"That was not some bookie that didn't get his payment on time," Ivy huffed. "Dead men can't pay back their debts."

All Alex could think to do was shrug. It didn't matter anyway, did it? That guy was dead and nothing was going to bring him back. A clean up team was on sight, she knew that for sure. They would take care of everything, including making sure he didn't come back from the dead.

Ivy had all kinds of questions swimming around in her head, and Alex could hear them clear as a bell. With all the excitement, Alex's control had begun to slip a bit. Maybe she was just tired and stressed like always. The last thing she needed right now was for her past to make an appearance in her present.

"Do you think it was one of them?" Ivy asked.

"No," Alex replied. "I don't see vampires behind every bad thing that happens in the world anymore Ivy, but thanks for the confidence in my recovery."

"Quit being such a drama queen," Ivy sighed. "It's just that you seem kinda spooked, that's all. I was just wondering."

Alex gave Ivy all of her attention. "Don't."

"Sorry."

"It's fine," Alex replied waving her off. "I thought I recognized someone in the crowd for a second, that's all. I was wrong."

"Ok," Ivy answered as she turned to the screen again. She didn't like that answer. Her face flushed red as she grinned awkwardly. Alex's sensitive ears picked up the sound of Ivy's heart as it raced in her chest. Why did she care anyway?

Inside his office, he could ignore the ringing desk phones and busy people on the other side of his door. But he couldn't ignore his personal line.

"Jason Stavros."

He always chuckled when Jason answered the phone. He could almost smell the alcohol he likely started the day with.

"Catch you at a bad time, did we?"

"I thought maybe I'd be spared the accusatory call from Strategic," Jason laughed back. "For the second time this week."

"Well I just left another crime scene wondering why my victim was drained dry," Coop replied. "And dumped behind one of *your* casinos this time."

"That's a good question, Agent Cooper. I was just wondering that myself."

"And what did you come up with?"

"Coincidence," Jason answered. "But don't worry, we are on it."

Because Jesse Cooper was the current lead agent for Strategic Asset Management's covert group, the Trackers, his team would have been first on the scene. Jason knew he'd be calling after last night.

"I'm not worried," Coop replied. "But you sound a little on edge. Why don't we drop by, say in fifteen, and you can run down the game plan for us."

"Coop, I've got a full schedule today," Jason sighed. "Why don't we meet later for dinner and drinks, my treat?"

"Sounds good," Coop chuckled. "I know the perfect place, off the Strip, just to be safe."

"You don't trust me Coop, after all we've been through?" Jason teased. "I'm hurt."

"Yea, right," Coop laughed. "See you around eight? You remember my favorite place right?"

"Unfortunately," Jason replied. "See you then."

"You're just gonna let him have time to circle the wagons," the young man asked as he passed the plate of bacon to his left.

"He can't circle shit without telling the Council first," Coop stated, taking the plate. "Jason might be hot stuff in our world right now, but he's still just a turned human in their eyes. He needs us to prove this didn't have anything to do with them. And we need their resources to find the box."

Jumping from Vegas to L.A and back was a bitch! Everybody was pretty much running on fumes

26

even with their secret weapon in a bottle. The last thing he wanted to do was play games with Jason Stavros. But last night they came up short again on any solid evidence, so they had no other choice.

His Team Leader, Xavier Ramos, looked beat. His usually perfectly coifed mane was messy and needed to be washed. He stuffed a piece of toast in his mouth as he looked over last week's autopsy report.

The twins, Kai and David Yun were arguing over who got the last piece of bacon. They argued over a lot of mundane things like that it seemed. *Maybe it's a twin thing*, Coop thought.

The two female members of the team, Erin Sinclair and Amy Proctor, sat quietly going over the scene from last night. The computer hacker and the teenage witch made this team Strategic Asset Management's crown jewel.

Then there was Sebastian Rayne.

Sebastian was the newest member of this team. He joined only a year ago, but, to Coop, it felt like he had always been here. He fit in perfectly and no one, on the team at least, minded that he was a newly turned vampire. They really didn't get a choice in the matter, but since he'd proven himself in the field time and time again, he was here to stay.

"Can we trust anything he gives us?" Amy asked. "I mean, turned or born, he's still a vampire, right? Doesn't that automatically mean he can't be trusted? No offense, Sebastian."

He just grinned as he picked up his cup again.

The others went back to their work. As Sebastian put down his coffee laced in human blood, he noticed Coop's eyes on him. "Something on your mind, boss?"

"I want you to go with us to Texas," Coop replied.

"Why?" Sebastian asked, trying to contain his excitement. "I mean, you said it would just piss her off. What changed your mind?"

"I think I want her pissed off."

Every eye was on him as he put the cup to his lips. Peering over the edge, he grinned.

"You said that could get messy," Xavier answered.

"Maybe a little mess is what we need," Coop replied.

They all went back to what they were doing as Coop contemplated what he was about to do. If she was going to be pissed and start killing, maybe she'd let him live to tell the tale.

CHAPTER 2

The entire floor had grown increasingly quiet as quitting time finally arrived. Bite, Inc. had just landed on Fortune's "100 Best Companies to Work For" list last month. Over the last ten years, Alex's little underwear company had gone from small Texas startup to international darling, much to everyone's surprise—especially hers. All she wanted was a way to escape her past and reinvent herself after all the years of being known only as a hunter of bad guys. Now, the only thing she's killing is the competition.

Various conversations reached her ears as her employees filed out of the office for the evening. Some making plans for drinks at the local, others making plans to pick up children from practice or dance class. Everyone seemed excited about the summer launch meeting though. Weeks of hard work, schedule changes, vendor meetings and party planning had finally come together. The launch would be on time and Alex had promised a bash to end all bashes if they met the deadline.

Switching off the evening news, she ran her fingers through her dark hair and sighed. Out of her high heels, her toes curled and popped while her arms stretched high overhead as she yawned. A feeling of pride swept through her. Everyone was talking about her company and everyone was wearing her underwear. It seemed like every young hot celebrity was wearing the comfy cotton t-shirts with the small vampire silhouette on the right sleeve these days. And she just laid claim to the hottest football player in the game as one of her models for the men's line. Nothing was going to stop her now.

She barely looked at the faces on her computer screen as she tapped her water glass with an uneven nail. With the mouse nestled in her hand, she stared at the imperfect faces made perfect by technology. You'd think she'd had her fill of perfect people. People that aged by centuries, not by every heartbeat. As she thought of those creatures, some perfect and all practically forever, Alex rubbed her burning eyes and stood.

Tapping the mouse, the screen went dark as she made her way to the floor to ceiling windows. It felt as though she were suspended in midair when she stood before the wall of glass. From here, the entire city stretched out before her eyes.

Her view through the glass was as spotless and clear as the sky itself. It was going to be another warm, fall night in Texas. All around her was noise she could ignore. Ventilation system, electricity—those sounds that took the place of absolute silence. A polished chrome desk lamp blazed behind her, casting a bright beam on the random objects beneath it. Alex closed her eyes to see last night's dream begin to play, the one where they torched that vampire inside a dusty old church. Then his voice echoed around the room as if he were right there.

"Hellclaw," someone whispered in her ear.

She pressed her back to the cool glass and opened her eyes wide. When she turned to face the glass again, all she saw was the night. No one stood in the sky. No one was perched on the ledge with fangs bared, ready to claim her as his next victim.

But the quick pops to the window surprised her. In the glass were two spider web-like cracks: one to the heart and one to the head. The lines radiated out from the center of each impact point like tiny claws. The ammo was heavy duty and special issue. She'd used it a long time ago to stop some of the toughest vampires in existence, thousands of years old. Why would someone use that kind of firepower on a human? If the glass hadn't stopped them, those bullets would have sent her heart through her chest and her brain would have ended up on the other side of the room.

"Bulletproof, asshole," she said as she backed away. Just the thought of what might have happened sent Alex into flight mode. Her brain screamed warnings as she fled from the building.

She grabbed the beat up leather briefcase on her way out. At the bottom floor, the guard lay across his neat desk, his brains sprayed over the small monitor. Monday Night Football was just getting underway as she ran across the polished marble floors to the exit.

Littered around the outside of her building were bodies—bloody and lifeless. Some of the faces were familiar, some not. Ivy's body was propped against her car door, eyes wide and dead. Her throat had been ripped out. The bright yellow dress she wore was stained with red. As Alex side-stepped bodies and blood puddles, there was silence. Sinking to her knees, a warm breeze pushed the scent of fresh blood and Ivy's perfume into her face.

Everywhere she looked was death. The bloody mess that used to be her best friend's neck was warm and sticky to the touch. The coppery smell burned her nose as Alex swallowed her anger and pain. As she reached up to close Ivy's eyes, a hand snatched her wrist with an iron grip. There was no sound when her mouth opened to scream.

Alex bolted upright on the couch. Her office was quiet and warm. She'd fallen asleep again; photos clicking by silently on the laptop sitting on the table in front of her. *Stupid dreams keep coming back*, she thought as she stood up. A cold sweat covered her face and her hands trembled as she swung her pack over her shoulder and picked up her keys. Inside the elevator, she coaxed her heart to go back to a regular pace so that the tremors would go away. The night watchman was fine—still glued to the monitor with a wave over his shoulder at her as she made her way across the polished marble floors.

Once inside her car, the Vanquish purred like a kitten. The tires smoked out of the lot and onto the almost empty street, as Alex blew past almost every car in sight.

Her mobile interrupted the music so she tapped the speaker function on the steering wheel without looking and answered, "Alex Stone."

"Yea, I know."

Alex had swerved into an empty parking lot and slammed the brakes before she knew it. The hairs on her arms stood up at the sound of his voice. The deal was no one contacted her, ever again. No matter what, they kept their distance and she kept her mouth shut. He had just broken the pact, the contract they'd made years ago. It didn't really matter why, just that it was now broken and she was pissed.

She cleared her throat and her hand trembled as she reached for the phone. "You have the wrong number."

Jesse Cooper's laugh scratched at her skull. It was exactly the same in every way. His voice made her stomach turn over. He was the last person she thought she would hear from after all this time. "You wish," he laughed. "You didn't answer my email, so I thought I'd get more personal. It was pretty easy . . . getting your number, I mean. You've lost your touch."

"What do you want Coop?" Alex asked as she prayed the queasy feeling in the pit of her stomach would go away. A sour taste kept returning with each swallow. The bottle of water in the holder had been there for a couple days, at least. She chugged it without a second thought and it did the job of washing away the lump that formed in her dry throat at the sound of his voice.

"You," Coop chuckled. "Did you happen to hear about the body in Vegas last night?"

"Yea, so?"

"So, it's a problem for us." Coop said with another chuckle.

"Sucks to be you."

Alex could hear voices in the background and glasses as they tapped together.

"Exactly," Coop replied.

"Bullshit," Alex hissed.

"Why would I lie about that?" Coop chuckled again. "Do you know how much paperwork I'm gonna be buried in, if it's true?"

Her phone beeped twice meaning she had a text message. An address and a time appeared on the touchscreen. "Forget it," she countered. "Go find Ben."

"I'm trying, but he's not answering."

"Not my problem."

"I could send the local PD after you at your office," Coop said. "Won't that look nice on every news outlet in the country?"

"You won't do that," Alex laughed. "The old man would have your ass for bringing that kind of attention to the program and you know it. You forget how short your leash is again?"

She heard him take a deep breath and cough long and hard. At first it seemed strange that he'd be sick. They never got sick as long as they were on the pills, but maybe he was off them now. Rumor was his team was pretty close to being the best, so there really wasn't much for him to do but bask in the glory—just like him to take credit for someone else's work.

"I don't have a leash anymore, little girl," Coop boasted. "Sounds like somebody's still a little pissed she got replaced."

"You didn't replace me," Alex sniffed. "I went out on med leave."

"As I remember it, you went out on crazy leave," Coop said. "What was it like to live in a padded room?"

"Go to hell, Coop!"

"Just for grins," he chuckled, "I framed the hole you made in the wall of the base bar with your head."

The line went dead before she could rip into him. How effective would that be over the phone though? Not very, and not very smart either. He took a big risk when he called, she reminded herself. Something big had happened. Something that superseded the agreement she had with them. An icy coldness crawled up her spine. Her brow became speckled with sweat and her skin immediately felt clammy. She opened the car door just in time for her liquid lunch to land on the pavement instead of her nice leather interior.

Jesse Cooper was called up from some B-team when Matt had to return home after his father fell ill. He was too cocky for Alex's taste, but she had to work with him anyway. Her father insisted he would step up to the challenge of Sandbox, but Alex had doubted it.

"He's ready, Alex," he said over the rare coffee chat he invited her to in those days.

"No, he's not," she replied sipping tea instead of coffee. "He's an immature jack-ass and he's gonna get someone killed."

Dr. Carlisle shook his head as he reviewed the report on Jesse Cooper casually. Alex had seen the report a thousand times and wasn't impressed. Who cares if he was Navy Seal trained; on the fast track to being one of the first black officers in that outfit. This wasn't the Seals and they weren't going to tracking vampires underwater. The feeling she had grew stronger the closer they got to the time for action.

"No one else has a problem with him," he continued. "He's doing well on the supplements and his field work is satisfactory. He stays."

As she shook loose from that memory, she swished the water around her mouth then spit out the awful taste her expelled lunch left behind. She popped a breath mint and eased her car back into traffic. An uneasiness filled her gut, she had other things to worry about right now. Things that didn't involve Coop and his vampire problem.

CHAPTER 3

"I thought you forgot," the young woman smiled. She backed away from the door to let Alex inside. "I was just about to call you."

"I got hung up, sorry," Alex replied, returning the smile. "How are you feeling tonight?"

The main living area was littered with boxes; some open and empty, others still sealed with packing tape. Styrofoam peanuts covering the wood floor like snowdrifts. She cleared a spot on the low couch, sat down on a stack of newspapers and waited for Alex to sit too.

"Better. Can I get you something to drink?" she asked in a small voice, almost like a whisper. Alex was slightly irritated by her meek demeanor, but this wouldn't take long.

"I can't stay long. I have another meeting, so I'll just wrap this up and get out of your way."

"You're never in the way, Alex," she replied. She took a quick glance at Alex then flushed red when she realized she'd been caught looking. "You look nice."

"Just left the office."

When Alex placed the ziplock bag on the coffee table the girl straightened her posture, nervous energy causing her to tremble. Alex could see it even if the girl didn't notice.

"What's . . . I usually drink . . .?"

"I know, but it's the last dose and I need to give it to you myself, just to be sure."

Slowly, she stood, crossed to the only window in the entire apartment and opened the blinds. Her shoulders slumped as she stared out into the night. Alex just wanted to do this quick and go. This one had gone on too long. The girl had become too attached. They always wanted more than Alex could give. She stood behind her and waited patiently for her to speak.

"So will I see you again?" she sighed.

Alex placed a hand on her shoulder and tried to keep up the game. This girl was just a girl, nothing more. Nothing like Alex at all.

The young woman took her hand as if it would disappear. Her grip was light and cold. Alex gave hers a squeeze just to be nice. What would it hurt to be nice? It was almost over anyway.

"You'll see me around, I'm sure."

"But not here, not anymore after tonight."

"No."

She faced Alex as if to challenge the decision, but all she did was wrap her arms around herself, bite her lower lip, and stare at her own feet. Alex could see the slightest hint of anger flare in her brown eyes. Then, just as quickly as it came, it went. She tucked her thick curls behind her ears and suddenly she was that worn down little junkie Alex had found in Tucson a couple of months ago.

Making a piss poor effort to hold back tears,

they sprang to her eyes anyway, sliding down her shiny cheeks like a sudden rain shower. "I thought . . ."

"I know what you thought, but you can take it from here."

"But what if I can't do this on my own?"

"Then you're screwed," Alex answered as the young woman pushed past and dropped down on the couch again. "Because the job is done and your life is yours to do with what you want."

"Can we keep in touch at least?" she sniffed as she wiped her nose on the dishcloth from the floor.

"If there's something you want to say, now's the time."

"Jesus! I just . . . like you and I was hoping we could be . . ."

Alex took a seat next to her on the hard cushion. She could still see the slight tremble in her body. She couldn't tell if it was from fear, hunger, or something else entirely.

"I'm not your mother or your girlfriend or whoever else you want me to be. I was hired to do a job and I did it. Start over, don't start over, I don't care. Just don't use me as the reason you don't even try. You have a second chance; take it. Be grateful that I let you live. I won't make that mistake again."

"Why didn't you just leave me where I was?" she mumbled as she rolled up her sleeve and pushed her arm out.

"Because someone cared enough about you to pay me to get you out," Alex replied.

"Who?" she sniffed and wipe her nose on the dishcloth again.

"I don't know and I don't care. I was hired to save you and that's what I did. Just say thanks and try very hard not to run into me again."

She turned her face away and pushed her arm out further toward Alex, who held the needle in her hand.

"It goes into your stomach muscle," Alex replied. "Lie down."

She did as she was told, dragged the shirt tail up and stretched out on the couch.

The injection had been measured perfectly, but Alex checked it anyway. She didn't want to have to come back here again because something went wrong. Before she gave her the final dose, she pulled the slip of paper from the front pocket of her bag.

"Here, read this and do exactly as it says. When I'm gone you'll have just enough time to grab a shower and get into bed. This will hit you pretty hard, so I don't want you to take any chances on falling or anything."

She turned her face into the cushion with a quick nod. The thin needle slid easily into the weak muscle. The girl flinched, just a little, as the contents entered her body with a slight burning sensation. There was the tiniest bit of blood as the needle came out and Alex rubbed the spot with a cotton swab.

With everything back in the plastic bag, she looked down in time to see the young woman's eyes roll up and her lids close. She pulled out a hooded sweatshirt and jogging pants. As she changed clothes, she gave Sara clear instructions.

"When the door closes, you will continue with what you were doing. Wipe down every surface, including the doorknobs with a bleach and water solution like we discussed. Read over the slip of paper before you go to bed then burn it. Do you understand what I've just told you?"

She nodded slowly and took a deep breath.

"Your name is Sara Benton. You've lived here for five years. You work at the bookstore down the street and you sing at a bar downtown on weekends. The names are on the slip of paper. Repeat."

Sara Benton repeated every word and would keep repeating until she showered and went to bed. In the morning, her memory of the last two months would be altered just a bit. Clear memories of night sweats and vomiting until there was nothing left would have center stage in her dreams. She was clean. And here in Texas she had a new start. Her favorite memories would be of the nurses and doctors whose pictures hung on her walls now. None of it was real though, not even the second mortgage. All made up and planted in her brain by an ex-assassin with skills far beyond simply killing.

In her mind, she kicked a bad coke habit. In reality, she was hooked on something more powerful than cocaine or heroin or any other drug known to man. The vampire bite: the feeling of giving into it is highly addictive. During feeding, a chemical is released similar to a hit of ecstasy, only ten times as potent. Most people never realized what was happening to them until it was too late. As long as you had a steady dose of your vampire lover, you were happy—even carefree. But go a couple of days without and you were scratching at your own skin for your next hit. That's how they hooked you and kept you coming back for more, which also kept the vampire fed on a regular basis without much trouble. Unfortunately for the human, it's no picnic and hard as hell to kick the habit.

Luckily or unluckily, depending on whom you ask, Alex was hired to find Sara and help her do just that; kick the habit. With her help, and a synthesized version of the supplement, Sara finally got clear of the thing that hooked her. This last visit was to wean her off that drug for good and for Alex to give her a bit of hypnotic help if she was ever to have a future without the bite of any vampire.

Don't go back to that life. The only thing you'll find is death—yours.

She wondered why Ben had insisted on her taking this job. This girl had just gotten hooked on the bite. She was human, completely. Alex could tell the moment she saw her. But the client was some rich fat cat with a secret life. This girl was either the result of that secret or knew way more than she should about it. Besides, Ben had already taken the fee and she wasn't asked to kill her, so it worked out pretty well for everybody. She stuffed her work clothes inside the pack, swung it over her shoulder and left the apartment for the last time.

Glad for the coolness of the evening, she dropped down in her car and blew out a hard breath. From the notepad on the cheap mobile phone, Alex erased all the information from the screen and the memory card. Then she called him. The line rang four times before he answered with a yawn.

"Hey."

"Hey," she said. "Did I wake you?"

"Just taking a little nap," he chuckled. "I gotta put my steak on in a few. Done?"

"Yea," Alex sighed. "Remind me again why I'm doing this?"

"Because we both know what goes bump in the night," Ben replied. "And it ain't all glittery and kind."

"I started doing this because I wanted to make amends for what I did when I worked for Creed," she sighed. "But the more I do this the more I realize that they don't want to be saved, Benny. They never did."

She heard Ben blow out a hard breath. Pain shot through his skull the moment she mentioned his name. He hated to hear her even say Mason Creed's name. When she lost it, it was because of the secret Ben and her father had kept from her. After leaving the hospital, she ended up working for Mason Creed as a way to punish them both.

Of all the vampires he'd come across—all the ones he'd killed—Mason Creed was the one he wanted to dust the most! What he'd done to her, what he'd turned her into, made Ben cringe sometimes. He couldn't understand how she even got mixed up with him in the first place. For one, he was a cheap club owner in those days. Two, his clubs were even cheaper than he was, and three, he was just an arrogant prick. But Alex landed on Creed's doorstep after she swore to bury Ben and Dr. Carlisle alive if they ever came near her again.

"You working for that prick was as much my fault as it was yours," Ben stated as he tried not to grind his teeth. "The past can't be undone Alex. If you want to stop, we can stop. This can be the last one."

"Not yet, but thanks for saying that," she replied, and then the line went dead.

_____

As messed up as it was, Alex Stone had a talent for killing. And Strategic Assets Management made very good use of that talent. The details of her contract stated she was to locate and return to Area 51 six human/vampire hybrids. Then she could end her relationship with Dr. Johnathan Carlisle and Strategic Assets Management once and for all. Sometimes the occasional side job, like Sara, would overlap with her contractual obligation to Strategic.

Of the six she was assigned to find, three had died of natural causes shortly after they were found. What else could they say? As for the others, one was in Vegas, one somewhere near L.A. and the last in Oklahoma City.

It was her job to get them back to 51. She didn't know why, and she didn't ask. If bringing them in would get her closer to real freedom, then bringing them in was her top priority. As far back as she could remember, it was all she'd ever been good at; tracking things. As a soldier, she did it for her country. As an assassin, she did it for money. Now, she was doing it to be free of her father, the program, and maybe as penance too—trying to save her own soul, before it was too late.

———————————

Life in Vegas was simple. If you had enough money, you could do anything, and Jason had enough to do whatever he wanted. As soon as he stepped out onto the patio of Coop's favorite place, Jason wished he'd never agreed to meet them there. He hated the smell of cheap meat and this place reeked of it. *Humans can put some of the worst shit in their bodies*, he thought as he made his way over to the group in the corner.

"We have to stop meeting like this, Coop," Jason sneered. "This place is a dump and the health department is probably on their way."

When he looked up, Coop's big smile made Jason want to snap his neck. He had some nerve summoning him here. "Well, I didn't think you'd actually show."

"What's a little *E. coli* between friends?" Jason replied as he eyed the burgers around the table. "What can I do for you, Coop? I'm in a hurry."

Coop looked him over. Jason could hear the laughter inside Coop's head and he found it funny that Jason Stavros, owner of half the Las Vegas Strip, was at a dive burger joint on the outskirts of town. Jason, however, didn't find it funny at all.

"I could get you one," Coop grinned with a wave of the bloody meat and bread in Jason's direction.

"No thanks."

"Are you sure? I thought you liked it rare."

"I like my steaks rare," Jason frowned. "I have no idea what that is."

They all laughed.

"Comes from the same place," Coop replied.

"Whatever helps you sleep at night," Jason chuckled.

Coop wiped his mouth and waved for another beer. "So, last night."

"What about last night?"

"Guy dumped behind one of your casinos, bled dry? Ringing any bells?" Coop answered.

"They were shooting a movie there, so don't make that sound like evidence in my murder trial," Jason replied. "And we're working on finding out if he was the actual target or just in the wrong place at the wrong time."

When Coop picked up his new beer, he almost emptied the frosty glass in one draw.

"See that's the real problem," he stated. "He was on a movie set, Jason. Working. So whoever did this was looking for him, specifically."

Jason sat back and took Amy's water with a grin. "Your point?"

"My point is that's number two. We need

information before number three pops up. Any ideas?"

"Working on it, I told you," Jason smiled. "You just let us handle it. We have jurisdiction on this one."

"Wrong," Coop huffed sitting forward. "When there are humans involved, that means we're in this up to our eyebrows! Two humans, two cities, it just screams our jurisdiction!"

"Coop," Jason sniffed matching Coop's posture, "It was my casino, as you so aptly pointed out, so relax, we are on top of this. I'll keep you posted."

"Posted? Gee, thanks! The reason we're involved is someone, correction, one of you is picking off humans," Coop sighed. "If you break the covenant, we get to break you."

"You have no real proof," Jason sneered. "So let us handle this." He stood and buttoned his jacket, nodded to everyone and turned back to Coop. "Have a good evening."

CHAPTER 4

Jason welcomed the end to this day. Something about the way the air felt as the earth turned away from the warmth of the sun helped to ease his aching head. Chills tingled the surface of his skin as he thought about what it would feel like to walk in the darkness again, even if it was just for the short hours between night and day.

As the temperature dropped, late afternoon turned into early evening. Soon, the sun would be gone and the moon would be the center of attention again. Jason loved the night. He loved the way people looked in shadow. Besides, to him, daylight was for work and serious things. The night was for fun.

A little pre-dinner sex, a quick snack and he would take advantage of the night once his video conference was done. His plans for the evening involved a pretty little starlet who chomped at the bit to get into the big budget movie being shot here. She called and emailed him going on six months now. Rather than make her beg one day more, he decided to meet her tonight for drinks and other things.

His current playmate rolled over with a small sigh as he watched from across the room, drink in hand. He could see his mark on her neck from where he sat. As the seconds ticked by, it healed slowly. After another second or two, the purplish bruise turned to smooth olive skin again. "The perks of being a vampire," he mused, as he took another sip from the glass in his hand.

Absently, Jason swirled his glass and he wondered why Conner Gale, the head of the Council of Pure Blood Vampires, had insisted on this meeting. Jason had kept secrets from the pure blood vampire that made him—his sire, Adam Craig—before but nothing that involved the Council. What could Adam have done to be left out of the loop on this one? He was one of the founding members of the Council, which meant he should be privy to everything that went on under their orders. So, why had Jason been asked to keep this secret and report directly to the head of the Council from here on out?

Doesn't really matter, he thought as he stood and stretched his naked body on his way to the shower. After all of his efforts, Jason would soon be inside the Council—the first turned vampire to do so. That fact alone kept his confidence high. It had taken him a hundred years, give or take, but now he was on the path to success and fortune beyond anything he'd imagined.

Several reinventions of his name and persona over the years had cost him friends and lovers, but it was worth it in the end. Jason was now right where he should be: the fast track to the vampire inner circle. That was really the point, wasn't it? Doing whatever had to be done to secure his status in both worlds. He'd killed enough of his enemies to build a reputation for being a man no one should cross. Now, he would have a new reputation for being the turned vampire that clawed his way into Council chambers and lived to tell the tale.

Under the hot spray of the shower, he covered himself in soap and washed her scent away. The mixture of sex and sweat disappeared down the drain. He scrubbed his nails and his face of any blood before he lathered once more and rinsed clean.

In front of the mirror, after a shave and a splash of his best cologne, he brushed his teeth and styled his hair. A quick check and he was perfect once more.

Her shallow breathing echoed all over the bathroom as he prepared for his video conference. He was reminded of the whistle of a kettle each time she exhaled. Their heightened senses came in handy sometimes, but other times it could be a deterrent. When he focused, the sound faded into nothingness.

Suddenly she appeared in the doorway with the glow of satisfaction on her pretty face. Nikki was one of his oldest friends and the only human he had ever turned. He'd been allowed to bring her into this world of excess and power only if he kept her close. Back then, he wanted her with him; couldn't imagine his life without her or Adam, but as he became more involved in the politics of being a vampire, his romantic feelings for her turned cold. She was his employee now and part time lover. He wasn't interested in much more and she seemed to be fine with that. But, one day he'd be expected to take a mate. Would they assume Nikki would be his choice?

"Why didn't you wake me," she sighed, sheet wrapped tightly around her body.

"You needed the rest," Jason replied.

She giggled as he passed her.

Inside his room-sized closet, Nikki eased her body on top of a low dresser and watched him pick out his clothes for the evening. Her green eyes followed him around the space and critiqued his wardrobe choices with a crinkle of her long nose or a girlish nod of approval.

"So . . ." she said as she studied her red polished nails.

Jason dropped the towel and pulled on his underwear. "So . . ."

"Big night, huh," Nikki stated. "Do you remember everything we discussed this afternoon?"

"Of course," he bragged. "And what are your plans for the rest of the evening?"

"Well," she cooed, "I thought I'd wait for you and we'd go to dinner or dancing or both."

"Sorry, I have plans after the call, but maybe Adam's free."

Nikki gave him a pout, but he just shook his head and continued to dress.

When he was ready, she tied the silk fabric around his neck and brushed his shoulders when she was done. Jason turned a smooth cheek to her and she gave him a quick peck. He left her in his closet still wrapped in a sheet and satisfied.

Once he was in his private office, he locked the door and poured himself a drink. He was ashamed to admit the idea of meeting with the head of the Council, even electronically, made him nervous. Secrecy aside, Jason felt the weight of his situation when he was invited to Council chambers last year. His star rose fairly quickly in the human world and had begun to shine in the most important vampire circles, both social and political. That idea pleased and scared him.

When the connection was made, Jason projected the image on the screen and waited for his host to appear. The title on the screen looked rather childish. *Welcome to the Council of Pure Blood Vampires Home Page, please wait for your party to join the conference.* He thought the greeting was humorous and needed a lot of work. It just seemed so 'old school'. The deep red script on a black background was hilarious. Maybe he'd mention that during the meeting. As he enjoyed his drink, classical music played in the background. He closed his eyes and eased down in the seat just a bit. He figured he'd hear a fanfare of trumpets before the head of the Council actually appeared. *How funny would that be?* he thought as the drained the glass dry.

"Comfortable?" he heard the voice ask with a slight chuckle.

Jason's eyes popped open to see the head of the Council smile at him from somewhere on the East Coast. He straightened himself in the leather chair with an apologetic grin.

"Sorry," Jason said with a slight bow of his head.

"I didn't hear you come on."

Conner Gale, Founder and CEO of Gale Enterprises and the head of the Council of Pure Blood Vampires, returned the gesture. His perfect smile and classic handsome guy features struck Jason all at once. If he hadn't been one of the richest men in the world and a vampire, Jason was sure Conner would be important in some other way.

"Don't apologize. I'm sure your day has been as long as mine," Conner replied. "I should apologize for making it that much longer with this, but it couldn't be helped."

"I understand, sire," Jason answered. "How can I help you?"

Conner shifted in his seat and the easy smile faded slowly. Jason couldn't tell where he was, but he seemed very uncomfortable there. He was wearing a gray sport coat and navy shirt. Without a tie, he looked like any other human Jason might come across at a meeting or some other social function. His brown hair was cut close on the sides, but wavy on top. His longish nose complemented his big green eyes and high forehead. He looked like a typical billionaire, if there was such a thing.

"Well I'd like to ask a favor if I could," Conner said.

"Of course, sire. Anything," Jason gushed like an awestruck teenager.

Conner smiled. "I'd like you to go to Texas and speak with Coop's contact."

Jason's heart began to race in his chest. He stood to take a bottle of plain water from the center of the table. It cracked open and he almost finished it in one long swallow.

"Why? If you don't mind me asking."

"I don't think Cooper is being completely honest with us," Conner replied. "My hope is to have someone from the former team on this assignment. I'd feel better if they were there to protect you and our interest in Romania."

Conner had a serious look on his face. Jason couldn't remember a time when Conner looked this serious about his safety. He had no faith in Coop's abilities either, but to have Conner voice that same concern and throw his confidence in Jason was something to be proud of.

"Our agenda won't be the priority."

Conner smiled again. "It doesn't have to be, Jason. I just want to be sure you are protected. So, you'll be on a plane first thing?"

"Of course, sire," Jason said as he stood. "But what will be the incentive to help us?"

"Offer your assistance with their current problem. The Council of Pure Blood Vampires will cooperate fully with their investigation if this former team member will accompany you to Romania. I think that will pique their interest enough, don't you?"

"I'll leave first thing in the morning, and I promise you they'll be on board," Jason stated confidently.

Conner laughed, then the screen went dark. Jason let out a hard breath as he dropped back down in the chair. One of these days his ego was going to get him in trouble. He didn't have the first clue as to how he was going to convince her to take the assignment. Then it came to him like a jolt of electricity to his heart.

Chapter 5

"You're leaving?" he yawned and rubbed his eyes. "I thought we were going to dinner?"

"Rain check," she replied with a pat to his foot as she rose from the edge of the rumpled bed, "I just remembered a meeting, so . . ."

He sighed, rolled over and stuffed the pillow under his head. A claustrophobic feeling came over her as she slipped one foot into her runner, then the other. The hoodie was still draped over the lamp. Once it was on again, the desire to be out of his apartment overwhelmed her. Her keys were where she'd dropped them. As she looked around to make sure nothing of her remained in this place, his sigh turned her in the opposite direction of the exit.

He leaned his naked body against the door frame as the light from the bedroom dropped a dim shadow over him. Rich, dark skin covered his well-defined muscles from every angle. The feel of that skin against hers was a momentary distraction from her long day. He was good at being there to help her release some stress, but this was not a permanent relationship.

"Will you be at the game at least?" he sighed, scratching at close cut waves of hair.

"Umm, I'll try," she said. "I've got . . ."

"A meeting," he interrupted the lie she was

about to tell. "Is this all I get from you? A quick fuck then you're gone?"

Alex had done this dance with one man or another over the last few years. It used to be that casual sex, or 'friends with benefits', was the thing. And he certainly never complained before.

"Was there supposed to be more?" she asked, standing in the middle of his living room, trying to get out the door before he said something to piss her off. "I thought you were okay with this."

With a sideways glance, he shrugged, "I guess I'll have to be, huh." He stepped forward and grinned, "Wanna go again?"

Alex shook her head as she backed away and opened the front door. "Next time." She was out the door and inside the elevator before the "walls closing in on her" feeling started to subside.

Once she was home and showered, she settled down with her laptop and a drink. Someone had sent her a news item from Los Angeles. The body of a young man had been found in a park two weeks ago. As she scanned the article, she wasn't sure why anyone would send this to her, then the picture at the bottom took her breath away.

"Damn," she huffed and speed dialed Ben.

"Hey," he yawned at her.

"Did you email me a news article tonight?"

"Nope," he yawned again. "Why?"

"Patient nine was found dead in L.A. a couple of weeks ago, that's why." She heard a rustle on the other end than a loud bang like he had just throw something against the wall.

"Send it to me," he groaned.

The ping in the background meant he received the email.

"He was one of the hybrids, right? I thought they were keeping them under lock and key at 51. What happened?"

"I have no idea," she sighed. "I thought you might know. I thought you sent that article."

"Not me," he replied.

"Let me know what you find out, if you can get that close. And Coop's coming here about that body in Vegas last night. You know why he's bringing this to me?"

Ben laughed. "Why would I? Me and him aren't exactly Facebook friends you know."

"I'll deal with Coop. Call my . . . Dr. Carlisle and find out what happened, please."

"You know, you can refer to him as your father, Dagger," Ben chuckled then exhaled. "You forgave me. Don't you think it's time to forgive him too?"

"You apologized," she stated. "He hasn't."

The line went dead. Once she was settled, she turned out the light and tried to relax. Sleep was not going to come easy after all.

Chapter 6

"Just tell him," Dr. Carlisle stated, in the condescending tone he always seemed to have when he spoke about anything that had to do with Alex. "Conner feels quite confident that Mr. Stavros will at least convince her to consider the offer and not turn it down out of hand, like she did you."

Coop hated the way he chuckled. Mostly because the slight was at Coop's expense. "Dr. C, that's probably not a good idea. Jason tends to come on a little too strong around women. She may toss him out the window before he can get to the point."

"And if she does, who cares?" Dr. Carlisle chuckled again. "Let him try."

Coop shrugged and sent the email with her name and business address to Jason. He asked if he should meet him there, but he had replied no. "He plans to be here first thing. Won't this be fun?"

All the press Jason could find on her suggested Alex Stone had a taste for young athletes. Not too young, but young enough to keep her rep solid in that world. Who would've guessed she was hiding such a great secret. He smiled looking over the pictures his contact had emailed to him. Even in this day and age,

Alex Stone being caught with a woman would turn some heads.

―――――――――――――

The next morning her office bustled with activity. Alex strolled in with breakfast in hand. In every unused space, boxes waited to be opened. The models came and went. Every department coordinator was busy with set up for the big meeting this afternoon. She moved through the boxes and people without a sound or a word spoken to anyone. No one really seemed to notice her at all.

As she passed the main conference room, her personal assistant was preparing the space. The projector mounted from the ceiling cast the company logo on the white wall at the end of the room. They placed leather bound reports at each chair. Water, pastries, sandwiches, coffee and soft drinks were lined neatly on the tables by the entrance.

Inside her office, Alex plugged in her laptop, opened the files, and pulled up the photos from last night for the meeting. Unfortunately, Coop's phone call was real last night and so was the dead body in Vegas. She couldn't ignore that, or him for that matter.

While Alex mulled over how to explain taking time off in the middle of launch prep, Ivy walked in, pushed the door closed then put her back against it. Alex glanced up then back at her computer screen. "Hey. What's up?"

When Ivy didn't answer, Alex looked up again.

There she stood, against the door, arms folded over her chest, eyes sparkling.

Alex picked up the stuff for the meeting and stopped in front of her.

"What?"

Ivy's full red lips spread into a smile. Her bright smile almost rivaled the sunlight as it poured through the windows. "You are a sneaky little bitch, aren't you?"

Alex smiled back, but she wasn't sure why, "What are you talking about?"

"He's standing in our lobby asking for you."

"Who?"

Ivy led the way down the hall toward the lobby. They stopped at the glass that separated it from the workspace. With the sound of Top 40 music swimming around them, Alex and Ivy turned to the glass together. Ivy hummed with the tune as Alex prayed for a gun. *Son of bitch!*

In the center of the room were two models, two huge bodyguards and one gorgeous, tall, dark-haired man. His tailored suit and leather shoes looked new and expensive. Against the shiny marble floors and overhead lighting, he looked human, almost.

It was obvious Jason Stavros took pride in his appearance. Judging by the way he stood, it was apparent that confidence was not an issue he struggled with. Alex rolled her eyes as his dazzling smile melted everyone else in sight. His longish nose had a small rise in the bridge. It had been broken long before he was turned; becoming a vampire wouldn't erase the past.

The face of the limited edition Zenith timepiece on his left wrist sparkled as he talked to the pretty redhead to his right. Against the rich fabric of the jacket sleeve, his watch looked even more expensive. Most young guys would throw a Rolex on their wrists to show how much they were worth, but a Tourbillon Quantieme made a different kind of statement. His accessory announced he had taste and the means to express it in the most unexpected ways. Wearing a watch that cost more than a Ferrari was pretty unexpected.

As she stepped back, her head bumped the wall with a hollow thud. "Fuck me," she whispered.

"I don't think Jason Stavros would mind doing that," Ivy giggled as she ogled him through the glass. "When did you meet him?"

"I haven't met him yet."

"Then why is he here saying you guys have a meeting this morning?"

"I don't know," Alex said as she placed her things in Ivy's hands. "I'll be right in as soon as I'm done."

When she stepped through the door, all eyes turned towards her.

The receptionist went back to buzzing phone and her models excused themselves politely as Jason turned in her direction.

"But . . . I want to meet him," Ivy whispered as Alex pushed her back through the door.

"Not now. Go."

Being a vampire suited him. The beautiful smile and bright brown eyes were offset by dark waves of hair so shiny it looked wet. His long arm came out as he approached. There was a nice 'just fed' color to his skin. Fresh blood gave their usually dull pallor a sun-kissed appearance that would last for hours. When he was close enough for her to smell his cologne, she committed it to memory in case she ran into him in a dark alley some night soon.

"You sure can clear a room," he said, as his large hand waited for hers. "Jason Stavros."

"I know who you are," Alex replied with a firm grip of his soft, warm, manicured hand. "What can I do for you Mr. Stavros?"

"Just a minute of your time, Ms. Stone," Jason smiled. "I promise it won't hurt, unless you're into that."

"Cute," she grinned. "Why don't you give me a call in a couple of days and we'll set something up. Say, when Hell freezes over?"

Jason laughed as one hand slid down the front of his Italian wool jacket, smoothing the invisible wrinkles. Then both hands disappeared into his pockets. "You don't really want to do this here, do you?" The temperature dropped slightly as he invaded her personal space. "Please. I'm just asking for a few minutes."

Unfortunately, Jason was right, she didn't want to do this in front of prying eyes and virgin ears. She stepped to the side and waved him toward the door as his two bodyguards followed them to her office. It had been awhile since she'd been this close to a vampire and

even longer since she'd touched one. The experience
then was not pleasant. Now, it wasn't just pleasant, but
oddly exciting.

Jason instructed his bodyguards to wait as he
followed Alex inside the office. As he turned to take a
seat, Alex felt a shiver roll through her body. His eyes
were like deep pools of chocolate. When he smiled,
his entire face lit up. No, glowed. His bronze skin
brightened and his silky hair caught the overhead
lighting, showing its true dark brown color. Most
people would chalk it up to good genes, but Alex knew
better. Supernaturally speaking, he had been born to be
immortal.

He sat on the small leather settee and poured
two cups of coffee in a very polite manner. She almost
said 'thank you,' but caught the compliment before it
left her lips. To thank him would be like admitting she
enjoyed his company. She wasn't ready to give him the
upper hand just yet.

She took the chair instead of the cushion next
to him. He gave it a pat and winked at her for good
measure. When she didn't take the bait, he dropped a
spoonful of sugar in each cup and a small bit of cream
with a shrug. The 'Mr. Manners' routine was meant to
keep up the illusion. But since she already knew what
he was, it was overkill and irritating.

He sipped his coffee with a calm expression.

Jason Stavros made the perfect poster child for
the modern vampire. He was unbelievably charming
and, of course, handsome as hell. With his chiseled chin

and high forehead, no one would dare to mistake him for anything other than the classic all American boy. From his handshake, Alex felt his preternatural power. He did it on purpose, let just a bit of it through. He was probably used to holding back to fool everyone into believing he was mortal—everyone but her.

Keep it cool and casual, girl. Her eyes locked on his to keep her focus tight. If she allowed herself to be the slightest bit distracted, she'd lose her advantage. *Don't let him inside your head.* Alex pretended she wasn't impressed with him. She crossed her legs and placed her hands demurely in her lap. He seemed to like that. From his expression, Alex could tell he liked his women in heels and short skirts. And, as with most egomaniacs, he probably liked to be on top too. "I get the pun, by the way. Bite. Very clever," he said slyly. The sound of his voice jumped her back to reality.

She shifted in the chair and moved her mouth into a small grin. It really was involuntary.

He grinned too, looking as though he wanted to feed right here in her office. For a one hundred and fifty year old vampire, he was most likely very skilled at holding back those long white incisors when he needed to be discreet. The idea of a vampire like Jason Stavros denying his true nature when he was so clearly aroused and ready to strike was amusing. Contrary to legend, vampires were not mindless, blood-thirsty creatures. The desire to feed uncontrollably was resolved years ago. In order to keep the cravings under control, some super smart, pure-blood created a substitute. Although it isn't real human blood, it does work as a suppressant during times when human blood isn't available. Alex prided herself on keeping up to date on everything that happened in that world, even though she tried very hard to stay away from it these days.

Usually vampires didn't deny themselves any opportunity to feed, but, if nothing else, he was smart. He knew something about Alex he shouldn't, or at least enough to keep him from trying anything. If he was so inclined, he could compel her to offer him a taste. Mind control was a neat trick, when it worked. But she wasn't susceptible to it and therefore, Jason was 'shit outta luck' in that respect. *Glad you've fed already handsome, 'cuz I'm not on the buffet,* she thought.

Jason cleared his throat to break the silence. "So, I guess you're wondering why I'm here."

"Not really. I think I know."

"You do?" he smiled.

"Yea," Alex stated. "Just give me their sizes and colors and you can be on your way."

"Sorry?"

"You want undies for your staff, right? . . . 'Cuz that's what I do, sell underwear."

Jason laughed as he stood and walked around the space in a casual way. He knew what he was doing. He wanted to appear approachable, safe, just another face in the crowd. But millionaires that constantly have their faces in magazines, newspapers, and on every social media outlet in existence were not just faces in a crowd. This guy had a status far above the rest of the world. Even Alex, with all she had access to, would be turned away from some of the doors opened to him.

Jason looked at the pictures and books as he checked her expression from time to time.

When he sat back down, his long legs crossed toward hers. He threw an arm over the back of the couch as he tapped her foot with his playfully.

"When Coop told me who his contact was, I was just as surprised as you are now. But this is just a simple request really."

"I'm not surprised Coop stooped to calling in the big guns to get me to listen to him. And I don't do requests."

"How about orders, do you do those?"

"Not from you," she laughed.

He smiled and loosened his tie slightly. A look of nervousness passed over his face then he was back in control. Like something he hadn't thought about just crossed his mind.

"You're right," he apologized. "But that may change soon."

"Right," she smiled, "In your dreams."

"Fine, call it a business proposition then. I'd like to propose a joint venture of sorts. We can discuss it in Vegas, you know, on neutral ground."

"What kind of business?"

"A young man was killed in Vegas last night," Jason said, "I'm offering my assistance with finding the responsible party. Coop says you were interested in helping with the investigation."

Alex smiled and shook her head. She eased forward on the chair, placed her elbows on her knees and sighed.

"Coop's wrong," she grinned. "As he so often is. I'm not getting involved in the investigation."

Jason nodded and matched her posture. "He says you are," he grinned, then waved her open mouth shut. "We can split hairs about it later."

"If they're on your head when I get to split them, I'm in."

Jason laughed full and long as she stared at his hands. Although they were soft, she was sure he had used them for pleasure and pain many times during his existence.

"Don't get yourself all excited," he chuckled, "I may surprise you before this is all said and done."

"There is nothing you can do that would ever surprise me," Alex smiled. "But, I am curious why the death of a human would interest you."

"Why wouldn't it?" Jason purred. "If we're being set up, we'd like to find out why."

"Of course you would," Alex replied as she tried to stand and get him out of her office. "But this has nothing to do with me. If you'd bothered to call first, I could have saved you a trip."

He jerked her back down then slid his thumbs over the veins on the back of her hands. As he studied them, Alex could feel warmth crawl up her arms. He wanted her to relax so that he could connect to her mind more easily. His tone was almost hypnotic as he spoke.

"I'm sorry for showing up unannounced," he replied. "We didn't have the luxury of going through proper channels."

Alex had forgotten how vampires could be, especially male ones. With healthy appetites for power, wealth, and sex, this man had a reputation that rivaled the most popular of athletes in the human world. And Jason's exploits were both well-documented and publicized.

Alex knew the public persona as well as anyone else in the free world.

"It's called a telephone," she answered as she eased her hands free. "And I couldn't care less about Coop's problems right now. Why would I help them?"

Jason pulled her gently to her feet, then led the way to the windows.

"For their survival, of course," he replied close to her ear. "Theirs and the rest of the human race." He pointed to the crowded streets below. "If there's a rogue element working its way back into human society, you'd want to bring it down as quickly as you could, wouldn't you?" He brought up his smart phone, then tapped the screen with his thumb. Pictures of Alex and a young woman at the window of an apartment popped up, one after another. "And then there's her." He cleared his throat then put his lips to her other ear. "She's pretty, but I didn't get that vibe from you."

"Maybe I'm bi."

"How trendy," Jason chuckled. "What happened to the basketball player, what's his name?" Her scent tingled deep as it went from his nose straight to his brain. And her body chemistry changed in a matter of seconds. He couldn't help but feel slightly aroused even though it took his focus away from why he was here for just a second or two.

"Football, actually," she responded as she faced him. "What's this gonna cost me?"

Her closeness sent him backward two steps. He didn't expect that and from the look on her face, neither did she.

"Not much," Jason answered. "If you agree to come to Vegas, those pictures will disappear forever. I'll send you the file to destroy yourself."

"What else?"

"Are you always this paranoid?"

"Occupational hazard," Alex stated as she pushed past him and stopped at the door.

"The Council of Pure Blood Vampires would like a face to face with you too."

"Why?"

"To ask you for a favor in exchange for my help with finding this killer."

"When?"

"The main conference is set in Romania for the week before Thanksgiving," Jason grinned as he pushed his hands into his pockets on his way toward her.

"Will I meet with the Council before then?"

Alex smirked at him.

He laughed, "I don't know."

As hard as he tried to keep it down, desire crept up as he closed the small distance to her again. She just stared into his eyes, but her pupils betrayed her. They dilated when he reached her personal space and she took a deep breath, then her hand landed on the doorknob before she spoke again.

"When you know, call me."

Jason was a little annoyed at Alex's dismissal. As the door began to open, he pushed it shut and leaned on it with a grin.

"Right now, they're asking nicely, Alexa," he purred as his left arm wrapped around her waist to pull her into his body, "don't make them insist." When he placed his back against the door, his lips stopped a few inches from hers.

"I can't just call up the head of the Council and say 'Hey! Mind if I drop by with a six pack for a little chat?'" he continued. "We do treat him with some respect you know."

He tightened his grip around her when he felt her try to move away. To his surprise, instead of a slap to the face, she placed her hand on the door at his ear and let her finger tease the edge just a little. *That's more like it!* When she moved closer he thought he might get that taste after all.

"Well, be a good little lap dog and tell the head bloodsucker I'd like some respect too. When he decides on a date and time, he can call me," she whispered. "You can even use my phone if you want."

Jason swallowed his rage and kissed her. The growl coming from deep inside him escaped before he could stop it, but it did cause a strange reaction from her. She trembled, very slightly, but she did tremble and her fear pleased him.

"I'll do that from the car if you don't mind," he said as he released Alex from his grip.

He opened the door and his bodyguards stood straight and tall waiting for him to exit.

He turned to her again, stepped close and breathed into her ear one last time. "We can help you with your little problem. Coop and his sidekicks are in over their heads, that's why they came here for you," he grinned and scratched at his cheek like a child as he took her hand. "Oh, and if you ever refer to me as anyone's lap dog again, I'll make you wish you hadn't. Are we clear?"

"Crystal," Alex replied with an arrogant grin.

Jason kissed the beautifully brown skin of her hand and left her office with a smile on his face.

He would like to say his incisors burned to drop in response to the anger he was feeling, but that wouldn't be entirely true. Yes, he did want to rip out Alex's throat for the 'lap dog' jab, but he also wanted to pin her to the door, push himself deep inside her and take his fill. And he was fairly sure she wanted that too, for a few minutes anyway.

Jason felt claustrophobic all of a sudden as the elevator seemed to take its sweet time to get to the bottom floor. A heat rose inside him and it threatened to erupt. The sweet smell of fresh air rushed inside when the doors finally opened. He practically ran out the sliding doors with his bodyguards on his heels welcoming more fresh air in his face. His driver appeared at the backdoor in a flash. Jason slipped inside the dark, cool space and took a deep breath. Alex Stone was definitely the right person for this job. She might have been trembling, but it wasn't from fear. It was from an energy she kept bottled inside her. An energy Jason wanted to unleash.

CHAPTER 7

"Mr. Ramsey is expecting you, Ms. Stone," the steward greeted her. Handing her jacket to the coat-check, the steward led the way down the foyer. "He's taking drinks in the main conservatory. Please follow me."

His steps seemed measured. As if he would forget how to walk if he didn't keep the exact same pace every time. She found herself keeping up with him, step for step. A large gold placard hung on the wall of the first room they passed through. The Grand Hall was just that, grand. Every few feet were expensive Persian rugs covering the dark wooden floors. Fine leather furnishings sat in perfect conversation circles throughout the entire space. She was sure the paintings were originals and the marble statues were probably on loan from some museum that didn't have room for them anymore.

"The Geller was first opened in 1901 by Francis H. Geller," her escort began.

Alex tuned him out after 'drinks in the conservatory' came out of his pinched lips. Who knew places like this still existed? A bastion to the white male ego that should have died a long time ago, *The Geller* seemed to be thriving, tucked away in a quiet corner of downtown. Everywhere she looked, men sat or stood in tailored suits smoking Cubans and drinking insanely expensive liquor from crystal glasses. No one seemed too surprised to see her. There were the occasional odd glances in their direction, mostly from the old money types.

"Who do you have to kill to get into this place," she thought she said under her breath.

"I could get you a list, if you'd like," he replied with a weird grin.

Alex felt her cheeks burn from embarrassment. "Sorry."

"No need to apologize, Ms. Stone," he replied. "I understood you were just being facetious." When they finally came to a stop, they were in the doorway of a slightly less grand room. Its golden placard said simply 'Conservatory'. The steward pointed to the small group of men in the center of the room. "May I have someone bring you a drink?"

"No thanks," she replied. "This won't take long."

"As you wish," he stated, then turned and walked away.

The air inside was cool and smelled of cigars. The excess reminded her she was just a guest and, even if she wanted, she would never be allowed here unless it was at someone's request. The man she was meeting, seated in the small group the steward pointed out to her, looked up and smiled. The three young men around him glanced in her direction, but continued their conversation. She moved inside. Masculine laughter filled the space as she stood outside the semicircle waiting for her host to acknowledge her presence.

Like the gentleman he pretended to be, Leland Ramsey stood, buttoned his jacket and extended his enormous hand out to her. His bulky body looked almost stuffed inside the expensive suit. But it was tailor-made for his build. His salt and pepper waves were professionally cut. His manicured nails and everything else about him screamed success. Even the dark honey tone of his skin announced that money really could buy anything, even a perfect complexion.

"Alex! You look wonderful, as always," he stated in a polished timbre. His parents were old Southern folks. Hard working and polite, Leland Ramsey grew up not too far from where they sat now. You wouldn't know it from his manner though.

He gave her a firm, but not too friendly handshake. This wasn't a friendly meeting. Maybe the handshake was to remind her of that fact. After quick introductions, the young men left them alone. Leland waved at the chair next to his and motioned for a waiter.

"I'll have another Dalmore," Leland stated.

"And for the lady?" the young man asked Leland.

"Nothing," Alex interrupted before Leland answered for her. She hated scotch and pretense. Both of which Leland seemed to revel in.

"Are you sure?" Leland said. "They have the best selection in the city."

"I'm good," she replied and the young man left.

"So how have you been?" Leland began the

conversation in a cheery tone. "Last I heard, you were in London introducing your new line."

"That was a year ago, Leland," Alex sighed.

"Really?" he smiled as he took the drink from the silver tray the young man held out to him. "How time flies."

When she crossed her legs toward him, it was unintentional—habit, really. She didn't want to give the impression she was interested in small talk. She wanted Leland to get to the point so she could get out of this place.

"You might run the hybrid program, but you don't run me," Alex said. "So, get to the point so I can get back to my real job."

He cleared his throat and placed the glass down with hardly a sound. "I do run you. At least until the contract is fulfilled, so get over yourself." The silver cufflinks blinked in the artificial lighting overhead as he adjusted them absently. "Now, I'm sure you've heard about the body found in Las Vegas last night?"

"Yes." A sharp pain stabbed at the back of her left eye. The body had a name, but that wasn't important, was it?

"You don't seem very surprised."

Alex turned toward him. "What do you want?"

"We'd like you to accept Mr. Stavros's offer to help us find out what happened," he replied.

Alex moved to the edge of her uncomfortable chair. "How did you find out . . . never mind."

Leland adjusted his posture, turning his head

toward her. There was meanness in his brown eyes as he looked at her. It seemed to belong there—in the eyes of a man who wouldn't give anyone the time of day unless there was profit in it.

As with most people in this business, the money he threw around was made the old fashioned way, by somewhat nefarious means. He thought since he'd made a new life for himself, he could treat most people like the help. What it made him, to Alex anyway, was a gigantic douche and as outdated as this club.

"We don't need their help with this," Alex replied. "Just have another team assigned to the investigation."

"No," Leland sighed as he tapped his phone. "You are hardly in any position to make assignments or turn down a direct order."

"I'm done cleaning up my father's messes," she stated.

Leland turned slightly in the chair, uncrossed his legs and glared at her. She felt like she was in the principal's office.

"Ms. Stone, we have an agreement. If you renege, the consequences would be dire." He tapped the screen of his phone then held it up for her to see. She was getting kind of tired of people doing that. "As the contract dictates, you are to locate all six hybrids. You've only found three and two of them are dead now. That makes this assignment even more important, don't you agree?"

The little grin on his lips dripped with hatred

and superiority. She hated it and him.

"Dire," she repeated. "That sounded like a threat, Mr. Ramsey." She laughed at him because she could see how angry it made him. "If I disappear, the consequences for you and Strategic will be more than just dire."

"You may bring us down, but what happens to you will be much more personal," he snapped at her. "The mental institution we put you in won't be as nice as the last one, I promise you that."

"Try it," she hissed.

His chuckle always irritated her. "Let's not get into a pissing contest over this. This isn't just *our* mess, it's yours too and you know that. We have to get in front of this before it gets out of control."

"It's already out of control," Alex said. "We should have left them where they were, living their lives without our interference."

"And we would have if someone hadn't started picking them off," he replied. "If Mr. Stavros has been given instruction to help us find out who and why, we should take advantage of this opportunity."

Alex pushed away the urge to grab him by the neck and squeeze until his eyes popped out of his head with every muscle in her body. From the moment she found out Dr. Carlisle was experimenting with human and vampire DNA, she knew it would only bring trouble. How he kept it off the books and funded was a mystery until she hacked his data files. Leland Ramsey was the money behind the project. It was Leland who provided Dr. Carlisle with the volunteers too. Where those women came from and where they disappeared to was still a mystery.

The six newborn babies, all male, were subjected to various procedures in an effort to create a being that would be immune to the bite. A creature that could not be turned and did not need to feed on blood to survive. And they didn't need to be on the supplement either. In short, a creature like her, only created in a lab, not born, as she was. Dr. Carlisle perfected the process in the six and then placed them with childless families in the real world. But then something went wrong with one of the hybrids, prompting Dr. Carlisle to order her to bring them all in for testing.

Alex knew returning those hybrids to the program was a bad idea, but she wanted out. She had successfully tracked down the strongest of the hybrids—the ones who survived through their teenage years anyway.

"They don't know the truth," Alex hissed. "What happens when the vampires find out what you and the good doctor have been doing all these years? What happens when they find out you've created a being that can't be turned by experimenting on one of their own? A being that you can't even find now! And what happens to the innocents caught in the crossfire?"

"Why do you care?" Leland asked, taking the last sip of golden liquid from his glass then placing it on the table between them. "They were a means to an end for you right? Isn't that what you said?"

"Go to hell," she answered. "If not for me, you wouldn't have found any of them! Don't forget that."

"Yes, we owe you a great deal," Leland grinned as he stood, "but, you also owe us and that's why you're going to do this and you're going to accept Jason Stavros's offer."

Alex stood, taking the arm he held out to her as they began to walk back the way she came. Through the Grand Hall, Leland delivered her to coat-check once more. Helping with her jacket, he remained quiet as they walked toward the front door. The doorman pushed it open with a bow, as he touched the brim of his cap.

Once outside, they both took a deep breath. A long black limo pulled up to the curb. Leland stepped close to Alex.

"Do this," he said, "and your contract will be fulfilled."

"You tell the old man I want his word this time, in writing," she replied stuffing her hands in her pockets as the cool breeze pushed at her. Leland stepped into her personal space, giving her a quick peck on the cheek.

"Of course," he said as he turned to the car again. His driver opened the back door of the limo. "Can I give you a lift somewhere?"

"No, thank you, Mr. Ramsey," Alex shook her head. "But you have a good evening."

The vampires were ahead of them on this one. Alex couldn't decide if that was good or bad. The only thing she knew for sure was that two hybrids were dead and she really did want to find out why. What she didn't want to do was work with Coop or Jason to do it, but maybe that was a blessing in disguise. She didn't have to use her own money and they would keep her identity safe if she agreed to help. Next stop was getting Sara out of the line of fire just in case someone mistook her for one of the hybrids.

Those poor kids, she thought as she drove through the city toward Sara's apartment. It was hard for her to imagine her father experimenting on babies. But what was harder to fathom was why no one had stopped him. At least the test subjects in her program had a choice. Each soldier was given the opportunity to turn Dr. Carlisle down. No hard feelings. Even after they found out that vampires and werewolves were real, shown proof, they could still back out. Babies couldn't do that.

Just thinking about it now made her head hurt. Of all the things she had seen her father do—of all the things she'd done under the guise of national security—she couldn't imagine taking an innocent child and subjecting them to experiments just to prove a point.

CHAPTER 8

The breezy afternoon turned into a windy evening. Alex felt kind of refreshed despite what she had to do. All the native Texans milled about the faux town square as the twinkling lights popped on one group at a time. "Ma'am," she heard the black suited businessman in the cowboy hat say as he passed briefcase in one hand, and mobile phone in the other. A grin moved over her lips. It was always so weird to see grown men in expensive suits and more expensive cowboy boots walking around like that was the most normal thing in the world. But around here, it was.

Everyone else, with light jackets and holiday Starbucks coffee cups in their hands, filled the square as the day came to an end. At this time of year, shopping was the local pastime, next to Cowboys football. For Alex, it would have been just one more day not unlike any other except for one thing, a piece of her life had been uncovered and she had to plug that hole before more secrets came out.

She put the phone to her ear in hopes of it going to voicemail. She hated to hear 'I told you so'. When he answered, Alex hesitated.

"You're late," he said. The gravel in his voice indicated he'd just woken up or hadn't been to sleep yet. It was hard to tell with him. It depended on the day whether or not Benjamin Palmer was the biggest jackass on the planet or the most understanding guy in the world. Tonight, he seemed somewhere in between.

"Daylight savings time ended yesterday," Alex replied. "So technically, I'm right on time."

"What's wrong," Ben replied. "Usually, me telling you you're late elicits a 'bite me' from you. You must be in deep shit right now."

Alex frowned. "I need an extraction."

"For who?"

"The girl."

"The girl you said no one would care about," Ben chuckled. "The bite junkie with the crush on you? Well, I never thought I'd live to see the day the Dagger was wrong about something."

Ben laughed hard as the sound traveled through the receiver and into the evening buzz of conversation around her.

"You done?" Alex exhaled.

Ben cleared his throat and chuckled again. "What happened? Why do you want to move her?"

"I got another call from Coop and a visit from Jason Stavros this morning. Stavros had pictures, so move her, tonight."

There was a weird silence on the other end of the phone. Then she heard Ben curse and glass break.

"How much does Stavros know?" Ben asked, with very little emotion.

"He thinks I'm hiding my *girlfriend*," she giggled. "But that doesn't mean he won't keep digging if

I don't go to Vegas."

"And how come Coop's still calling you?"

"Because you wouldn't answer the phone, apparently."

Ben let out a long sigh, "Coop knows he's burned every freaking bridge he had with me. He can go to hell for all I care."

"Well, they need my help with something," she said, "and it involves Jason Stavros."

"Like what kind of help?" Ben replied.

"The bodies . . ."

"Yea."

"Hybrids," she almost whispered for some reason. "My assignment."

There was the emotion Alex had expected from Ben when she told him the girl had to be moved. Now she was afraid she really was in deep shit. He hated Ramsey more than she did.

"How did that happen?"

"I don't know, and apparently neither does Strategic."

"They're just trying to keep you tied up with them, Alex," Ben groaned. "Don't believe it."

"What happened in Vegas last night was real Ben," Alex huffed. "So now I have to help them or I'll never get out of that contract."

There was an edge to Ben's voice when he spoke. He never got mad about anything. But, then again, he never liked Jesse Cooper that much either. "Why can't they solve their own damn problems? They left you in that fucking place without a second thought! You don't really owe them anything, Alex."

"Yes I do," she answered as she stood to continue to her destination. "The program wasn't going to come to a crashing halt because I lost it! They had to move on. I understand that."

More glass broke and cursing from Ben and Alex's heart began to race. The vibe coming across the air waves sent her senses into overdrive. She could hear all kinds of things on the air around her, random conversations from buildings, and cars as they passed along the street a few yards away. And everything mixed with Ben's anger and fear as Alex tried to focus again.

"Ramsey threatened me," she said as she walked slowly toward the girl's apartment building directly across from the town square. "Can you get the girl moved please?"

"Yea," he replied. "What are you gonna do?"

"I have something to take care of," Alex replied. "I'll—"

All of a sudden, a searing pain shot through her temples stopping her in her tracks. The sound of sirens from blocks away popped inside her head. As the emergency vehicles came closer, her palms began to sweat and her vision sharpened without her trying.

As the vehicles pulled up in front of the building she was headed to, two uniformed police officers stepped from a cruiser, followed by EMTs and a bright red fire truck. She stopped just short of the crowd that was gathering in the square. Suddenly, everything went into slow motion. The gurney being pulled from the back of the ambulance while more police arrived for crowd control gave Alex a queasy feeling. She opened her coat to the breeze as she turned in the other direction.

"Alex," she finally heard Ben yelling. "Hey! What's going on?"

She moved as slowly as she could so that no one paid any attention to her.

"Forget the extraction," she said in one short breath.

"Why," Ben asked. "What's wrong?"

When she reached her car, she placed one hand on the hood to steady herself. Taking several deep breaths, the nausea began to subside and the sweat began to dry from the strong wind in her face.

"She's dead." Alex hung up on Ben as she climbed into the car and sped away.

Nice weather aside, the place hadn't really changed much since the last time he was there. And, just like then, Jesse Cooper was looking for a girl. But not just any girl it turned out. The little tomboy with the big attitude had skills he had no idea existed, in anyone, especially a sixteen year old high school junior from Texas.

In the Navy, when the brass says jump, you don't have to say how high; you just jump and hope you made the cut. Jesse Cooper, Navy Seal and all around great guy made the cut. Forgoing desk duty after being injured on assignment, Coop decided to take the assignment no one else wanted. To retrieve and deliver a new recruit to some hush hush outfit stationed at Edwards Air Force Base. Or the outlying building to be exact. No one knew what the hell was going on out there, but there had been a lot of activity in the summer of 1993 and it had everyone talking on base.

Coop just wanted to get back on active duty, so he took the shit assignment to bring back this new guy and deliver him to Area 51 in 72 hours. Easy. He spotted the fresh face private nervously craning his neck to see Coop over the crowd that deplaned at an annoyingly slow pace. *Southerners never seem to be in a rush to do anything*, he thought, waving at the kid in khakis.

"Lieutenant Cooper," the young man stated with perfect salute. "Welcome to Texas, sir. I'm Private Hanson. I'll be your driver while you're here, sir." The handshake was firm, and he held it for the right amount of time before he let go of Coop's hand.

"Nice to meet you Hanson," Coop replied. "Do I have time to hit the head before we go?"

"Yes, sir," Hanson nodded in the direction for the restrooms a few feet away. He took Coop's duffle and waited outside the entrance.

After a quick pit stop, they were on the way to pick up the new recruit. Coop flipped through the pages absently. His driver chatted about the city and landmarks he might want to see while he was in town.

None of that really mattered. Coop just wanted to pick up the kid, maybe get a bite to eat and a beer, and then get back to the West Coast. San Diego put this place to shame. Sunny skies, beautiful beaches and women to match; he was ready for a nice little break after this assignment was over. And he was certain a high school kid wouldn't know the first thing about where to have a good time around here. As he scanned page after page, he wondered why there were no pictures of this kid in the file. Maybe it was just an oversight. Paperwork was never the military's strong suit.

"So, how long are you going to be here, sir?" Hanson asked.

"Just a couple of days," Coop replied. He cranked up the a/c when he felt a bead of sweat roll down his spine "Is it always so hot here?"

Hanson chuckled, glanced in the rear, then to his left to change lanes. "Sorry, sir. After you've been here for a while, you hardly notice it. Yesterday was 101! This is a cold front around here." He tapped the temperature gauge over the a/c unit in the dash. It read 95 degrees.

As he remembered, he could almost feel that heat. Then he remembered what she looked like back then. She stepped inside the fancy coffee shop and looked directly at him and Private Hanson. It was pretty hard to miss them since they were the only people in the shop dressed in military uniforms. Thrown over her shoulder was a leather backpack. It looked brand new. Over the years it would become worn and beaten, but she never went on a mission without it.

"Lieutenant Cooper," she asked. "I think you're looking for me."

"I don't think so little girl," Coop remembered laughing as he and Hanson stood. No one told him he was looking for a girl.

"I'm Alex Stone," she stated as the pack dropped in the empty chair between them.

Coop could feel his caramel colored skin blush bright red. Embarrassed was an understatement. "Sorry sis, I didn't know, and there were no pictures of you in the file."

She grinned, shrugged and sat down. "Don't worry about it. I'm used to it, trust me."

A quick glance in Hanson's direction and he could see the confusion on his face too. Why would the U.S. military recruit a teenage girl? This had to be illegal and just a little freaky.

"How old are you?" Hanson whispered. "I mean, you have to be eighteen to join the service."

"Yea, I know," she stated.

"This is some kind of joke, right," Coop said with a grin. "My buddies pull a prank? What are they paying you, sweetie? Where are those assholes!"

He looked at her and he knew it wasn't a joke. Now he was really scared.

"I don't know where the assholes are and this is not a joke, unfortunately. We should get going," she stood, pulled the pack to her shoulder and waited for them to lead the way.

Hanson tried to take her pack, but she brushed him off. Coop got the feeling that she didn't let people do things for her if she didn't have to. She didn't say a word to him in the car, in the airport, or on the plane. And once they arrived at McCarran, a more official escort waited for her and he was dismissed rather abruptly. Jesse Cooper would not see Alexa Stone again for five years.

"She's moving again, when she stops I'll send the address," Erin's voice boomed in their earpieces and Coop jumped back to the present. She and Amy stayed at the hotel to do research on the last victim.

"Thanks," Coop replied.

"How long do we have to be here, Coop?" Kai whined. "I thought we were getting a little break after Vegas?"

"We don't get breaks. Besides, Vegas was a detour," he answered. "We were headed here in the first place remember?"

He was glad to sit on the patio of a Tex-Mex eatery on a beautifully cool evening in downtown Fort Worth, Texas. Who wouldn't? Chasing corpses across three states was tough enough. But having to do it on almost no sleep and bad fast food was just asking a little too much. This place may as well be a five star in NYC compared to that.

"And if we can't get her on board, then what," David added.

"We go to Plan B."

"Which is?" Xavier jumped into the

conversation.

Coop eased down in the chair and stared up at the stars. "I'm working on it."

All at once he noticed it. The whispers and glances all around them. Even the wait staff gawked and whispered to each other. Their public image was that of personal security to the rich and famous. If you were anyone and you needed the best security team money could buy, your money would buy them. They could be seen escorting dignitaries one week and rock stars the next. That's why mostly everyone under the age of thirty knew who the Trackers were on sight.

Coop should have been able to pick up the sounds from across the patio instantly, but his power was off tonight. Well, it had actually been off for the last few months. The doctors had tweaked his formula three times and he still had moments where nothing worked the way it should have. Tonight was one of those nights. He took another pill and washed it down with the last of the Budweiser.

"Should you be popping those things like that, boss?" Xavier whispered, waving for the waiter. "I mean, that's like the fifth one today."

"Who are you," Coop coughed, "my mother? Don't worry about it. I'm fine."

Xavier shrugged as the twins, Kai and David, fidgeted in their seats. Coop didn't want to admit that Xavier might have a point. If he did, then he'd have to admit he was scared too. The effects were not lasting as long and it was getting harder to focus and heal. One of them would eventually report it, but until then Coop could fake it, couldn't he?

"The ladies at that table over there would like to buy y'all another round," the skinny waiter said, as he placed a frosty pitcher in the center of their table.

Everywhere they went, women bought drinks and dinners. Last year, a diplomat's daughter tried to buy the services of the entire team for a night. She wasn't looking for protection though. Coop winked at them and turned back to the team.

"Sebastian's got point once we get her location," Coop began. "We'll be waiting at the bar. Watch your ass with her and make sure you're not followed."

Sebastian gave him a nod even though he was still focused on the table of pretty women in the far corner.

"Hey," Coop sniffed as the chip he threw bounced off the back of Sebastian's head. Pretty boy looks and an innocent but killer smile, he had been a surfer in his other life. In this life, he was the best tactical agent Coop had ever seen. "What did I just say?"

"Once Erin locks her location, bring her to you in one piece and make sure nobody follows."

"Good boy. Now as for Stavros, this assignment is important, so check your tablets for the agenda and updates from home. We go in as usual—world famous security specialists to the stars. We keep him safe and try to get as much intel on what's really going on with them as we can."

"Why Romania? I mean, was somebody trying to be funny or something?" Xavier asked as he poured more beer in his glass. "They do know Stoker made that shit up, right? And right before Christmas, really?"

Xavier always looked like he was flexing, but he was just cut like nobody's business. Warm brown skin and beautiful brown eyes, he took to weapons like a kid to candy.

"What," Coop chuckled. "You got plans for the holiday? Playing Santy Claus at the Y?"

"No," he smiled. "But, I do have a few ho, ho, hoes I'd like to get close to!"

Male laughter shook the glasses on the table and turned heads.

Kai and David bumped fists then emptied their glasses as well.

Even though they were not identical, they were a lot alike. As the demolitions team, Coop was always surprised at the ways they could completely destroy any target they were given.

"Well you're gonna have to put that on hold if we end up escorting Stavros to Romania, sorry."

"If," Sebastian chimed in. "I thought it was a lock?"

"Not quite," Coop sighed. "SecDef and the head of the Council are still working out the logistics for foreign soil. Since he actually carries a passport that says he's a U.S citizen, we should call the shots. But *King Biter* says since he's a vampire, he's not really a citizen of any country but theirs. It's a stupid argument if you ask me."

"Whatever," Kai sighed. "We have bigger problems than babysitting Stavros right now."

"Yea, but they may be involved, so we have to get as close as we can," Coop replied pouring another glass of beer.

"And, if they had anything to do with the deaths of our two operatives," Xavier added, "we should be the ones to bring them in. And then there's the matter of the Box missing."

Sebastian downed his warm beer and stood up, wiping his mouth on the white napkin in his hand, his blue eyes giving off a radiant shine as he ran his fingers through his blond hair.

"While you gents argue over that, I'm going to go and thank the ladies properly."

"Don't take too long," Coop said. "You're on the clock, son. And no snacking between meals either."

"Yea, yea, clock," he mumbled as he walked away. "No snacks, got it, Dad!"

Chapter 9

She stopped to give her eyes time to adjust to the dim light of the alley and the scent of trash that replaced the burger odor from the shop across the street. Huddled around an old metal drum, figures, illuminated by the fire as it danced in the breeze and mesmerized by the flames, moved only slightly as she approached.

Upon closer inspection, the men passed around a bottle as their friendly conversation continued. The cleanest of them turned when she kicked a bottle in her path. He moved one step to his left to make room for her at the fire.

"What took you so long?" he smiled at her.

"Sorry. I had to see a friend about something," she replied.

The bum she stood next to led the others away, but the tall man remained.

His tan jacket was clean and fit him perfectly. His fresh haircut, high and tight, and slightly gray at the temples didn't give away his age, only his place of employment. The brass that hung from the front of his shirt was mostly hidden from view by the jacket. The U.S. Army pin on his collar sparkled by the fire light. His hands were stuffed in the pockets of his khakis and the brown leather of his boots, worn from years of use, were not Army issue. She guessed he didn't want to ruin a good shine standing in a cruddy alley.

"Care to elaborate?" he said.

"On? Oh . . . not really," Alex answered.

"Okay, what's new then?"

"Not much. Launch should be on time, for once."

"That's a good thing, right?" he grinned.

Alex shrugged as they continued to watch the dance of the flames.

"At the risk of sounding like a bad movie character," he said. "We gotta stop meeting like this."

They faced each other and his left brow went up slightly as he waited for a reply.

"It's safer this way."

"Yea, but my office is much more comfortable," he chuckled.

"Good point," she sighed, then turned back to the fire.

Scratching at his cheek, the man blinked a couple of times then he sighed. "Are you sleeping any better?"

"A little, I guess."

"You guess?"

"It's hard to tell," she replied as her eyes scanned the alley and the men behind her. They were still sharing a bottle and talking amongst themselves. "*Better* is such a relative term when it comes to sleep, don't you think?"

"Relative to what?" he replied.

"Is it better to sleep and have dreams about

being killed by monsters," Alex stated. "Or, not sleep at all and think about it anyway?"

He looked around to make sure no one heard what she said. The homeless men who lived in this alley were veterans and Captain Thomas Gilchrest did his best work down here. Doling out free mental health services and sometimes money for a safe place to sleep for the night, he got help from people like Alex.

"Most people have dreams about being chased, hunted. Usually it's just your subconscious trying to work out something your conscious mind can't," he whispered. "I'm not sure why you're making them monsters though."

"Do you remember the first time we met?" she asked as he moved closer to her.

Her discomfort displayed itself almost immediately. She pushed her hands inside the kangaroo pocket of her hooded sweatshirt. Absently biting her lower lip, he knew she didn't like to talk about that time.

"Yes, I remember," he answered.

"What did you think?" she asked in a hushed tone. "Of me, I mean."

"I thought how strange it was for a young woman to be in a military psych ward."

"What did they tell you about me?"

"That you'd seen combat, but what kind and the details of your assignment were classified," he answered. "I was just there to assess your ability to return to active duty."

"You told them not to send me back," she said as

she faced him.

An easy calm suddenly replaced the tension she displayed earlier. Dr. Gilchrest took a step back, but kept eye contact with her. "Yes and I'd do it again. Combat was no place for you then."

"Then where should I have been, doctor, in your professional opinion?"

He stepped back into her personal space expecting her to retreat, but she didn't. Stupid of him to think that someone like her would be afraid of an almost retired Army psychiatrist carrying twenty pounds of extra weight his personal physician had told him to lose.

"In my professional opinion," he said, then cleared his dry throat. "You should have been at a 'kegger' having your first drink of cheap beer, like every other twenty-one year old in America. You should have been falling in love, studying for finals, waking up hung over; anything but what you were ordered to do in that desert fifteen years ago."

Alex dropped her head and closed her eyes. "Can't change the past." The fire crackled and popped as silence fell between them again. "I do appreciate you seeing me off the books, doc," she said as her eyes opened and she backed away.

"Well it's the least I could do after all the financial help your company has given this outreach program," he smiled. "Not many people take the time to care about what happens when wars end. No one comes home the way they were when they left."

"Don't I know it," she said, mostly under her breath. "I'm glad to help."

"Am I helping you at all?" he asked as he followed her down the alley toward her car. "I really want to help you, Alex."

"You are, I swear."

"I don't feel like I am because you won't open up to me for some reason. You can trust me."

"I've probably told you more than I should have. Too much information can be dangerous."

"For who?"

"You," she answered. She stopped at the curb, turned and held out an envelope stuffed with cash. "I'm headed to Vegas for a couple days, so I won't get to see you next week."

"That's too much," Dr. Gilchrest insisted.

"How do you know?" she smiled. "Besides, your funding is coming up for review. You might need this to keep you going till then."

"How do you know so much about me?" he asked as he took the envelope. "Should I really be worried? About you, I mean."

"No, you should worry about these guys. They depend on you, Dr. Gilchrest."

"What about you?" she heard the doctor shout as she crossed the street to her car.

"What about me?"

He stepped up to the mailbox, leaned on it as his arms crossed over his chest.

"Who do you depend on?"

Alex opened the door, put one leg in and waved as she dropped down inside.

"Myself," she yelled as she drove away.

CHAPTER 10

She took the darkest streets to her building on purpose. Covered in shadows, she could use them to draw the young man that was following her out. He dropped in behind her a few miles back. At first she thought it was just a coincidence. Maybe he was just going in her direction, but when his lips began to move, she knew he wasn't just singing to his favorite tune. He had a receiver in his ear. When she focused, she could hear a low hum from the transmitter in the air. Funny how some things never change. Even with the kind of technology available to Strategic, all they could think of was to put a tail on her. Coop had to know she'd make him before he got too close. Didn't he remember what Alex was capable of? She guessed he'd either forgotten or never really knew in the first place. Too bad for his errand boy.

The parking garage was quiet as Alex climbed from the car, pulling her bag with her.

She held her keys in her hand as she made her way toward the elevator. She pressed the button and waited for the steel box. Then, dropping the bag to the ground along with her keys, Alex forced her foot into his gut. He caught the right she threw and slammed an open palm into the center of her chest.

The elevator doors opened just in time. Falling

through, Alex jumped out of the box just as the doors closed again. He ran and she gave chase.

At the top of the ten story structure, they stopped.

Moving cautiously, Alex could smell his fear in the air around them.

The young man found himself on the ground when Alex's right fist connected with his squared jaw. Spitting out his own blood, he struggled to stand. Her elbow crashed against his cheek, before he could speak, spinning him around and slamming his back against the low wall around the roof.

It had taken so little effort to pluck him from the ground and hold him over the side of the building that she surprised herself. He couldn't speak because her hand was wrapped around his neck.

The stranger's icy blue eyes began to turn a pale pink as she cut off his air supply. Letting him go without a second thought, she turned away with a sigh.

Walking calmly toward the stairs she paused again.

Not giving a second thought to how she would dispose of the body, she was more worried that he wasn't screaming on the way down.

Peering over the side, a few feet below her, he clung to the building, looking up and grinning like an idiot. Those blue orbs, glassy, but big, stared up innocently.

Adjusting his grip on the building, he grunted, "Coop sent me." As he inched closer to the top he blew out a hard breath. "You're not gonna give me a hand?"

Alex planted her hands on the ledge and shook her head, "Nope."

The young man slid one hand up and turned his head slightly. The black script letters of his tattoo, only visible at a certain light spectrum, jumped out at her.

"He just wants to talk to you."

"I told him I'd think about it. Where is he?"

When he swung a muscular arm over the ledge, she backed away, "He's waiting for us down the street."

Once he dropped, safe again on solid ground, he leaned over and spit out more blood. He wiped his bloody fingertips gracefully on a handkerchief from his jacket pocket.

"Whatever's going on is your problem, not mine."

He followed her back to the elevator and pressed the button before she could.

"He said you'd be like that, but he told me not to take 'no' for answer," he mumbled as the elevator made its way up.

"And, what do you think you can do to change my mind," she asked, spinning around.

"Well, I could beg, but that won't be pretty," he grinned sweetly. "It's just one drink and some conversation, that's all."

Back at her car, Alex tossed the bag in the trunk and waited for him to get in.

"So," she said without looking at him. "Where

to?"

His blue eyes locked on hers again. When he grinned, his pearly white teeth were just visible behind rosy lips and perfect cheekbones. "Not far from here."

Her phone buzzed. She popped it in the holder and pressed the speaker function.

"Guess who!"

"You mother . . ."

Sebastian found it hard to focus with her anger all around the small space. From the passenger seat he couldn't get away from the scent.

"I've been called worse," they heard Coop sigh. "Anyway, we're in a nice little bar about a mile from where you are. See ya in a few?"

"I got kicked out, remember? Call Ben," Alex groaned with a quick glance at Sebastian.

Coop pushed out a long sigh and this time they heard someone ask if they could really trust her. Sebastian could smell the spike in her temperature at that remark and it scared him.

"You took the easy way out and he's not answering. You heard from him lately?"

"Nope," Alex replied. "He's probably avoiding you too come to think of it."

Sebastian smiled as he buckled up. "Lucky us," he said with a low laugh.

Coop's laugh brought a frown to her pretty face. Sebastian placed his hands on his knees and waited for further instructions. He also made sure to turn his head so she could see it. Poised just over the large vein in his neck, that tattoo made him an official member of the Trackers even if he was a vampire. And by the way her heartbeat changed, she didn't like that at all.

"Sebastian can get you here safely," he heard Coop say. "Don't let the handsome face fool ya though!"

When the line went silent, she shot the phone the finger then turned to him.

Warm, like a blanket, her scent wrapped around him. It felt good to be this close to her for some reason. Sebastian had to admit she was something of a loose cannon, but he liked that. Like the moment when he crossed over, dark and frightening, Sebastian was almost disappointed she didn't seem to like him or the situation.

Just like him to pick a crappy biker bar, Alex thought as they eased into the makeshift parking lot. The light poles sat at odd angles that threw weird shadows everywhere.

They sat in the dark of the car with nothing but the sound of her breath to fill the awkward silence between them.

"Um . . . we should get inside," Sebastian said. "He just wants to talk, that's all."

"Just so you know," Alex replied as she opened the door. "I'm gonna finish what I started with you earlier if this goes sideways. Are we clear?"

"You really should try decaf," he replied, then slammed the car door with her. "Look, my orders were to bring you here and to let you know your status has been upgraded, so . . ."

"My status *was* no contact. What changed?"

"You'll have to ask Coop," he sighed. "He's in command."

"Coop," Alex laughed this time. "How many asses did he have to kiss to get that job?"

Sebastian shrugged as he led the way to the front entrance. "He's always been a Team Commander."

Alex stepped into his personal space and took a deep breath. He smelled good. Nice expensive cologne and that fresh out the dryer smell to his clothes. "No, he hasn't."

CHAPTER 11

Her vampire escort waved and shook hands like he was politician. She felt like she should know these people, but no one looked familiar until his face came into view.

At the pool table, Jesse Cooper hardly looked like the brash young Navy Seal Lieutenant she met all those years ago. If not for the Navy tattoo and brilliant smile of his, he'd be a stranger too. The yellow nine banked, then disappeared in the pocket in the far corner. The eight followed shortly thereafter and the guy Coop just beat slapped a hundred in his outstretched palm and cursed.

"Thanks," Coop smiled as he waved with the new bill. His companions clapped and hooted as the man disappeared into the crowd. "Not bad for an old man, huh?"

Sebastian stepped up to the table and jerked his thumb in Alex's direction.

Coop's hazel eyes peered over one broad shoulder and danced when he saw her. That was another thing she remembered about Jesse Cooper—animated facial expressions highlighted by beautiful hazel eyes.

"*Ay dios mio*," he harped with a shake of his head. "Damn girl, you . . . you look like hell!" They all laughed as he took her chin in his hand and examined the bruise with one eye. She pulled her face away and stood perfectly still as he walked around her slowly.

"You look great, actually, even in that get up."

"She tried to throw me off a building," Sebastian replied as he lined up a shot. "I'm fine though; thanks for asking."

Coop chuckled, doing a double take. "I told you to be careful."

"I was careful," Sebastian smiled.

"Well, she let you live, so she must like you."

"Can she like me less, 'cuz that hurt."

They both laughed as Coop turned, stepped up to Alex and placed his hand to her cheek.

"So, how long has it been?"

She pushed his hand away and smiled. "Not long enough."

"Ten years," Coop sneered down on her. "You missed me. Admit it?"

With a shy bat of her eyelashes she stepped closer to him. "I missed the rash I got from poison ivy on that mission to that rainforest more."

"I did offer to scratch it for you, but . . ." he chuckled.

That collective laughter just irritated her. And Coop circling her like a buzzard didn't help the matter any.

"Nice place. Meth den closed for the evening, I'm guessing," Alex said.

Once Coop was back in her face, his smile faded and his pupils dilated.

Every vein in his neck and upper arms popped out at once and she could smell the change immediately, excitement—sexual excitement to be exact. His own Tracker brand etched over that vein in his neck; she remembered when they were all marked for life.

"Just trying to make you feel at home," he chuckled.

"What's the emergency, Coop?" Alex asked as he continued to move his eyes like he would his hands if she allowed him to touch her, ever. "I've had about all the excitement I can stand today. Stavros shows up at my office. Ramsey summons me back to the fifties for a little chat and you send the boy wonder to bring me to this shit box for a talk. I'm here, so talk."

"The box is gone," he hummed, turned and sat down on the edge of the pool table.

"What box?"

"The Sandbox."

"When?"

Coop grinned. "January."

"It's been gone almost a year," she frowned.

"Three years to be exact," he smiled at her.

She laughed, but what she really wanted to do was find the quickest way off the planet. That cryogenic crypt was supposed to be virtually impenetrable. The only way to open it was to remove one of the four biometric cylinders used to seal the lock. But not just any one of the cylinders, it had to be the right one, and only three people knew which cylinder would open the cage.

Sandbox was the name of the mission to capture Tristan Ambrose. As the leader of Hellclaw, he commanded the largest of the vampire clans back then. Hellclaw pretty much stuck to the classic vampire persona. They hunted humans for fun. Fed without permission or regard. Tristan broke every rule the Council of Pure Blood Vampires handed down. Life within the walls of his compound was that of legend. Weird devices used to slowly extract blood from the victims were found after he was captured. As Alex remembered, walking around that place was like being on a horror movie set. It gave her chills to think of it even now.

Coop laid a cue stick over his lap and held it at both ends as he stared at her. All the movement behind her had stopped. Except for the *Best of CCR* on the jukebox, no one made a sound. When she looked into the mirror on the far wall behind the tables, all eyes were on them.

"He's been loose all this time," she said. "Why come to me now?"

"The body in Vegas was one of the hybrids," he replied. "And that makes two."

If she started running now, maybe they wouldn't catch her. But once you start, you never stop. And there really was nowhere she could go that they wouldn't catch up to her eventually.

"That's too bad," she whispered.

"So, I need your help," Coop replied.

"Can you connect the deaths to Tristan?" she

asked as her stomach began to flip. "Do you even know where he might be?"

"Not yet," Coop answered, "but . . ."

"Then, no."

Before she could step away, the slim end of the stick struck her cheek and snapped her head to the right. When a drop of blood landed by her toe, she smiled as she wiped her mouth with the back of her hand. She ran her tongue along the inside of her mouth as her gaze lowered on Coop where he stood.

"Let's try this again. Two hybrids are dead. I'm not asking you, I'm telling you!"

"Get over yourself," she grinned.

He'd never actually hit her before, so his backhand, as weak as it was, took her completely by surprise. Someone righted her from behind and she pushed them off as she stepped back in to the line of fire. The taste of her own blood sent adrenaline through her entire body.

"Don't fuck with me, Alex," Coop growled in her face. "I'm not in the mood. Your contract isn't up yet. You still work for us, don't forget that."

"My contract doesn't include helping you clean up your own mess," she said. "If you lost him, you can find him without me."

He was fast, but Alex had always been faster. She blocked the right fist as it sailed toward her face, twisted his arm behind his back and pushed him into the pool table.

She turned quickly as one of the twins stepped

up to her. He found himself on his knees when she struck his Adam's apple with a quick jab, taking his wind. Then the other tried to force his foot into her right side, but she caught him by the ankle, jerking him forward. With the front of his shirt in her fist, she slammed him down on the small table that shattered like it was built from toothpicks. When her fist came down, it landed squarely on his chin.

The Latino, muscled and angry, attacked next. He pulled her away by the collar then shoved her into the wall. She dodged the right jab and he was stuck, up to his elbow in the sheet rock. Alex forced his head into the wall and his perfect nose exploded on impact. He howled like a wounded dog.

Suddenly, almost iron arms wrapped around her from behind.

"Okay, you win," Sebastian growled. "Don't make me hurt you!"

"Haven't you learned?" she groaned with a hard stomp to the arch of his right foot. "I like it rough!" She heard the bone break over his roar as she turned to face him.

Too quick for her to dodge, the back of his hand crashed against her cheek and stars danced through her head. Like a top that spun out of control, Alex landed in a heap on the dusty floor with Sebastian over her with a guilty look on his face. For some reason, he reached down to help her to her feet and he was too vulnerable for her to ignore.

She saw two of him, so she split the difference

and went for it. With enough force to move a small car, she planted both feet in the center of his chest and watched him fly through the air as if attached to a wire. Everyone in his flight path scattered.

He stopped because he crashed into the jukebox; otherwise Alex was sure that kick would have sent him straight through the wall and brick on the other side, no problem. But she was glad it was silent now, even if it took the destruction of a really nice machine like that.

The chair splintered over her shoulder and she was on her knees.

Coop jerked her up by her collar with some effort. When she landed on the pool table, he stood over her as he rubbed his shoulder. "This is a direct order. You remember those, don't you?"

"Vaguely," Alex laughed up at him. "What I do remember, clearly, is I never took them from you!"

"This order isn't coming from me."

"Then who?"

"Secretary of Defense."

She swallowed hard, pushed his hand away from her chest and sat up. "I don't take orders from him anymore either."

He let her swing her legs over the side, but kept her in place at the edge of the table.

"I'll let you tell him that," Coop smiled. "Meanwhile, we'll meet with Jason Stavros, in Vegas by the way, then . . ."

Her finger touched his lips and she shushed him. A playful and sexy grin moved over her face as she slipped down from the table. Coop shuddered when she kissed his cheek softly, stepped back, and shook his head slowly.

"I already got threatened by Stavros this morning, so save it. Whatever you're doing to keep them happy and hidden is not my business. I'm not going!"

"Don't think I'm not above having you arrested on live T.V. to get you on that plane," he smiled back.

"Go home Coop and take the Power Rangers with you. You were supposed to keep Tristan on ice and the hybrids alive. If it was him, then that's their blood on your hands. If the Council gets wind of what really happened, I'm not gonna stand in front of you when the shit hits the fan," she said as she turned.

The young men, beaten and bloody, blocked her attempt at a really cool exit.

"If this is Tristan's work," he said, "he's not going to stop until he gets what he wants. I saw film from the Sahara. I can't imagine what it must have been like to walk through that for real."

"No, you can't," she whispered again.

"Then help us, Alex," Coop replied. "I know you still see that in your dreams."

She did sometimes still see the bodies Tristan and his followers left in their wake. Mothers and fathers fed upon by their own children. The children Tristan turned into monsters to amuse himself. When Night Command had to destroy them, Alex couldn't shake the images from her head for a long time. They were all pretty messed up after that, Alex most of all.

Pure cold anger filled her at the thought. If she gave into it, she'd put Coop's head through a wall. Instead, she just stared at him. He smiled and gave her a small salute. "Let her go. That's an order."

They parted and she passed between them at a leisurely pace.

Once Alex was outside, she stepped up to a large SUV.

She took a deep breath, slammed her left shoulder into the side of the vehicle and stifled the scream she desperately wanted to let out. Her shoulder snapped back in place with a low pop and she sighed. Inside the safety of her own car, Alex let out another long breath and headed home for a handful of painkillers and a bottle of Jack so she could sleep.

If Coop were smart, he'd be gone by morning, but he wasn't actually known for his smarts. Sending a rookie after her was dumb. The old Alex would have killed him without a second thought, sent the ashes back to Area 51 in a FedEx box. But Alex wasn't as impulsive as she once was. She thought about every move she made at least three times before she actually made it. It was safer that way.

As she walked through her living room, she grabbed that bottle of Jack, then stepped out onto the balcony. Her view of the sky was filled with stars and the darkness beyond them. She took a deep breath and let it out slowly. Once the white noise was shut down, she could focus on the sound her heart made. The easy rhythm she'd grown accustomed to had been replaced by a sound she didn't like; the sound of fear.

On top of the city, nothing had ever hurt her. Nothing could enter unless she allowed it and she never allowed anything in she couldn't control.

Besides, other people's thoughts rattled her lately. Here the only thoughts were hers.

But with Coop and the Tracker team here, trouble had entered the world she had carefully constructed all those years ago. And that voice in the back of her mind she tried to ignore, wanted—needed—to be heard now. It screamed for attention like a spoiled child as her head pounded and her teeth chattered.

When her smartphone vibrated in her lap, the voice stopped.

"Hey, what happened to you tonight?" Ivy chirped. "You missed a great game."

"Sorry, I got caught up on something," Alex replied.

"You work too much," she giggled. "You're the boss, you know. You have people that can do that for you."

"Yea, well, I like working."

She heard Ivy sigh.

Alex took one last look at the city as she pushed her battered body from the chair.

"Yea, well, there's a difference between work and what you're doing," Ivy laughed.

"Next game, I promise," Alex replied on her way

back inside.

In her bedroom, she kicked the beat up Chucks off her feet, put down the almost empty bottle as she sent them flying in to the corner. She pulled the t-shirt over her head and it landed on top of the baggy camo shorts she let drop to the floor by the bed.

Inside the bathroom, she flipped on the light and stared at her own reflection.

"Yea, yea," she heard Ivy say. "Promises, promises. So what was so important you blew off your bestie?"

"Just going over some stuff for the launch, that's all."

"You're not a very good liar."

"Don't tell anybody, okay?"

Ivy didn't laugh that time. "What's wrong?"

"Nothing."

"Alex . . ."

"Listen, I gotta grab a shower so . . ." Alex tried to laugh.

"Call me when you're done. We can talk like we used to, all night if you want."

"Can't," she answered. "Kinda tired. How about we meet for coffee instead?"

She heard that sigh again. "Sure, see ya in the morning."

Alex hung up before she got out the 'bye Al' she always ended their conversations with.

The hot water bounced off her body at a soothing pace. Her head dropped forward and she welcomed the water streams as they ran over her scalp and down her face.

After, as she prepared for bed, she hoped the pills would kick in soon.

She climbed between fresh, cool sheets. Alex held her phone in her hand as she scrolled through the phone book for the right number. No names, just numbers. She knew every number by heart and to whom they belonged by looking at them. She found the one she needed, sent a text and settled into her pillow.

Alarms and other countermeasures in the penthouse had been checked and double-checked; no one would sneak up on her tonight.

Alex pulled the blanket up to her chin and closed her eyes.

As the dull ache of her head began to ease, it was replaced by the voice that echoed deep inside her brain. That small voice was sending a warning she couldn't quite hear, like trying to listen through a wall or keyhole, the words soft and barely audible to her inner ear. Nothing irritated her more than trying to either silence it, or turn up the sound so she knew what to do next. Once she could make out the warning, she was surprised at the message: *You have to go or people will die.* The voice hardly ever went against her on anything. It had always kept her safe and off their radar. Now it was telling her—no, ordering her—to go back to a life she barely escaped. *Find out before it's too late.*

Jason and Adam waited patiently for them to call, video screen and speakerphone ready.

When his assistant put the call through, Jason sat back on the sofa and Adam turned the entire chair around to see.

Only Coop's image appeared on the screen. "Gentlemen," he smiled, drink in hand. "Nice evening."

The first thing Jason noticed was his busted lip. Although it wasn't puffy, it was split and still bleeding. The sight of fresh human blood triggered something deep inside him. He and Adam sat back in their seats at the sight.

"Cooper," Jason replied trying not to look at the tiny streak of red on his mouth as he smiled. "What happened to you?"

Coop cleared his throat, licked at the fresh blood and rubbed his bruised chin with a grin. He adjusted himself in the chair and waved the others over from off screen.

When his battered team sat down, Jason laughed and Adam just stared in disbelief. Sebastian was shirtless, an ice bag on his ribs. His pale skin was purple and yellow and they all moved slowly, more slowly than any of them should have been. Xavier held a matching ice bag to his nose and the twins had black eyes and blood on their clothes.

"What the hell happened?" Adam huffed as he emptied his glass and slammed it on the table. Coop held up his hand when Sebastian opened his mouth to speak.

"Alex happened," Coop answered. "We had a slight misunderstanding."

"I can see that! But what happened?" Adam huffed again. "Did she bring help?"

"Not exactly," Coop shook his head. "I'm gonna need a couple more days."

"You'll be dead in a couple more days," Jason laughed. "What's the hesitation?"

"Obviously whatever you threatened her with just pissed her off," Coop chuckled. "I asked you to let me handle this."

"And look what happened. You got your asses kicked by a girl," Jason continued to laugh.

"She'll do it, don't worry," Coop replied. "I just need a couple more days."

"One day," Jason huffed. "I'm giving you one day and then we go with a better plan. Mine." He hung up on Coop and took the drink his assistant had prepared for him.

CHAPTER 12

Ivy always felt dirty after. No matter what she told herself, she just felt dirty. She pretended it was the conversation that had kept her interested in this relationship for so long. But that was the lie she'd repeated so many times that it had almost become truth before she knew it. It was the sex. And not just sex, but sex that defied anything she'd ever experienced with a mortal man.

For the entire game, all she could think about was getting here, being with him in all the ways he could think of, and now she hated herself.

She stumbled from the bed and into the shower; his fingers missed her arm as she rushed from his side. Under the harsh spray, wave after wave washed away his scent and sweat, but there were things not even a hot shower could wash away, not completely. She could scrub and scrub and it would always be there just under the surface. Shame.

When Ivy stepped out, he stepped in with a playful slap to her butt like guys do. He knew she hated it, which is probably why he did it.

The comb skipped through her long dark hair. Its teeth caught the tangles at the end, but the pain didn't even register. Neither did the long strands she pulled loose from the comb. She twisted the black band around her wet hair and bunched the wet mess on top of her head as best she could. She'd have another shower when she got home.

Barely dry, Ivy left the bathroom to get her clothes. *Too bad I didn't bring a clean set*, she thought. At the bathroom mirror, she started her makeup.

She tried to cover the bruises his fingers left around her neck. Her next thought was of the new lie she would tell just in case. She didn't recognize her own reflection anymore and that made her angry, then sad, then angry all over again. Time passed so quickly when you were enjoying the dangerous and forbidden. But when your eyes open and you don't recognize your own face, it's time to stop. Had she stuck to that logic, she wouldn't be in this mess in the first place and she damn sure wouldn't be in this mess with Mason Creed.

By the time she realized she was daydreaming, he was out of the shower, dry and dressed while she continued to cover the bruises with makeup.

Creed eased his long body on top of the counter, crossed his legs gracefully, and gave Ivy the sweetest smile. "I could help with that if you wish," he nodded toward the purplish discoloration on her neck. "It'll only take a couple of drops of . . ."

"That's okay," she interrupted him. "I got it, thanks."

"Suit yourself," he sighed. "So, same time next month? I have to be out of the country during the holidays, so maybe we could meet earlier in the month for a change?" That beautiful twinkle in his eyes just made her nauseous.

"No," she exhaled. "No more next month. This is the last time. We're done."

He laughed that laugh she hated now. All light and airy like a girl.

"Done," Creed smiled. "Are you sure? I mean, you're paid up till the end of the year. I don't give refunds." He laughed again and she wanted to smash his head into the mirror.

"Call it an early Christmas gift."

Before she could step away from the sink, he had her by the wrist.

Creed stood tall behind her, his gangly arm coiled around her, then he jerked her back against him. He rested his squared chin on top of her head; his image in the mirror gave her an innocent smile. The muscles of his arms pressed against her stomach made it hard to breathe, in addition to the cologne he wore at every engagement that had been her favorite right up to this moment.

"When you've done what you promised," he hissed at their reflections. "Then we're done, understand?"

"Creed, you're hurting me," Ivy pushed out a quick breath.

"Answer me," Creed growled as his arm tightened. "Or I'll do more than a love bite this time! Do you understand me?"

Ivy tried to take a deep breath, but couldn't

manage enough air for a meek reply, so she nodded quickly.

"Good," Creed snapped as he forced her pelvic bone into the sharp edge of the sink. "And the next time you decide to assert yourself with me, don't." One rough peck on the cheek and she was out of his grip. He watched as she used the sink to steady herself on shaky legs. "Besides, we have so much fun together, Ivy." Creed turned on his sweet smile again as he led her gently from the bathroom. "How can you say we're done?"

Ivy continued to dress as he sat on the bed and admired his manicured nails as if she weren't there at all.

Just a few hours ago those same fingers tangled in her hair. She felt so much pleasure from his seduction all she could do was pant and weep and beg for more. Now she just wanted to scratch his eyes out with his own hand.

Dressed with her purse tucked securely under her arm, she turned to him as she fought back tears. To look at him now, her flesh crawled as the memories of their years together shamed her.

Mason Creed, just a few feet from her, was all deep brown eyes and dirty blond hair worthy of any shampoo commercial. He'd earned every dime of his fee that increased with every year that passed her by. Vampire or not, he would still have women from all over the world glad to pay any price for his services. Up to now, it seemed fair.

His soft lips brought images of sin and self-loathing that made her head ache. And his rock hard body that she couldn't wait to undress now made her want another shower as she allowed the lust to peek its head out over the sight of him.

Ivy tried to make her words strong, but she pleaded in a southern drawl instead.

"I can't do it! I thought I could, but I can't, sorry."

"Sorry," Creed mocked her as he stood up again. "Give me one good reason why I should just let you back out of our little agreement?"

"Because maybe it's not true," Ivy snapped through gritted teeth. "Maybe it's just a rumor. A way to get him out in the open, then put him back in that cage, this time forever."

Creed sighed as he circled around behind her as if he would pounce any second.

Ivy held her breath. His low growl made its way into her ears, spilled over her skin and sent chills everywhere. "Just do what you're told for a change," Creed hummed in her ear. "You made him a promise Ivy. I intend to make sure you keep it."

"All she'll say is she was hurt on that last mission," she replied. "She won't go into any detail. We had the best hackers in the country trying to find anything on her during that time. Nothing exists anywhere in the world."

"You're pathetic," Creed growled into the nape of her neck. She fully expected to feel his teeth cut through her skin, but he nuzzled her ear instead which sent a shudder through her body. "Best hackers my ass! You're useless! Remind me what I need you for again?"

"I'm the closest thing she has to family," Ivy sniffed. "She listens to me. She trusts me more than anyone else in the world. If she knows the identity of this Dagger person, I can get her to tell me."

"You better. And don't forget that other thing."

Ivy cocked her head as she met his steely gaze once he was in her face again. Suddenly tears streamed down her cheeks. She swore she could hear the drops hit the fine carpet under her feet.

A sick yellow hue had replaced his brown pupils. His perfect features distorted by his true nature. His long white fangs gleamed in the pale hotel room light as his tongue move slowly over them.

"You're fucking insane," Ivy barked. "I might be able to search the house, but how am I supposed to get a blood sample from someone who incinerates her trash for God's sake?"

His movement was too fast for her to track him. He was behind her again, her ponytail in his fist, lips on her ear leaving it damp from his breath.

"That's your problem. But if you don't, the alternative will be much worse. I'll make *you* bleed. And I promise it won't be quick or painless. Get it, then we're done. Refuse, and I'll drop your corpse on her doorstep!"

Creed's push sent her into the door a few feet

away.

Ivy screamed when her finger jammed on impact.

"I hate you," she whimpered as she scrambled away from Creed. "She should have killed you when she had the chance!"

"Yes, she should have," Creed bragged. "But I'll give you one guess about who she will kill without a second thought."

"Not if I tell her what you've been doing over the last year," Ivy whined as she held her hand to her chest. "I'll tell her everything. She'll burn Vegas to ground to get to you. All of you."

"Is that what you tell yourself when you're spying on her and lying through your teeth about who you really work for? Do you really think she'll grant you forgiveness just because you throw my name out to save your own ass?"

A roar of a laugh shook the floor. When her tears began to stream down her face again, Creed laughed harder. He followed Ivy around the room until she was pressed against the far wall. Creed seemed to delight in the way she cringed. She knew he loved the smell of fear and he had told her once or twice that hers was like fine wine.

She watched as he knelt down and put a finger to her tear stained lips.

"She won't care," Creed whispered. "You've betrayed her, Ivy. And once you've lost her trust, she's done. Alex never looks back and never forgives. You'll need us when that happens. We might be able to keep her from killing you."

"Go to hell," Ivy huffed. "I'm inside, which is more than *you* were able to do the whole time you had her under your control. Why do you think they chose me over you Creed? Because I can deliver what you couldn't."

"Cocky bitch, aren't you," Creed said as he snapped her finger back in place and kissed her hand as she screamed. "They chose you because you're weak and greedy. Do you think you coming to me was just a coincidence? He knows you like the back of his own hand. Everything you think and feel. He knows you crave all those nasty little things we do. You tell me it's over, then I get that call, that desperate plea for my services. How can I refuse when you sound so wounded? How could I say no when I can smell you all wet and wanting over the phone? You can barely make it through the month without what I offer you. You need me Ivy. Admit it."

Ivy burned red as he laughed harder. Without the physical strength to match his, she was helpless and at his mercy. Then she smiled and she could see that it struck him as an odd thing for her to do.

"You say that like you're doing this out of the goodness of your heart," she sneered. "You do it because you're paid to. And you like the perks that keep that heart of yours beating. You should bear that in mind before she finds out what you've been doing and rips it from your chest!"

He jerked her to her feet and dropped Ivy at the front door.

"When did you get a spine?" He picked up her purse then clamped his hand around her neck with a slight squeeze. "Killing you would be way too easy," he spit out. "Just do it Ivy and don't take too long. I hate waiting. Do what you're told and I'll let you live out the rest of your pathetically short life!"

Ivy rushed toward the elevator before Creed changed his mind and killed her right there. Once inside, she took slow deep breaths to calm her heart as it pounded in her chest. Her hands shook as the elevator moved toward the bottom floor. Ivy closed her eyes tight, the vibration of the machine soothed her all the way down.

When the doors finally opened, she followed the shiny tiles to the exit. The valet took the crumpled ticket and the windy evening pushed away what was left of her fear.

In that moment, Ivy realized she had the upper hand. Even if she couldn't get the blood sample, Alex had to have something in her house about that last mission. Something, anything that made reference to the operative known only as 'The Dagger'.

Screw Creed. He was the one that was afraid, afraid of Alex. Afraid that Ivy was the one in control of her and what she could do to Creed. The valet smiled bright when Ivy slapped that hundred dollar bill in his hand. For the first time since this all started, Ivy did have some level of power. And she would use it to eliminate her enemies, starting with the one person with absolute power over all of them.

"How long are you going to stare at that," she purred. "Are you expecting it to come to life?" Her lips touched the back of his neck and he shuddered slightly. "Welcome back from the sticks darling. It's time to put that away and focus on me."

One pale hand slid inside his shirt leaving an icy path from his chest to his abs as she hummed some tune in his ear. Jason's muscles tightened as her nails rode over his skin playfully, at first. He felt the sensitive skin just above his right nipple separate when she drew blood with a quick scratch. Nikki was in his lap before he even registered the pain. Her slick tongue licked at the blood as it appeared then she covered the wound, including his hardened nipple, with her mouth and began to feed.

Jason dropped the electronic tablet to the carpeted floor then tangled his fingers in her golden hair. As his body temperature dropped, hers rose as she drank his blood slowly. The pressure of a growing hard on began to build as she drank and teased him. He barely noticed she had unzipped him until her now warm hand wrapped around his erection. With every stroke, she sucked harder at his chest and he almost came. When her mouth stopped its agonizing pull, he felt her hand slow its pace too. He opened his eyes to see hers blood red, like her lips covered in his blood.

There was a thin layer of sweat on her brow. Her pink tongue made a quick trip around her lips to clear away his blood then she kissed him softly on the cheek. How sweet she looked to him perched on his lap like the perfect pet. The smell of her wetness and his blood mixed inside his lungs when he took a deep breath to clear his head.

"Be ready when I return. This won't take long," Jason said as she tucked him back inside and zip him up again.

She shook her long blonde hair as she eased from his lap down to her knees in front of him. "Should I shower?"

"No, not without me."

Her soft giggle used to excite him. Her pouty mouth and pointed little nose gave her an angelic appearance. But he knew under all that was the devil; the devil he'd grown to love in an odd sort of way. You couldn't really call what he felt for her desire. It was more like a simple need for physical contact. From the moment he laid eyes on her, he had been physically attracted to her. She was beautiful. But he was human when he first met her and the power she had over him, over all men, was undeniable. Once she was like him, the struggle for domination began. Nikki liked being in control and so did Jason. She liked being chased too. Before he was turned, he pursued her with a passion. Little did he know just how dangerous getting what he wanted could be. He pecked her on the forehead and pulled her to her feet as he stood.

"Don't forget the notes I prepared for you," she sighed as he buttoned his shirt again. "He may ask some of those questions. You should at least sound like you know what you're talking about."

Jason smiled at her. "What would I do without you?"

"Let's hope you never have to find out," Nikki replied. "Now go, or you'll be late."

As he made his way to his private office, he thought about what a lethal pair he and Nikki were once upon a time. Adam's enemies fell quickly back then. No one could kill like Nikki, though. Her signature, deadly flowers. With a passion for plants and a green thumb like no one else, Nikki used the world's most deadly flowers as weapons on many occasions. Who would turn down beautiful flowers from a beautiful woman? No one.

When he reached downstairs, it was quiet. He'd gotten used to the silence around him. Comfortable and comforting, Jason built this sanctuary as a gift to himself. One hundred and fifteen years ago he was born to dirt poor immigrants just arriving in America. When he was old enough, he began working the docks for absolutely nothing. He swore no matter what, he'd make it in this land of opportunity and show them all. Even if all of the people he knew then were dead, it still felt good to prove he wasn't just some immigrant with no future.

Jason surrounded himself with the best of everything because he could. Nothing was out of his reach. And if it were, he'd figure out a way to get it. That's how he ended last year owning half the infamous Las Vegas Strip. And once this conference thing was in his rearview and he'd secured his seat in the chamber, he'd get the other half too.

For him, this assignment wouldn't take much effort. He was dealing with humans after all. Jason was sure he could convince Alex Stone to join the team again. The assignment was only a week and then back home in time for Thanksgiving. Who would turn down a chance to work for Jason Stavros? Not even Alex could afford to turn him down. And she did seem enticed by his offer.

Chapter 13

One week later, all the media services, print and digital, in the country buzzed with the news. Jason Stavros and Bite, Inc., i.e. Alexa Stone, were in talks to join forces early next year. Jason and Alex would be in Vegas to discuss a joint venture. The gossip rags, however, speculated about a personal relationship between them. That was even bigger news than a merger.

She shook her head and tossed the newspaper in the trash.

"Okay," Ivy hummed. "Tell me, again, how you don't know Jason Stavros."

Alex shook her head again as the team filed in to continue yesterday's meeting she missed.

They looked scared. They looked angry. They looked confused.

Alex stood slowly and smiled. "I am not selling this company. Nobody is losing their job." They looked at each and back at her. "Trust me."

When Ivy laughed, everyone else did too, even Alex.

"So what's up then," Dan chirped from the far end of the table.

"I'm just kicking around some ideas for the Fall line, that's all," Alex answered. The low whispers of excitement rolled around the room. Even Ivy looked more excited.

"Nice move," she sang. "But Jason Stavros is not our target market, is he?"

"Maybe not, but he has access to the Tracker team and they are," Alex agreed. "They'll be perfect for the new men's line, right? Young, handsome, and cool. Every Steven Seagal wannabe wants in that outfit, right? And they're hot right now. Just what we need."

Everyone agreed.

"I want to see mock ups and print ad samples by the end of the week. Locations for three shoots, someplace warm, please." She sighed, they laughed.

"Why y'all still sittin' here?" Ivy scolded with a grin. "Get to work."

The room emptied out quickly as she and Ivy faced each other.

"So what's really going on?" Ivy whispered over the rim of her coffee cup.

"I don't know what you're talking about," Alex shrugged.

"Don't lie to me. You know I hate that."

"I'll only be in Vegas for a couple days," Alex answered, "Some details to go over with Stavros."

"What kind of details?"

"Just some loose ends, no big."

"You can't do that here?" Ivy sighed.

"You know me," Alex smiled. "Any reason to go to Vegas." Ivy didn't smile back. "Don't look so worried. I thought you'd be excited, happy."

"I am, but I just wish you woulda kept me in the loop on this," Ivy replied as she scratched so hard her colorful scarf fell loose.

"What happened to your neck?"

Ivy slapped at Alex's hand and gave her a nervous laugh.

"Doctor says I'm allergic to that new perfume. You know, the one I got in Paris last month? Last time I buy anything French."

They parted company at Alex's office door. She watched Ivy walk quickly down the hall, tugging at the scarf wrapped around her neck all the way.

Alex walked around her office as she looked over the schedule Jason had sent for the conference. Standard *Meet and Greet* on the first morning. The next day, lunch at the hotel then an afternoon session with Jason, who represented the largest vampire houses in North America.

Even the Wolf Pack and the Warren Coven would be in attendance. That hasn't happened, ever. Vampires, Werewolves, and Witches in the same place at the same time, how could she refuse?

On par for something like this, all the names were tied to businesses in case this fell into the wrong hands. But she knew the code and protocol they had created a few years ago.

Alex shredded the agenda, sat back down and dropped her head on the desk.

"I'm so screwed," she whispered to no one, then raised her head when her desk phone buzzed.

"Alex," her assistant's voice came over the small speaker. "There's an Esmeralda Warren on one. She says you're expecting her."

"Put her through," Alex raised her head and straightened her clothes as if she could be seen through the phone. The small beep announced her line open. Alex opened her mouth, but nothing came out.

"I know you're there," the sweet sound of her voice oozed through the small speakers. "I can hear your leg shaking."

"Hey Es," Alex said after a sip of cool water. "It's good to hear a friendly voice."

"Don't try to sweet talk me," Esmeralda replied with a girlish giggle. "What are they doing there, Alexa?"

"Coop needs some help. And, before you ask, Ben's ignoring him."

Alex heard her let out a long breath, then she laughed.

"I wasn't going to ask because we keep in touch. Unlike some people I know who refuse to even drop me an email just because she now owns some fancy underwear company."

"This keeps me busy, sorry. I've been meaning to call, I swear."

"Right," she replied, "Just like you were meaning to come for a visit over the summer?"

Alex grinned as she turned her chair away from the desk to see the sun sitting high like a bird in the blue skies outside her window.

"The summer launch took longer than expected. I was coming though. I had tickets and everything."

When Esmeralda laughed, the deep throaty vibrato brought her brown eyes and slim mocha colored hand as it rested on her chest to Alex's mind. A very southern belle kind of a gesture, but on her it was charming and sexy, and that made Esmeralda hard to forget.

Esmeralda Warren hailed from New Orleans. Her family was one of the oldest in those parts. Some say her lineage dated back to the free people of color who lived in the French Quarter. But Esmeralda had never admitted that, and Alex had never really asked. She and her husband lead the largest coven in the world, practically, so it didn't really matter how she got the power, did it? Esmeralda and Morgan Warren were feared and respected in the supernatural community and that's what mattered most.

"So, why you?"

"Strictly business," Alex sighed. "Besides, the Trackers have been assigned to his detail. Since when do they do protection for the vampire elite?"

Alex wiped her suddenly sweaty palms on her skirt.

"To the rest of the world, Jason's human, Alex," Esmeralda laughed again. "And for the world's most famous rich guy, nothing but the best will do!"

"Are they still the best? I mean, they've been running interference for rock stars for God's sake. How hard can that be, really?"

"You really believe that's all they've been doing?"

"Why should I care what they do these days?" Alex groaned. "I can't get involved in this."

"Sounds like you're already involved. Look at the bright side, at least you get inside Stavros's inner circle. I hear he's quite insatiable. When was the last time you . . .?"

"Never mind," Alex cut her off with a laugh. Esmeralda laughed even harder. "Why are you bugging me anyway? Don't you have a broomstick riding class to teach or something?"

"Bitch," Esmeralda giggled. "Don't get fresh with me. I called because I just got the agenda and low and behold, there's one of your aliases, in very small print mind you, accompanying the most delicious vampire ever. Makes a girl wonder, you know?"

"About?"

"About why you think this is a good idea."

"This was not my idea. Someone else started this and I'm getting dragged in," Alex said.

Esmeralda's silence, though short, chilled Alex to the bone. Even with her penchant for the dramatic, she was never at a loss for words. "You haven't been in the game for a long time. Do you even know why they're bringing this to you?"

Alex didn't know how to answer her without lying. "Not yet."

"Then, don't do it," Esmeralda sighed. "You've created a fabulous life there. Why mess that up by getting involved in Strategic nonsense again?"

Esmeralda sighed again and let out a low yawn. "So are you coming to Romania or not?"

"I haven't decided yet."

"Well we're dying to see you, even if it means having to spend a week in a godforsaken hole covered in snow," she sighed. "We've missed your beautiful face."

Alex picked up the receiver. "I miss you too."

"Then it's settled," she heard Esmeralda cheer. "We'll see you for the Solstice. You can come to the celebration. Oh please Alex, please?"

The celebration of the Winter Solstice, for this coven of witches and warlocks at least, was like an out of control rave on steroids. After the boring ceremonial stuff ended, the real fun would begin. Music, food and drink with lots of 'Lollapalooza' style love throughout, the Warren Winter Solstice Celebration would be by invitation only. Alex still didn't remember her first foray into partying with Esmeralda and her husband Morgan. What she could still remember was lots of booze, music, and party favors.

As Creed's right hand girl back then, wherever he went, she went. If he received an invitation to anything, his personal bodyguard was always at his side. No one turned down Esmeralda and Morgan Warren, not even Mason Creed.

"Maybe, if we have time."

"Come on," she purred. "You had a great time at the last one."

"I still don't even remember most of it," Alex

laughed.

"Well I do, my dear sweet Alexa Stone," Esmeralda cooed. "And you had the time of your life, trust me."

"On that note, I must bid you *adieu, ma chére*," Alex smiled. "Let that gorgeous husband of yours know I said hello and I'll let you know when I've decided for sure about the trip."

"Alex?"

"Yea."

She heard Esmeralda's deep breath and then she exhaled.

"Blessed be and remember one very important thing."

"What?"

"Remember that I love you," she replied.

"Blessed be and I love you too."

Alex placed the receiver back on the base then stood and crossed the room again.

Her head rested on the warm glass and she wondered who was pissed at her and trying to get her attention. She was in again and she was sort of looking forward to it.

CHAPTER 14

It was good to be home. Jason sat back as he read his newspaper and waited for the dreaded call from on high. Conner had begun checking up on him like he was a ten year old. One of the rules of working for the Council was reporting to Conner on the status of Alex Stone.

When his phone rang, he took a deep breath, popped his neck and answered.

"Good morning, Conner," Jason sang through a fake smile.

"Good morning to you," he replied. "How was Texas?"

"Warm and sunny; New York?"

"Cold and snowing," Conner chuckled. "Perfect holiday weather."

Jason straightened himself in his seat and thanked his butler for the tomato juice with a quick nod. Nothing would please him more than to have New York buried in snow, phone lines down, so that he didn't feel like one of Conner's children calling *daddy* for permission to breathe.

"I expressed our willingness to help and she seemed interested. I'm confident she'll do the conference. She just wants to flex her muscle first."

He heard Conner clear his throat. "As I can see

from the *Times* this morning. How exactly is this going to help us?"

"It'll keep the human press busy for a while," Jason answered with confidence. "Having us meet in Vegas will give them something to chew on."

"Really," Conner huffed. "Because it seems to me they'll be on your tail twice as much trying to get a shot of the two of you doing other things. How are you going to control this situation now that the human press thinks you're joining forces with their *golden child*?"

"They're not that hard to control, Sire," Jason laughed. "They'll chase any bone I throw out, like hungry dogs."

"And what about her? Will she do the same, or are you the *hungry dog* in this scenario?" Conner asked in a low tone. "If you don't think you can handle her, say so now."

"I can handle her," Jason replied. "I know that Romania is important. I know it's my job to convince the others that our best defense is to stay united. And I understand if Tristan resurfaces, all of this goes to hell. I will have her on our side, I swear it."

"Well if you manage that one," Conner replied in an uncharacteristically cheerful tone, "we'll talk more about your new role in Council chambers."

"Absolutely, sire," Jason said, with a big smile on his face. "I'm sure she'll cooperate fully once she understands what's at stake."

"Don't say that unless you know it for sure, Jason. I've been very pleased with you up to now.

Pictures can be explained away," Conner stated firmly. "I don't like regretting my decisions."

"Have I ever let you down?"

"No, but there's always a first time and you won't get a second chance. Are we clear?"

"Crystal clear, sire," Jason replied, as his excitement died as quickly as it came.

A long pause, then he heard what sounded like a door closing in the background.

When the line went dead, Jason started to breathe again. If he didn't do exactly what he'd promised, he'd stop breathing sooner than he thought.

In the next minute, Coop had joined him on the terrace with a cup of coffee and a hangover from last night. He sat quietly as Jason scratched on a notepad and sipped on a dark brew in a mug right next to him.

"Listen Jas," Coop mumbled. "I know I sorta messed up the other night, but . . ."

"Messed up? Messed up is an understatement," Jason replied, still scratching away on his notepad. "Your little stunt could have done more harm than good. Someone might have gotten hurt or killed."

"But no one did," Coop huffed. "She's fine. We're all fine."

Jason put his pen down and turned in Coop's direction. He put his hands in a prayer pose in front of him and blinked. "Maybe we should let her lead the team then. She seems much more suited to the task than you."

Coop smiled, rubbing his chin. "Based on what

exactly?"

"The fact she took on your entire first string without a problem," Jason smiled back.

"Whatever," Coop growled. "I told them to take it easy on her anyway. It was my call and it turned out just as I planned."

Jason tilted his head to one side and continued to smile. He could smell Coop's sweat as it came to the surface. The candy smell was almost too sweet for him.

"Barely," he hissed. "You promised me someone with experience. Who knew it would be *Little Miss Underwear*? Lucky for you, I was able to salvage this before it got out of hand. Having Conner spare your life is my gift to you, Coop, but don't press your luck. You're almost out of time, don't forget that."

Coop wiped his brow with the back of his hand. He coughed several times, washing back the mucus with the coffee.

"I've got all the time I need, but thanks for your concern," Coop grinned.

Jason stood slowly as he smiled at Coop.

He walked to the brick wall surrounding the terrace and looked over. The humans below were clueless, like the one seated with him, testing his patience.

When he turned, Coop was sweating more. He poured water on a napkin and wiped his face again.

"You're getting weaker by the day," he stated. "You said she'd be happy to help. She's not. I put my reputation and my head on the block solely on your word that you could deliver a way to get to whomever is after all of us. That she would help you find a cure for what's killing you. She just might do that, or just kill you for what you've done."

"Let her try," Coop responded as he pushed out his chest. "She's been out of the game too long." He stretched his legs out in front of him and put his hands behind his head.

"It's good to have confidence," Jason smiled as he walked up to Coop. "But don't get ahead of yourself. Our alliance is still in its infancy as far as the Tracker program is concerned. After three centuries of being what I am, I can still see the true face of human kind from time to time."

His personal butler entered with a grave expression on his face. He leaned in, delivering the news as if he were reporting the weather.

"When?"

"Our contact in the police department says three days ago," he replied.

Jason's good day was going south pretty quickly. "Have my car brought around please."

He nodded and disappeared inside again.

"What's wrong with you?" Coop coughed again. "You look like your dog just died."

"Get back to work. I'll bring her here myself."

"She won't go anywhere with you, Stavros," Coop laughed as Jason put his phone to his ear. "Let us bring her."

"Do as you're told," Jason said stepping closer to Coop. The sweet smell of his body was putrid to Jason. "I'm going to get her."

Chapter 15

"These stone walls have seen so much," he mused. "So much loss and pain and blood over the centuries. Now, it was ready for hope. Hope for an existence long denied my kind; a co-existence in a world that still considers us monsters of myth and fairytales."

He ran his hand over the smooth tabletop as he thought about everything and nothing at all. He hated to wait, but wait he would until they reported success or failure.

While he waited, the twelve year old Scotch his sons had given him on his birthday kept him company. After almost two thousand years he thought it funny he still celebrated such things. But the boys insisted on a party after some business was concluded and he agreed, halfheartedly.

Oddly, he found himself looking forward to it now.

Then this came up; old business he thought was finished twenty years ago. And that business is why he waited in the main hall of Council chambers for his team to return with good news, he hoped.

He poured one more short glass for himself, then dropped his head back against the high back of his chair and closed his eyes. Images popped up in the dark of his mind. Some good, like the moment his eldest son was born. Others, not so good, like the day his wife died.

Conner Gale, founder of Gale Enterprises, the top biomedical engineering company in the world, counted himself blessed. His company had led the pack in everything from artificial hearts to biopharmaceutical advancements, like vaccines for various diseases and the creation of the synthetic blood product used by most of the vampire population.

His many charitable contributions gave him a status in the human world very few have achieved. This human world may never know the supernatural existed, and most days he was glad. But lately he had to consider the possibility that their secret wouldn't stay a secret for long. That weighed heavy on his mind tonight.

His eyes opened when he heard the doors yawn on their hinges at the far end of the empty hall. They walked in one after the other, haggard and hungry from their latest adventure. Someone was missing, however.

"Where's Michael?" Conner asked, as they made their way across the open space.

"He's following a lead on the woman," Aiden replied.

The team stopped in a straight line in front of him, bowing politely. Then his oldest son stepped forward. He brooded, which signaled their failure to complete the task they were given.

"Sorry," Aiden sighed as he rubbed his hands together as he was prone to do when he was agitated or disappointed in himself. His mother had done that. "He was gone by the time we arrived. The house was empty and my contact says he and the woman have already entered the United States."

Conner just nodded. He waved them all forward.

He waited for them to be seated in the chairs on either side of him before he spoke.

"I don't have to tell you how disappointed I am."

All nodded with their eyes cast down.

"Not in you," Conner continued. "But we seem to be one step behind him at every turn. Either we have an informant in our midst or we're not as good as we think we are."

Aiden sat forward and poured himself a drink, then one for his brother Sean, who was seated next to him. "Had the humans told us sooner, maybe we would have been able to recapture him. God only knows where he is by now."

"He had help," Conner sighed. "He couldn't have done this without it."

Aiden pushed the bottle toward Conner, who sent it in the opposite direction. His other two sons, Zu and Raphael, who looked more haggard than their brothers, poured a vial of blood in their glasses.

"We have to consider the possibility of a traitor inside the Council," Zu sighed in his West Indian accent. "But we've been so busy tracking his sarcophagus we haven't had time to look into it yet."

"Speaking of which," Conner sighed. "Where is

it now?"

"My lab, under guard," Sean replied. "I'll take a look at it in the morning."

Conner nodded again and emptied his glass. "Get some rest, all of you. I'll meet you at home. We'll talk more in the morning."

They stood and Conner hugged each of his sons.

As they walked slowly across the empty floor of the hall, he moved around the table and watched them until they reached the large wooden doors leading out.

"Hey," his voice boomed through the space. They turned as if they were one person in response to Conner's call. "Let me know when Michael has returned."

They all smiled and waved at him as they disappeared from his view. He could hear the echo of their conversation and laughter move slowly away as they did.

Chapter 16

Alex glanced up from her work to see Jason narrow his focus on her. He was still as a photograph. With everything that had happened over the last few days, it seemed only logical he'd show up on her doorstep to whisk her off to Vegas. To everyone, it was a romantic gesture meant to prove that there was something more than business going on between them. To her, it was proof the vampires were just as scared as the humans were about the body count.

When Jason blinked, his irises turned pale amber then back to deep brown as he stared at her.

"What?" she sighed as she tapped on the keyboard.

"I'm sorry about your friend," Jason said as he closed his laptop on the seat next to him.

"Sure you are," Alex replied without even a glance at him.

She ignored him as he crossed the small space between them. He closed her laptop and pulled it away before she could protest. As he sat down next to her, he placed it on the tray in front of them, then pushed it all to the side.

"I mean it," he said as he took her hand in his. The tips of his fingers moved down her palm. "I didn't do it either. You have to know that." When his fingers

153

stopped at her wrist, he wrapped them around it and she could feel her pulse jump beneath his grip.

"I wouldn't be here if you had," she replied. "And neither would you."

"Who was she to you, if not a lover?" he asked, as his lips lightly touched her palm.

"Does it matter?" Alex sighed. "She's dead now. If I'd left her where she was, maybe she'd still be alive, even as bite junkie."

Jason pulled her arm up and ran his nose over the vein in her wrist. She felt that chill again, but it was different from when they kissed.

"Or not," she heard him whisper, his warm breath on her wrist caused the vein to throb. "You saved her for a reason. The problem is someone didn't want her saved."

As much as she knew she should, she couldn't pull away. The way his lips brushed her skin, then his tongue traced the bluish-green vein back to her palm, made her head swim.

"Obviously," she whispered to the top of his head.

He looked up at her. "Sorry."

She let her right arm rest on top of his left, his hand almost swallowing hers. When his fingers slipped through hers, he curled them down as they pulled hers into a double fist. In his grip, shoulder to shoulder, she was caught, literally and figuratively. Ordinarily, she wouldn't let any vampire this close to her—hell, any human either—but it seemed safe in a dangerous kind of way. Obviously he wanted something from her besides sex. It was written all over his face. He had an agenda, like most people did, but his wasn't quite clear just yet.

Strange to be so close, but feel so far away, Jason thought. She would warm up to him, but it wouldn't go as smoothly as he wanted to believe. Aside from the sexual attraction between them, Jason could also tell she had a natural distrust of people in general, not just vampires. Usually, he didn't give a damn what humans kept locked inside their heads because he could get to it, if he wanted. But he couldn't with her. Every time he tried, he was rewarded with a sharp pain to his right temple and nothing else. Alex Stone was much more than she appeared to be, so much more. He'd never come across any other human who could block his telepathic abilities. Not one that could match his speed, stamina, or intellect, not one. Then she was pushed into his life and all bets were off. Which made him wonder what he was really more excited about. Being on Conner Gale's short list or being Alex Stone's next lover.

Physical closeness was all an ordinary man could have with her. He wouldn't be able to enjoy the wealth of emotions Jason was sure Alex had at her command; she wouldn't let him. All the average Joe would ever know was one part of her, Jason was very sure of that. But for him, an immortal with the gift of telepathy, connecting to her mind while he seduced her would be an experience beyond description. But he had tried to move too fast back in her office and ended up back at the starting line. Now, he would have to work back up to square one, on her terms, unfortunately.

So as his body touched hers, he tried very hard not to even attempt to use his abilities on her. Could he possess her, fully, without that edge though? Would she allow him inside so that they shared in each other's emotions? The idea drove his temperature up. Just the thought of being able to hear what she wanted from him, what she wanted him to do to her, caused his heart and his body to crave the taste of her blood and the feeling of being so deep inside her she wouldn't want anyone else but him.

It had been almost one hundred years since he had to seduce a woman with only his prowess. He raised her wrist to his mouth again and took a deep breath. Her perfume had faded hours ago. Now her true scent had surfaced and it was a combination Jason had never encountered before. Most women smelled of cheap knockoffs or very expensive perfumes and soaps. She didn't. He wasn't sure what his nose had discovered, but it was wildly sensual, almost inhuman. Odds were it was just his desire that made him believe she wasn't just human. As with anything forbidden, being told you can't have someone makes you want to disprove that theory. He could have anyone he wanted, even in the slightest way. A woman like Alex was too rare for just anyone. And Jason wasn't just anybody. Jason was somebody no one had ever denied.

The sound of her heart as it raced in her chest sharpened his attention to the moment. Her body temperature had risen, however slightly, as he held her to him. But her thoughts were locked away in her brain, a brain he couldn't enter. Without thinking, his fangs dropped. Long and white against her brown skin, they came to razor sharp points as they gently touched her vein. Jason's mouth watered at the thought of one long taste of her blood.

"Don't," she said in his ear. The vibration of the raspy spoken word shook his insides.

He heard the blood as it flowed like an angry river. It teased him without shame. It called his name, dared him to taste it. Jason licked at her wrist and hoped for a different answer.

"I'm asking you not to," she repeated.

His teeth retracted, then he dropped her hand and turned to her. "Just a taste, one taste," he moaned.

"No."

Her denial never crossed his mind. She seemed so willing just a few seconds ago, or maybe it was just wishful thinking.

"I won't hurt you, Alex," he said as he picked up her hand again.

"You can't hurt me, Jason," she replied, pulling free of his grip.

Just as he felt the urge to take what he wanted, the co-pilot appeared and announced their approach. He picked up the stray cups of coffee and asked them to prepare for their landing in Las Vegas.

Jason packed his briefcase and buckled up. So did Alex.

She suddenly grinned at him. He couldn't help but grin back because she was so hard to deny. Later, he'd have another chance; he knew that for sure. But a different approach was in order. She was different from the others he'd conquered and controlled—mostly because he couldn't control her at all.

―――――――――――

Jason was pleased that Alex agreed to join him for breakfast the next morning. He wanted to apologize for the night before and start new. If she didn't trust him completely the plan wouldn't work. He would turn up the charm, get her trust, and prove to Conner that he was the right choice.

He continued his phone conversation as she approached the table. When his bodyguard held her chair, she smiled and took his hand as she sat. Jason shook his head slightly as the young bodyguard flushed red. Young men can be so easily manipulated. Young vampires were too busy trying to control all the changes inside them, so it was understandable that an attractive woman would distract them with very little effort.

"That was Coop," Jason said as he placed his phone down on the table. "We'll meet for lunch. See where we are on all of this."

"Great, "Alex replied.

After she dumped too much sugar and cream in

the small cup of Colombian coffee, she stirred it slowly, eyes fixed on it. Jason watched her, still trying to figure her out.

From the moment they met, there had been a distance between them. One of her making, of course, but it was there when he kissed her that day. It was there on the plane last night when he took her hand in his. He could still smell her blood lingering around his nostrils. And it was here now, deep and wide, and Jason had no idea how to cross it.

"I have a couple of meetings this morning," he continued as she stirred and stirred. "What about you? Anything planned until lunch?"

She just shook her head as the mocha colored liquid spun around and around.

"Shopping? That's always fun during the holidays," he said. Alex cut her eyes up at him with a frown. "Fine, you're not a shopaholic," he chuckled. "I just thought maybe you'd need something to help pass the time, that's all." He gave her a bow of his head to apologize.

"I'm sure I can find something to amuse me till then," she replied.

"I'm not sure if that's good or bad," Jason replied.

"Relax," Alex grinned finally, then took a sip of her coffee. "I promise to be a good little girl."

"I bet you're better when you're not," he said absently, as she wiped her mouth and stood. The bodyguard helped her with her jacket.

Before Jason stood, she was over his shoulder, her hand kept him seated. She leaned over and put her lips to his ear. "I bet you are too."

Her lips brushed his ear with such a light touch that he shuddered. After she thanked the bodyguard for his help, she walked away without even one look back.

"Follow her," Jason told the bodyguard. "Don't get too close, but keep her in sight. And remember, she's just a pretty woman, Oren. There are lots of them in Vegas."

"Yes, sire," Oren replied. "You can count on me."

CHAPTER 17

The kid in the really expensive suit would be easy to lose, so Alex kept her casual stroll down the sidewalk.

With a loose grip on the phone in her jacket pocket, she waited for their signal. When it buzzed, she stopped in front of the Monte Carlo, put the device to her ear and pretended to talk. Her shadow appeared a few feet away, hidden from the bodyguard's view by a high fence covered in black plastic bags.

She had to admit it was a good idea.

As she inched closer to the makeshift construction barrier, a crowd of teenagers blocked his view and the switch. Behind the fence, Alex handed her jacket to a woman approximate in height and weight with a smile. The decoy stepped out onto the sidewalk and the vampire followed.

"Nina will keep him busy for hours," Sebastian smiled as he led her down the dimly lit tunnel.

"This won't take that long," Alex replied as they headed toward sunlight again.

At the end of the tunnel, Xavier and the twins sat on a low wall as people passed like zombies on their way to wherever. Xavier tossed a box at her along with a jacket.

"Thanks," she said. "Everybody ready?"

"Coop says she's expecting you," he replied. "He says you owe him a grand, by the way."

"So what's the big secret," David said. "Where are we going?"

The sleek black GMC Yukon sat next to a steel gray Maserati GranCabrio Sport, top down. The back lot was quiet for a Friday morning, but all the action was inside the casino, even on a Friday morning.

"You three are headed here," she said and she texted Kai a name and address. "Just tell him Alex sent you. He'll take it from there." Then she turned to a very surprised Sebastian. "You're with me."

David tossed the keys to him as she got in the passenger side.

"Don't forget to thank the man when you're done," she yelled. Both of them waved as they burned away. "See you at lunch!"

Sebastian wasn't sure if he should be scared or honored, but he enjoyed the wheels he sat in now. As he blended into morning traffic, she entered an address in the GPS, then eased the seat back with a yawn.

"So, where to, boss?"

He caught the little grin on her face from the corner of his eye.

She tapped the navigation screen and shut her eyes. "Just follow the nice lady's instructions and relax."

"I'm relaxed," he replied. "Don't I look relaxed?"

"I'm guessing you've fed," she grinned and

ignored his attempt at being cool even though he wasn't at all. His death grip on the steering wheel made that obvious.

Sebastian chuckled, turned down the radio and rolled up the windows. He should be able to hear her perfectly over the wind and music. The gesture, she figured, was mostly for her benefit.

"I have. But if you're offering, I could use a quickie!"

She turned her head toward him as it still rested against the seat.

"I'm not," she yawned again. "This lead might have something we can use, so I need you to stay focused, that's all. And for the record, I don't do quickies."

"Noted," Sebastian replied.

"You boys known Alex long?" the old man croaked as the twins inspected each gun carefully. Government issued C-4 and caps were packed carefully in the other case with the ammo.

"Not long," Xavier replied. "You?"

The old man, his weathered leathery skin stretched and folded in long grooves around his cracked lips, grinned. "Long enough." He stifled a witchy cackle as he packed the cases in front of him with special weapons.

Sleek lines polished to a high shine, both Stealth Recon Scout .338s fit snugly in their black cases. There were two more cases with two P226 X-Six Sig Sauers each resting on the table beside the rifles. Modified to carry the custom ammo, their wood grip plates were polished and brand new. He closed each one, then tapped the counter top for the twins to pick them up.

The twins each took a case and followed the old man and Xavier outside again.

Small dust clouds swirled around their feet as they packed the SUV.

"Tell her I heard this guy has a prototype she might be interested in," he said as he slapped a piece of ragged paper into Xavier's palm. "He's in L.A. Good huntin' fellas!"

"Do you get the feeling he knows something about her we don't?" David sighed from the back seat.

Xavier nodded, but kept silent. Kai just slumped in the passenger seat and sent Alex a text that they had the weapons and a lead in L.A.

"We should get a full bio on him by tonight," Xavier finally said. "The doctor erased her file and everything on that last mission. We're supposed to find out why. So just do what she tells us and finish in one piece."

Kai's phone buzzed with a response. "She says get a plane ready for L.A. by the time they get back."

Chapter 18

She sidled up to Sebastian with sex oozing from every pore. Alex could hear her tiny sniffs here and there and the soft purrs as they floated through the air. Sebastian did as he was told, one eye on Alex, the other on the woman as she moved around him like silk.

"Vampire," Alex grinned.

Kit Blaze, high priced call girl and Shifter, frowned as she circled and sniffed.

"No kidding," she squealed, then shook her head. "That's a shame. Can he—"

"No."

Kit stopped and placed an elbow on his shoulder then she shook her head slowly.

"That really is a shame."

In the most graceful turn Alex had ever seen, Kit was on the sofa, feet curled underneath, still oozing sex, coppery waves of shiny red hair framed her long face. She motioned for them to join her. The slant of her eyes and length of her long nose left no doubt she was a feline shifter.

"You sit right next to me, handsome," she purred to Sebastian. When he sat, she laid her head on his shoulder and took his hand. "So what can I do for you, Alex?"

"Just a little information."

"Like?"

"Any weird requests lately?"

Her giggle was so sweet. "Honey, there's no such thing in this business."

"It's important. Coop said you might have a client that's connected to the vampire world. Specifically an old clan called Hellclaw."

"If it were that important, he wouldn't have sent you here empty handed asking for confidential information."

"Who says I'm empty handed?"

"He doesn't count," Kit replied then rubbed her nose against the back on Sebastian's hand. Alex saw him shiver.

She placed the tiny glass bottle on the table between them; Kit's eyes lit up as she moved to retrieve it. "Um . . . you were saying about that appointment?"

Kit crinkled her pointed nose and sat back again.

"Just one, calls himself *Mr. Hollywood*. We usually meet every first Wednesday of the month, but he didn't show for his last appointment and hasn't called to apologize."

"What was the request?"

"Virgin blood," she pouted then giggled again. "But he's human, so I'm guessing he was asking for someone else."

"Does *he* have a real name," Alex grinned.

Kit laughed, "I'm sure he does, but I didn't ask and he didn't tell."

Alex tilted her head and sighed. "You've never

seen anything with his name on it?"

Kit shook her head, "Sorry." Kit's head dropped back on Sebastian's shoulder and she took his hand, placed it on her thigh, and moved it up and down slowly. "Wait. I did get a wire transfer once."

Kit stood and crossed the room with her finger between her teeth and a whimsical look on her face. At a dainty little desk in the corner, she picked up a pink Post It note, scribbled something on it and crossed the room again.

When she placed the small piece of paper next to the glass bottle, she looked up at Alex.

Taking the bottle, Kit took a big sniff and purred. Alex could smell a faint hint of lavender and jasmine on her hand, even though she'd held the bottle only briefly. Courtesans were said to routinely use essential oils to soothe or arouse their clients. She figured Kit liked the lavender scent best because legend tells of the Greeks and Romans using it to soothe lions and tigers. Since Kit was a feline shifter, it made sense that she'd prefer that oil over any other. And jasmine, of course, was an aphrodisiac among other things. So just a few drops in a hot bath or the bed and the effects could be explosive for both people.

Alex stood and Sebastian followed. "He ever ask for something like that before?"

"Never," Kit purred as she held the bottle like it was the Hope diamond. She cocked her head as she stared at the glass in her hand. "I think he's a lawyer too."

"Why do you say that?"

"I overheard him talking about some big deal with a studio that's up for sale. That's the name of the bank the wire transfer came from. That's all I have for you."

Alex stepped up and held out her card to Kit. "If he calls, give me a heads up. Thanks, Kit. I owe you one."

"My pleasure," she winked at them. "And don't think I won't call in that favor one day."

Back in the car, she stared at the slip of paper in her hand. Some things never change. Hiding money in a bank in the Caymans wasn't very original.

"You need our computer geek to hack that bank, find out who this guy is," Sebastian asked.

"Yea, and I want it before we leave here," she said.

Lunch was a waste of time. Disappointed at the lack of real information Coop had to offer, Alex agreed to take the assignment, if for no other reason than to show Coop how to conduct a real investigation.

Stretched out on the California King bed, she wondered what the hell she'd really agreed to. Alex squeezed her eyes shut. The idiot that let the box go should be executed, in her opinion. If Coop's word could be trusted, the box would be secured and returned to where it belonged soon. Tristan Ambrose free to turn and build another Hellclaw clan was not just a bad idea, but the biggest bad idea ever. Without the ability to feel remorse, he was quite possibly the world's oldest sociopath. He thrived on chaos and craved adoration. Her fight with him had left her close to death, with Tristan sealed inside what amounted to a refrigerated coffin for what was supposed to be forever. Turns out, forever meant twenty years, give or take.

The time had gone by fast, she thought, as the images of that last mission blew through her brain. She could just smell the sand and feel the scorching heat as she trekked across the desert toward the cave where he and the last four members of his clan lay. Back then, daylight slowed them down, powers all but depleted during daylight hours. She began to pop orange glow sticks on her way down the narrow tunnel toward the crypt. After she'd secured the target, she'd radio for a retrieval team to bring in the 'box' and transport him to wherever they planned on keeping him on ice. Then, the charges the new guy, Coop, had built would be placed around the space and blown when everyone was clear. Easy.

The closer she got to the crypt, the stronger the scent of decayed bodies grew. At the entrance to the main vault, she stopped to pull the ash and silver stake from her boot before she pushed the door open with her foot. One by one, torches hanging from the walls of the vault lit like magic. In fact, it probably was some kind of magic, as she remembered.

One rule when dealing with sleeping vampires, dispatch them quickly. Although they may be weaker during daylight hours, you don't want to take a chance because even weak, they'd be stronger than you. And she didn't. The woman and the young boy were the first to go. Alex tapped their hearts quickly, turning them to dust. From across the room she heard a growl. Before she could turn around, she immediately felt the kick to the center of her back. She threw the stake backward with all her strength as she sailed toward the far wall. Forcing her body around in mid-air, she saw his eyes fly wide open before he disappeared into dust too.

When she slammed into the wall, her breath was forced out of her lungs. On her knees, she took a deep inhale as the last of his followers stomped toward her. This one was big, really big and really mad. Based on his size, he'd probably been Tristan's personal bodyguard. One of his arms looked to be the size of both her thighs put together. Solid muscles were everywhere. The roar shook the dust from the walls, making the fire from the torches flicker.

He raised his massive foot and just missed her as she rolled away, still trying to get her breath back. Once her lungs grabbed some air and held onto it, her head cleared and her vision sharpened on him. Based on size alone, she'd never be able to take him. She knew that. What she needed was a clear shot to his heart. The good thing about muscle heads like this one was that they moved slowly. Each strike may have been powerful, but he was too big to move as fast as she could.

Alex climbed to her feet and began her attack. Kick after kick landed squarely, but didn't do much but piss him off. He slapped her away like a fly and she flew over the crypt, then rolled head over heels into the wall again. Luckily, the stake was in her path. She snatched it from the ground, and as he raised the six-inch thick stone used to close the crypt over his head ready to make her a pile of gooey vampire hunter, she launched the stake at her mark.

He laughed as he looked down at his chest. It barely pierced the skin. His ribcage was too close to steel, which kept the stake from reaching his heart. Alex jumped away from the stone lid tossed at her, and used the stone box as a platform to project herself at the creature. With all the strength she had left, she plunged her foot, stake and all, through his chest. His entire body burst into fiery ashes that left her leg, up to her knee, covered in black soot.

She landed on her feet with a smile. As she turned, his hand wrapped around her neck before she had time to think. Tristan was awake and pissed.

"They sent a child after me," he sneered, as he held her by the neck high on the dusty wall. Heat from a torch next to her burned her ear and made her right eye water.

Forcing the memories back took effort on Alex's part, but she closed the door on that encounter then shook his face from her brain. She couldn't trust herself with those memories right now. Right now she had a decision to make.

One reason after another popped in her head for not taking the assignment. Jason Stavros was number one with a bullet. Everywhere he went, the press followed. He couldn't sneeze without a report on what tissue he used to wipe his nose on the evening news. She had noticed the well-placed news items about their relationship on the net this morning too.

Hints of the 'merger' had begun to appear on business and entertainment pages by noon. And, of course, the gossip sites buzzed about a secret romance between her and Jason too. That little sound bite could have only been planted by the vampire council as a smoke screen to cover her sudden appearance in his life. When the ball started to pick up steam on the "Romance of the Year," Alex hoped no one would come up with a ridiculous amalgamation of their names like every other famous couple had. Jason would think it was amusing, but then again, he liked the attention this would bring. In fact, he seemed to welcome it with open arms. Alex hated the press, but she understood why they had to be manipulated as part of the plan. They served a purpose.

Relax for God's sake! It's not like you're on this one by yourself like before. They sent you into the tomb alone. You fought the toughest vampire ever and you survived. This will be a walk in the park for you as long as Jason listens and follows instructions. Alex thought to herself as she laughed out loud, rolled over on her side and stuffed the pillow under her head. Her eyes were heavy and hungry for sleep. *Then, I'm in big trouble*, she yawned big. *Because he is going to challenge everything I say and do.* After a few minutes, she felt the approach before the knock on the door came. As she eased from the bed, she pulled the Nine from under the other pillow. As she crossed the living area, she flipped the safety off, then peeked through the peephole. *Damn.* She opened the door slowly as she held the gun behind her back.

"Speak of the devil," Alex replied as he stepped inside.

"You were talking about me," Jason stated as he unbuttoned his jacket.

"Thinking about you," Alex answered, then sighed and placed the gun on the table. "Thinking about the assignment and how to handle you I mean."

Jason laughed as he took a seat on the couch and waited for her to join him there. Once she did, he eased closer and she let him. One arm went over the back of the couch behind her head, the other hand moved cautiously around her neck. His fingers barely touched her, but she felt the heat like a flame. So he wasn't hungry, not for blood anyway, but she could see the need in his clear brown eyes.

"I'm not used to being 'handled' but I promise to do what you think is best," he whispered on her lips. Before she could respond, his mouth covered hers.

Her brain flooded with endorphins and her body responded to his touch and his lips and the smell of his cologne threatened to swallow her whole. A tug-of-war began. She pulled his hand free of her neck and it went to her crossed legs. As they crawled under her skirt, his fingers left a hot trail from her knee headed to a place she wasn't quite sure she wanted to let him go yet.

She grabbed his hand and placed it back on top of her skirt and shook her head.

"This is not a good idea Jason."

The sparkle in his eyes grew brighter as he stood. She took his hand and let him pull her into the bedroom. She didn't remember the balcony doors being opened, but when Jason pulled her into his arms and kissed her again, it didn't really matter. Before she knew it, they were on the bed. His hand eased under the skirt once more. This time, she let him reach his destination. All of the emotion she kept tightly bound began to unravel as his fingers worked their magic.

"Tell me again how this is a bad idea," she heard him whisper as she unzipped him and eased her hand inside. His deep moan bounced off her eardrum and sent a shiver up her spine.

Just as she felt him slip inside and begin an easy push and pull that brought an ache to scream his name, she bolted upright. She was alone still. Just in case, she scanned the room to make sure it had been a dream. When she dropped back down into the bed, she cursed herself and him. Then she laughed. When her muscles began to relax again, she pushed from the bed and entered the bathroom to turn on a cold shower.

"Very nicely done, Mr. Cooper," Creed smiled. "I have to say, I didn't think you had it in you!"

Coop smiled too. He didn't have the heart to give credit where credit was due. And he really didn't have to. His job was to get her to Vegas and he did. Maybe he used Jason as bait. There was nothing in his agreement with Creed's new boss that said he couldn't. He'd been hired by him to betray his country and his team in order to get the remaining members of Night Command to Vegas for more money than Strategic had ever offered him. And he had. For Benjamin Palmer, Matt Wolfe, K.C. Becker and Alexa Stone, the end of the line was here—where it all started.

Ben would be here soon. K.C. had fallen off the map, but until they found a body, they were still looking. As for Matt, well, Coop had done something that might cause a war between the vampire clans and the wolf packs, but it had to be done.

His host handed him a nice fat envelope and his pick of any woman under his roof for the night. For a day and half worth of work, twenty five grand wasn't a bad payday. He could pay his bookie and still have enough to tide him over the weekend.

"Thanks," Coop said as he thumbed through the stack of cash. "Nice doing business with you again."

Creed laughed, gave Coop's knee a pat and walked away. He returned with an empty glass. He sat it down on the table and the crystal goblet caught the light overhead. Creed's slim hand stroked the glass as two females joined them on the couch.

One placed herself in Coop's lap. The other sat behind him on the back of the couch.

Creed pushed himself to the corner of the sectional to watch the show.

When the door opened again, the man was carried in and placed gently on the carpet.

Propping one long leg up and opening the bottle of Jack in his hand, Creed poured two glasses with a grin. Coop picked his up and watched Creed pour blood in his own glass.

Coop and Creed watched with fascination as the women began their seduction. As one undressed herself, the other undressed the man on the carpet. The marks on his neck and chest meant they had been feeding on him for a while.

He was dazed, but feeling no pain as they moved around him on the floor, biting every unmarked part of his body. When he was completely relaxed, they heard a low moan from the floor.

When one of the women sank her teeth deep into his neck, he screamed. The other handed her a crystal goblet and they watched as it filled with the man's blood. She handed it to Creed and went back to feeding. "Don't forget to leave the mark," he said as he stood to leave. "Leave the body where they will find it."

Coop watched as they drained the man dry, leaving the mark as instructed. Coop sat back, turned up the bottle of Jack and almost choked as he tried to take it all in one swallow.

"Not too much Coop," Creed chuckled. "You have a date, remember?"

"I know," he replied. The sound of whimpering coming from the trio on the floor caught in his ears. He couldn't shake his head hard enough to ever get the sound of their victim dying, slowly and painfully right at Coop's feet, out of his mind. He took one last shot, accepting the burn as it went down. Then he stood on wobbly legs as the room tilted just a little. "Sorry, Matt," he whispered as his vision cleared and he left his friend in the hands of certain death.

CHAPTER 19

She bolted up in bed, grabbed her neck and yelled, "Matt!"

The feeling of teeth ripping through her flesh and draining her blood out was too real. Her hand was clean though, as she pulled it away. She hadn't had a dream of being bitten in a long time—not since she left Night Command. Back then, she dreamed about it all the time. The room-temperature bottle of water was empty before she realized she was done drinking.

Her call went straight to his voicemail. She would have just chocked it up a wrong number, but that was Matt's voice on the greeting. She didn't leave a message. Maybe she shouldn't spook him just yet. And the number she had for Becker had been disconnected. "They're both fine," she told herself as she got dressed for drinks with Coop and his team. It was just a dumb dream and nothing more. "You can't keep jumping every time you have a dream about the past, Alex," she continued.

On the walk to the bar, she thought about Matt's brother, Lucas, but stopped herself. She wouldn't intrude in their lives unless she had to, and she didn't, not yet. Matt would be home soon. As for Becker, last she heard, he was doing contract work for whoever paid the most, somewhere in Los Angeles. After Strategic, he had disappeared. She only knew where he was ten years ago because he sent her a Christmas card and it had his business information on it. She never could understand why he had sent it, but she tossed it in the trash and never thought about it again, until now.

The bar here was a little better than the one in Texas, but not by much. She stepped inside and immediately wanted to go back to her hotel. They were at a table toward the back as she made her way to them through the crowd of people.

Coop coughed and laughed as he retold stories of their adventures; stories of a time when Alex felt like she had a lifetime to look forward to. But that was an illusion, and the reality was she was just a weapon; they all were.

"So she tells the old man where he can put that commendation . . ."

His entire body shook when he laughed and the sweat poured from his skin even though it was cold inside the space. The others laughed just as hard; only they didn't seem as sweaty as Coop.

"So they let you quit?" Kai hummed as the bottle of Patron made its way to Alex.

"It was a little more complicated than that," she replied.

Taking a shot, she passed the bottle to her right.

"But you did leave the team," Sebastian added as he passed the bottle. "And the old man let you?"

"That's a story for another day. Right now Coop's gonna tell us why we're really going to Romania."

Coop cleared his throat. One more shot and the bottle was empty. He flagged down the waitress and ordered another bottle.

"Strategic owes Gale a favor," he answered. "That's all."

"Stavros has his own security for that," Alex replied.

"Please," David jumped in. "Those biters aren't as good as we are."

The group of men laughed, but Alex just stared at her hands. She could feel them about to shake. She could feel something else too—trouble.

"Why are you letting them do this?" she asked Coop. "They won't survive a real attack and you know it."

"Alex, come on! Don't be so paranoid," Coop frowned.

Alex moved her eyes around the room, but she couldn't see anything but people, humans. The music and voices made it hard to concentrate, but something was there, in the crowd, watching them.

"Where's the box, Coop?" she asked.

Coop reached for the new bottle, but Alex pulled it away.

"I don't know," he coughed. "I'm the one trying to find it, remember?"

Alex took a deep breath. Coop's body chemistry

180

was different than before. It was bitter and strong and stung her nose as he continued to sweat like they were sitting on the sun. The sugary sweet smell replaced the bitter one and Alex felt her stomach turn over.

"Jason Stavros is bait, isn't he? Tell me now before this gets out of control and I can't help you."

"What's she talking about, Coop?" David asked as the bottle slid into his open hand.

"I have no idea," he coughed. "Stavros is the client, Alex, that's all."

"*Move!*"

When the whisper came everything slowed down around her.

Coop raised his glass, but his smile faded as it shattered in his hand and alcohol splashed everywhere. They all saw the red stain on his shirt as he fell from the chair.

At first, Alex thought it was just in her mind; the sound of a gun over all of this noise. The hammer clicked, the muffled radio transmission announced, "Wait for a clear shot."

Glass shattered in all directions as Alex crawled toward Coop as fast as she could. Bullets whizzed overhead and cut through the walls behind them. She barked at the others to scatter to protect the civilians and find the shooters. Maybe there were two, she wasn't quite sure, but she knew one had to be a pro.

When she reached Coop, he was on his back laughing at the ceiling.

As the stain grew on his chest, Alex almost

choked on the sweet smell as it poured from his body. Her hand pressed down on his wound with the tablecloth. Suddenly, he smiled.

"Well, looks like I won't be making that trip, huh?"

Alex yelled for someone to call 911 then looked down into his bloodshot eyes.

"Sure you will, then you're gonna tell me what you did."

Coop coughed and blood seeped from the corner of his mouth as tears slid down the side of his head. "You're not gonna like it."

She tried to stay calm, hoping he would start to heal. But he didn't, and the sickly sweet smell crowded out the oxygen and she felt choked and faint.

"When you're healed, I'm gonna kick your ass!"

Coop smiled, teeth bloody, "Can't heal anymore. Too tired." His eyes closed as the smile faded.

"What did you do?" she yelled. "Coop!"

In the distance she could hear sirens and someone behind them through the mess of glass and furniture. She pulled Coop's gun from his belt and aimed at the intruder without one glance.

Coop grabbed the hand still pressed on the wound, pulling it away from his chest. He took a deep breath and she could hear the fluid fill his lungs.

"Made a deal with the devil," he coughed. More blood poured from his mouth. "Benny . . . you got his whisper didn't you?" He shook his head as blood oozed from the sides of his mouth. "Find him, Alex. You're the only one that can now. It's almost too late."

"Too late for what?"

With the sound of chaos all around her, Alex looked over at Sebastian as he kneeled and checked Coop's pulse.

"We have a team on the way, but the cops are already here," he said in her mind. He pushed the gun aimed at his heart away and held out his hand. "You can't be caught up in this, Alex," he said out loud.

Alex ignored his hand, shoved the gun in her waistband and walked to the bar to wash away the blood. With the wet towel under her arm, she followed Sebastian out the back door.

At the bottom of the short stone stairs the black SUV sat idling with the others inside, angry and scared. Kai and David sat in the third row together.

"You lost them," she frowned, as she climbed into the center row seats.

"Lost? I didn't even see anybody," Xavier hissed. "Did you?"

He looked at David then Kai through the rearview. They shook their heads at him and shrugged. Alex punched the back of Sebastian's seat.

"There were two! One human, one vampire! I can't believe you lost them!"

"They were long gone by the time we got through the doors," Sebastian replied as he frowned. He felt her punch through the seat. "We couldn't risk any humans getting caught in the crossfire or wannabe photographers catching a glimpse on a camera phone!"

"Damn," she whispered.

"Stavros had eyes on us," Xavier interrupted. "Maybe they caught them."

"Then let's ask him," she stated.

CHAPTER 20

The rapid knock at his door woke him from a deep sleep. Even though darkness still hung behind the drapes, he could feel the sun about to rise again soon. He climbed from under the blankets, wrapped himself in his thick robe and opened the bedroom door.

"Sorry, sire," the guard huffed. "But there's trouble."

"What kind?" Jason asked, as he backed up and dropped down on the bed again.

"Human kind."

Jason stood, crossed the room and disappeared inside the bathroom. When he appeared again, he was dressed in casual clothes, taking the bottle of real blood the guard held for him. "What happened?"

"Jesse Cooper was shot. The woman and the team are headed back here," he replied, eyes on the floor.

Jason stood tall as he stared at his bodyguard. He could see the fear all around him as he stepped into his personal space.

"Get Cooper back, dead or alive," Jason hissed. "Before sunrise!"

The SUV pulled up to Jason's front door. Armed guards waited, ready for them. The others were immediately patted down and their weapons taken. When Oren stepped up to Alex, he seemed confident she would let him do the same to her.

"Don't fucking touch me," she growled at him.

Her grip tightened on the gun as he took one step back to reach for his under his jacket.

"It's fine, Oren," they heard Jason say.

Alex pushed past Oren into the foyer with her weapon pointed at Jason's heart. A commotion erupted behind her as Jason's guards tried to get to Alex before she reached Jason, only to be stopped by the young men with her.

"If you think I had anything to do with this," Jason stated calmly as she pressed the barrel of the gun to his chest. "Pull the trigger."

His eyes locked on hers as she tried to bring herself to send a plain bullet through his chest. It wouldn't kill him, but it would hurt like hell. Then the muzzle of someone else's gun tapped the back of her skull.

"Don't be stupid," she heard Adam's voice behind her. "This was not our doing and I'm only going to say this once. Put the gun down."

When she didn't, he took the safety off and pressed the cold steel hard against the back of her head. There were two choices. Have her brains splattered all over Jason or drop the gun. She released the magazine and caught it in her free hand. Jason took the gun and magazine as Adam stepped in front her, his gun still aimed at her head.

Adam moved the gun closer to her forehead, eyes an angry yellow, as he stared down at her, "Don't ever do anything like this again or I will kill you!"

"Sire, don't," Jason said, "It's over."

He handed her gun and ammo to Oren then Jason pulled Adam away from her. In her personal space, Jason stayed focused on her. "Please escort these young men back to their suite. She stays here until I return. Adam, could I speak with you in private?"

"We're not leaving without her," Sebastian stated tight jawed.

Jason looked in his direction. "Yes you will, won't they Alex?"

He could tell it pained her to give them the order, but she did. She could do that now that Coop was gone. She could order them to do whatever she wanted them to do.

Reluctantly, they were escorted out.

"Damn," Xavier huffed as he paced around the room on his mobile. "Is he dead or not?" The others watched him try to get confirmation on Coop. The cleanup team reported Coop missing when they reached the hospital. "Find him!"

When he threw his phone, it just missed Kai's head as it crashed into the far wall.

"Now what?" Kai asked as he picked up the pieces and placed them on the coffee table.

"We wait to see if they find him," Xavier hissed

back.

Sebastian just stared out the window as his friends grieved their loss in their own ways. He could hear Erin tap away on her computer as always. She was trying to hack the security system from the club to hijack the feed and see if anyone appeared on camera. Amy cried on David's shoulder while Kai and Xavier sat pensively a few feet away.

"You think Alex is okay?" Amy asked in a weepy voice.

"I'm sure she's just fine," Kai harped. "I'm sure she and Jason are having drinks by now."

"Why would you say that?" Amy replied. "She lost a friend tonight too."

Xavier stood up and shoved his hands in his pockets. "You think she cares about that? This puts her in charge, Amy, of us!"

Amy looked almost angry at his statement.

"So?"

"So, what if she's the reason Coop's probably dead?!"

"She was with you at the bar," Erin sighed as she wiped at her eyes.

"That don't prove shit! All the connections she still has . . . this could have been a set up from the beginning!"

"Stop it," Sebastian jumped in. He took a deep breath and pushed it out slowly to calm his nerves and get rid of all the fear. He couldn't block their feelings right now. "We just need to stay calm and try to think clearly about this."

Xavier dropped down on the couch with a groan. "Think clear! How? Coop's wounded, dead maybe! And she's down there with Stavros doing what, playing cards?"

"If the vampires didn't do this," David joined the conversation. "Then who's left? The dude in the box hasn't surfaced yet and we're not sure he ever will. Alex was with us and we're pretty sure she's not working for anyone else. So, where does that leave us?"

No one had an answer.

Inside Jason's office, Adam paced back and forth as Jason sipped a drink and followed him with his eyes. Part of the problem was the way Jason had spoken to him in front of the humans—he knew that. The other part was, as much as Adam wanted to, he couldn't hurt Alex or anyone on her team. They were useful right now. They were important to the plan and if Adam killed any one of them, Conner would kill him, no doubt about it.

"Don't get too full of yourself," Adam growled. "I am still your sire."

"Yes, I remember that," Jason stated as he placed his almost empty glass on the edge of the desk. "And I didn't mean to embarrass you in front of the humans, but it had to be done. You were ready to blow her brains out, Adam. I couldn't let that happen."

Adam sat down, locked eyes with Jason, and then picked up the glass that still had a small amount of liquid to empty it. "I wasn't going to pull the trigger. She didn't need to know that though."

Jason took the empty glass from his hand. "My apologies then, sire. I've seen that look in your eyes before. Just trying to avoid an inter-species incident," he chuckled. "That's all."

They stood and embraced. Adam's power resonated through Jason with a shockwave of pain, however slight. "My love for you will never wane, but my trust can," he whispered in Jason's ear. "Be careful."

CHAPTER 21

"You ready to talk without trying to kill me?" Jason asked.

They'd sat by the pool for almost thirty minutes without exchanging one word. Alex watched the door and Oren watched them while Jason stared at her with no real expression at all.

"Sure," she grinned finally. "Let's talk. Who shot Coop?"

"How would I know?" Jason answered.

"This is your town. How would you not?"

He tapped the table with an irritated look on his face. She almost believed that he had no clue what happened tonight, but something told her he did.

"Because I don't concern myself with what happens on that end of the strip," he replied.

"What's on that end of the strip," Alex asked.

"Humans," he answered. "What they do to amuse themselves is of no importance to me. What happened tonight was not my doing. I hired the Trackers, remember?"

So maybe he had a point.

"Maybe you shouldn't have," she almost whispered.

"Too late now," Jason replied. "It's done. The real question is who were they really after?"

"Me?" she laughed. "You think it was me? Why?"

Jason sat forward, "Why not! Ever since Strategic decided to bring you in on this, bodies have been almost dropping out of the sky! What's that tell you?"

Alex wanted to drive the leg of her chair through his heart. She had never asked to be brought into this at all. They knocked on her door; or rather kicked it down would be more accurate. Now Coop was probably dead and she was stuck leading this team into unknown territory.

"That you and Strategic have pissed off the wrong people," she replied.

"Or maybe you have," he sighed. "The two men that were killed, what's your connection to them?"

"I don't have one," Alex stated.

Jason's mouth twisted into a crude smirk. His eyes changed color and the muscles in his shoulders and arms flexed as if he were about to attack.

"Of course you do. Just like you had a connection to that girl and to this team that no one else knows about." He eased forward on the chair, placed his forearms on the table, one on top of the other. "We can do this one of two ways."

Sometimes it was best to take a second to consider your options in this type of situation. She was surrounded by vampires. Her team, too far away to be of any help, and as if they'd help her anyway at this point—they probably thought the same thing, that she had set them up. He couldn't read her thoughts, so she had that in her favor. But he was strong and had the numbers on his side.

"I'm under contract with Strategic," she stated. "I find new recruits for the program."

Jason's grimace turned to an amused smirk then he chuckled. "And?"

Alex shrugged. "And that's it. I'm all over the country, the world. I see all kinds of people. I'm good at gauging whether or not someone would be a good fit for the work, you know."

"So Dr. Carlisle let you opt out of fieldwork to be a recruiter for a top-secret government agency?" he smiled. "Bullshit!"

"Look. The original team, including me, were getting too old for this kind of work," she smiled back. "We're not going to live forever. Who better to keep the program going than someone who lived it! Not just anybody can do this job. It takes someone special. I find them and send them to Dr. Carlisle for evaluation."

"And if they didn't pass his evaluation," Jason replied.

"CIA, FBI, NSA," she giggled. "They're always looking for new people."

He nodded knowingly at her. Without telepathy, he couldn't know she was lying. Easing back in the chair again, Jason's body relaxed. She could see his shoulders and arms return to their normal size and shape. He believed her.

"I've got work to do if we're done," she said as she stood. When he didn't follow suit, she walked away.

She didn't look back until she was outside the gate and headed down the path to the hotel. Maybe that had bought her a little time, maybe it hadn't. One day, the truth would come out; all of it. The vampires would find out that Dr. Carlisle had used their DNA to construct those hybrids that were now dead; all but one. And whoever that someone was would find out that she wasn't constructed—that she was born the old fashioned way. Of all the hybrids, she was the strongest and the oldest, and the only one left on earth. One day all supernatural beings would be introduced to the world and everything would change. And one day, her secret would come out too. The secret she had kept since that day in desert when Tristan Ambrose revealed her fate and sealed his own.

Chapter 22

"This is Area 51 Lab," the female voice announced. "Can you hear me okay?"

"Yes, we can hear you just fine, Emily. Anything to report?" Adam answered.

"Yes, sire, but you're not going to like it," she replied in a solemn voice.

"Is he too far gone?" Jason jumped, palms sweaty.

They could hear noise in the background, doors slammed, voices rumbled in confusion.

"No, Mr. Stavros," she sighed. "He's just gone."

Jason almost choked as he put his glass down, "What? What do you mean gone?"

"He was being transported from x-ray back to his room," she answered. "Someone took him sire. I'm sorry."

Adam crushed his glass in his hand as he yelled, "You had better be joking, Emily!"

"I'm sorry, Adam, but I'm not. He's gone and we lost ten guards."

Jason asked Nikki to leave.

"He was practically comatose! How did this happen right under your nose?"

"Someone on the inside helped, I'm sure. We're going over all the employee files now to see who's missing or new at the facility. We'll find them."

Jason slammed his fist down on the machine. Its shiny pieces dropped silently to the carpet. Remnants of the coffee table piled on top of them.

"Stupid," he hissed as he paced in front of a silent Adam. "Damn!"

His mobile rang and he cursed again to see that it was Conner. Adam shook his head, but he answered anyway.

"Jason," Conner sniffed, "I've been calling for a few minutes. Is there something wrong with your office phone?"

Jason looked at the pieces and shook his head again. "Sorry. It's been acting up all day. Um . . . the humans are here, safe."

"Good," he sighed. "I'd like to speak with her if that's possible."

Jason could feel his stomach turn. "Of course sire, as soon as she's ready, we'll call you." He took a shot of tequila and prepared for the worst. "Sire, there's been a development with Jesse Cooper."

"Has he made a turn for the worse?"

"No, not exactly."

"What then?"

"He's been taken from the facility, we're . . ."

When he roared the feedback stung Jason's ears and Adam jumped at the sound over the small speaker. "You let someone take him from the facility?" Conner barked.

"Sire, I just got word myself . . ." Jason huffed before being interrupted again.

"I want them, all of them, on video conference in one hour! Do you understand me, Jason?"

"Yes sire."

The phone folded up in his fist, the sharp edges cut his palms as he let them fall to the floor next to the rest of the mess he'd made. He emptied the bottle of Patron, washed the blood from his hand at the bar sink and dropped back in the chair.

"Do you know where they are?" Adam whispered, still staring at him.

Jason shook his head slowly.

"Find them!"

Adam stomped from the room; doors slammed and glass broke in his wake.

When they pulled up to the front of the junk yard, they spotted her on the hood of her car. The expensive sports car didn't stand out as much as one would think. The vehicles scattered around the dark lot were all expensive. From antiques to the most exotic machines on four wheels, the gravel parking lot looked like Barrett Jackson on auction day.

She slid from the car as they pulled into a space.

Xavier grinned as they all looked around, "What is this place?"

"Dog pound," she replied, as they followed her toward the chain link gate.

There were old Junkers piled high on either side. More lined the path deeper into the property. Pulling the gate open, Alex led the way down the narrow path.

"This is a junkyard, not a dog pound," Kai sniffed.

Sebastian took a deep breath as his incisors dropped and his muscles bulked.

"Whoa! What's wrong," Xavier whispered as he reached for his weapon.

The night air brought cheers and howls from deep within the property. Barks, blood-curdling screams of pain, and anguish flowed overhead. When the circle of people came into view, Alex just stood still. The others drew their weapons and waited for her signal.

"I wouldn't do that if I were you," said a sweet voice from behind them.

When Kai spun, she had his gun and he was on the ground before he knew it.

Sebastian charged, but didn't make it very far.

Two big men in partial wolf form stopped him. He growled and spit as they slammed him to the ground and held him there. David and Xavier both stopped short when the sniper beams hit them in their chests. Alex raised her hands slowly as she smiled at the woman.

She turned in a full circle to show no visible weapon under the jacket she still wore.

The woman smiled back and then whipped out her hand to slap to Alex's face. She laughed when Alex spit out her own blood. "I thought I told you not to come back here!" she yelled.

"I just want to talk to Lucas, that all," Alex

replied, as she rubbed her cheek.

"Talk or screw," she laughed.

Alex continued to smile with her hands behind her back. "Talk. He's not real good at multitasking."
The woman laughed as she pushed Alex toward the noise and the team behind them.

Alex and the woman stood in the center of the large circle.

The team was being held at gunpoint on their knees a few feet away.

"Brothers and sisters of the Pack, we have visitors! Humans and their pet bloodsucker," she yelled, as she walked around the circle with pride. "The best the Tracker organization has to offer—which explains why the humans are in such bad shape these days!"

Alex followed her with her eyes as the crowd roared and booed.

The woman turned to Alex; her round eyes a deep sapphire, teeth long, white, and dripping with saliva. She pulled her wavy, dark hair into a ponytail as she circled Alex.

"You're interrupting our recruiting session," she hissed.

"Sorry, I just need to talk with Lucas, then we'll leave you to it," Alex stated politely.

The woman kicked her in the small of back and the dirt puffed up around her when she fell to the ground. Rolling just in time, the woman's foot slammed down where Alex's head had been. Jumping to her feet, they circled each other like gladiators.

"Can I be of any assistance to the great and powerful Alexa Stone?" she purred. "Lucas isn't here."

Alex cracked her neck and knuckles in preparation for the next attack.

"That's all you had to say, Deanna. Let him know I came by, okay? I'll call him later."

When she started to back away, Deanna howled.

Alex stopped, slipped out of the jacket and pushed up her sleeves.

"I don't think so," Deanna purred again. "If you want to leave, without a severe limp that is, you're gonna have to get past me! If you think you can do that old lady, let's play!"

Deanna's razor sharp nails cut through Alex's thin t-shirt. Shortly after, thin ribbons of blood appeared on her torso, stinging as the wind blew over them.

When she looked up, Deanna's fist caught her chin, and then the tip of her cowboy boot cracked two ribs when she kicked Alex into the air. She hit the ground right in front of her team. Each breath sent an icy sharp pain through her chest as she rocked slowly.

"Stay put!"

Back on her knees Deanna took Alex by the hair before she could get to her feet.

"That was a bitch move," Alex stated as she pulled her hand from her hair.

"I am a Bitch," Deanna laughed and the crowd roared.

"Good point!"

The crowd roared again as Deanna tossed Alex like a rag doll to the other side of the circle. Alex rolled to her back in time to see Deanna as she flew through the air, big knife in her hand and rage on her face. With both feet, Alex kicked her back to the other side and was on top of her before she could react. She twisted Deanna's arm behind her until she dropped the knife. Taking out one knee, Deanna flipped Alex over her back.

Alex's foot shot back in a flash and Deanna was on her back, Alex sitting on her chest with the tip of the silver knife to her throat.

As the blood slid down the blade, Alex was close to taking her life and it felt good!

"This is for the 'old lady' crack," Alex glared down on her and slid the tip over her skin.

Deanna screamed when her flesh opened and her blood seeped out.

"Stop!"

The crowd parted and the cheering stopped when he came into view.

The others were pulled to their feet and pushed into the ring, weapons tossed at their feet.

"I said stop, now! Put the knife away, Alex. I'm here," he stated in a half growl.

Alex stumbled to her feet and backed up. Staking the knife in the ground as she spit out more blood. He pulled Deanna to her feet and pushed her into the arms of two big men.

When he stepped up to Alex, he wiped her

bloody lip with a piece of cloth from his pocket.

Lucas Wolfe was tall and all lean muscle—bare arms sweaty and tight—with a Pack tattoo etched in the reddish brown skin of one broad shoulder. His wavy curls shined black in the moonlight.

"She's still pissed at you," he whispered with a smile.

"I can tell," Alex replied holding her side.

Lucas waved the others over and they followed him down a trail between the cars.

The fighting noises started again as they disappeared behind a heap of rusty parts and old tires. The lights of the office drew them closer, and Lucas told the guards to wait outside as they entered the small building.

He took the chair behind the desk, Alex the one in front. The others stood silently behind her. "Nice of you to drop by," Lucas grinned. He looked at Sebastian and winked. "You should have told them you wanted her to think she was winning. They looked like they were worried about you."

Alex glanced back at them then turned back to Lucas. "They don't know me that well," she shrugged. "I kinda owed her that one anyway."

"Right," he laughed. "Drink?" He placed a bottle of Jack Daniels and two glasses between them. "Sorry boys, I think she needs this more than you do."

He poured the golden liquid in the glasses and slid one over to her.

It stung going down, but she swallowed two

before she shook off more. "I need to find your brother," Alex said as her brain cleared.

Lucas frowned at her then took two more shots. "He's . . . gone."

"What?"

"He's gone, Alex," Lucas replied. "It's been about three months."

Alex could feel his pain as he took another shot. Her stomach dropped when he looked at her, tears in his brown eyes.

"The training ground was attacked," he continued with a pained expression. "The potentials were killed and Matt was taken. His trail went cold about a week ago."

"Where?" Alex sniffed.

"Los Angeles," he sniffed back. "That's why we're doing this recruiting session. I won't stop until I find my brother."

The large teeth extended well past his full bottom lip.

The team's guns were drawn. Alex stood slowly, telling them to stand down.

"How's your father?"

Lucas retracted his canines when she asked that question. The look in her eyes eased his pain slightly. "He's not doing well and this didn't help. The cancer is spreading too fast. It's just a matter of time. I don't want him to . . . not without knowing."

The problem with Werewolves is that they are susceptible to human disease. More human than wolf, they could contract any virus or bacteria or be overcome by cancer and even AIDS. The current Alpha Male, Roland Wolfe, had led this pack for almost 75 years.

His two sons, Lucas and Matthias, were his pride and joy, and both possessed the traits needed to lead the pack for the next few centuries.

As the oldest, Lucas would take the lead, but Matt would be the next in command. Now that was not going to happen. Now Lucas had to appoint someone, or mate and hope for a son.

"Of course," Alex agreed. "Anything I can do, tell Roland to call me."

Lucas smiled and nodded. "I'll let him know."

She stood and Lucas rounded the desk, taking her in his arms. He smelled of wood and ash for some reason. Releasing her, he walked to the other side of the small office and opened the safe. Lucas puled the shiny case from the bottom, he held it out to her. "I believe this is what you're looking for?"

Alex hesitated, but took the case from his hand. She handed it to Kai then pushed him slightly toward the exit.

Lucas led them back through the stacks and away from the crowd to the gate. "Don't forget about us," he said holding the gate open.

"I won't, I promise," she replied letting her lips linger on his scruffy cheek.

Once outside, Alex turned and watched Lucas as he disappeared inside the gate again. He didn't even look back.

Chapter 23

Jason changed clothes and left the house with Oren. Down the path to the casino, he called Alex again. This time she answered.

"Finally," he huffed. "Where the hell are you? I've been calling for almost an hour!"

"Sorry, Dad! I had to see someone," she said in an amused tone. "What's the rush?"

"The head of the Council would like to meet you and your team in twenty minutes," he shot back. "How far away are you?"

"We'll be there in five," she answered.

"Wait for me in the lobby," Jason snapped and hung up on her.

"Problem, sire?"

Jason stuffed his hands in his pockets and picked up his pace. "Nothing a few dead humans won't solve."

"Any humans in particular, sire?" Oren chuckled.

Jason smiled, "Not just yet, but thanks."

"Get back to the penthouse," she ordered as she pulled the second briefcase from the back of the SUV. Alex handed one to Sebastian and kept the other. "He's meeting me in the lobby, so you don't have much time."

They watched her slip her torn and bloody t-shirt over her head and wipe her body with several tissues soaked in water. "Sebastian, I need you to push these back in."

He looked down her body to see the small bump on her skin. Two ribs sat out slightly. "On three," he said and placed his fingers on the spot. When he put her right hand on his shoulder, he counted, "One . . . two . . ." Before three, he pressed hard and the bones popped back in place with a muffled sound. Her knees buckled but he caught her before she hit the ground.

She put the jacket back on and zipped it up. "What?" she frowned. "Get going!"

When they disappeared behind the building, Alex popped a mint, took a deep breath and walked slowly toward the front doors of the casino.

Jason spied her as soon as she strolled inside, looking like she didn't have a care in the world. As though the most powerful vampire in all creation hadn't waited for an hour to speak to them. Jason was scared to death.

The case in her hand, Alex moved through the people without a ripple. No one noticed her in jeans, a leather jacket and no makeup. She could be anyone.

"Where've you been?" Jason asked, pulling a scrap of paper from her hair. "Mountain climbing?"

Alex pushed his hand away, "I had to take care of some business. Why?"

He stepped closer and took her arm. "Don't go anywhere else without protection again, do you understand?"

"You're being a tad overprotective," she hissed, jerking free. "I'm fine!"

"I need you to clean up, quickly. We have a video conference in ten minutes," he hissed. Oren led the way to the elevators.

Alex glared at Jason through the glass on the inside of the elevator doors. He glared back.

Inside the warm conference room, Jason took a seat at the round table. In front of each chair, a black leather portfolio, bottled water and a pen. In the center of the table, audio equipment and a state of the art holographic image device. It was very impressive, even Alex had to admit that.

To sit without pain was impossible. Usually, to heal, she'd take six painkillers and pass out. That was not going to happen tonight. She'd have to suffer through it with two aspirin instead.

When the blonde woman entered, every eye was on her. She smiled and moved gracefully through the room; turning on the equipment and then dimming the lights before she took a seat at the wall behind Jason.

Slightly shorter than Jason's six foot three inch frame, Adam Craig moved just as gracefully to take a seat next to him. His gold pinky ring winked at her as he opened the leather-bound book and scratched on the paper inside. Gold cufflinks against the white shirt that peeked out caught her eye next. His gray wool suit, Armani probably, and silk tie—red, blood red—with a gold tack that symbolized his house at the center, all added to his appearance.

When her eyes moved back up to his face, she saw a finely chiseled chin.

Smooth skin without scars or blemishes. Narrow nose, deep set eyes and high forehead completed his perfect face. Haircut, fresh and shiny in the pale light of the room.

"Visiting the wolves was not a good idea," he said to the tablet under his hand and not at her.

"I was just seeing an old friend," she grinned. When she reached for the bottled water the pain shot through her body and rattled her teeth. "Did I break some rule or something?"

He looked up with a less amused expression. He sat back, dropped the pen.

"As long as you're in this city, you will do as you're told," he stated firmly. "So yes, you did break a rule. The Pack is off limits to you right now because of your relationship with Matt and his brother. Keep in mind that you're working for us. We don't associate with them unless we have to, understand? The head of the Council is not much for games and nothing that has happened up to now is very funny."

"Who I associate with is none of your business," Alex stated just as firmly. "So, if you could just get to the point of us being here, really, we'll be on our way."

"You're here because you're helpful to us," Adam replied. "If you become more of a liability than an asset, we'll cut you loose, if you're lucky!"

"And if we're unlucky?"

Every muscle in his face twitched into a grin so evil, she held back a shudder. He probably knew it.

Alex smiled when she smelled his anger. "Kill us and you'll die too!"

"Are you sure? It seems to me the Tracker team has pissed someone off! We'd be doing someone a favor if we just ended you right now!"

An image appeared like an apparition in the center of empty space. His voice rumbled all over the room. "That's enough, Adam." The hologram floated above the table for everyone to see. "Good evening," he smiled, green eyes sparkling bright, ashy brown hair immaculately styled.

"Conner Gale," Jason announced, "This is Alex Stone and the current Tracker team."

He seemed to be everywhere at once, his smile still in place.

"Ms. Stone, it is nice to finally meet you. I'm sorry it has to be under these circumstances."

"I'm sure," Alex replied. "Where's Coop?"

He smiled again. He didn't blink or flinch or seem to have any kind of tell.

"I was told he was back at 51, isn't that right Jason?"

Alex held her hand up and Jason closed his mouth.

"Our contacts say someone took him from there." She rubbed her chin and sipped from the bottle again. "Was it you?"

Conner moved slightly and blinked once.

"No," he replied. "We have a team searching Vegas as well."

"How does someone walk into a supposed secure installation and walk out with a body?" she said. "Who took him?"

"We have no idea," he hissed. "We want him back just as badly as you do, believe me!"

"Why? What were you going to do with him?"

"If we could have save him, we would have. If not, he was to be turned by morning."

The air felt stale and cold all of a sudden. Her palms began to sweat and her leg trembled.

"Under whose orders?" Alex asked softly.

"Mine," Conner answered in the same manner.

"It's my understanding the Trackers still take orders from the Pentagon," she stated. "They are still agents of the United States military, and as such, take orders from the Secretary of Defense. So why would he just let you turn one of our agents at will."

Conner cut his eyes to his left for a second then back to the group.

"The Secretary and I have an understanding," he stated. "The Trackers are contracted to do work for the DoD from time to time, but Strategic Assets Management is owned by me now. My company has been working on a cure to the side effects of the supplements, but we needed the original team to work on what went wrong. Team Commander Jesse Cooper, Colonel Benjamin Palmer and you are the only living test subjects now. Cooper was in the first stages of degeneration, with breakdowns at the cellular level causing severe muscle pain, weakening of the immune system, and slowing of his healing abilities."

Alex opened her mouth, but nothing came out. She almost emptied the water bottle and another appeared over her shoulder immediately; the blonde female vampire nodded at her on the way back to her seat.

"Coop was not a member of the original team," Alex said in a low tone.

"He is, however, suffering from the side effects of those pills. If we don't find him soon, he will die. With your cooperation, I may be able to find a cure."

"Define cooperation."

He fidgeted slightly, looked away, and then looked back at her. "I think if we were able to examine you and Colonel Palmer, we could figure out what's going wrong. Only you and he seem to be fine, you especially. Are you so selfish that you wouldn't even try to save your friends if you could?"

As hard as she tried, Alex knew her expression changed at his comment. Conner dropped his gaze and leaned forward at the screen.

"I'm sorry. That was rude," he continued. "But we're running out of time. I can't force you to anything you don't want to do, but I hope you consider the alternative before you say no."

Alex watched the sun rise over the distant mountains. She dressed quickly and knocked on their door before 7am. Kai answered, bed headed and glassy eyed as he yawned.

"Hey."

She nodded at the guards as she eased through the door. A faint cigar odor still lingered in the air. He scratched at his leg as he stumbled away with a nod in the other direction when she asked where Sebastian was.

Alex pushed the door open slowly and stuck her head through first.

His entire body was covered in the blanket like a corpse, barely moving as he inhaled and exhaled. When the blankets rose, it took almost a minute to fall, like he had taken a deep breath and held it.

She stepped inside, stopped at the foot of the bed, unable to tell where his head was in the mass of blankets.

Sebastian coughed and rolled. When the blanket fell away, he looked up at her, blue eyes glassy, but clear. "Hi."

"Hi," she replied. "Sleep okay?"

His bare arms came out and he stretched his body long. "Yea, you?"

Alex shrugged and stepped back as he sat up straight. "Where's the other case?"

He pointed between his legs underneath the bed.

"I'll get that when we're done," she said. "Buy you guys some breakfast?"

"Can I asked you a question first?" he yawned and stretched.

"Sure."

Adjusting the blankets around his waist, Sebastian stared at Alex with a serious expression on his face. "What did Kit want to know about me?"

Alex couldn't hold the grin as it pushed at her lips. He grinned back.

"Remember when I tossed you off that building?" He nodded and yawned again. "You caught yourself."

"So."

"How do you think you did that?"

He smiled bright. "Skills!"

Alex laughed. "Not quite." She sat down next to him, then pushed herself against the headboard. When he turned to her, he looked afraid. "You weren't actually holding on to the bricks."

"Yea, I was. I could feel them," he smirked and nodded like a six year old who'd just been told there's no Santa.

"You were levitating," she said plainly.

He blinked, twice; then frowned. "What?"

"Levitation," Alex pronounced every syllable. "Apparently, you inherited the power of telekinesis. If your sire could do it, then you will too, eventually."

The bed shook as he laughed at her. His eyes watered and his shallow breath caught in his lungs for a few minutes. When he composed himself again, he turned to her with a slightly less serious look on his face. "So," he cleared his throat to keep from laughing again. "Why would the call girl care?"

Alex sat forward, folded her legs in front of her and eased her face close to his. The amusement faded quickly from his posture and his lips. "If you have never had sex, in mid-air, you're missing out."

He seemed to let that sink. "I've never been able to do that before."

"Anybody ever throw you off a building before?"

"No."

Alex stood and turned to him. "You reached out, instinctively, to catch yourself. Your focus was on not falling. Eventually, you'll be able to do it without a second thought. It's pretty freaking cool, actually."

"Cool as shit," he replied. "Can all vampires levitate?"

"It depends," she answered. "Some things develop over time and depends on what your sire could do. Obviously, yours had telekinetic powers. Some are telepaths—mind readers. Others, shifters. I guess you could be taught to do those things, but telekinesis seems to be your dominant power."

From the look on her face, he guessed he should have known these things already. Unfortunately, he didn't ask very many questions about what it meant to be a vampire. His sire, a beautiful thief, didn't offer up any information either. All she told him was he'd live forever, practically, and be stronger than any human being ever imagined. That sounded pretty good considering his situation back then.

Sebastian Rayne, rising star in the surfing world, had been paralyzed in a competition almost ten years ago. At the height of his career he faced a wheelchair, with his mother as his caretaker for the rest of his life. He couldn't ask her to give up her life to care for her paraplegic son, so he jumped at immortality without a second thought. Later, he realized his mistake.

"I need a quick shower," he yawned again.

Alex just stood as he stared up at her. He raised an eyebrow and so did she. When he smiled so did she.

"I'm naked," he stated.

"Okay," she shrugged.

He cleared his throat and pulled the blanket with him when he stood. As he moved by her, she turned to see the blanket fall to floor and him disappearing inside the bathroom.

"Nice ass," she whispered as she moved toward the bedroom door again.

"Thanks," he yelled, slamming the bathroom door closed.

There was a long stretch limo, four SUVs and armed guards waiting when they returned to meet at Jason's home behind the hotel. Alex warned Sebastian not to let that case out of his sight, not even for a second. He swore on his life he wouldn't. As they followed Oren inside, radios crackled and men spoke into their hands, with eyes hidden behind dark glasses, weapons under long overcoats.

The temperature dropped a few degrees and the wind had picked up again. A gust pushed them through the front door as Jason and Adam came into view.

Jason approached with a weird look in his eyes. He was angry, but scared about something too.

"Something's happened," he said to the group.

"You found Coop?" Xavier asked almost as if he were afraid to hear the answer.

Jason stepped up to Alex, laid a hand on her shoulder. "It's . . . Matthias."

Alex felt her heart sink into her stomach then she stepped back. "Where?"

"A few miles outside town," Adam replied as he joined them in the center of the room. "We've notified Lucas. He'd like you to meet him at the compound. The car is waiting."

Without so much as a sorry, Adam marched through the front door on the phone like he'd just announced snow in the forecast. Alex couldn't get enough breath in her lungs to yell, or breathe for that matter.

"We'll go to 51," Sebastian whispered to her. "Unless you want us with you."

"No," she said.

"We should stick with you tonight," Xavier said.

"No. I need you guys to see what you can find

out about what happened at 51," she said heading for the door. "I wanna know who took Coop and where."

"I might have some contacts that'll talk to me," Sebastian sighed. "There's a club on the other end of the strip where they hang these days. We'll see what we can come up with."

CHAPTER 24

As the car pulled up the winding drive, her palms began to sweat.

Everything looked the same, exactly the same. The cactus spread throughout the property. The stone lawn out front and transplanted brush around the covered porch were still immaculate.

When her car came to a stop, the door opened and a young werewolf waited. A hand appeared and she took it. He helped her from the car with a slight grin on his face. Maybe he recognized her or maybe he'd been told about her connection to Roland and his sons. Show respect to those who have the respect of your superiors. Until he was told otherwise, she was sure Lucas had told all of them she was welcomed here.

"Welcome, Ms. Stone," the young man stated, "Lucas is expecting you."

The Great Room was well lit with a fire raging in the corner. The fireplace was big enough for a human being to stand upright in it. That was probably the point.

"I'll let him know you're here," the young man announced as he disappeared around a dim corner.

In a few minutes, she could hear heavy footfalls down the hall. His scent was strong, as strong as it was the other night.

"Sorry," he said entering the room in a slight jog. "I got hung up."

In his arms, Alex found she missed the safety he'd always made her feel when he was around.

"Father will be down shortly," Lucas stated. "Can I get you a drink?"

"I'm good," Alex said. She followed him to the bar at the back of the room where he poured whiskey in a shot glass and smiled at her. "Lucas . . ."

"Don't say it," Lucas said. "People have been saying that to me all day."

"I'm sorry," she replied. "What have you found out?"

Lucas shook his head as he emptied the drink then poured another. "Nothing yet."

"I can help."

"No you can't," he said. "This is Pack business."

He nodded toward the couch and they took a seat. The fire crackled and Alex felt her nerves do the same. When Matt first brought her here, Lucas was not too happy. He never liked outsiders, especially human ones. And he really didn't like her. The longer she trained here for that last assignment, the more Lucas seemed to always be around. Before long, he took over for Matt. Of course he was a better tracker and fighter, so it made sense he'd trained her to fight, to track any target and survive in the wilderness. And as young girls often do, she developed feelings for him that went well beyond teacher and student.

"So," Lucas's low voice brought her back to

the present. "What are you doing here, Alex, with the vampires?"

"Favor for a friend," she lied. "I was hoping Matt could help me. . ." she trailed off when the frown formed on his face.

"Help you with what?" he asked.

"I need to find Becker," she lied again.

"We haven't seen that guy in years," he growled. "Do you think he's involved in this?"

"I'm not sure."

When he grabbed her arm, she didn't try to jerk free. "Alex."

"Lucas," she tried to remain calm because he wasn't. "I will do everything I can to find out who did this. When I do, I will deliver them to you, I swear it."

His grip eased up, but he took her hand and pulled it to his cheek. Her skin tingled when he brushed his lips against the back of her hand. He kissed her hand then placed it on his leg, keeping it there with his own. The warmth of his skin snaked up her arm and scattered through her body.

"You shouldn't be involved in this," he whispered. "You have bigger problems right now."

"I can handle it," she sighed.

Before she could stand, he'd taken her face in his warm hands and kissed her. A brilliantly passionate kiss that made her head spin and sent chills everywhere. She'd never known him to be so forward with her. In their past, he'd treated her like a sister. He'd even referred to her as such on several occasions. Now he was kissing her like they'd been lovers once, or that he wanted to be now.

"Lucas," she exhaled, as she pushed away.

"Sorry," he said with one last peck on her cheek. "I used to think you'd be a kid forever. The feelings you had for me, I couldn't return them, not then."

"You were my very first kiss, real kiss," she replied with a squeeze of his warm hand. "And I knew you and Deanna were promised to each other then, but I still had a massive crush on you."

Lucas smiled at her, "Same here."

They stood and turned to the doorway when they heard the sound of footsteps in the hall. The disturbance in the entryway meant only one thing. Lucas stood as he pulled Alex with him.

He hardly looked like a man whose body was being eaten away by cancer. But the hand carved cane he used to walk said differently. Alex had never known him to depend on anything or anybody. But his uncharacteristically slow rate of speed made it clear to her he really was sick.

Roland hugged Lucas, then turned his wolfish grey eyes to Alex as he placed the cane in front of him and held on with both hands. He sighed, then he smiled at her. His reddish brown skin stretched over those high cheekbones and the chandelier lights danced in his eyes.

A silver mane of hair sat on his broad shoulders and smelled of spices she couldn't quite put her finger on.

"Let me look at you for a second," he said. "I

can't believe you're here."

Alex took two steps and she was in his strong arms. The smell of sandalwood puffed up through his shirt when she squeezed him tight and his cane bumped her on the butt as he rocked her in his arms.

"I'm so sorry, father," she said, voice muffled in his broad chest. She held on so tight. His arms were still strong and squeezed her close to him. As he rocked them slowly, she didn't want to let him go, but he pushed her gently from his grip and smiled down on her again.

He leaned on his cane again as she stood before him. He touched her face with a strong hand as his face registered his pleasure to see her again.

"I'm glad you're here," he whispered down to her.

"Whatever you need," Alex whispered in his hand.

"We need nothing right now," Roland grinned at her. "But those who took my son from me. Do you know who they are?"

"Not yet, but . . ."

"When you know, I expect you to tell me and only me," Roland said. "Do you understand?"

"Yes."

Lucas cleared his throat as he appeared behind Roland. "Father, I can handle this. You should rest. Alex and I . . ."

"Have lost someone you both love," Roland growled. "I have lost a child, a part of my soul. Your grief has limits, mine does not!"

Roland nodded slowly and led the way out the back door. The smell of burning wood and the sound of fire as it crackled interrupted the night songs.

The stone circle appeared before them, created when he was Shaman of his tribe. Two hundred years later, he was leader, but would pass the mantle to his only son soon.

Roland entered the circle first, chanted as he sat down on a stone in the center. When he was done, Lucas led her inside. Roland directed them to the stones directly in front of him; where he wanted them to be.

Alex watched the flames in the pits around the outside of the circle as they danced in the breeze and red embers floated up toward the stars.

"Roland, I came here . . ." Alex started.

Roland raised a steady hand and she fell silent.

"I know why you came here," Roland replied. "Matt told me he had a dream about you a few days before he was taken from the training ground. He was expecting you to show up."

"I had one about him too," she admitted. "But I didn't know what it meant until now."

"He tried to warn you."

"I think so," she nodded.

Roland stretched his legs out in front of him. He placed his hands in his lap and tilted his head to one side. She could see the relief wash over him and Lucas. "Where should we look?"

Alex took a deep breath. "I don't know, but he

was close when it happened, very close."

Lucas stood and began to pace behind her. "What does that mean?"

"Our connection has weakened over the years, Lucas. I don't know exactly where he was. I'll keep trying though."

Lucas sat back down and stared at his father. Alex could feel his fear and his anger, but she wasn't prepared to do anything about it. Her path would take her far from here this time.

"I haven't used blood to track in years," Alex explained. "I'm surprised I was able to feel what I did after all this time. The case I picked up has a sample of his blood. That's why he left it for me. So maybe I could track him in time. I still may be able to get something from the sample. I'll try tonight if you want me to."

"You do that," he huffed. "In the meantime, I'm going out to find my brother's killer the old fashioned way, hunt!"

Roland didn't try to stop him as he left. They could hear doors slamming and then car tires rolling away from the compound in a hurry.

"I'm sorry," Alex said as she took a seat next to Roland.

"It's not your fault," Roland replied. "Lucas is angry and so am I. I didn't expect to see you, but when Lucas told me you were here, I let myself believe it was because Matt had connected with you and he was still alive."

"I wish I'd come sooner," Alex tried to keep the

tears from falling. Roland stretched a long arm around her and kissed her forehead.

"I do too."

His text surprised her. Jason asked her to meet him at the fountains. How could she have refused such a strangely human request as that? The walk helped to clear her head. Jason's voice popped inside her brain from across the street. He waved her over like an excited child.

His bright smile, casual dress and tousled locks almost hid him from her eyes. But he wanted her to see him surrounded by humans and no one the wiser.

"You almost missed the beginning," he smiled and kissed both cheeks. "It's the best part."

He pulled her in front of him and wrapped his arms around her shoulders.

As the lights and water performed and the music filled her ears, Alex relaxed against him. His body was less firm than earlier and he was warmer than she was.

"Okay," Alex laughed. "What's going on, Stavros?"

His hold tightened and his chuckle made her back tingle. "I like being around . . . people," he sighed. "It reminds me of when I was like them. That's our little secret."

"My lips are sealed," she laughed.

"Let's hope."

He pulled her back and they emerged from the crowd hand in hand.

Jason led her to a bench and pinned her in the corner.

"We won't get in the way of the Pack. How's Roland?"

Alex kept her hands in her lap as he stared directly in her eyes. He liked to do that.

"He's lost his son. How do you think he is?"

"Conner will speak with him tonight," he whispered. "He will offer whatever assistance they need to find the murderer."

"That's decent of him," Alex replied. "Why's he doing that? You guys don't exactly give a damn about each other's wellbeing."

Jason laughed a really normal laugh.

"We may not be best friends, but no one is glad to see Matt dead."

"And if it was a vampire?" Alex asked.

"We'll cross that bridge, *if* we come to it," Jason replied.

The crowd cheered a few feet away and she turned her attention to the sound. "Right."

Jason wanted to change the subject. All this talk of death and revenge was spoiling the moment for him. "So, how do you know Kit Blaze?"

"Who says I do?"

Jason grinned and she grinned back. The

slightest bit of fire still left in her eyes as she stared at him. "I was told you and Sebastian paid her a visit the other day."

"So?" Alex smirked as she stood and they began to walk toward Jason's property again.

"Why?"

"I was bored," she replied.

"Bored," Jason chuckled. "Did you pay for her services for the boy or yourself?"

"Why?" Alex sighed. "Jealous?"

"Hardly," Jason chuckled. "But I am curious as to why you'd visit a call girl just to talk."

Alex turned to him when they reached the main entrance of the casino entrance. "She knew Coop. I was trying to see if he might have told her something he shouldn't have."

Jason took her hand as they walked through the casino and through the back doors leading to his private residence. When they reached the front door, Oren opened it as if he had been watching from the peephole.

"And, did she?" Jason asked leading her out back to the pool area.

"Did she what?" Alex asked.

"Know anything," he chuckled. "Why are you making this so hard?"

"It's fun winding you up," she replied pulling him to a stop at the edge of the pool. Bringing him closer, she kissed him. He was surprised and pleased at her forwardness. Although he was used to taking the lead, it only seemed right that she did.

At first, the kiss was innocent, almost sweet. Then she began to let go of her defenses and allow a rage to escape her. Jason didn't mind at all.

———————————————————

Hot and wet, his mouth moved in greedy pulls at first, but when Alex pulled him closer, he slowed the pace and gave in to her silent direction.

When he moved her toward a staircase that led up to his private balcony, she barely noticed. He held her hand tight, but she could only focus on her desire to reach their destination.

Once on the balcony, she pulled free of his grip and stepped back a few inches to catch her breath. The balcony doors opened with a wave of his hand and Alex could smell scented candles and see a bottle of champagne as it chilled next to the bed.

"Was this the plan or did you just wing it?" she asked breathlessly.

"Sixteen-year olds wing it," he replied in the same manner. "I always have a plan."

He backed inside and opened the bottle. Pouring one glass, he took a sip and she took the bottle. "Very ladylike."

Alex laughed as she took a drink from the cold bottle. "Is that what you want me to be right now, a lady?"

Climbing into the bed and tossing her shoes over the side, Jason joined her.

Alex climbed on top of him and they eased

down into the bed together.

They tugged at each other's clothes like horny teenagers and once there was nothing more to take off, she took control.

———

She moved over him like silk. She did all the things he liked to do to his conquests like she was reading his mind. But what she didn't do was offer him a taste. And his body was aching for it right now.

As he was invited inside her, that blood hunger surfaced. It pushed at his groin and bounced around his body like a pinball. Over and over they came, shaking the glass in the windows and pulling the sheets loose underneath them. Jason flipped them over and entered her again, deep.

"You haven't offered me a taste," he growled, voice hoarse.

When she stretched her arm out, her wrist brushed his mouth.

He smiled, incisors dropping slowly.

———

Alex thought she could hear the gums separating as they descended. As much as she tried to deny it, all of her senses were still heightened. No matter how much she wanted to suppress her own skill, she grew stronger with every passing day. Humans were never any threat to her, but now that she was surrounded by supernatural beings again, and she had to use the skills she was born with as a hybrid. She hated it, but she had no other choice.

She connected to his mind almost instantly. It was easy because he was focused on the taste. Like everything else she hid from the world, she rarely used her telepathic abilities anymore. In this situation, it was necessary to keep Jason from taking too much of her blood. She still wasn't sure what it might do to him.

The prick of one tooth sent a familiar pain through her body. It scratched the thin layer of skin at her wrist and his eyes closed as he took a deep breath.

Alex let him lick the thin stream from her arm, but kept him from sinking both teeth in and feeding the way he wanted to.

Later, when he was asleep, Alex dressed and left him there.

Downstairs, she almost made it without being seen. Nikki stepped out of the shadows, low growl in her voice.

"Sneaking off," she purred. "Did you pick his pocket or something?"

Alex smiled as they walked to the front door. She turned to Nikki and plucked a long hair from her sweater. "I've got an early meeting, need to get some sleep."

"He can be quite demanding," Nikki smiled as she opened the door.

"You would know," Alex replied then stepped out onto the porch.

"Yes, I would."

"Tell him I'll call him later today. We'll do lunch. You're welcome to join us," Alex grinned.

"No thanks, but I'll pass that along," Nikki grinned back. "Um . . . for the record, it won't last. Jason has a weakness for human women. Always has, especially ones like you. I tolerate it, but remember one thing, he's not for you. His future is with his own kind."

Alex stepped back in Nikki's face and forced her against the door with her closeness. She took a deep breath, nose grazing Nikki's neck; her slight shiver made Alex grin.

"Don't worry. You can have him back when I'm done. I don't care about his future. The present is enough for me."

One soft, quick kiss to Nikki's cheek and she was off. She could hear Nikki cursing as she got to the end of the drive and the gate opened slowly.

CHAPTER 25

No one wanted to really talk about the shooting from the other night, or Matt's death. And Sebastian had called in every marker he had in the city and still came up short. Now what?

He was up two grand, but it hardly mattered. If he went back to Alex with nothing, he'd stake himself. The twins on one side and Xavier on the other, Sebastian folded the last hand with two pair.

"Hey," Xavier barked. "Where you going?"

He walked away, saying he'd be back in a few minutes.

The bar down the street was a bust, and so was the strip club Kai talked them into going to downtown.

Sebastian didn't have the heart to tell them all the women were vampires and the only reason they paid them any attention was for the chance to hook them to the bite.

He finally convinced his friends to leave and hit the poker tables for a while. He wasn't sure where Kai would have heard about that place, but they were safe now, back at their hotel, losing money like normal people.

He sat down in the bar and people-watched. From his position, he could still see his friends and Jason's guards all around them.

He wondered what Alex was doing right now. And he wondered what the cases were really for. He stuffed a hand in his pocket for his room card, but he pulled out a slip of paper instead.

The obviously battered and worn stock paper appeared in his pocket for a reason. He wondered why he'd have a flyer from a strip club from over twenty years ago. The picture was faded and the colors, he could tell, were once bright neon.

The words 'Grand Opening' were barely noticeable at the top of the page.

This bar catered to a particular type of human—the type who craved the bite and came there to feed their addiction. Its clientele, strictly female; their fee for membership, one hundred dollars. For that small amount, all their dreams fulfilled the paper said. No request denied. No fantasy beyond their reach.

Like any good drug, the vampire's bite is highly addictive.

But unlike the manmade drugs of today, there is no reason to chase that first high. The more you're bitten, the better it feels! And you'd do anything or pay any price for the experience. And they did!

Before he could toss the paper away, something caught his eye.

At the very bottom, scrawled in almost illegible handwriting was a note.

"She deceives you all," he whispered to no one. "The bite consumes all who seek its embrace forever."

Sebastian folded the paper carefully then tucked

it back in his pocket as he stood.

He stopped at the poker table. "I'm headed upstairs."

"Too much excitement for you," David chuckled.

Sebastian gave them a fake smile and waved over his shoulder as he disappeared in the crowd again.

His steps were deliberately slow. He needed this time to slow his heart and control his anger. If not, one of them would die.

"I should be back in a couple of days," Alex stated. She swiped the screen to see the images one by one. "How're things going there?"

She heard Ivy pushed out a hard breath, "Fine. Don't try to change the subject. What are you really doing in Vegas? Does it have anything to do with the guy they found a couple weeks ago?"

If she even hinted at that being part of the reason, Ivy wouldn't stop asking questions Alex didn't want to answer. Ignore Ivy and she was liable to board a plane an hour later. When they were kids, Ivy was the most popular girl in school. She never bothered with formalities like introductions. Not knowing her was your problem. And if you did know her, everyone wanted to know you. For a teenager who hunted vampires, being known was not a good thing.

"So," Ivy said from the other end of the line. "Spill it, Stone."

"I'm doing what E! News says I'm doing," Alex

giggled. "Secretly dating Jason Stavros and plotting to sell my company to him because I might be pregnant with his child."

"Shut up," Ivy sighed. "Don't tell me then. I'm only your best friend in the whole world is all and you're keeping secrets from me. Not cool, Alex."

Her first thought was to tell her best friend in the whole world the truth. Jason Stavros was a vampire—the principle player in a meeting of all things supernatural. She and the Trackers would be his personal security team at a super-secret meeting she was still unclear about and she would more than likely die in Romania if she failed. *Yeah, tell her that.*

Instead she opted for the lie. "Save it," she replied jokingly. "I'm just trying to talk Coop into getting me access to the Trackers, for the campaign, remember? Our bread and butter?"

"Whatever," she heard Ivy giggle. "Where is he by the way?"

"I have no idea," Alex replied. "Probably in the bar picking up twenty-somethings."

"Yea, well, take care," Ivy stated. She was dismissing Alex, which was so unlike her. "Call me when you're on the way home. Don't make me come looking for you."

"Yes, mother."

The line went dead and Alex was kind of glad. As she continued her work, she glanced at the bed through the open door. Matt's silver case sat on the bed, unopened. Every time she tried to reach for it, her hands shook and her head ached. But she couldn't avoid it much longer if she was going to find out what really happened.

Chapter 26

"When were you going to tell us?" he asked as he shook the glass, causing the wine to spin inside. He stood in front of her for almost ten minutes without a word.

She looked up from the computer screen only briefly. "Tell you what?"

Sebastian emptied the glass. When it slammed against the far wall, she didn't flinch. She didn't even stop until he pushed the screen down, clicked it closed, and a small beep announced sleep mode.

Alex sat back on the couch and stared at the machine. After a few seconds of silence, she reached for the computer again. After the night she'd had, she didn't have the strength to figure out what this kid was so pissed about. Maybe if she ignored him, he'd just go away.

Sebastian swept the device from the table and it flew across the room and landed in pieces on the floor. "You're bitten!"

The timbre of his voice shook the glass in the windows. The vibrations echoed around the ceiling as she stood.

Alex stayed calm as she walked over to the remnants of her laptop and scooped them up in both hands. After she dumped the bits on the dining table,

Sebastian stood in her personal space as she turned around, body rigid, fangs bared.

"I'm not bitten, but if you're offering . . ." she giggled.

He put everything he had into the backhand. His hand even stung a little.

Alex bounced off the bulletproof glass and slid down to the carpet.

Sebastian picked her up like a puppy and tossed her to the other side of the room.

She crashed into a floor lamp and ended in a heap next to the front door. When she started to laugh, Sebastian roared.

She shook her head and wiped at her own blood as he approached again.

"You lying, self-righteous bitch," he barked. "How can we trust anything you say or do now? You could be connected to whoever did this to you even now! Who are you working for?"

Trying to push herself from the floor, she sighed, "Nobody."

At first he raised an open hand, he paused then brought down a fist as hard as he could. Alex hit the floor again and laughed.

He split her lip with that blow and her forehead bled, slightly. "I should just kill you now and save us all a whole lot of trouble," he growled at her.

Alex stood tall and faced him. He was the one

to put some space between them when he sensed it. Danger always had a bitter smell, almost sour. He felt her rage burn the air around them as her face contorted to scream at him. "Do it!"

Sebastian had never seen this kind of pain before, not ever.

Alex no longer looked like the woman he'd met days ago. She was no longer cool, calm and collected. Although still beautiful on the outside, the storm of emotion that erupted from her was hard to look at. It was grotesque, and even harder to believe.

She took a deep breath and kicked him in chest with everything she had.

"Disappointed, Sebastian?" she hissed as she stood over him. "Did you think I was one of the good guys? Innocent and brave. Righteous! I wasn't!" She plucked him from the floor with ease then slammed him high against the wall. "I was human and weak! And every time I told myself that it was the last time, I'd do it again and again and again!"

She dropped Sebastian to his feet then she forced her knee into his gut. When he doubled over, that same knee bloodied his nose sending him back into the wall. The blood he coughed up splashed her bare foot.

"Do you know what it's like Sebastian? Wanting it all the time? Needing it every day?"

Once he was upright again, she pressed her body

against him, her nose slid over his neck and stopped on his ear, then she exhaled.

"Scratching at your own skin until it bleeds! Begging for that first break of skin, feeling like you were on fire. Then they bite and it all goes away. All you can feel is blissful pain! And when it's all over, all you want is to burn in hell!"

Alex steadied him on his feet, stepped away and shook her head at the floor. When he tried to move away, she caught him by the neck, squeezing off his wind pipe.

"I have never known a need like that before. Pure lust! Pure desire and the only way to satisfy the hunger was to let one of you feed on me."

Before she knew it they were stretched out on the floor, she on top of him as she moved against him, and exhaled hard against his ear again.

"And I did. Every night I'd find some hungry little newbie and let him take his fill and then I'd take his life!"

She straddled Sebastian, held him to the floor by one hand and smiled like she was just this side of insane. When he tried to sit up, she forced him back down, his head bounced off the floor with a thud.

That's when she let him feel her power—her real power. Even if he wanted to, he wouldn't have been able to free himself from her grip. And that grip was nothing compared to the one she had on his mind. She slithered inside his head like a snake, pushed past his mental blocks like they weren't even there.

The pictures formed slowly then there was a full-fledged movie played inside his head. Faces blurred, but it didn't matter. She showed him how she fed her addiction to the bite and how she covered her shame the only way she knew how, killing! She let him enjoy the pleasure and then she made him feel the pain.

Over and over again, Sebastian felt each one die at the height of his pleasure. He tried to force her out, but couldn't. His body ached for her the way theirs did. He screamed the way they screamed; the way she did each time. And when she was done, she pulled him to his feet and sat him down gently. So much pain he thought, too much pain for anyone to have to bear. When his head spun, his knees buckled and she let him fall to floor.

After the pain in his head stopped, he opened his eyes to see the bottle of blood as it loomed over his face. Sebastian took it in a shaky hand, crawled to the wall and sat up against it. Alex slid down next to him with a bottle of Patron in one hand and two shot glasses in the other.

Every muscle ached, as he drank slowly at first. The sensation was like a really bad hangover. The blood eased the fire in his gut, but didn't erase what he'd seen. Finishing his blood, he took the shot glass and they drank.

"How'd you find out?"

Sebastian opened his mouth, but nothing came

out. He took another shot and it burned going down. He pulled the piece of crumpled paper from pocket. The chicken scratch didn't seem familiar, at first, then he saw a flash of recognition move over her face.

"How long has it been?" Sebastian whispered because he couldn't raise his voice any louder.

Alex took a shot and put the bottle down between them. "Ten years, two months, two days," she replied with a far off look in her eyes.

He turned his head toward her and she looked lost. "How did you sever the bond? I mean nobody goes cold from that . . . do they?"

"No they don't," Alex sighed. "You either beg to be turned or you beg to die."

"So . . ."

"I died," she said with a pat to his shoulder as she pushed up from the floor. "And you owe me another laptop."

CHAPTER 27

This place was tacky way back when. Now it was just plain sad. Nothing had changed in over twenty years. The neon sign blinked and buzzed as she passed. The steel door was a joke. Even the rapidly aging bouncer made her laugh inside.

Alex wouldn't have been caught dead within a hundred miles of this place under any circumstances, but she had to be here. This was the beginning of the yellow brick road for her, unfortunately. As Creed's right hand, she protected him with her life. Fueled by hate, Alex Stone went from full-time soldier to part time enforcer and lover of one Mason Creed. Worst mistake of her life.

Gramps checked the fake I.D. she presented with his good eye. He eyed her, then the license again. After a few seconds, he let her pass.

Inside she almost laughed out loud. Same paint scheme, same cheap ass furniture, and incredibly bad artwork on the walls. This stuff had left cool in the dust ages ago.

Alex slipped the money under the glass separating her from the woman in the booth and waited for her change. The woman pointed a long fake thumbnail toward the ratty curtain behind the booth and said, "Have fun honey."

This would have been the perfect situation for gloves or a full decontamination suit, Alex thought as she tried not to really touch the curtain to pass through to the other side.

What was most likely dust or Anthrax floated to the floor as the fabric separated. She held her breath and stepped to the other side. The vibrations from the bass hit her in the chest as she walked through. The lights on stage drew her attention to the dancer.

He danced around the small stage alone. His abs moving in time to his music as the women screamed and clapped and waved money in the air. When the pants came off, the crowd went wild.

On his knees, the dancer crawled seductively to the edge of the stage and took the dollar in his teeth. His admirer, a healthy girl with platinum hair, Lee press on nails and tight jeans fanned herself as he pecked her on the cheek and slid to the other side of the stage.

Her girlfriends cheered and ordered another round.

Alex took a stand at the bar.

She watched the crowd of women from this decade surrounded by remnants of the last. Some of these women were too young to remember those days; some weren't even born yet.

Whoever said women couldn't be as raunchy as men should come to this place on a Friday night. The bouncers around the stage were prying women off the dancers like pull taffy.

When the bartender dropped a white paper

napkin on the bar, he waited for her order with no expression at all really.

"Tequila," she said. "And I need to speak with Creed."

The bartender poured the tequila without the slightest acknowledgment of her request.

She slammed the cheap liquor and tapped the glass for another. The hundred she put under the glass got his attention quicker than before.

He reached for the money and Alex reached for him.

His wrist was weak—no upper body strength either. She guessed the fact that she was a million times stronger than him might have had something to do with this not being that hard. And he didn't reach for the sawed-off under the register because he knew he wouldn't make it.

"Creed ain't here," he growled as she let his arm go. He massaged his wrist and poured her another drink.

"He's always here," Alex replied slamming the shot. "Get him now."

He picked up the phone with his good hand. "Who's lookin'?" he sniffed.

"Alex," she replied.

When he repeated what she said, he hung up and said Creed was on his way down.

Mason Creed fancied himself an entrepreneur. This fine establishment was one of three he owned and operated within the city limits. However, it was the only one catering exclusively to women, thus explaining the poor attention to detail when it came to the décor.

But this crowd was too drunk to care. They were here for another reason.

They were here to get a chance to see the men behind the red door just off stage right. They were here to escape the mundane and walk the tightrope for a few hours every weekend.

Creed was the man with the plan, and his plan worked beautifully.

Each and every weekend, this place filled with lonesome widows and bored housewives; horny singles and wispy wallflowers. And every weekend they came here to forget the last five days of the week. They drank and danced and waved money in the air for the chance feel like the most beautiful girl in the world.

The objects of their desire danced at their command.

They writhed and gyrated to upbeat tempos or slithered and posed to what passed for 'mood' music in this place. All the while picking the ones they'd take behind the curtain; the ones who would give anything to be in their arms, if only for one night.

Creed had been center stage back then; the biggest draw in this place. Now he owned it.

When he spotted her, he noted how easily she fit in here. She was a few years older, but nothing else had changed. Perched on the stool, she looked bored, classic disposition. As his enforcer, Alex was feared and desired at the same time. His competition tried on several occasions to lure her away, but she stayed with him. He let himself believe it was because she loved him, but in the back of his mind he knew it was for a different reason. So he was content to be the one she shared her bed and her blood with back then.

Now he imagined what she'd do when she found out her very best friend in the world had taken over those duties. That thought amused him so much right now. The first opportunity he got, he'd spring that on her and watch as it brought her to her knees.

When it was clear to him she was alone, he gave the bartender a nod and stopped a few inches behind her. "You lost?"

Alex turned on the stool and smiled. "Nope."

"I know you don't need a job, so what are you doing here?" Creed smiled as he took the whiskey from the bar.

"You should seriously consider redecorating this place," she replied, then led him to a dark booth in back.

She smiled as she slid into the faux leather booth and sent his drink back to him. "I see you're still drawing them in like flies," Alex grinned. "Or should I say keeping the bait on the hook?"

Creed laughed and tapped the glass with his pinky ring. "Just giving them what they ask for."

When the next dancer hit the stage, the lights

went low and the music slowed down.

Still covered in shadows, Alex could see him clearly. The costume was laughable. Black tuxedo pants and opera cape; hair slicked back, giant iron cross at his throat.

When the cape fell open a collective gasp sailed around the room.

His chest, bare and slick with body oil, the muscles rippled and flexed as he pulled at the string so the heavy fabric around his broad shoulders slid to the stage. Alex recognized Jason's young bodyguard, Oren, immediately. Sometimes blackmail material just fell out of the sky in this town.

"You like that, huh," she heard him say. "Remind you of someone does he?"

"Lose your touch Creed? Girls not screaming for you the way they used to?"

"Oh I still keep them screaming," he winked, "My talents are best enjoyed behind closed doors these days. My clientele, well let's just say they like their privacy and they pay very well for it. I'd be happy to pencil you in, for old times' sake."

"Tempting as that sounds, I just came here to talk," she replied.

"If you say so," he answered. "I don't remember you being much of a conversationalist in the old days, though. I remember you being eager to please me, which of course is how it should have been."

Alex pulled the crumpled piece of stock paper from her pocket and tossed it over to him.

Creed looked almost afraid to touch it, but he pressed it out and smiled when he looked up at her. "I've updated that if you're interested."

His wry grin and low chuckle made her want to scratch his eyes out.

"Somebody slipped that to one of my guys tonight," Alex stated as she took his glass and emptied the contents on the cheap carpet. She pointed to the note scratched at the bottom and Creed just smiled.

"You think I did this? I didn't," he replied, waving his empty glass at the bartender with two fingers in the air at him. "Looks like someone's sending you a message, but it's not me."

"I know someone is sending me a message, Creed. I want to know who."

Creed and Alex fell silent when the bartender dropped the glasses on the table and walked away.

"How would I know?" he groaned. "We haven't seen each other in ten years."

"My guys were in your place downtown. When they left, this was in one of their pockets."

Creed pushed the paper away and frowned. "And?"

"And coincidence is not in my vocabulary."

"Maybe it should be."

"Maybe you should just tell me what I want to know."

Creed sighed again and raised his glass to her. They toasted, but Alex didn't drink.

"I can't begin to imagine how someone came

across a twenty year old flyer, let alone explain how it ended up in the pocket of one or your 'guys'," he stated.

"You should probably try to figure it out then because I would hate to see anything happen to all this beefcake," she smiled, "especially him." She jerked her head toward the stage.

"Are you threatening me? That is not a good idea," Creed growled.

"Really?"

"I'm a law abiding, taxpaying businessman," he continued. "This isn't the Old West, you know. You can't just come in here, guns blazing, and expect me to blink."

He put the glass to his lips, but she pulled it back before the liquid touched his mouth.

"Here's what I can do," Alex purred. "I can make sure the Council finds out how much you actually make off this place. I'm sure they'd be very surprised to see the real numbers versus what you send them every quarter."

Creed gave her a full fanged smiled, "And now you're calling me a cheat? I've killed trash like you for less! You think you're better than me now, Alex? However you were able to kick it, underneath you're still just like all the pathetic sheep that crawl in and out of here every weekend. You're only one bite away from scratching at my door again, begging for your next ride!"

It wasn't easy to kick the affliction that was Mason Creed, but her hatred for him made it far less difficult. On Esmeralda and Morgan's doorstep, Alex begged them to help her. With Roland Wolfe's help, Alex died. To sever that bond, to separate her life force from his, she had to. Death was easy. To bring someone back from it; that was hard. That was a power only a select group of people had. A Shaman and a Wicca combined their powers and brought the only female hybrid in 600 years back from the dead. She couldn't really remember very much, but she did remember how painful it was to come back from the darkness. Esmeralda had said that one day, she might remember what happened while she was dead, but Alex was in no hurry to find out.

Alex put her finger in his glass and sucked the whiskey as she stared at Creed.

"Ouch, that hurt Creed," she giggled. "As for you killing me, get in line. You forget I know what really happened to your sire that night."

"That was self-defense," he growled.

"Most people just quit a shitty job working for a giant asshole," Alex smiled at him. He growled again as his fangs retracted.

"You don't quit your maker," he hissed. "And that's what I went there to do, but he decided me dead would be better than just giving me my freedom." He shrugged boyishly. "Okay, so I tried to blackmail him into it. He could have just cut me loose instead of trying to separate me from my head!"

Alex dropped her gaze to his trembling hands. Creed and his maker had been very close back then. She showed him proof of just how connected Cyrus was. Money laundering, prostitution, drug trafficking—nothing was taboo for him. Creed had a way to break free and Alex thought she saw a way to walk away from that life forever.

Cyrus had given her a key to his private quarters. For the elimination of his enemies, she was paid very well. But in order to get close enough to get to his secrets, she had become his lover, thus earning his trust and that key. He was her first vampire, not Mason Creed. When Creed found out, he went ballistic.

"You turned me down time and time again," he had yelled at her that night. "And you succumbed to him! Why?"

Back then, she thought she had feelings for Creed. Maybe not love, but she did have a strong desire to please him. He'd taken her in after the hospital when none of her friends gave her a second thought. And he'd convinced her, begged her, to do this for him and they'd both reap the benefits.

"I did it for you," she whispered. "You told me to do whatever was necessary to get the information." He shoved her against the wall. "I did it for you."

"Liar," he barked in her face then snatched the briefcase from her hands. "You're just like all the other pathetic sheep in this world! I thought you were different! I thought . . ."

Creed marched into Cyrus's office and demanded his freedom and enough money to start his own business. Cyrus laughed. Cyrus told them both he'd known their plan all along. Played along because it amused him and he'd beat Creed to her blood. That's when Cyrus drew the gun and put one in Alex's right shoulder and thigh. Then he drew the machete that sat on the stand on his desk. He'd bragged about the witch doctor he'd killed for that machete. They fought and Creed came up with the weapon held high. One hard swing and Cyrus' body fell back and his head rolled next to Alex on the floor.

As his body and head burned to cinder, Creed wept like a baby. To see him still affected by that memory almost made him seem human. Then she remembered all that Creed was capable of; the guilt and pain he made her feel in punishment for her sin against him. She straightened her posture then locked eyes with him.

"When you sent me after that information, you promised me you'd take that to the Council. Do you know what I had to do to get that close to him," she hissed at him. When he grinned at the glass in his hand, she remembered how much she hated him. She didn't have to be able to read his mind to know what he was thinking. But every time she tried, a pain shot through her brain. That wasn't supposed to happen.

"Yeah," he sighed with a quick sip from his glass. "You did it for me. I remember."

Alex grabbed the side of the small table to keep from breaking his nose. "I brought you enough proof to bury him with the Council. They would have just given you his holdings if you'd just done what you said you were going to do!"

"You don't know that! Humans . . . You think everything's so fair! Like you, I did what I had to do to survive."

"You owe me," she hissed as she sat back again. "I'm here to collect."

Creed slammed his glass down and it shattered. "Alright!"

"Good boy," she winked. "You have exactly two weeks, then the Council starts asking questions you don't wanna answer."

Alex balled up the paper and stuffed it inside her glass. Then she lit a match and dropped it on top. The small flame lit up Creed's face. She pushed the glass to the center of table and left him as it burned.

Just being back in this place, being that close to him made her want to pour gasoline over her head and light a match. Outside, the desert air cleared her mind.

Sebastian jumped off the hood of the car and met her halfway. "Well?"

"Something's changed," she said in a low voice. "We're in trouble."

"What does that mean," Sebastian frowned.

"I couldn't read his thoughts, at all, that's what that means."

"Nothing?"

Alex shook her head. "I couldn't even get a buzz, Sebastian. His mind was different, stronger than before. Like a pure blood."

Sebastian stopped in his tracks, "That's impossible! He's turned right?"

"He's only about seventy or eighty years old," she continued. "I don't understand."

"How do you know it's not just you? I mean it has been awhile and you're still aging," Sebastian replied. "Maybe you're just out of practice."

She was out of practice. She heard his thoughts as clear as her own right now. What surprised her was he didn't think she was crazy. He thought there had to be a way to test the theory. There had to be a way to be sure it wasn't her, but Creed that changed somehow. They'd figure out what problems that would cause later.

"Where are they now?"

Jason paced back and forth, clenching his jaw.

"Headed west," the man he had put on them, replied.

"What happened at the club?" Jason huffed. "How long did she stay there?"

"Not long," he answered. "She didn't look too happy when she came out, then she and the young one headed west. I won't lose them."

"Thank you," he mumbled.

"My pleasure, sire."

Jason tossed the phone on the desk and scratched at his head. Too many things were out of his control, and he included her in that. He didn't like being out of control, not in his own city! He'd given Creed some space on this, but now he was starting to regret that decision.

Alex Stone knew much more about them than she should have for a human. Even with her past, she couldn't be privy to the kind of things Creed was hooked into, could she? He sat down and decided to not play nice guy anymore.

Chapter 28

Slanted shadows fell across his desk as the sun rose. He'd waited practically all night. He'd done a lot of that lately. Waited for his funding, waited for medical supplies and drugs, waited for his patients to get better. But drugs and supplies are always late. The funding, never enough, and his patients never seem to get better. Even with help from donors like Alex Stone, he still struggled to keep the outreach program alive most months.

Dr. Thomas Gilchrest tried to keep the faith though. Maybe one day his clinic would be empty and he'd have to take up golf to kill time between outpatients. Unfortunately, it's never been that easy. Sometimes coming home was the hardest part of ending a war.

His third cup of coffee was cold, ice cold. He thought maybe he should try to sleep as he pushed away from the desk, dropped down in the center of the room in a plank and did push- ups. With every push he tried to forget the job he'd agreed to do. The job that involved a doctor/patient relationship that shouldn't be broken. But were they really doctor and patient? Technically, Dr. Gilchrest still worked for Strategic, even if Alex didn't know that. And she hadn't actually been his patient anyway. After the hospital, he was ordered to 'accidentally' run into her in London. His cover, a medical conference on PTSD. He brought up the subject of his outreach program casually and she seemed genuinely interested in helping. The plan worked. It was Alex who offered to subsidize the program if his funding came up short. In return, he listened and offered advice. It seemed simple enough.

At first, it was mostly about the stresses of a successful business. Alex had gone from invisible to the spotlight in less time than she had imagined. It had become harder for her to find time for herself or her interests. She never really said what those interests were, but Dr. Gilchrest guessed it was important to her to continue doing whatever it was she was doing. She did speak about her best friend a lot. Dr. Gilchrest got the impression that this woman was very important to her—like family. They'd started the business together, but most of the capital had come from Alex. Ivy brought the clients and design ideas. Alex said Ivy could talk anybody into anything and without her, that business would have died a long time ago. Dr. Gilchrest found that hard to believe. Alex seemed to have a certain quality he couldn't quite put his finger on, but you wanted to be around her for some reason. He stood and stretched long. The kinks in his tired back fought him, but gave in as he bent over and touched his toes.

The one thing she never talked about was her past. As much as he tried to gently guide her down that path, she never took the bait. His assignment was to find out how much she remembered, but in order to do that, he'd have to get her to admit it ever happened in the first place. Then one day over beers in some dive downtown, she asked him a very odd question.

"Do you believe in evil?" That question sounded so juvenile. He could barely see her hooded eyes locked on the glass in her hand. They sat in a dim corner booth as she slumped down in her seat like his teenage son.

"Sure," he answered, "Why do you ask?"

She just shrugged and emptied her glass. "Want another?"

"Sure, why not."

The look on her face was unreadable. She was so still he couldn't even tell if she was breathing. Then she straightened up and grinned.

"Do you believe some people are born bad? Created like that, I mean?"

"I believe acts of violence are learned behavior," Dr. Gilchrest replied. "Usually, people that do violent things have witnessed or experienced some sort of violence themselves, abuse of some kind."

"But what if they hadn't?" Alex whispered, as she leaned on the table. "What if their purpose in life is to destroy? Feed on . . ." she stopped suddenly when the waitress appeared with more beer.

"I don't think I understand the question," he said.

"Never mind," she flushed. "I was just . . . nothing. Finish your beer."

At that moment, Dr. Gilchrest remembered overhearing something he thought was strange at the time. Sitting outside the Director's office, the voices could just be heard through the closed door. He remembered hearing the words 'feed' and 'capture', but they didn't make sense to him at all. The two men kept referring to 'her' which he could only assume was the new patient in the locked ward. The young woman had come back from a classified mission with nightmares and memory loss.

It was rare to see a young woman in a Military Hospital psych ward in those days. The only time he actually saw her was in the mess hall or out in the yard for exercise. Outside of that, she was locked away on a private wing that was guarded by two Marine escorts at all times.

Her doctor, Dr. Marcus Slaten, and his nurse were the only staff with access to that wing. Her case was never discussed at staff meetings and reviews, and she was never alone in the mess hall or the yard. No one could get within shouting distance of her, ever. He'd overheard that conversation that day by mistake. Now he wished he'd never met her.

After the Director was released and or reassigned, Dr. Gilchrest found himself reassigned as well—back to Washington. He wasn't sure if they were suspicious of him or, again, it was just dumb luck that he was on a plane to Washington a week after hearing her doctor and the Director.

The gossip was she was a part of some 'super soldier' project that had gone wrong. The orderlies were always talking about it on breaks. He just laughed and told them to stop with the silly rumors.

"Come on, doc," one of them chuckled. "You gotta wonder why no one goes into that wing. Is she cleaning her own room and stuff? And you can't even sit on the same side of the room as her at chow without one those guards getting twitchy. Makes you wonder."

"Yea," another laughed. "Makes you wonder that she might go postal if you say hi to her! I hear she just got back from an assignment in the desert and freaked out! Be glad we don't have to deal with that one."

He never really listened to the gossip that spread around the hospital back then. Orderlies talking about the weird patient in the private wing doing strange things in the middle of the night. He thought they were just trying to scare each other. But when he met with Strategic for the first time, he thought maybe they were right.

"After the hospital, she disappeared," Dr. Jonathan Carlisle announced at their first meeting. "We'd like you to try and find out what happened during that time."

His conference room at Area 51 was dimly lit and stuffy as Dr. Gilchrest remembered. Back then, a large black phone sat in the center of a rectangular conference table. The Secretary of Defense on speaker phone. No fancy projected image on a screen. No Skype.

Dr. Gilchrest flipped through the report. Redacted lines of information made it hard to grasp what kind of assignment or what really happened. "Why don't you know?"

Dr. Carlisle eased back in the leather chair as he tapped the folder in front of him with his pen. The chilly stare reminded Dr. Gilchrest of some of his more disturbed patients back at the hospital. His mouth opened, but the man on the phone interrupted.

"Thomas," the Secretary stated. "We really need your help on this. You had some contact with her in the hospital. We just want your impression of her now, if you have time."

"Mr. Secretary," Dr. Gilchrest cleared his throat. "I had one meeting with her before I was reassigned. She probably doesn't even remember me."

Dr. Carlisle interrupted this time. "She'll remember you. Trust me."

"Alright, but what do you want to me say? If I start asking questions, won't she get suspicious? I would if someone from almost fifteen years ago just walks up to me out of the blue and starts asking about my mental stability."

"You're right," the Secretary continued. "We'll arrange for you to run into her in London, next month. She'll be there and we've booked you as a speaker at a conference on PTSD at the same hotel. She won't put it together. You can run into her, buy her cup of coffee or something and let us know how that went. No strings, Tom. None at all."

He sighed as he looked around the empty house and remembered the past again. With his wife and youngest son visiting the oldest at Stanford, Dr. Gilchrest braved the weekend alone. So he waited patiently for that monthly phone call. He lay on the rug and stared at the dark chandelier, then blinked. In an odd sort of a way, if it hadn't been for her, he wouldn't have been able to send one son to Stanford and the other to the most prestigious prep school in Maryland. If not for her, he wouldn't have been able to pay off his mortgage ten years early and take his wife on a cruise this year.

But the price was to monitor someone he'd come to consider a friend. To report back on her progress had started to make him feel like the biggest asshole in the room.

He straightened up when the phone rang. On his feet, he hesitated, took a big breath and picked up the mobile. "Hello?"

"You're an early riser, doctor," the voice chuckled.

"Not really," he replied as he took a seat behind his desk again. "I haven't been to bed yet."

"Well, then we should get started so that you can get some rest."

"Of course, Mr. Secretary," he said. He sat back in the chair and closed his eyes. "There's not much to report this month. I've only seen her once and that was only for a very brief moment or two. She was contacted by Cooper and went with Jason Stavros to Las Vegas."

He heard the Secretary of the Navy clear his throat. "We expected that. Has she told you anymore about the dreams?"

"No, sir. Just that a friend was in trouble," he answered, rubbing his eyes. Dr. Gilchrest could feel the pain behind his lids grow. His pulse had quickened and his palms were sweaty.

"She didn't mention what friend," he exhaled.

"No, sir," Dr. Gilchrest replied.

"Just keep me updated on her movements if you can," he said.

"Yes, sir," Dr. Gilchrest replied. "There is one other thing, sir."

"Yes?"

"She's afraid of something or someone."

"Really? Interesting," he replied. SecDef sounded as if he were excited all of a sudden. "How do you know for sure?"

"Just a feeling," Dr. Gilchrest replied as he realized he shouldn't have mentioned that.

"So nothing she said or did?"

"No, but I've been monitoring her long enough to pick up on her cues."

His chuckle seemed rude and completely unnecessary. If she was in trouble, they were supposed to help, right? Wasn't that what they said they were here for? To help her if the operation went wrong and she needed them?

"That's good," he said finally. "Very good. I expect confirmation on that as soon as possible. You have to take the initiative on this one, Tom. It's very important to know what's spooking her."

When the line went dead, he was glad. He tossed the phone on the desk then headed to the kitchen for another cup of coffee. As the machine hummed and purred, and his mug filled with fresh coffee, he rubbed his temples. With the full cup in front of him, he dumped in powered creamer and sugar as he contemplated what he had gotten himself into.

She wasn't what they said she was. She wasn't just a soldier with PTSD. She was cautious, careful. And she had a heart, a big one. She cared about the Vets he helped and she cared about the people closest to her. She seemed broken in the hospital. Maybe she was and maybe they wanted to keep her that way, but why?

"How did she look?" he remembered Carlisle's question seemed odd to him. At their last real meeting, they met for lunch at Hank's Oyster Bar on Dupont Circle one nice Saturday afternoon. He remembered because they had a table on the patio.

"She looked like a successful businesswoman," Dr. Gilchrest replied. "And you were right. She did remember me."

"She has an eidetic memory," he seemed to say with pride.

"She also has a great life. I don't think you should worry about that missing time anymore."

"Why do you say that?" he asked as he looked over menu. "Did she tell you what happened to her? Where she was? What she was doing?"

"No, but she seems happy now, so why does it matter?"

They placed their orders with the surly waiter.

"It matters, Tom," he replied. "I need to know that she's back to her old self before we bring her back in."

The waiter returned with two beers and a dry 'your order will be out in a minute,' then left again.

"Bring her back in for what?" Dr. Gilchrest asked.

"We have a new assignment for her," he answered. "Pretty simple, but important."

Dr. Gilchrest was confused. From everything they'd told him, she was out of the program; had been for years. Now Dr. Carlisle wanted to bring her back in. Why would she even consider a return to covert operations after all she'd accomplished on her own?

"Jon, I only spoke to her briefly," he sighed. "I can't assess her stability after a five minute conversation. How am I supposed to get her to talk to me?"

His grin surprised Dr. Gilchrest a little. A big platter of raw oysters landed in the center of the table. Napkins, crackers, lemons and a small bottle of Tabasco too. A pretty young woman helped their grumpy waiter bring it all out. She smiled as she placed two white plates on the table between them.

"We've set up everything you'll need for your foundation," Dr. Carlisle said as he took two big shells to start. A couple of splashes of Tabasco and a spritz of lemon, then he swallowed the gooey meat with a nod of approval. "She'll check you out first, but everything is clean and above board."

Dr. Gilchrest was speechless. He'd only mentioned wanting to start an outreach for homeless vets in passing. He looked through the portfolio Dr.

Carlisle placed in front of him in disbelief.

"How did you do this so fast?" he practically whispered.

"The perks of working for the government," Dr. Carlisle chuckled. "Don't worry, she'll want to help you. That's your in."

Dr. Carlisle was right. She did want to help. And she helped him more than any of his other benefactors. He considered telling her the truth almost every day. But he could never bring himself to do it. But what if he did now? What would she do?

When Strategic confided in him that she was not just any soldier, but one involved in a special project, it all made sense to him. The way she guarded her words. How self-aware she was. The things she said to him before she left for Las Vegas. As far as he knew, she was still under their control. And if he let himself think too hard about it, he had helped keep her under their thumb by following orders. Dr. Gilchrest absently stirred his coffee and pondered his situation. *Why not follow orders? You're a soldier too,* he told himself. *I'm a doctor, psychiatrist,* he corrected. *What's best for your patient?* "She's not my patient," he said out loud.

Chapter 29

It was just a shell now. Just a pretty wrapper that would soon be emptied of its contents then cast aside for good. He turned back to the mirror and smiled as he admired his new physique. Of all the things he imagined for his future, he never thought he'd be in a new century with a new life and a brand new body, at least compared to the old one.

A nice young body was just what the doctor had promised him and he had delivered—someone unrecognizable to his enemies, but who would be revered and respected by his friends. Tristan couldn't care less how Dr. Carlisle had acquired the volunteers. When he paid that kid to hack the computers, he was just looking for something to lead him to the identity of the Dagger. He never imagined he'd find a wealth of other information in the process.

He knew his old body had too much history attached to it now. That's why this ritual was such a great idea. As Tristan Ambrose, he had made more enemies than he wanted to count and had very few friends. Those he called his family were long gone and were not friends in the traditional sense anyway. Being locked in a frozen cage for years left little opportunity to meet new people. Although he had brain function, he couldn't stop the experiments on his body. His jailer,

Dr. Carlisle, as he heard many call him, took samples of blood and tissue almost every day. He would play awful music as he worked in the lab. Once he heard a voice use the term 'classic rock' several times during one of their sessions. Tristan knew if he ever escaped, the first person he'd kill was the guy from the 'classic rock' station the doctor always listened to.

Then one day, his brain was awake without the sound of rock music blaring. Then his eyes blinked open and his thumb twitched as his body temperature warmed. At first he thought it was a trick. The doctor was hidden in a dark corner somewhere just to see what would happen next. Harsh lights overhead burned his eyes, but after a few minutes, he was able to raise his hand to shield them. An hour later, he was able to sit up, and found himself on a steel table with only a pair of thin cotton pants to cover his lower body. The ice coffin hummed next to him.

Tristan looked around the room, caught his own reflection in a mirror across from where he sat. He barely recognized his gaunt image. Silvery pale skin covered his bare torso and head. His once lively blonde hair was frostbitten and brittle from the years spent refrigerated like old meat. As he slid slowly from the table, his bare feet landed on the broken glass on the floor underneath them. Inky red and thick, the frozen blood stuck to his skin as he walked gingerly toward the mirror.

His exotic blue eyes were now dull and lifeless. The skin was tight and cracked, but not as bad as it could have been. He remembered a sharp pain spike behind his eyes as his body temperature rose even more. At the ice coffin he studied the lock carefully. There were four empty slots for the biomaterial that held the mechanism in place. On the floor, three smashed vials that held the material.

Tristan dropped to his knees and sniffed the samples. He tasted each one too. He'd track down the owners and make them pay for what they'd done to him. He began to rise, but stopped. His eyes scanned the floor again. Three vials. Three vials. An anger grew inside his rapidly defrosting body. Where was the fourth vial? Just as he was about to trash the entire room, the door opened and two hooded figures stepped inside. Behind them came Giselle. And the rest, as they say, is history.

Shaking off his memories, he remembered that he was now a sire without children to lead. Tristan's *children* feared him in the past. He understood that. He liked it that way as a matter of fact. What he needed then were offspring willing to give their lives for his survival. Now his methods had to change because the world he knew no longer existed. His new vessel had friends, buddies as he called them, and they went on trips together. They dined and played and wooed women together. As a group, his companions thought themselves better than the average human male and they went to great pains to prove it.

And, with this new body would come new possibilities! He was looking forward to the future again. The 21st century was living up to the hype so far, but he had just been brought back a few hours ago. He didn't want to get ahead of himself. There would be time to stake his claim on this new society. There would be more than enough time to rebuild his clan and put into motion his revenge on those who imprisoned him. The prize he was promised in return for his cooperation would soon be his as well. Then he would teach them not to trust a twelve hundred year old vampire with a grudge.

He could feel the human fading inside him now. Screaming and begging to be set free—promising all sorts of riches for a second chance. In the next 36 hours, the original owner would slowly die out like an old car battery. Soon, his voice would be just a slight irritation, then nothing at all. By the time he reached the Northwestern United States, Brice Campbell, legal counsel for the world's most powerful and famous, would be reborn. But Tristan would retain his memories, skills, and ideas. Everything would be embedded into the new owner's consciousness.

Tristan Ambrose, once a powerful presence in the old world, had come to the new one to pick up where he left off.

Tristan studied his new physique with the curiosity of a child.

He touched and stretched and pulled at every limb and digit. He took stock of how well defined each muscle was, for a human anyway, and decided he'd been given the best of the lot of hopefuls. He even admired his manhood as he held it gently in his hand. What woman could resist him?

As the ritual dictated, he would be able to recall anything Brice knew. A long incantation, a sacrifice of some kind, and twenty-four hours later, Tristan's consciousness was transferred to Brice's body. For the next few hours, Brice and Tristan shared this body, but it was Tristan that took control of it. And, from legal tome to the face of his latest conquest, Tristan had access to all his knowledge and dirty little secrets.

For now, Brice was still very much trapped inside his own head for lack of a better explanation. He considered that Brice had no idea what he had agreed to when Creed approached him with the offer. Meeting through a woman Creed referred to as a 'call girl,' Tristan figured the term to be a modern reference to a paid whore. He didn't have all the details on how Brice had been talked into the deal, but Brice jumped at the chance the way Creed told it. It wasn't Tristan's fault he didn't ask the right questions. The man was an attorney for God's sake! He laughed and continued to take stock of his new identity.

Brice, as he was eight days ago when he took possession of Tristan's sarcophagus, would fade into oblivion soon enough. His soul extinguished to make room for a new one, Tristan's. As the minutes ticked by, Tristan began to understand just how human he was right now. He felt the cold tile of the bathroom floor under his bare feet. He could only hear the hum of the machine in the next room and the buzz of the florescent lights above his head. And he felt hunger, growing and gnawing at his insides. He'd considered using Brice instead of taking over his body, but he decided against it. Humans could be too easily tortured and turned to trust sometimes. To hold on to Brice's soul was fruitless. He'd served his purpose.

Tristan turned back to the mirror and focused on his face in the harsh bathroom lighting.

From his Korean mother, Brice had inherited the slightly almond shaped eyes and soft features inherent to the race. The genes from his American Caucasian father gave a rugged edge to those features. It worked for him though. And at six feet and two inches, he had a commanding presence that Tristan liked most of all. His forehead was smooth except for a tiny scar just at his right temple, which caused him to frown at the discovery.

"What happened here, Mr. Campbell?" Tristan listened closely, then shook his head at the reflection. "Really? That was dumb."

As he continued down his face, Tristan noted his longish nose and strong cheekbones. Very regal, he decided with a nod of approval. He needed a good shave and possibly a facial, but that would have to wait, he told himself and Brice.

His lips, pinkish and thin, didn't please him at all. However, his teeth looked strong and would make wonderful fangs once they came in again. His dark hair, thick and well cut, shined in the light over his head.

He turned his head left then right and decided

his ears were too small. Maybe in this age that wasn't such a flaw, but a few centuries ago small ears were a bad omen.

"God, I would have hated to be born this way really," he huffed and squinted at himself. "You're so ordinary."

As his brown eyes moved down his body, he was pleased with it overall. But Brice had been soft in places he could have taken better care of. With Tristan in the driver's seat, his diet would change quickly. Once he fully inhabited this vessel, everything about it would be different, better, perfect.

The last thing he would have to do was ingest the entire blood supply of his old body.

He turned and leaned on the doorframe to stare at the refrigerated casket in the far corner of the massive master bedroom. It hummed as it kept his old body intact. The bitter cold held the parts together while they were drained of blood.

The device attached to the bottom captured every last pint of precious, pure ancient blood. When the two gallon bottles were filled, the shell would be allowed to writher to dust. He'd already picked the perfect urn for his remains.

The ritual had worked according to plan. After the final step, Brice Campbell would be perfect and forever. He might look like him on the outside, but he wouldn't be Brice Campbell on the inside any longer. He'd be Tristan Ambrose, a fourteen-hundred-year-old vampire with the world at his feet.

Tristan stepped back inside the bathroom but the knock on the door didn't interrupt his taking stock of his new self.

She strolled in with a bundle in her arms.

Round and plump, it slept peacefully against her breasts. He noticed those the second he opened his eyes. They hovered over his face hidden inside her clothes, which only made him want them more. She placed a flask on the table then turned to him.

She may be considered older by today's standards, but Tristan was sure she had experiences to share and ways to sway a woman to his favor in the modern world. Her big brown eyes sparkled behind long lashes as she looked down on the baby in her arms.

"You'll drink that first," she nodded at the flask. "Then, you'll have to start slowly once the blood is replaced," Giselle said as she rocked the baby gently. "Newborn blood helps with the transition. And I hear it tastes like the finest wine in the world."

"First born, I'm assuming," Tristan hummed as he continued his inspection of the child. "What's in the flask?"

"Different things to help that body ingest your blood; keep it down," she smiled. "And, as promised," she smiled down on the child in her arms. "The mother will be quite happy with his replacement, so no one will ever know the difference."

Tristan came from the bathroom without even a towel to cover himself.

She glanced up, but didn't seem startled by his

nakedness. Maybe women were more relaxed about such things now. Or as he thought, she had experience; but compared to him, she was still a virgin.

"Why couldn't I have both mother and child?" he asked as he drew a finger down the child's face then licked it with a smile. Warmth spread through him from the taste of the baby's sweat. *How perfectly delicious*, Tristan thought. His mouth watered as he imagined what the blood would feel like on his tongue. He imagined it to be sweet and thick as it made its way down his dry throat and filled his empty stomach completely. The first taste of human blood was an experience he'd never forgotten.

"Because you won't be strong enough," Giselle scolded. "I've warned you about the transition in the final stages. It will be painful, very painful until you are fully yourself again. Don't treat this lightly, Tristan Ambrose. That would be a tragic mistake."

Tristan stepped back and bowed to her and the baby.

"I am in your capable hands, Giselle."

"Yes, you are, and I will not fail you as long as you do as I say. Now, you should eat something and then get some rest. I will wake you at midnight. I've taken the liberty of having your lunch prepared and set on the patio. It is a beautiful day; enjoy it as a human would."

Back at her side, Tristan let his eyes move over her body as he slid his hand down her back. When it rested on her round butt without protest, he smiled down on her. Beautiful olive skin everywhere he looked and it all smelled so wonderful, even with his human senses.

"You will wake me before midnight. If I'm going to experience the final hours of this day as a human, I'd like to see what it's like to take a woman as a mortal man."

"As you wish," she hummed and shuddered when he gave her butt a squeeze.

His stomach growled so loud, it shocked him. Giselle just giggled.

"Hunger," he groaned. "How can they stand being so weak all the time? They are slaves to such miserable desires as hunger and sleep. What happened to this age of man? There's no passion left in them! No craving for blood and pain! I miss the old days."

He picked up a pair of slacks and slipped them on. Once his white dress shirt was buttoned, Tristan slipped his long feet into a pair of loafers and turned to Giselle again.

"Find Sasha and Creed and have them report to me in Las Vegas once we return," Tristan sighed. "I guess I'll have to eat regular food to get this to stop."

"Well you only have to endure such agony for a few hours more," she laughed. "And then you will truly be yourself again. Then, God help us."

After he tucked in his shirt and made himself presentable, he leaned into her and placed his lips inches from hers.

"Yes," he whispered as his tongue licked at her

red lips. "God help you all!"

Chapter 30

She'd been quietly pacing in front of them for the last ten minutes. Every time she stopped, Sebastian held his shallow breath hoping she'd speak, but then she started pacing again without one word. Kai and David looked like they would pass out from the boredom and from the looks of it, Xavier was about ready to shoot her.

"Umm . . . Al? You gotta say something," Xavier finally gathered the courage to say. "We got your back. Just tell us what to do."

Alex stopped, went down on her knees as if she were going to pray then looked at them. Her gaze stopped on Sebastian and his cold flesh goosed from the chill.

"How much do you know about Night Command?" she asked calmly. "I mean the old program."

They all looked at each other and nonverbally elected Sebastian to speak. Maybe it was because she seemed to trust him or that he was a vampire, but he cleared his throat and adjusted his posture on the couch.

"We know you guys were on a similar formula as we . . . not me, but you know. And that the formula was flawed. The med team didn't find out until the others started exhibiting side effects." He felt the sweat rolling down his spine as she stared at her hands with a strange frown on her face. "Dr. Carlisle changed the formula, but it didn't last long. Coop is or was pretty sick. If he hadn't been killed, he would have died anyway, probably."

Alex looked up into his eyes and he felt his body tense. "Of what?"

"Cell degeneration," Xavier answered tentatively, drawing her full attention to him. Sebastian was relieved to have her focused on someone else for a few minutes. He couldn't explain why though.

"Cell degeneration," she whispered to herself mostly. With her eyes back on Xavier, she looked sad all of a sudden. "And is that happening to you too?"

Xavier just nodded and the twins followed when she turned her eyes on them.

"Just not as bad," David replied. "The new formula seems to be slowing down the process in us, correcting it even, but we don't know for how long. Coop and the others weren't so lucky. Becker," he shook his head like he didn't want whatever image Becker's name conjured up to stay in his mind. "He got the worst of it."

"Meaning?" she asked as she moved closer to him.

"The way his body just started to fall apart," Kai interjected. "It was really bad, Alex."

"Why? What did Dr. Carlisle say was the reason?"

"They were too human," Sebastian jumped back

in the conversation. He felt confident again. He wanted to show her he was strong.

When his friends turned to him too, confusion smeared over their faces, he knew he'd said one word too many.

"Too human," David and Kai said in unison. Then they looked at Alex. All of them.

"And you're not too human?" Xavier asked.

Sebastian could smell fear, but not his fear or his friends'. It was her fear he could smell. Rich and full, her fear, like her scent, fascinated and excited him. Although, to look at her, his companions couldn't possibly know she was afraid, but he knew and that made him more afraid.

She stood and put some space between her and the team. Walking over to the window, she stood there, still and silent. Sebastian wanted to turn off his sense of smell for now the fear had turned to something else. It grabbed his heart and squeezed tight. He felt his chest seize and his heart struggled to get free. Sometimes, if he went too long without real blood, he'd get this way, but he wasn't hungry. Then the thought dropped in his brain and he jumped from the couch before he knew what he was doing.

"You're not human at all," he croaked before he passed out.

Alex focused her energy around his heart. The others caught him as his knees buckled. She didn't want to, but she had to stop him. Unfortunately, Sebastian was smart. He had put it together a lot sooner than she thought. Now she had to figure out how to erase the whole conversation from his mind and theirs without too much pain to herself.

She thought about just telling them what she was, but they wouldn't understand, she decided. How could they? They still believed hybrids were created in labs with drugs. If she told them the truth, she'd have to tell them the supplements were created from her DNA, not by a man everyone thought was a freaking genius. Dr. Carlisle used her blood to create those pills and had never told anyone, except for Ben, the truth.

He never talked about her mother or where she disappeared to. Never once did he ever mention her name outside of their brief affair and Alex being the result. She remembered asking questions only to be shut down at every turn. He erased any trace of her mother from the records. Ben knew very little about her or where she came from, but he agreed to help Alex find those answers. That's why she cut the deal to train and monitor the hybrids in the real world. So she could at least have access to the program and maybe find some answers. But the more involved she became in the assignment, the less time she had to investigate her own existence. Then her own company needed more attention, so, for a fee, she agreed to do other things.

What she knew about her own abilities, she learned through trial and error. Most of what a full vampire could do, she could do. She did, however, learn she had telepathic abilities early on and that talent always came in handy. It was especially handy tonight.

"Dude," he heard a familiar voice from a distance. "Hey. Sebastian. Open your eyes."

He forced his eyelids open as they all stood over him. Kai held a small glass of blood under his nose; moving it back and forth. His stomach turned at the scent.

"You okay?" Xavier asked as he and Erin helped Sebastian to a seated position on the couch.

Alex sat next to him, taking the glass from Kai's hand. "Maybe you should drink this. It might make you feel better."

Sebastian shook his head and it felt like his brain rattled around inside. He pushed the glass away, he tried to stand, but he just fell back against the cushions with a moan.

"What the hell happened?" he was finally able to whisper.

"Well," David replied. "You passed out."

"Why?" he asked once he was poised with his head in his hands.

"You tell us," Xavier chuckled.

Kai stood, dropped to the floor then laughed. "Like a sack of blonde potatoes."

They all laughed but he felt like someone had just beat him over the head with a sledgehammer.

Alex began to rub his shoulders. "I think you

might have gotten some bad blood. Jason's doctor said you should probably sleep it off." She placed the glass on the table in front of him. "Sip that. It'll make you feel better."

Chapter 31

Nothing could be better than this.

A beautiful day gave way to a more beautiful evening in the deep woods of Montana—fresh water stream, crisp mountain air and no one for miles—just the way he liked it.

Benjamin Palmer, ex-Tracker Commander and all around boy next door type, scratched at his five o'clock shadow and his honey colored buzz cut as he watched the sun begin its descent.

He whistled a cheery tune as he chopped more wood for tonight's fire.

It looked like one more round of snow, but he didn't mind at all. He had enough food, water and José to last another week or two.

After he split the last log, he stacked the pieces in the sack and slung it over one shoulder. He swung the ax over the other as he made his way back to his cabin.

Some night bird mocked him from above as a doe kept pace with his stride and Ben took it all in with a smile on his face. This life was good and he was right where he wanted to be.

The only thing missing was . . . there wasn't anything missing, nothing at all.

At first, the smell of burning wood filled the air.

Then the steaks he had grilled earlier.

But what stopped him dead in his tracks was something else; something that wasn't supposed to be here, in the deep woods of Montana, not now, not tonight or ever.

He dropped the sack of wood and tightened his grip on the ax. The snow at his feet crunched as he distributed his weight evenly between them. The night began to glow from the two inches of snow cover that had fallen only this morning.

A hint of musk found its way up his nostrils and they flared. A sweet smell of perfume chased it and the hair on his arms stood up.

Very still, Ben rolled his blue eyes up when a shrill giggle rustled in the leaves and sent a sprinkle of white powder down from above. When she touched down in his path, the girl smiled from ear to ear.

"Well, you're a hard man to find," she giggled again. "Even for me."

"If I'd known you were looking, I would have made it a little harder," Ben replied. "Just for grins."

"I like a challenge, Major," she laughed. "Gets my juices flowing."

Ben smiled and let the blade end fall toward the ground. One stroke up and he'd cut her in half before she blinked.

The young girl continued to smile, but kept her distance.

Her pallor was dull, but that only made her easier to see in the growing darkness.

The worn leather of her brown boots matched the belt holding the baggy jeans around her waist. Soft cable knit sweater, cream colored from the looks of it, swallowed her even though she was built almost like a linebacker he'd known once, but with more curves.

Ben imagined she'd just stepped off the bus from some place nobody had ever heard of when she was taken and turned into a creature with a lust for blood. And at her age, any kind of blood would do, even that of the innocent.

Her stringy brown hair was pulled back and knotted at the base of her long neck—pieces of it picked up by the breeze. Acne scars hadn't yet disappeared, so she was newly turned. *Poor kid*, he thought.

"That's Lieutenant Colonel," Ben replied. "But I don't think we've been properly introduced."

She bowed politely in his general direction, "Sasha. And it is a pleasure to finally meet you, Lieutenant Colonel Benjamin Palmer."

Ben bowed back. "You can call me Colonel Palmer, if that's easier for you."

Sasha smiled and took two steps toward him, then stopped.

Ben wanted to be polite and give her a chance to state her piece and go. When he shook her off, the smile disappeared. "So, Sasha, what can I do for you this fine evening?"

The low growl came out of nowhere.

A twig snapped and Ben swung the ax backward

as hard as he could. The young vampire only had enough time to blink once before he exploded into fiery ash.

When Ben turned back, Sasha was gone, but her laughter echoed over his head as he ran.

At top speed he reached the cabin in no time. He slammed and locked the door, even though he knew that probably wouldn't stop her.

The front room had been ransacked—papers, clothes, and broken glass were everywhere.

Ben grabbed his keys, phone, and anything he could use and shoved it all in a backpack.

Before he could stand up straight, a fist to his chin sent him sliding down the wall a few feet away. He could hear Sasha's laugh somewhere in the dark.

Ben's eyes adjusted when the lights popped on, but he was in her grip again before he knew it. One headbutt and Sasha dropped to her knees as blood poured from her nose through her fingers. Ben picked himself up, still seeing stars.

"That was not nice," she laughed then licked at the blood that slid from her nose. "You haven't even asked if I wanted a drink."

Ben's feet left the floor again when she kicked him in the center of his wide chest.

His nice wooden table splintered like toothpicks when he landed on it. He looked up just as Sasha wiped her nose and popped the bone back in place.

"I'm afraid I don't keep your brand around," Ben moaned as he stood in the pieces of his table and shook his head like a dizzy dog.

Sasha smiled and cracked her knuckles.

"I prefer my meals fresh. The fake stuff doesn't have the same bite, you know?"

"I'll have to take your word for it."

"Look, I just want to know where to find the hybrid," Sasha sighed. She dropped down in the big chair and crossed her legs as she wiped her bloody nose clean on the sweater. "If you tell me the truth, I'll let you keep some blood just to be fair."

"Hybrid? I drive a pickup. Sorry, darlin'."

"I'll run you down with it if you don't tell me what I need to know," she frowned.

"I don't know what you're talking about," Ben shrugged. He took a stool from the bar and sat down a few feet in front of her. "Now, I don't wanna sound rude, but I've got some stuff to do, so if you don't mind . . ."

Sasha's slightly pretty face became an inhuman mask right before his eyes. Bright yellow pupils, long white teeth, and her spicy scent made Ben's mouth go dry. But he just smiled at her and waited for her reply.

"I'll leave when I get what I came for. I could just start removing limbs if that would get this over quicker."

"If you were gonna kill me," Ben smirked. "You would have done it already. My guess is you were given specific instructions. No goin' off script, right?"

"Whatever," Sasha sighed. "You're not being very cooperative Colonel. It's a simple matter of telling me what I need to know and then I'm out."

Ben laughed as he stood to pick up the bottle of tequila from the floor. Thank God it didn't get smashed or he'd really be pissed.

He took his seat again, cracked it open and took a long draw. It stung going down, but that only lasted a few seconds before the cut in his mouth sealed itself.

"Who's asking anyway?"

"My boss, I mean sire," she giggled. "Still getting used to that word."

"Oh yeah? What house?"

Sasha smiled and caught the bottle he tossed over to her. She matched his draw and tossed it back.

"Hellclaw."

Ben almost dropped the bottle, but his knee helped him save it. The booze wasn't going to help his dry mouth this time. He just hoped she didn't notice his hands as they shook.

"That's . . ." he swallowed the lump in his throat as his eyes locked on hers. "There's no one left to start that up again. Those practices have been forbidden by the Council anyway."

"Really?" she teased as she pulled her feet into the seat underneath her. "I guess no one told my sire."

The ax lay only a few inches away, but Ben didn't think he'd beat her to it.

"Whatever. Why are you looking for this hybrid anyway?"

"My business," Sasha snipped. "You gonna tell me or not?"

"Probably dead," Ben replied. "That's what I was

told anyway."

He stretched his legs out long and folded his arms over his chest.

"Where's the body?" she mused as she stood to reach for something in her pocket while she approached him.

"Bones by now. That was almost twenty years ago." A wad of money landed in the crook where his ankles crossed. "What's that for?"

"You can keep that, if you tell me where to find any descendent that might exist," Sasha purred again. "We'd like to be sure. You understand, right?"

"Not really," Ben laughed. He stood and kicked the money back at her, "But helping you kill a human being . . . for the chump change you just tossed down . . . it's insulting really."

His laughter angered her. He could see the change in her body and even smell the anger like smoke in the air.

Sasha stepped back and sat down again. "How much then?"

"Let's see, betray my country and give up classified information that could get me life in Leavenworth? What to do . . . what to do?" he rubbed his chin and turned his eyes to the ceiling.

"I'll let you live out your pathetically short life for the information and we'll call it even," she yawned.

"Even?"

"The things you did," she frowned. "An entire clan destroyed and for what? Myths, fairy tales."

"If that were true," Ben sighed. "You wouldn't be here trying to cut off my arms and legs for information, now would you?" He scratched at the stubble on one cheek, then smiled at Sasha. "How about you go back to your sire and tell him I said he can crawl back into whatever hole he came out of. There is no hybrid and there is no Hellclaw. Not anymore."

At the front door he waited for her with a hand in his pocket and a grip on the phone inside.
"You sure you wanna do this, Colonel?" Sasha asked as she passed him. "I mean, it's a one-time offer. Once I'm gone, it's off the table and open season on you."

"Won't be the first time," Ben chuckled as he opened the door wide. "Thanks for the visit."

Sasha stepped onto the porch and it lit it up like Christmas. She turned and waved at the figure as it moved toward them.

Ben wished he'd picked up that ax now.

Moving with confidence and ease, Ben could tell he was old, very old, even though he looked to be no more thirty. And his face was familiar for some reason. Then he realized he'd need the ax and possibly a tank if he wanted to hurt this one.

When the man's face was in view, it was too late.

He caught the fist Ben threw, wrapped his hand around Ben's neck and pushed him back inside. When Ben's back hit the wall, the man smiled like the cat that ate the canary.

His wrist opened with a flash of pain, then pleasure—pleasure like he hadn't known in years. Blood flowed easily as Ben struggled to breathe.

Tristan Ambrose smiled as he stared at the mark on Ben's wrist, written in elegant script across the blue-green vein he just tapped. The strange little words popped off his skin as he smeared blood across it.

Forever etched into their flesh once indoctrinated into the group, the mark could only be seen at a certain light spectrum. Vampire vision was perfect at all of them. And the Tracker members underwent a surgical procedure, he was told, to allow them the same benefit.

"*Bi Mete.* Someone has got to tell me what that means one of these days," he chuckled as he took one last taste of Ben's blood.

Ben groaned and struggled to get free as he kicked his feet at Tristan like a fidgety child.

The blood was filled with tequila and lots of vitamins and minerals. "Good little soldier to the core," Tristan laughed to himself.

"Inside joke," he heard Ben whisper.

"I love jokes," Sasha piped in.

Before he realized, Ben was propped against the wall on the floor, paralyzed, as the man stepped away and Sasha took his place.

"Seems the joke's on you, Benjamin," Tristan said from the chair Sasha occupied earlier. "I guess they didn't let you in on the secret, huh?"

Sasha fed slowly, but stopped when she was told.

"He's refusing to help us, Sire. But he and the woman are close. Watching her beg for her life might bring his memory back."

Tristan wiped his mouth then placed the bloody fabric on the arm of the chair.

Sasha sat down next to Ben, licked his wrist and the wound closed.

"Leave her out of this," Ben groaned. "I don't know who you are, but you've got the wrong guy."

"I don't think so," Tristan hummed and straightened his tie. "It's going to be such fun jogging your memory, Benjamin." He laughed again as Ben struggled to stand. "Before I'm done, you'll wish you'd just given me what I asked without having to play this game."

Ben made it half way up, but dropped to his butt again with a thud.

"Let me save you some time," he chuckled. "There's no hybrid, so you and the Amazon can leave now."

He watched the man wrinkle his long nose as Sasha stood to pour gasoline everywhere. The smell started to grow stronger as Ben stared at the man, trying to figure out how they knew each other.

Sasha opened the big windows by the front door as Ben tried not to cough from the fumes.

"When I get what I came for. Let's start with the location and then work our way up. How's that sound?"

"Sounds like you're fishing," Ben sighed. "So I guess we're gonna stand here and watch the paint peel then, because I got nothing to tell you that you probably don't already know."

He'd given up standing. He couldn't feel his legs anymore.

The man strolled to the front door without a word. His walk, the way he swung his arms, held his head high, was so familiar.

"The others were so much more forthcoming with the information," he finally replied. "Which came in handy since pieces of my memory have been erased Benjamin. I'd like to know why?"

"The others?"

"Yes, Becker and Wolfe. They fell so easily. They gave you and the woman up, begging for their lives in return."

"Bullshit," Ben coughed. "Who are you?!"

He stepped up to the open window and stuffed his hands in his pockets.

Then the memories flooded Ben's head, buzzing around like flies.

"Oh my God!"

He smiled and even on a different face, it was frightening. His cold expression reminded Ben of the last time he'd seen Tristan in that tomb. Alex, bloody and fighting to stay conscious, managed to tranquilize the toughest son of bitch vampire ever and drop his body in a refrigerated container for transport. Once the lock was in place, her own blood was the final seal, Alex collapsed to the dusty floor at Ben's feet.

"Surprised? So were your friends, right up to the moment they died," he chuckled. "I told you I'd be back."

"How'd you do it? You were a block of ice! Air tight and buried," Ben whispered. "How did you do it?!"

Tristan turned on the balls of his feet and walked back up to Ben. He reached down to pull him to his numb legs, then held him against the wall.

"I asked you a question. Why can't I remember who made me that block of ice? Whose blood did you use to seal me in that tomb?"

"Mine . . . it was mine."

"Not just yours," Tristan growled. "There were four blood types keeping the lock engaged. By the time I was freed, one had been stolen—the most important one as far as I'm concerned. If you continue to lie to me, I may get angry." Then he smiled again. "Who can tell me what I need to know? You or the girl?"

Ben tried to move, but couldn't. "Like I told her and now I'm telling you, Tristan, they're all dead."

Tristan moved in close, putting his lips to Ben's ear. The hot breath escaped his mouth and Ben barely felt his feet leave the floor again.

"I don't believe you," Tristan whispered.

An icy chill ran up his spine as Tristan's slick tongue slid over his ear.

Ben screamed when teeth pierced his vein in his neck and his entire body went numb.

He barely felt the floor when he landed in a heap at Tristan's feet. He watched as those feet walked away, then Sasha jerked one of the curtain panels from the window and lit it.

Tristan checked his watch as he waited patiently at the door. When everything around them caught fire, it didn't take long before red and orange flames were all Ben could see behind them.

Smoke began to burn his eyes and Ben felt his body rise over Sasha's shoulder and they followed Tristan outside.

"Last chance, Colonel," she laughed with a hard slap to his butt.

"Bite me," Ben groaned as Sasha dumped him into the back of the SUV and slammed the door with a girlish giggle.

Ben closed his eyes at the sound of breaking glass and cracking lumber. He couldn't watch the cabin his father built as it burned to the cold ground.

"Dagger, run," he whispered, then gave into the blackness so maybe it wouldn't hurt so much if he woke after.

CHAPTER 32

"How's he doing?" Jason asked. Alex could hear the click of his keystrokes during the entire conversation.

"Better," she replied, doing the same. They had this in common she supposed, workaholics to the end. "Did your doctor find anything in his blood work?"

"Not yet," she heard him sigh. "He'll let me know if anything shows up. It's strange that he would just drop like that. There are very few things in this world that can do that to a vampire, even one as young as him."

"Maybe it was just bad blood," Alex stated. She didn't want Jason asking too many questions.

"Maybe," he said. "Well, I need to finish some work, so I'll see you later?"

"Me too," she answered. "Later."

Tossing the phone on the nightstand, she went back to her work. Ivy had filled her inbox with contracts and photos over the last few days and she was behind in answering them. And her constant texting was a distraction Alex couldn't afford right now. With heavy eyes, she reviewed and changed page after page of contracts and photos she didn't like. Then the big yawn she'd been trying to hold back came. Stretching the kinks out of her back and arms, she finally pushed the tablet away.

Her fluffy pillow pushed itself underneath her head and she gave in to its call for her to rest. It was so easy to forget why she was here. It was hard to keep pretending she wasn't enjoying the action though.

When she felt her body begin to relax, she sighed. How could she like being in the middle of all the mess and mayhem that seemed to follow these people all the time? Easy. She used to be that kind of person before this. And as much as she tried to deny it, she was good at this and she liked the way it felt to use her powers again.

Suddenly she realized Ben hadn't answered any of her texts. Should she be worried? "He's fine," she told herself. "Whenever he's at that damn cabin, he forgets the world exists. He'll call tomorrow."

Dreaming wasn't really something she did, so when the images began to pop up behind her eyes, she just let it happen. A forest, huge trees topped with fresh powder filled the dark in her head. The smell of pine and burning wood flared her nostrils. She saw flames in the distance through someone else's eyes. The teary eyes blinked as the sight bounced away from their view. A burning came to her throat and she forced a cough out, then the voice jumped inside her head. '*Dagger, run,*' it shouted.

Alex bolted up in bed still coughing. She could still smell the faint odor of smoke inside her mind. She rubbed at her eyes and checked her phone. It was fifteen minutes later than when she laid her head down, though it seemed a whole lot longer. When the smell disappeared, the coughing stopped. Emptying the bottle of water on the nightstand, her phone beeped twice. A blank text box appeared, sender's number blocked. "It happens," she told her suspicious mind. She needed to get up anyway. Deciding it was the wrong number, she pulled the tablet over and checked her emails again. Nothing new from Ivy was a good thing.

It was time to get ready for the big meet with Jason and Conner Gale. Alex found she was excited about this meeting. Maybe it was the opportunity to actually meet Conner Gale in the flesh. She wanted to impress him for some reason. Was it because he was a very powerful man and having those kinds of friends was useful? Or could it be she was just looking forward to being the first human to be inside council chambers one day soon? Jason mentioned that might be a possibility, if they were successful in Romania in a couple of weeks. Beep. Beep. It was Jason reminding her she had thirty minutes to meet him at his residence. She replied with a smile and an 'I'm on my way'. The next beep brought the number five to the screen.

Alex checked the sender—still blocked. Slipping into the tan shift dress she'd chosen, a funny feeling came over her. Maybe it was Jason trying to make her nervous. As she swept her hair up into a ponytail, she slipped her feet into the orange fabric heels and checked herself in the full length mirror. She was ready.

Inside the elevator, her phone beeped again. This time the number four appeared bright red against a black box. She decided it was Jason playing around. She sent him a 'bite me' to which he replied 'later' then a question mark.

The feeling in the pit of her stomach became a brick. Another beep with the number three popping up like a jack in the box sent her internal alarm into overdrive. Trying to call Jason as she moved quickly to the exit and up the concrete path leading to his residence, Alex didn't think this was cute or funny anymore.

One more call to Jason went directly to voicemail again. Beep. The number two sat on the front of a cartoonish bomb, fuse burning down. The gate was open when she reached it. His security was at the front door waiting by the limo. Alex started to run when she got the next text with a number one on fire on her screen. The last beep came with four letters: B O O M, sending her into a full sprint after she kicked the heels from her feet. The front door opened and Jason appeared with Oren out in front. When she yelled his name, the car exploded and she took in a mouth full of smoke as she was propelled backward by the force of the blast.

Chapter 33

He couldn't imagine spending this much time in the sun just a few years ago, but here he basked in its light and enjoyed it, strangely enough.

Stretching his legs out, Tristan closed his tired eyes and took a deep breath. The air here was heavy with salt from the ocean somewhere in the distance and toxins from the smog above. But to his surprise, it didn't bother him as much as he thought it would. Even with the sun beaming down, he felt only a slight irritation from its rays.

The more of the substitute he drank, the less uncomfortable he felt in the light of day. Giselle was right. All he had to do was drink at least one bottle a day and he could walk in the daylight hours unharmed.

Dining al fresco was a pleasure! Beautiful young women greeting him at the door, escorting him to the best table on the patio and offering themselves in that wordless way excited him. More beauty taking his order and calling him by name made him feel special again.

Little did they know, the Brice they knew was gone for good. If they wanted a tumble with the new and improved one, they'd have to offer him more than just a pretty face.

His leisurely brunch kept getting interrupted by phone calls though. After the client, an up and comer in the action movie genre, left with a smile on his almost legal face, he decided to stretch the breakfast meeting into a little *me* time.

The first call from his assistant was to tell him his new suits were ready.

A couple calls were about some contracts needing to be signed before the end of the week. The one he was hoping for hadn't come yet—the one from Jason Stavros's camp granting him an audience.

Tristan hated waiting more than anything he could think of.

When he was the leader of Hellclaw, he waited on no one! He snapped his fingers and things got done! He need only wish and everyone in his house made it so. Those times were grand and he would have his family back, soon.

Dropping the black card on the silver tray his waitress left, he slipped his sunglasses on with a decidedly happy feeling in his chest. Once he gathered what information he needed from Stavros, maybe he'd let him live. The device wouldn't kill him, or so he hoped. And if Tristan had him killed, that might set into motion something he wouldn't be able to control right now. He had no house to speak of just yet, no one to fight the opposition. This would take time. Luckily, he had it to spare.

Leaving the waitress with a healthy tip and his private number, he walked through the little gate and mixed in with the late afternoon pedestrian traffic, making his way back to his office a few blocks away.

California, as much as he hated to admit it, was starting to feel like a good place to re-establish himself and his house. After all that time buried underneath the world, he found this place suited him, suited his plans for the future.

The lovely Karen smiled when he walked through the door.

"How was the meeting?" she hummed as she gathered little pink pieces of paper with things scribbled on them. She followed like a puppy dog to his office.

"Outstanding, Karen," Tristan replied. "Did I miss anything?"

As they entered the spacious room with a fantastic view of L.A. County, with one wall of very thick glass separating them from the sky, Karen took a seat in front of the large desk, note pad in hand.

"Well, the studio called and they're ready to discuss those changes to Gray Russo's contract. Looks like you were right again, Brice. They won't say no if the star is bright enough!"

"Good," he smiled, tapping the keyboard and waiting for the computer to come to life.

"And, Mr. Stavros's rep called," Karen said with glee. "He's ready to speak with you on Tuesday afternoon."

"Speak? I believe I asked for a meeting, a face to face."

Karen took a deep breath and one step forward, "I tried, Brice, but all I can get right now is a conference call."

Tristan turned away from the computer, ready to berate her for her failure, but stopped himself. Although the real Brice would have verbally assaulted Karen, then asked for forgiveness later, he decided on a much different tactic.

"Then I guess I'll have to settle for that," he replied. "Thank you for all your hard work on this."

Her cues were not very subtle either. He could pick up the excitement she telegraphed by blushing like a virgin and swaying on her high heels at his ego stroke. "Thank you, Brice. I just wish I had gotten you that face to face."

Tristan was only slightly irritated that he had to wait an entire weekend before he could get what he wanted. And then it was just a phone call. This would all change once he was back at the top of the food chain again.

"I guess that's still a good thing," Tristan replied. "Was my gift delivered at least?"

She smiled big and nodded her slightly oversized head at him, happy that she had made her boss happy. "Yes! I confirmed delivery a few minutes ago."

Tristan scanned his memories for Brice's relationship with Karen.

Karen Anderson started with this firm when she was fresh out of college. Her plan was law school, but she married straight away and failed to give her now ex-husband children. He left her with nothing, so she took this job as a paralegal just until she could get back to school.

She found she liked this better, or rather she found she liked Brice's affection and promises he never kept to help her get into law school, so she stayed. Still holding on to the hope that he would make good on his promises to her, she runs his office as he expects and keeps her bed warm in case he calls.

"Brice, you've tried to get close to this guy for a year! Could you be a little more excited?"

Tristan gave her a sideways glance as she brushed her thin lips with the end of her pen.

"You're right, Karen. As always."

He stood and took the chair next to her, taking her hand.

She blushed bright red and gave him a girly bat of her long fake lashes.

She is rather pretty in an ordinary sort of way, Tristan thought. He could see why Brice gave her moments of pleasure so she'd stay. She was smart and hard working as well. He could tell from the way this office ran so smoothly. No one looked worried and particularly happy he was back because she kept everything running like a well-oiled machine.

"I don't say that as often as I should, do I?"

"I . . . um . . . you show your appreciation in other ways," she whispered nervously. As if someone could hear them behind closed doors, her grip tightened on his hand. "I can't complain."

Tristan cupped her tiny hand in both of his and smiled.

"But I can do better at showing you how much I appreciate everything you do around here. Without you I'd be up a creek."

"Yes, but I'd be right there with you, always."

"Thank you."

He kissed her hand, felt the shiver as it stomped through her when he moved his lips to her wrist then back to her palm.

He entered her mind as easily as he would a child's. As his fangs dropped slowly, she slipped into a trance-like state. And when he pierced her wrist, the smell of blood and expensive perfume filled his lungs.

Sweet and clean, her blood entered his mouth with the feel of silk over his tongue.

Again, he would have to tell Giselle she was right. His first taste of warm human blood was just as sweet as he remembered. So sweet, he wanted to scream.

He had to force himself to stop or she'd be hurt. He licked the wounds and waited for them to heal before he released her mind.

"Are you alright," he whispered as Karen blinked several times.

"Yeah, I must have zoned out. I'm sorry, what were we talking about?"

"I was thanking you for being the best assistant any man could ask for," he chuckled as he kneeled in front of her.

Hands on her thighs, he pushed the pleated skirt up.

Again, she trembled, but didn't protest.

"What . . . what's gotten into you Brice," she giggled. "I've never seen you like this. And we've never done this here! I mean, you've always insisted on being discreet."

"Oh, well, I'm turning over a new leaf," Tristan replied as the fabric travelled up her thighs. "When I feel like doing something, I'm going to do it!"

His long fingers crawled playfully under the skirt.

Her thighs trembled as his thumb brushed over the sensitive mound of flesh between her legs.

"I . . . like it . . ." she whispered as he stroked.

Tiny puffs of air escaped her lips with each flick of his thumb. The scent of her sex came up and she moaned. Pulling her to her feet, he held her close as their eyes met.

"Take them off."

She obeyed as quickly as she could, being locked to his body.

Once her dainty panties were on the floor, Tristan led her to the small leather couch on the other side of his office. He took a seat, but she stood and waited for his next instruction. Karen stared down on him as his hard-on pressed against the fine wool of his pants. As her heart raced in her chest, his kept the steady pace it had when he'd fed. He smiled when he noticed the pen and pad still in her hand.

"You can put that down, if you want."

They dropped to the low table with a tiny sound as she nodded like a drone.

Tristan pushed the table away with his foot, held out his hand as she kneeled before him. "When we're done here, I'd like you to take the rest of the day," he whispered with each stroke of her mousy brown hair as she rubbed his thighs slowly.

"Why?"

"Because we're having dinner tonight and I want you to get something nice to wear, red of course. You pick a place, big booths and low lights, and I'll be there."

"But . . . why," she sighed as his hand slipped inside her blouse and squeezed her breast to tease the nipple to diamond hardness.

"We're celebrating," he replied. "You worked so hard to get me this meeting, Karen. Not only are you getting a bonus, you're getting a fantastic night on the town with me! I'd like everyone to see the talent I have and be so very jealous."

Her flushed face was warm to the touch, eyes dilated with pleasure. "You don't have to do that. You're my boss, it's what I do!"

"Oh, but I want to! You'll hurt my feelings if you don't accept."

Her hands shook as she unbuckled his pants, eased the zipper down carefully. From her expression, Tristan could tell he'd improved on Brice's attributes.

She caressed with the hands of an innocent. Scared of what she saw or just inexperienced, she fumbled in the art of seduction.

Again, he hunted his memory for his encounters with her, he found mundane sex at her little apartment.

He never kissed her. She never even got undressed when they had sex. He was a poor teacher—a failure at the simplest of lessons on how to please a woman.

Tristan took her hand in his, guided her in the dance. He adjusted her grip as he relaxed and enjoyed. When he was ready, he positioned her straddled over his lap.

Karen let out a long breath as Tristan guided her over his erection.

Hands on her hips, he moved her slowly up and down. As her wetness covered him, her breath became labored. Her eyes closed and her head rolled back as she moaned and cooed.

"Tonight, after dinner, I'll do much better," Tristan whispered. "Tonight I'll show you how to please me thus pleasing yourself, do you understand?"

She just nodded as her body shuddered and she stifled the scream he so very much wanted to hear. As her orgasm waned to a low pant and one final shudder, he lifted her from his lap and placed her gently on the cushion. When she was ready to leave, Tristan opened his office door and smiled at her.

"I'll meet you around eight," he said.

"Of course," she sighed like a school girl. "I can't wait."

He hoped he was dreaming, but when he tried to raise his head, the pain was real.

Ben rolled to one side and his stomach flipped.

On his back again, he took several deep breaths to quiet his empty stomach. Once it settled, he eased up on his elbows and opened his eyes, one at a time.

The room, dark but cool, felt like a cave more than a bedroom.

The only real pieces of furniture were the bed he was lying on and the nightstand next to it. A card table in the far corner had one ratty chair pushed under it. A large mirror sat against the wall behind it. To his right, one door, cracked enough for him to see the harsh light coming through and what looked like the end of a claw foot bathtub. To his left and slightly behind him, another door, closet probably.

When he finally noticed the breeze, he rolled his tired eyes up to see a fancy ceiling fan pushing air down from above. As good as it felt, he wanted to get up, but couldn't. He wanted to run, but his legs were heavy and his arms started to shake.

He dropped back down in the bed and groaned. Silence filled the space until he coughed and it felt like his head was going to explode.

It was hard to breathe, but he filled his lungs with air and still couldn't pick out any familiar scents. A concentrated effort to find something he could track was impossible with the headache, so he wouldn't be able to find a sound outside these four walls that would help either.

All he could smell was himself, and he was pretty ripe.

"Shit," he whispered.

The bolted and steel door that led out of the room swung open. Ben's eyes closed tightly as more harsh light stung them, so much that they began to tear up.

It slammed shut and he was afraid to open his eyes. Taking another deep breath, he recognized the scent—her scent. That girl, Sasha, stood somewhere in the dark and watched him suffer.

"Hey," her voice popped right next to his right ear. When he jumped, she giggled.

Ben tried to push her away, but when he reached out, he came back with air.

"Time to rise and shine," she chirped in the other ear with another giggle.

He kicked in the direction and missed.

The light overhead popped on and Ben moved his arm quickly over his face and screamed, "What do you want? I'm trying to get my beauty sleep!"

Sasha laughed as she pulled at his ankle this time. His body moved slowly over the bare mattress and his knees bent when they reached the end.

When he opened his eyes, she was sitting at the card table smiling.

"You're beautiful enough," Sasha smiled. "Sit up."

Ben pushed up with both hands. Once he was slumped over his own knees, he raised his head slightly and smiled back.

His stomach was doing flips like crazy now, but he had to keep whatever was trying to get out down. He wasn't going to let her see him lose it like that, even if she was probably the cause.

"Where are we?"

"Home," she replied. "Tristan's home anyway."

"And where is he by the way? I'd like to thank him for the hospitality so far."

Sasha uncrossed her legs and leaned forward to place her elbows on her knees.

"He'll be with you shortly. How do you feel?"

"Like shit, you?" he frowned.

"You should probably stop fighting it and just let it come up," she sighed.

Ben's stomach flipped again, but this time it felt like someone had just kicked him in the gut. The next one came shortly after and he locked his abs in place with all the strength he had left.

"Let what come up?" he was barely able to speak as a bitter taste formed in his dry mouth.

"Tristan gave you a little something to clean you out, so to speak. He likes his volunteers to be clean, fresh."

"I didn't volunteer for anything," Ben snapped, pushing up from the bed. He was surprised his legs held him up. But not surprised at the next kick of his now angry stomach.

"Sure you did," she replied standing up as well. She was almost as tall as he was.

Before he could say anything else, the contents of his stomach had other ideas.

The bathroom door slammed into the wall as he almost jumped through to get to the toilet.

When his mouth opened, the first wave of green pea soup shot out. As the force of the convulsions racked his body, his organs moved out of the way of whatever he was given as it raced up his throat and out into the nice white toilet bowl.

Laughing as she sat on the edge of the tub, Sasha turned on the spout and held a red washcloth under the cascade. When the cold cloth landed on his back, he thanked her before another wave of soup escaped his body.

"You're very welcome," he heard her say over the noise of his stomach as it emptied.

Chapter 34

"You're sure you don't want to go to the hospital?" Adam asked, as he sat next to her in the back of the ambulance. Her ears were still ringing, but at least he didn't sound like he was in a tunnel anymore.

"Yes," she replied. "I'm fine. How's Jason?"

"Some silver burns to his hand, but nothing that won't heal. Oren got the worst of it. When he heard you yell he pushed Jason back inside."

The anger burned as she swallowed it like a bitter pill. "How bad?"

Adam rubbed his neck as he looked down at his feet. "He's out of commission for at least a couple of weeks, maybe longer. The shrapnel was silver based, so . . ."

"I'm sorry. I didn't put it together until it was too late."

She felt Adam's hand rubbing at her back in a slow motion. He was trying to soothe her.

"It's not your fault," he said in a low easy tone. "If not for you, it could have been much worse. Oren will recover and Jason is practically unscathed."

Adam shook his head as they watched the scene in front of them. Emergency crews from the police and the bomb squad scampered around like busy bees trying to keep the scene contained.

News crews were camped out at the gate, held back by a heavy security presence. She could see paparazzi in trees and on top of cars across the street from the back wall angling for the best shot. There had to be more guards at the wall or they would have scaled it already. For now, the police were doing a good job of keeping them at a safe distance. That was a good thing. The last thing she wanted was her picture splashed all over the world looking a smoky mess. Ivy would freak out. She would have to call her as soon as she got her phone back from the techies.

"We should get you to the hotel, your team is worried about you," Adam said, helping her stand. She dropped the blanket in the back of the truck and thanked the EMT for the assistance with her wounds. After, she slipped her feet back in her heels and tried to steady herself, but wavered slightly. Adam placed his hand at the small of her back. "Careful."

"Thanks," she replied as she looked down the drive at the chaos on the other side of the gate. "I can't go through that mess down there."

"You don't have to," Adam grinned. "Follow me."

He took her dirty hand and led her around the tangled steel that used to be Jason's limo. She could smell charred metal and burnt leather. Through the gaping hole that was his massive front door, they entered the house. Everything in the blast radius had been shattered and broken. Adam maneuvered them around the crime scene techs and local LEOs to Jason's private office. She was starting to get that feeling in the pit of her stomach again.

Adam released her hand as he moved further into the room. There was a faint smell of smoke, but for the most part this room was unharmed. Behind the massive desk, he pushed at a paneled wall that she thought was just a bad décor choice on Jason's part. The hinges yawned as it opened. She could smell dampness as the air rushed into the room.

"No cameras and no mess," Adam grinned at her.

Alex moved cautiously toward him. "Is this how you get the bodies out?"

He laughed as he stepped into the dim doorway and helped her through.

The landing was made from big wooden planks, new and expertly installed. She felt like she was suspended in midair as they stood side by side. He pushed the secret door closed and she heard the latch snap back into place.

"This property used to belong to a bootlegger back in the day," he said as he took her hand to lead the way down a narrow flight of concrete steps. The stone walls were damp and looked like they would crumble if she touched them, so she held tight to Adam's hand as they descended. "He used to get the booze from his warehouse to the speakeasy through this tunnel. Jason thought it would be useful to keep this intact," he continued. He smiled at her as they reached the bottom. "Turns out, he was right."

A steel catwalk would lead them to the other

side, which had overhead, dim antique lighting. At the other end were two brand new steel doors.

She kept the space between her and Adam small. Mainly because she didn't trust the catwalk and she was having trouble focusing in the dimness because her head pounded and her body began to ache. Adam, on the other hand, moved like he knew the place like the back of his hand.

"Just a few feet more," he said. "Those doors will put us into the hotel basement."

"Great," she answered, trying to sound like she was just as comfortable here as he was.

Once they were at the steel doors, Alex heaved a sigh of relief. Adam punched a code into the electronic keypad attached to the door. It sprang open and released a breeze filled with the smell of detergent and bleach. Alex was grateful for that smell. It meant she was safe on solid ground as she stepped over the threshold. He reached for a shelf next to the exit that held a stack of facial wipes. She took them and wiped at her face and hands as they walked.

"You might want to call Ms. Rose," Adam said as he handed her his phone. "I understand she's frantic." He took the dirty wipes then dropped them on the cart in the hallway as they passed.

"Shit," Alex huffed as she dialed and her heart pounded in her ears.

It barely rang once and she heard Ivy voice blast over the speaker: "Adam Craig, you bastard, you've been ignoring my calls all night! Where's Alex?!"

"Hey," Alex giggled, "It's me, Ivy. I'm fine."

On the service elevator ride all the way to the penthouse level, Alex listened to Ivy yell at her for not calling sooner, then cry because she was so scared something really bad had happened to her. At the end of the conversation, Alex promised to call back later to explain everything. Adam took the phone she held out to him. Maybe she bought herself some time to come up with a good lie, she hoped.

The device vibrated and Adam frowned at the screen. "Jason wants to see you."

"Sure," she replied.

The doors opened onto a well-lit and expensively decorated hallway. Heavy security on the floor meant automatic weapons, sophisticated surveillance and really big guards in combat uniforms. Adam explained the entire floor had been vacated, except for Jason, Alex and the team. When they were ready, Jason would make a statement to the press. Alex was not expected to join him, but she could if she wanted. However, the statement would be a joint one and she would not be allowed to make a separate one.

"Fine, but I'd like to see the statement before he makes it," she said.

"Of course," he replied. He pulled her to a stop in front of a door just a few feet from the Executive Suite at the end of the hall. "Don't you want to freshen up first?"

She caught her reflection in the mirror on the opposite wall. Her dress was now a completely different color than it had been a few hours ago. Soot and ash streaked her arms, but she looked better than she thought she would under the circumstances. There were bright red scratches on her forearms and cheek, but they were healing. She untangled the band around her ponytail, combed her fingers through the strands and tied it back up.

"Happy?" she smirked at him through the mirror. "Let's go."

Adam shrugged and waved her toward the end of the hall.

Of course, Jason had the largest suite on the floor. A four bedroom, three-bath mini-oasis with a wall of glass overlooking the city was one hell of a place to recoup from an assassination attempt. Inside, the entire place smelled like freshness and food.

"Thank God," she heard Sebastian's voice before he sailed around a blind corner at her. He lifted her from her feet, holding her tightly against his solid body. "You okay?"

"Yeah," she huffed, trying to breathe. He placed her gently on her feet again. "Where's everybody?"

"Xavier and Erin are making dinner," he said with a nod toward the glass wall that separated them from the night and the city skyline. "He's in heaven right now."

She looked over to see Xavier, Erin and Kai as Xavier placed massive steaks on a stainless steel grill. Erin and Kai set a big glass table with candles in the middle as a place setting. When they noticed her, they all rushed inside.

After assuring them she was fine, again, they went back outside with Sebastian in tow.

"Amy and David are with Jason," Adam said. "The study is this way."

Jason's scent overtook her senses as she took a deep breath. He was just on the other side of that door and he was fine. That made her feel better for some reason. The door opened and they stepped inside to see Jason at the desk, while Amy and David sat side by side on a small couch as they looked at a computer screen.

Adam cleared his throat to get their attention.

"Damn," David croaked taking her in his arms. "You had us worried, boss."

"Yeah," Amy chimed in as she gave Alex a quick hug too. "Glad to see you in one piece."

Alex just smiled and nodded. She was tired of saying she was fine, especially when she didn't feel very fine.

Away from the desk, she could see the bandages on Jason's right hand. She could also see the scratches that matched hers on his the right side of his neck. Because he was still pale, they popped out on his skin as if lit from inside.

"Could I speak to Alex alone?" he asked. "Please."

Adam escorted them from the room, closing it softly behind him.

In his faded jeans and t-shirt, Jason Stavros,

millionaire playboy, looked like Jason Stavros, starving artist. His usually styled hair was loose and still slightly damp from a recent shower. She could smell his shampoo as he moved slowly toward her. Maybe she should have taken a shower after all.

His good hand touched her face and he frowned. When his fingertips touched her wounds, it stung just a little. "You look like hell."

Alex kicked her shoes off as she stepped into his arms and accepted his embrace. "I feel like hell, thanks," she said into his shoulder. "I'm just glad you're okay."

He held her at arm's length for what seemed like forever. Then he led her to the couch, took a knee in front of her and shook his head. The warmth of his hands eased the pain in the stiff muscles of her thighs.

"It could have been much worse, if not for you," he said lifting her feet to the table. He stepped over them and sat down next to her.

"That's what I get paid for, right?" she replied, easing her aching head to his shoulder. "Taking a bullet for the client?"

"That was no bullet," she heard him whisper.

"Bullet, bomb, same difference, right?" she giggled. "Speaking of which, where are we on finding out what the hell happened?"

"You could have been seriously hurt or worse," he said as he shrugged her head from his shoulder.

"You too."

"I wasn't."

"And neither was I."

———————————

Jason didn't have the strength to argue with her about this tonight. To see her this way just made him want to fold himself around her and keep her safe, but she didn't really need him like that, did she?

"You need a drink," he said as he crossed to the liquor cabinet next to the door. He dropped a couple of ice cubes in a short glass and poured his best whiskey over them. He placed the glass in her waiting hand, and then he sat down again.

"Thanks," she said, and took the drink like she did everything else, with confidence.

"Better?" he asked.

"Some," she answered. The cold glass against her forehead, Alex closed her eyes. "So, where are we on the bomber?"

"Why?" Jason snapped at her, jerking the glass from her hand and then dropping it on the table, surprised it didn't shatter. "The others can take care of that right now. You're done being a bodyguard for the night!"

He expected a fight, but she just stared at him with tired eyes. The kiss surprised him more than anything else. As her desire pressed against his senses, he lost his anger and replaced it with lust. Quicker than he thought, he was aroused by her lips on his, her tongue took control, her hands underneath his t-shirt.

Then she stopped and pulled back every emotion like reigning in a wild stallion.

"Sorry," she whispered.

"Don't be," he whispered back as he tried to move her closer again.

She moved from the couch and was at the door before he caught her in his grip.

"I need a shower," she said as she checked her dress with a shake of her head. "A really long one."

Jason wanted to sweep her up into arms and not let her go until he'd had his fill of all of her, but he pushed down that thought and pressed his forehead to hers.

"Not too long," he said. "Dinner's almost ready."

They emerged from the office hand in hand and Alex asked Sebastian to show her where her room was. She winked at Jason as they left the suite.

Inside the kitchen, Jason waited patiently for her to return to him. Every voice in his head told him not to be jealous of the young vampire she seemed to favor over the rest of the team. She was his and he wouldn't let a newly turned vampire best him for the affection of a woman.

Chapter 35

The news coverage unfolded before him on mute. Just the thought of hearing one more reporter call this a terrorist attack made his stomach turn. But what other choice did he have, really? None. If the real truth came out, the world as they knew it could explode into chaos.

Conner sat back on the couch in his hotel room with a fierce desire to kill someone for causing all of this commotion, but he didn't know who to blame. Aiden's contact inside the FBI kept them briefed as the investigation unfolded. Zu, his third son, had a direct line to the Mayor's office. He'd been roommates with her son in college. His connections to high-level officials, even through their children, were helpful. Because Jason was a pretty big deal in Las Vegas, the Mayor had pledged to put every law enforcement agency in the city behind the investigation. Zu could get the latest information with a phone call.

But Conner was still nervous about what had happened today. Was it a coincidence, the attempt to eliminate Jason as Conner and his family arrived in town? And why a bomb? There were much more efficient ways to kill a vampire these days. Ways that didn't leave such a mess. Of course, the human government was uncharacteristically quiet. Conner was sure they had some team of super geeks in league with Alex Stone and the Tracker team to find the guilty party. Or they were pissed the bomber failed. Jason was certainly no threat to national security. But maybe this wasn't about Jason. Maybe this was about Alex Stone. That thought created a throbbing pain behind Conner's eyes.

"You feeling alright, Con?" Aiden asked from the other side of the long dining table.

Conner gave him a nod as he put the glass of blood to his lips. "Yes. I'm just concerned about this mess."

"Well, we'll get it under control. Jason should make his statement in a couple hours; after Ms. Stone has reviewed it, of course," Aiden chuckled.

"Of course," Conner growled then took another sip. "Have Jeffrey contact Adam and let him know I'd like to have Jason and Ms. Stone for an early dinner tomorrow night, would you?"

Aiden gave him a strange grin then made the call.

She wasn't really interested in the small talk going around the table. In the open air, high above the city, they enjoyed a home cooked meal like regular people. Jason was the perfect host. His personal security team stayed inside the suite, watching them closely through the glass. Even Adam kept his distance. Alex glanced inside from time to time to see him on the phone with a serious look on his face.

"Alex," Jason cleared his throat and the conversation died down. "The team tells me you're going to L.A. Kinda sudden, isn't it?"

"Yes," she spoke up after Sebastian kicked her under the table. "This can't wait, sorry."

Jason gave her a nod, but didn't look like he believed her. "Be careful," he replied.

"We'll be with her," Kai chimed in. "Don't worry. She's safe with us, right Sebastian?"

"Absolutely," Sebastian smiled.

Jason wiped his mouth politely and looked at both of them with a hard expression. "She'd better be or it's me you'll answer to."

Kai looked insulted, but he gave Jason a nod anyway. Sebastian, on the other hand, looked to Alex like he wanted to throw Jason from the balcony.

"We understand our responsibility," Sebastian hummed with a sip from his glass. "We look after our own."

Amy stood and took her plate and Jason's with her. "Nobody said we didn't Sebastian. I think Mr. Stavros just wants to be sure we're being careful, right?"

"I think Mr. Stavros is implying we'd let something happen to her," he growled as he pushed his empty glass away.

"Oh, I'm not implying anything of the sort," Jason smiled at him. "I'm telling you, her safety comes first."

"You think we don't know that?" Sebastian

grinned with a glint in his eyes.

Jason pushed his glass away as well, then sat back in his chair with a same glint in his eyes. "I think it's too easy to get distracted by all the young flesh that inhabits every corner of that town. You won't be there to hunt, Mr. Rayne. If something happens to her on this trip, you can be sure that you'll be the hunted."

Alex placed her hand over Sebastian's on the table and his mouth closed.

"Nobody's getting hurt or hunted, Jason, so relax," she interrupted. "It's a quick trip to La-La land and that's all."

By the time she and Jason made it inside the suite again, her team was gone and Adam told them Jason's personal security would patrol for tonight. He and Jason disappeared inside the office again. She thought about trying to focus on hearing the conversation, but her head hurt so much that she decided the added pain wouldn't be worth it.

Alex eased back against the soft cushions of the plush sectional sofa and sighed. The padded back and seat molded to her body as she willed her muscles to relax. The pain pills she'd popped earlier would kick in soon. After that, it wouldn't matter what happened, she'd be too relaxed to care. Pulling a stray blanket she found on the arm of the sofa over her legs, her head dropped to the decorative pillow in no time. With some effort, she was able to dim the lights using telekinesis. It hurt like hell, but worth not having to actually stand to do it.

The tension she had felt all through dinner and the testosterone display afterward started to melt away as the drug spread through her bloodstream. The last muscle to relax was her brain. Image after image of the explosion dissolved away at her command. All around her was the blissful sound of silence. She couldn't hear the guards outside in the hall. She didn't hear Jason or Adam behind a closed door a few feet away and that was alright with her.

She hadn't even heard him come out or Adam leave until Jason's fingers stroked her hair gently. His tenderness made her forget she was angry with him for picking a fight with Sebastian earlier. He eased his thigh under the pillow that held her head so comfortably.

"You can stay here tonight if you want," he whispered, as his fingers eased through her hair.

"I just wanted to close my eyes for a few minutes," she replied as she rolled over to see him stare down at her. He brushed a stray piece of hair from her eye and kissed her softly on the lips.

"It's been two hours," he said in a low chuckle. "I've already made the statement to the press."

She sat up to yell at him for not waking her, but when she saw the concern in his eyes, she didn't have the heart. Kicking the blanket off her legs, she gripped the back of the couch to keep herself upright. She kissed him and immediately her need for him grew stronger. Once she straddled him and his hands were under the thin t-shirt she wore, what was left of her anger disappeared. His hands were so soft, but strong. She'd unzipped him before she knew it.

"Hold on," he moaned. "Not here."

He pushed them both from the couch and carried her down the hall to the master bedroom. The door slammed shut and locked, as Jason maneuvered them down into the softest bed she'd ever been in. With him between her legs, his mouth took hers again with a passion that exploded through her entire body. Like the other night, they undressed each other like horny teenagers. But, unlike their last encounter, he hesitated to take her.

"What?" she sighed, pulling his bottom lip into her mouth. "You don't want to?"

Jason pinned her hands to the mattress in an effort to slow down the pace. The more her naked body touched his and the way her mouth teased as it pecked at his throat, the harder it was to resist the need gnawing at his insides. The animal wanted to feed, now. The man wanted to claim her for his own.

"More than I should," he moaned as she tried to get him inside her. "But I want all of you this time, not just what you're willing to give me."

Positioned between her legs, Jason felt the warm liquid on the tip as he nudged at her opening. The muscles in her thighs tightened with every inch that disappeared inside her. He moved at an agonizingly slow pace—for himself and for her, as he discovered.

She moaned with each deep thrust, pulled at his waist with powerful legs because he still had her hands in his grip as she struggled to free them. As much as he wanted to, he wouldn't allow himself to rush this time. He wanted to make her beg. He wanted her to purr like a cat then scream his name for the entire building to hear.

She flipped them over so that she was on top. Then she smiled down on him with her eyes on fire with desire. "Don't move."

As she left him on the bed, she took the sheet with her to the other room. When she climbed back on top of him, he thought she was going to plant the ice pick she had in her hand into his chest. Instead she drew it across her palm with a low hiss. "Open up."

Jason pushed up on his elbows. Her gesture felt more like an insult than an offer to let him feed from her the way he wanted. Never in his history of sexual encounters had he been denied the pleasure of the bite this way. Human and vampire alike begged for his bite before, during and after sex, sometimes. But not the great and powerful Alexa Stone, no sir! Rage flared his nostrils.

"Really," he growled. "Why can't I take it the old fashioned way? You won't regret it, believe me."

He tried wrap his arm around her, pull the sheet away and tried to flip her back underneath him, but he couldn't. Her hand pressed against his chest and forced him back down. The blood, that he could smell now, seeped through her clinched fist. It dropped on his chest and crawled up his nose. His brain tingled, screamed at the intrusion, but his mouth watered for a taste. Against his will, his mouth opened wide and accepted the hot, sweet fluid with gratitude. As it coated his tongue, he swallowed her offering with a deep moan he couldn't hold back. Tiny stars exploded behind his eyes as he squeezed them closed. Wave after wave of heat and desire swept through his stomach and his muscles tightened.

The assault on his senses started immediately. As she pressed her body down over his rock hard mass, she rolled her hips, and Jason wanted to scream from pleasure. His nails sank into the tender flesh of her waist and she hissed his name.

As his incisors dropped to razor sharp points, his gums burned and itched in anticipation of more. His mouth watered as her wetness covered him below. She drew her index finger along the edge of one fang and heard the soft skin separate. As her finger slipped into his mouth, he flipped them over which put him back in control, on top, where he needed to be now.

She sucked in a deep breath as her blood filled his mouth. Thick and hot, her blood ignited a flame inside him he was not expecting. His thrusts became as urgent as he sucked at her finger like a baby. With each mouthful, her body expelled even more wetness and he ventured deeper and deeper to see just how far he could go inside her.

She moaned and he pushed and fed until Jason thought he would lose control. Lost in the act of taking his fill, he released his hold on her finger to press her hands above her head on the mattress as the pain to come reached epic portions. He couldn't remember ever feeling a desire for blood or sex like he did now. As much as he tried to hold on, he felt the need to release, to be freed.

"Now," he heard her gasp.

Alex hadn't felt a sensation like this in a long time, if ever. He was thick, hard as hell as she guided him inside once more. The mound of sensitive flesh ached as his shaft brushed over it with every stroke. She had no idea how much he filled her up until this very moment. Moving in precisely the right manner and angle, Jason's grip on her wrists and the way he fought to keep from finishing before her, sent Alex over the edge.

He released her hands to plant his on the headboard with a grunt. She took his bottom lip into her mouth as he brought them both to the top of a climax neither would soon forget. He coaxed her to come with him with his hoarse voice and throbbing cock. He plunged in deep once more, buried his face in her neck and demanded her full surrender. Their voices mixed together as they came at almost the same time. Jason's body shuddered several times after Alex had given in. As he lay helpless on top of her, she kissed his ear and he sighed.

The quiet was sweet and soft as it settled around

them. Jason rolled down into the bed, placed his head against her shoulder without a word. She could feel his manhood, expended and wet against her thigh. She always hated that, but tonight it didn't seem to bother her at all. Tonight, she had given in to a vampire's will and that didn't seem to bother her either.

Her other lovers never made her feel this way before. What she wanted from them was strength and knowledge for how to please a woman, not just a vague idea of sex. What she got were immature ramblings and premature conclusions. But Jason had proven to be the exception. How could she go back to 'am I doing it right' after having 'I can do no wrong?'

"We're still meeting with Conner for dinner tomorrow night," Jason whispered as her head lay against his. "I just remembered."

"Sure," she replied. She pulled the tangled sheet around her body as she left his side. After she gathered her stray clothes, she entered the bathroom. "I should be back in time."

Jason jumped from the bed and reached the door just as it closed, "Where are you going now?"

"Back to my room," he heard her say from the other side of the door. "I need to get some sleep."

He pushed the door open and watched her at the sink as she splashed water over her flushed face. She tossed the sheet at him as she looked at his naked body. It fell silently to his feet. He wasn't in the mood to cover himself, why should he?

"You can sleep here," he grinned. Suddenly his bandaged hand began to itch and he tried to scratch it through the thick gauze. A searing pain radiated up his arm and his head began to spin. She caught him before he lost his balance.

"Whoa," she said, helping Jason from the bathroom to the bed again. "Let me check that before you make it worse."

Jason felt the cool air against his skin as she lifted the bandage. Now it burned and throbbed at the movement of the cloth. "Ouch! That actually hurts."

Alex gave him an annoyed stare as she crossed over to the minibar against the far wall of the master suite. She returned with two bottles of fresh blood. "Drink both of these, then get some sleep. I'll see you tomorrow night."

Jason watched as she placed one bottle on the nightstand and opened the other. The sweet copper smell sailed up his nose and he was ravenous. But it didn't smell the way her blood did and somehow he knew it wouldn't taste like it either. Disappointment and anger filled him. He thought of one last taste from her to get him through the night, but she tightened the bandage around his wounded hand and pushed the fake stuff at him with a shake of her head.

"Call me when you land in L.A.," Jason yawned, finishing the first bottle. The next one in his grip, he turned it up and swallowed its entire contents in three big gulps. She tossed both empty bottles in the trash can next to the nightstand. "You didn't answer my question," he yawned big again.

As Alex tucked him into the soft bed, Jason's mind clouded. He felt as though he were suspended on a peaceful sea of Egyptian cotton sheets, giving in to the call of sleep even as he tried to fight against its pull.

"That wasn't a question," he heard her say from miles away.

Searching his brain, he couldn't remember the last thing he said either. And as the softness surrounded him, the blissful beginnings of a deep sleep began to take over.

Her suite was relatively quiet, even with six people within its three bedrooms. She checked the first bedroom as Erin pecked away on the computer at the desk, headphones snug on her head. Amy asleep in one queen sized bed and the twins softly snoring in the other.

"Everything okay?" Erin whispered as she pulled the headphones free when she noticed Alex at the door.

"Yeah, great," she replied. "Have you found anything yet?"

She frowned at the screen shaking her head. "Not yet. Still going through the traffic cam stuff." Her finger tapped at a black limo at the bottom of the screen. "That's Jason's driver. Not sure where he's headed, but I'll keep tracking him."

An endless stream of cars and people scrambled

around the screen double time: Alex in awe of how Erin could keep up with the action. There were at least twenty black limos mixed in with the traffic. How the hell could she track one car in all that mess?

"That just gives me a headache," Alex said rubbing at her temples. "Can you let them know to be ready by nine?"

"Got it," she saluted with a small grin, snapped her headphones back on, and then went back to the computer. "Oh, I did find out who that wire transfer came from." Erin handed Alex a yellow sticky note. "It's a law firm. The account belongs to that guy," she said pointing at the note.

"Brice Campbell," Alex stated. "Perfect name for an ambulance chaser, don't you think?"

She had to admit it was the first bit of good news since this whole thing started. Even if it was just a name, it was way more than they had a few days ago.

"I'll send you his full bio in about an hour. Check your tablet," Erin yawned.

"Nice work," Alex said as she stood to leave.

"Thanks, boss," Erin smiled at her, put on her headphones again and went back to work.

Making her way down the short hall, light was visible under the door of the room at the end of it. Alex knocked and opened it when she heard Xavier invite her in. He sat in the center of the bed as he cleaned a berretta in striped boxers and a white undershirt. The door to the bathroom was cracked, steam coming out and she could hear Sebastian as he sang in the shower.

"He does that," he shrugged, turned his head slightly then yelled, "Hey! Alex is here. Hurry up!"

They heard him yell he'd be right out, but the song got louder.

Alex just nodded. "Anything on the bomb yet?"

"No," he replied. "But as soon as we get the preliminary report, the twins can tell us what signature was used and who might be in the system for that."

"I'm having dinner with Gale and Jason tomorrow night," she said as she stepped inside and sat on the edge of the bed across from Xavier. "He wants to discuss the conference, mostly." He began to put his gun back together without looking at it once. "And he probably wants to make sure I didn't try to kill Jason."

Xavier smiled, placed the gun on the nightstand. "Did you?"

"No," Alex smiled back. "You?"

His laugh was hearty and full. "Well, that's two down."

When Sebastian came from the bathroom, his head was covered with a towel. His black t-shirt and black boxer briefs stretched over muscles and other things quite nicely, she noted. He sat down next to Xavier and smiled.

"What's so funny?"

They both shook their heads and he shrugged them off.

"So can we trust this guy we're going to see in L.A.?" she asked.

Xavier straightened his posture, "Pinkie? Yea, I

think so."

"You think so," Alex sighed. "We're going to L.A. on 'I think so?'"

"It's the best lead we have on who took Matt. We check it out first. If it's a solid lead, we hand it off to Lucas and the pack." Xavier replied. "That cuts down on the mess they'd make if we sent them straight to Pinkie."

Sebastian joined the conversation. "You know Lucas better than anyone, Alex. He's an Alpha-Were with a bad disposition. Someone killed his brother. You think he's gonna ask questions without breaking some bones?"

Alex yawned and stretched as she stood to go. "Fine. Get some sleep you guys. We've got a lot on our plates for tomorrow."

"See ya in the morning," she heard Sebastian say as she closed the door.

Inside her bedroom, she stripped away her clothes that smelled of Jason and sex, grabbed a quick shower and settled into the bed. It wasn't as soft as Jason's, but it was good enough for the few minutes of rest she needed to start a new day.

CHAPTER 36

It was hard to imagine Xavier ever being in this crowd. As a Zoot-suited band took the stage, Alex followed him to a deep red booth in back. The dancers filled the floor and soon guys in pork-pie hats and girls in full skirts and perfectly coiffed hair jumped and flipped to swing music.

Her day had been spent in meetings for Bite's summer launch; theirs, meeting with the L.A. office of Strategic. Funny how a program of six had become a worldwide organization seemingly overnight. She didn't expect to be invited to the meeting, but she was kind of hoping she'd at least get to see the doctor. But she was sure he was checking up on her first. Getting what he could from them before bringing her in.

"You sure he'll be here?" she yelled into Xavier's ear.

He nodded as he flashed two fingers at the pretty bartender. Her dark hair was pulled into a bun at the base of her neck. With red, red lips and a nice rack, she pulled two cold bottles from the cooler and slid them across the bar to their waitress. Peggy, the waitress, dropped them on the table and Xavier dropped a twenty on her silver tray with a wink that she returned with a bright smile.

The band finished their set and was replaced

with a digital song styling of Frank Sinatra. Glad for the break on her senses, Alex sat back and emptied the bottle before Xavier. She felt out of place all of a sudden. Xavier, however, was dressed like every other guy in sight. Fancy bowling shirt, pleated slacks, and leather oxfords on his long feet. He belonged. He didn't mention that this was a swing bar and everyone would be dressed in the fashionable attire the era was known for. In her plain black t-shirt and black jeans, Alex looked like an outsider.

Xavier tapped her when their host strolled in flanked by two muscleheads. He may have been about Alex's height, but sandwiched between two 'redwood trees' he appeared compact, small.

The straw trilby sat perfectly on his round head. His left hand was hidden inside the pocket of his baggy slacks—the cuffs lay on top of brown loafers polished to a high shine. A silver chain attached to his wallet dipped almost to his knee as it came around his left side and disappeared under his tan and brown silk shirt. Like Xavier's, it was pressed and clean beyond clean. There was a thick gold chain around his big neck and a golden cross. On his right wrist, a big golden wristwatch, its diamond encrusted face blinked in the overhead lighting.

Pinkie kissed a few heavily powdered cheeks of the women he passed. They smiled and preened for him. Shaking hands with the men escorting them, he hugged and kissed them as well. Knowing nods and winks went on through the crowd as he moved toward them.

"Pretty popular guy, huh?" Alex said.

"He owns the place," Xavier replied as he stood. He looked nervous to Alex, like he was about to meet the President or someone equally as important.

Pinkie's companions stopped at a respectable distance as he approached the booth. Xavier towered over him, but Pinkie embraced him in a bear hug that lifted Xavier from his feet. They laughed, then Xavier leaned in and whispered in Pinkie's ear, both grinning at Alex. After a proper introduction, a bottle of Dom appeared on the table.

"I always start a new relationship on a high note," Pinkie smiled at her as he poured.

"We appreciate you doing this on such short notice, Pink," Xavier said as he handed a glass to Alex then took one for himself. Pinkie raised his glass and they followed. The sound the glasses made as they came together was lost in the noise of the bar.

"Anything for you X, you know that," he replied. His glass was empty then refilled by one of the silent bodyguards before Alex had finished her small sip. "And the lovely Alex Stone, of course. You sure are keeping much better company these days, Xavier. I'm jealous."

She was sure he was trying to figure out why they were together and if it was more than just business. "We won't keep you," Alex stated pushing the glass away. "We know you're a busy man."

Pinkie grinned, blushing a little. "So let's get down to business."

He emptied his glass and smiled at them. When

he slid a slip of paper her way, she was almost afraid to look. She unfolded it slowly, like it might explode.

"Offshore bank," Pinkie continued to smile. "Caymans. Guy's not very original, is he?"

"Not very, but I've seen this name before," she turned the paper toward Xavier. He stuffed it in his pocket.

"So did I do good?" Pinkie chuckled.

"Very," she smiled brightly for him. "Thank you." Xavier tapped Pinkie's knee with the fat envelope of cash under the table. Pinkie laughed as he handed it to one of his bodyguards.

Alex slid the wrinkled piece of paper across the table. "Time for one more favor?"

Pinkie didn't touch it, just glanced down then back up at Alex and Xavier with that same grin on his face. "Tall order."

"If it's too tall, I'll understand," she replied as she balled the paper in her fist.

"That's a government hack, in case you didn't know."

"I know."

Pinkie tipped his trilby back with the rim of his glass. "That's federal time," he frowned. "If I get caught."

Alex glanced at Xavier then back at Pinkie. "Then don't get caught."

Pinkie's sudden boisterous laughter shook the entire table. "Don't get caught, she says," he chuckled. "How much time do I have?"

Alex sighed, "Not much. If you can't do it, say so

now. I have another source I can go to."

Pinkie laughed again, but not as hard. Xavier looked at Alex and shook his head. She wanted to punch Pinkie in his round face, but she didn't. "There is no other source sweetheart. If there were, I'd know about him."

She noticed the thin layer of sweat forming on his shiny forehead now. He was playing games and wasting her time. Time they didn't have right now. Back in the day, if you wanted something off the books, the list of sources was short, but sweet. Today, any clown with a gangster dream could blackmail their way to equipment deemed *Government Issue*.

"It's a big world, Pinkie," Alex smiled. "You can't know every player in this game."

"Maybe not, but you came to me for a reason," he returned her smile. "'Cuz I'm the best and the only!'"

"I came here because X said you were the man to see in this town," she replied. "But sometimes a man may not be the best choice and there are other places to look for a hacker."

His tiny ears turned red. She'd insulted him, on his own turf. Most wannabe arms dealers don't like that. Alex didn't really care.

"If you think you can get that for cheap and on the fly, give it a try girl! You'll be back though, I guarantee it!"

Helping her from the booth, Xavier shook Pinkie's hand while Alex sent a text to Sebastian to pick them up now.

Pinkie stood, reached out and took Alex by the elbow. He gave it a squeeze as he pulled her close with a wicked grin. "Where you gonna go?"

She glanced at his stubby fist around her arm. "The Mistress."

All the color drained from his face. His grin and his grip slipped away at the same time. Adjusting the hat on his head again, he stepped out of her personal space.

"Sanguinosa," he hissed crossing himself. "You ain't getting in to see her. You ain't got that kind of juice. No fucking way!"

Alex knew the Mistress was a last resort, but this guy wasn't as connected as he wanted everyone to think he was. Being in debt to the Mistress wasn't a good thing. Fortunately for Alex, it was the other way around.

"I'm gonna ask nicely, Pink," she smiled, tapping his smooth cheek softly. "Don't worry."

His nervous laugh didn't surprise her. The Mistress was legend all over the world. Some of the most powerful men on the planet occupied the pages of her black book. Politicians, athletes, movie stars, you name it. And Pinkie, though a big deal on this rung of the ladder, wouldn't get an invite to clean a bathroom in her place.

"You're gonna have to do more than just whisper sweet shit in your boyfriend's ear to get close to her," he chuckled and winked.

Alex winked back and Xavier followed her out

of the bar. Once outside, she took a deep breath as they walked quickly down the sidewalk, meeting Sebastian at the corner. Climbing into the waiting SUV, Alex took shotgun, Xavier, the back seat.

"Well," Sebastian said pulling into traffic again.

"Pinkie gave us that same guy Erin found," Xavier sighed. "But he was a dead-end on the other thing. So we're going to see someone called the Mistress, right Alex?" He hit the back of Alex's seat when Sebastian slammed the brakes.

"No way," he yelped, looking at Alex, then Xavier in the rearview rubbing his chin. "Sorry, dude."

It was going to be a long night, Alex reminded herself as she checked her hair and makeup one last time. All the extra attention was for her meeting with the Mistress, not Conner and Jason. They were just men after all. Impressing them was easy, but the Mistress was a completely different animal. She reminded the others to be ready when she returned and on their best behavior when they were at Ashblood Manor. And no weapons. That was the main rule of the house. It was a place of pleasure and business, but not war.

"Wow," Jason gushed as he opened the door and laid eyes on her. "We should meet with Conner Gale every night." She stepped inside, doing a little spin when he asked. His heart pounded strong in his chest.

Alex wanted to believe it was because she excited him in her black body-con dress and high heels, but she knew otherwise. The residual effects of her blood kept his heart beating at a regular pace. He probably just thought he'd fed well.

She stepped up to him and straightened his silver tie. Against the white dress shirt and black jacket, it popped. The small black tie tack was the crest of his house, *Vrykolakas*. It was understood, when meeting with the most powerful vampire on the planet, that you would show pride in your house. As subtle as the pin was, it was still Jason's way of proving he knew who and what he was in this world.

"There," she said. "Now you're perfect."

"Not quite," he said, holding up his bandaged hand. Taking her right hand with it, Jason placed a soft kiss on her knuckles, "But, you will be the most perfect creature in the room tonight. He won't know what hit him." He held out his arm brimming with power, power she had given him.

Alex smiled, took the arm he held out to her, and let him lead her from the room.

Jason felt the heat of his lust for her as they discussed what Conner would expect from them tonight. They needed to show a united front. Alex agreed to let him take the lead. She didn't agree to answer any personal questions about herself or be treated like a frail woman. Jason laughed.

"That's not what I'm asking," he said. "I want you to act like a leader tonight, like you want to lead this team on this assignment."

"I am," she replied.

"No, you're not," Jason countered. He turned slightly toward her. "You're acting like you're doing us a favor, like we're an irritation to you. This is important Alex, to all of us as it should be to you. Act like it."

In her eyes he saw anger then concession. Those brown orbs softened as she considered his assessment of her behavior so far. He was surprised.

"Alright," she sighed as she sat back and lowered her gaze to her hands. "I will try very hard to convince Gale I'm on board with all of this."

Jason smiled. "Thank you."

She took his good hand, the one with the insignia ring, and kissed it. "For now."

Jason's desire spiked when she was close. Maybe he was starting to chip away at that armor she always seemed to wear.

"So after we're done, how about we pick up where we left off last night?" he said keeping her hand in his.

He pulled her wrist up to his mouth and lightly kissed it until the vein popped to the surface. Running his tongue across her skin, he couldn't shake the memory of having tasted her blood. As he moved his lips to the palm, he felt hungry again. He was, most of all, very anxious to get this meeting over and get her back in his bed.

"I can't," she whispered. "I've got plans with the team, sorry."

Did he hear her right? He raised his head and dropped her hand abruptly.

"What plans?" he asked.

"I promised them a night on the town," Alex replied.

Jason wasn't sure why his temper suddenly ticked up a notch, but it did.

"Where are you going?"

Alex shrugged as she stared into his eyes. He hoped she couldn't see how angry he was getting. But suddenly, he didn't really care. How dare she deny him?

"Mind if I tag along then?" he forced a smile. "I love bar hopping."

She grinned and shook her head. "Sorry, Jason, just us tonight. I want to get them out of the hotel for a while—away from big brother. You understand, right?"

"No, not really," Jason replied as he took her hand in his.

———————————

"Jason, are you okay?" Alex asked in a calm tone. His hand was hot and trembling.

She'd hoped this wouldn't happen, but he hadn't had enough of the substitute to clean her blood from his system. And he wasn't immune to the side effects. This was her fault. She shouldn't have let him feed from her in the first place.

He shook his head, a thin sheen of sweat formed on his brow. When he released her hand, he looked confused. "I'm not sure."

Alex pulled a bottle from the small refrigerator and handed it to him. "Drink, now."

He did as he was told, emptied the entire bottle then closed his eyes. When his head landed on her shoulder, she could still feel him trembling. "Maybe some residual effects of the silver," he whispered. "Another taste from you might help," he said with a weak grin.

"No, it won't," she replied as she wiped the sweat from his brow with a tissue. "Just finish that and you'll be fine."

As he drank, she felt his pulse begin to slow down. That was a good sign. As his body cooled, the fear inside her began to die down. From what she had learned over the years, her blood held properties unlike those of regular human blood. For a vampire, a turned one anyway, it caused a spike in body temperature and also healing abilities. Jason's damaged hand would have taken much longer to heal without what he took from her last night. Now, because her blood had sped up the process, he'd almost be back to normal by morning.

"I guess I'm just stressed about tonight," he said with a slightly embarrassed grin on his handsome face. The warm color of his skin had begun to fade to pale as his body reached a normal temperature, for him anyway.

"Yeah, me too," she said as she checked his bandage again.

The skin on the top of his hand was smooth and pink, but on the mend. No longer cracked and peeling, the paleness had returned to his fingers; his nails clear and hard as steel like before.

She tightened the white gauze and gave his hand a pat when she placed it on his knee.

"Looks pretty good, huh?" he asked. There was that sparkle in his eyes again, which made her feel better. If he followed her instructions, Jason would be back to normal and her blood would be so diluted that its effect on him would be null and void.

"Just keep drinking the substitute, Jason," she said. "You're healing just fine."

CHAPTER 37

There was something very weird about being here tonight. The delicate furnishings and clean linens reminded him of a proper lady's boudoir, not the bedroom of a modern-day courtesan who happened to own the most expensive brothel in Las Vegas.

She took great care with herself, her charges and her clients. Every dream was possible here, but at a price and within reason, her reason. You'd be hard-pressed to find anyone who would ever disagree with her or her rules. And no one ever had, as far as Michael knew.

At the full-length mirror that leaned against the wall, he straightened his tie and slipped back into his jacket. Once he was dressed, he sat down in the wingback chair to slip on his shoes. He stood when the door opened and she entered the room in a red dress that wrapped around her curves. With red lips and a porcelain complexion, she smiled. Her jet black hair, parted down the middle, hung to her narrow shoulders in bouncy waves.

"I trust you enjoyed your evening," she said as she adjusted the knot in his tie.

"Yes," he answered with a soft kiss to her cheek when she was done. "And as always, Mistress, your services were impeccable."

Mistress Bianca smiled at him again, took his

arm and they left the room together.

At a leisurely pace, the two of them walked down the softly lit hallway speaking in a quiet tone. It wasn't a library, but being inside the walls of Ashblood Manor could be a learning experience, if you paid attention. Michael always paid attention when he was here. He enjoyed all of the services available to the discerning client whenever he was in Las Vegas. Sometimes sex, sometimes not. Sometimes he just wanted someone, other than his family, to talk to. Sometimes, like tonight, an exceptional massage and bath were on the menu for him. To have a beautiful woman bathe you after fantastic massage was the perfect end to a long week of bad leads and dead ends.

And Ashblood Manor always had fresh humans on hand for a cocktail that defied description. Mistress Bianca always accommodated her special guests in that respect. Her charges were healthy, willing and able to grant all requests.

"So," she continued. "How's your father?"

Michael chuckled. He'd heard the rumors. Everyone had. His father and the Mistress had been hot and heavy a little while back. She'd stopped taking other clients during that time too. No one could remember her doing that before.

"He's good, I guess. Busy with this chaos around Jason Stavros."

"Yes," she sighed. "Awful mess. Well, do tell him I asked about him, would you?"

He gave her pale hand a friendly pat. "I will."

When they reached the bottom floor, all the activity surprised him. People practically ran in and out of the main salon. With boxes of alcohol and bags of ice and trays of glasses, Michael thought it seemed like a holiday or special occasion he'd missed.

Bianca pulled him inside the room with a grin. Usually there would be men sitting around talking or glued to smartphones or tablets waiting for their escorts to claim them, but not tonight. Tonight the couches looked extra soft and fresh flowers adorned the tables all around the space. Bartenders stocked the shelves quickly. At the back of the room, a long table was set for a buffet of some sort. Then he caught the scent of fresh food in the air.

"Humans coming tonight, Mistress?" he asked.

"Yes," she replied as he offered her a barstool. "Some out of town guests and an old friend."

Michael took it all in—all the activity and preparation. "He must be pretty special. Anyone I know?"

She just smiled as she adjusted the vase of live red roses on the bar in front of her. "I don't think so."

Michael leaned on the bar next to her, his curiosity piqued. He'd never known her to make such a fuss over just anybody. This kind of attention was reserved for dignitaries, Presidents, Sheiks, those kinds of people, his father even, but not just any human with a few bucks to spend.

"Come on, Bianca," he smiled big for her. "You can tell me."

"Don't you dare try to use that sexy smile on me, Michael Gale," she purred, taking the martini that was just placed in front of her. For Michael, scotch, neat. "It's not a secret anyway. Alexa Stone and her team will be here tonight."

Michael's heart jumped in his chest for some reason. "Really? Business or pleasure?"

Mistress Bianca frowned, then emptied her glass. "If you knew Alex, you'd know business is her pleasure, unfortunately."

Michael emptied his glass as well and tapped the bar for another one. He'd read the stories online like everyone else, he was sure. Alex Stone had her pick of young humans. Athletes, musicians, artists. She was no stranger to arm candy. He never imagined her coming to Mistress Bianca for companionship though.

"She needs no help in that area," he heard her giggle. The bartender placed fresh drinks on the bar for them both. "Trust me."

"Then what kind of business would you have with someone like her?"

"Long story," she replied then sipped her drink. Her green eyes twinkled like emeralds. "Would you like to meet her?"

"No," he stated with a little laugh.

"Why not?" she asked with a bat of her long lashes. "How long has it been, Michael?"

"Long enough," he answered then emptied his glass again. "Too fragile," he said, mostly to himself.

"Them or you?" Bianca said turning his face to

her.

"Stop trying to fix me up," Michael frowned at her.

As still as a statue, Mistress Bianca blinked at Michael. The blood in his body ran cold at her expression. She was the only one who knew his secret. Bianca never told anyone about the human he'd fallen for all those years ago. About how he was ready to tell his family and marry her. His first real love died giving birth to their child. They were both laid to rest on this very property. And, in seventy five years, she'd never told anyone, as far as he knew. But she did try to set him up from time to time, mostly vampire women, but sometimes she'd throw a human at him, just to trip him up.

"Fine," she purred on his lips. "But you can't hide forever, Michael. Don't let this life pass you by. You'll regret it."

"On behalf of the Council of Pure Blood Vampires," Conner stated as he raised his glass to the loose circle they formed at the bar. "We thank you for saving Jason's life." A deep rumble of 'hear, hear' went around those assembled as the men in attendance followed Conner's lead in raising their glasses to the lone female in the group.

Alex had never known vampires to be so gracious to humans, but then again she'd never known humans to save vampires either. This really was a new game now. Conner and his sons watched her closely. The eldest son, Aiden, just sort of glared at her and Jason from his place at his father's side. She got the distinct impression that he didn't trust them.

"I'm glad I was there," she replied. "I'm just sorry Oren was injured. How is he by the way?"

All was quiet around the room at that question. They glanced at each other as if she'd just broken some unspoken rule.

"He's improving," Conner stated. "Slowly, but we're hopeful he'll make a full recovery. Thank you for asking."

"I guess he owes you one too then," Aiden added as he stared at her over the rim of his glass.

Alex couldn't tell if he was just being an ass or serious. The perpetual smirk made it hard to tell. "No one owes me anything," she replied.

Jason's arms appeared around her waist as he pulled her into his body.

"I owe you my life," he said as he placed a soft kiss on her cheek. "And I can't think of a better protector for this conference than you."

Conner's green eyes flashed an angry glance at Jason. She just couldn't tell if it was because of the kiss or the statement. As the oldest vampire in the room, Conner Gale may not feel owing a human your life was something to be proud of, but Jason didn't really seem to care.

"Yes," Conner smiled. "We're honored that you've agreed to lead the Tracker team to Romania.

Secretary Carter and I had a lengthy discussion just a few hours ago on the subject. He is expecting a full report from you and the team on your return."

Conner's expression turned serious. "This conference will bring together fifty of the most powerful in the supernatural community. The world is changing. We must change with it. Soon, we won't be able to hide in shadows. Too soon, we may be forced to come into the light."

"But why me?" Alex asked. "I'm nobody in your world. I was a hunter, remember?"

He grinned. "Yes, but somehow you gained a certain level of respect in our world. It's time to put that to good use."

"You have more power and respect than I'll ever have, Mr. Gale."

"Conner, please," he smiled.

"Conner," she replied. "How is my presence going to help you?"

"When the price was placed on Tristan's head, it was because we knew he was dangerous. We knew he wouldn't stop until he had every human on this planet living in fear of us, of him. That's not what we wanted. We wanted to coexist. We still do."

"You are completely engrained in every aspect of human society. No one even suspects creatures like you exist. So this meeting is for what, exactly?" she asked.

"To find out who agrees with our plan to stay under the radar and who may feel the way Tristan did," Conner answered.

"And how did Tristan feel?"

Conner exhaled, "That we should be the dominant species on this planet. The Council controls our numbers for a reason. Right now we can accommodate our population quite comfortably. If Tristan had his way, we'll be overpopulated in a very short amount of time, comparatively speaking. We won't let that happen. Now or ever."

Alex stepped up to the bar for a something stronger than wine. Memories of the places they had saved from hordes of greedy, ruthless vampires that fed without rules and fought over what little food was around swirled in her brain.

All those small remote places no one else cared about. People nobody missed. But when the blood frenzy spilled over into the more important parts of those countries, Night Command was called in. U.S. interests were being threatened. Allies with money that could potentially benefit the American people had to be protected.

Mexico, Africa, South America, even Australia. They were just a blur of blood and bodies now. Strategic Assets Management could go into any one of those places as a U.S. contractor and clean house virtually undetected. And they did.

"Why don't you just go after him yourselves?" she asked as she turned back to the group.

"We are," Aiden joined the conversation. "But his reach went further than we anticipated. Before he was captured, he put groups in play that no one knew about, not even Strategic. While he was on ice, literally, they were working to keep his plan alive."

"So, you need our help," Alex stated at Aiden.

"Yes," Conner answered before Aiden could bark at her. "We need your help. You studied him, tracked him. We need you to do that again."

"If I do this," she stated to Conner "No holding back information. No secrets between us and by that I mean you and me." She extended her hand to him.

Conner didn't hesitate. As his hand gripped hers, he felt Aiden's anger and heard Jason's heart race. "Then we have a deal?"

"Yea, we have a deal," Alex replied.

"Good," Conner answered. "I'm just sorry Oren will not make the trip. He was looking forward to it."

"I'd like to see him," Alex added as Conner guided them to the seating area a few feet away.

"Let's relax, shall we," Conner said as he waved Alex to the empty cushion next to him on the couch. Jason was forced to take the arm chair on one end and Aiden the one at the other as Conner made himself comfortable next to Alex. "Now, you were saying something about wanting to meet with Oren? Don't you trust us?"

Alex angled her body toward him. She'd learned a few tricks when dealing with vampires, especially the old school ones. They like directness. Try to hide or deceive and they will shut down. And since she couldn't read their minds, she had to rely on her confidence to get what she wanted from Conner Gale.

"I just want to ask a few questions about that day," she replied. "He made a stop before returning to the hotel. I'd like to know why."

The others excused themselves and left the suite.

"How do you know that?" Aiden asked.

Alex turned her attention to him and grinned. "Traffic cam footage."

"When did you get the footage?" Jason asked, suddenly very interested in the conversation.

"Last night," she answered.

"And you're just telling me," he said. "What does it show exactly?"

"He made a stop at a coffee shop. Went in, met with someone, and came out with a box," she said. "We think it was the device."

Jason became uncomfortable. He straightened his posture in the chair and straightened his very straight tie. "I don't believe he betrayed me."

"I didn't say he did, but he made the stop and picked up that package."

She should have mentioned the discovery before now, but Jason didn't hold the cards anymore, Conner did. Then she remembered seeing Oren on stage at Creed's club—that should come out soon too. But without Conner's permission, she wouldn't get in to see Oren at all. An angry wave hit Alex's brain. Jason was pissed.

"Who did he meet?" Conner asked, drawing her attention away from Jason and his anger.

"A woman," Alex answered. "Erin's still working

on cleaning up the image. Maybe asking him will save us some time."

"And if I don't give you permission to see him, question him, what then?" Conner asked in an innocent tone. He took a sip from his glass waiting patiently.

Alex swallowed hard. With an inhale, she reminded herself how the game was played. A show of defiance will get her nothing. But a show of courage and respect for his authority might just get her inside Council chambers where Oren was being kept.

"I'll keep trying to find out who wants him dead," she nodded at Jason. "I would think the Council would want us to clear this up before Romania. The only person that may be able to do that is Oren."

Conner seemed to mull it over, but Aiden was not biting.

"Bullshit," he hissed. "We saw the same footage and it was crap!"

She smiled at Aiden and his smug arrogance that glowed like a beacon.

"Yeah, I know," she sighed.

He grinned back. "Then what could you have possibly gotten from it? Even the police weren't able to make out anything really and it was their equipment."

"I didn't get it from the police," Alex answered.

"Then where it come from," Conner asked.

"Let's just say there are all kinds of people watching from above," she grinned. "You just gotta know who."

Aiden sat forward in the chair, put his glass

down on the cocktail table in front of him and frowned at her. "Government satellites? You're talking about spy satellites."

Alex laughed at him. Jason placed his elbows on the arms of his chair and his hands in a prayer pose at his lips to hide his grin. Conner crossed his legs and sipped his drink quietly.

"Well," she gave him a childish frown. "Yeah."

Aiden's devilish grin pushed slightly at the corners of his mouth. "Well, I'm impressed! Did you get the number from the phone that texted you before the explosion too?"

"No," she sighed again. "It was a burn phone, unfortunately."

"Lucky for them then, huh," Aiden did the same.

"That wasn't luck. Whoever did it wanted me to save him. They're trying to get my attention. They have it now and next time, I'm pretty sure I won't get a heads-up."

"Then you should up your game, little girl," Aiden replied, picking up his drink again. "Because next time someone will die if you don't."

Alex emptied her glass and placed it on the table. "You don't have to worry about my game, junior. No one's dying on my watch."

Jason knew how arrogant all the men in the Gale family were, but Aiden was the most of the bunch.

His appearances in the gossip rags with one beautiful mannequin after another on his arm were more irritating than his tremendous ego.

"Let's hope you're as good as you think you are," Aiden continued. "Or he's as good as dust already."

"If you think you can do better, you can take the assignment," Alex replied.

"I wouldn't want to make you look bad in front of your people," Aiden bragged. "Besides, isn't that what you're getting paid for?"

"Aiden," Conner spoke low. "Don't be rude to our guests."

"Sorry, Con," he grinned at Alex.

"Its fine," she grinned back. "What I do takes skill. I don't expect a rich man's son to be able to keep up."

"I have skills you can only dream of," Aiden growled.

"Sleeping with the Police Commissioner's daughter does not take skill," Alex replied with a frown. "I know too many people that have been there, done her."

When he stood, so did Jason.

"Enough," Conner stated. "Would you excuse us, Aiden?"

"My pleasure," he growled again and left the room.

"You have your meeting," Conner continued as he stood watching Aiden until he was out of sight. "But don't think I will let you accuse one of ours without solid evidence. Do you understand me?"

"Yes," Alex answered as she and Jason stood to shake Conner's hand.

He led Jason and Alex to the door, then the elevator in silence. As the numbers ticked off, he turned to Jason first, taking him in his embrace. Jason felt Conner's power through his entire body. When his brain connected to Jason's, it felt like a hand squeezing his grey matter like a sponge. "Be careful and don't let your guard down with her."

"Yes, sire. You can count on me," Jason's brain replied quickly. He wanted Conner out of his head. Just like that, he let go and Jason felt slightly dizzy.

Taking both Alex's hands in his, Conner kissed both her cheeks softly and smiled down on her. "It was very nice to finally meet you," he said. "I look forward to seeing you again, after you return from Romania."

She looked confused, but she nodded and stepped closer to Jason as the doors of the elevator opened. They stepped inside together. Conner waved as the doors closed.

"Damn," she sighed leaning back against the wall. "He is . . . all kinds of scary!"

"Yeah, he is," Jason agreed with a sigh of his own.

He turned to her, still looking stunned. "Why didn't you tell me about the footage?"

"Because you told me to act like this was important," she replied, eyes turned up watching the numbers tick down. "If I have to clear everything with you, then I look like I can't lead a team of sled dogs, not to mention bodyguards."

He turned forward again shoving his hands in his pockets. She was right.

The doors opened on the bottom floor and they walked through the busy casino side by side. The limo pulled up quickly.

"Well," Jason finally said to break the tormenting silence. She was thinking about something he wasn't privy to and it irritated him more than he wanted to admit.

"Well, what?" she asked without even looking at him.

"Aren't you going to tell me where you're taking your team tonight at least?"

"Just out for a little quiet fun," she said.

"There's no such thing in this town," he replied, taking her hand. Maybe if he touched her, she'd change her mind and want to stay the night with him. Maybe if he kissed her hand, her wrist, she'd stay in Vegas until they left for Romania. But as she turned her body toward him and he moved in closer, he knew none of that was going to happen.

"Ashblood Manor," she whispered.

Jason blinked. He thought he'd heard her wrong. She didn't just say Ashblood Manor. When she didn't smile or tap his chin playfully, he sat up straight, dropping her hand to the seat as if it was burning, hot silver.

"How do you know about Ashblood?" he asked,

almost afraid to hear the answer.

"That is a long story," she said, turning his face to hers.

Her kiss was soft on his lips. The gentle way she smoothed his furrowed brow with her thumb relaxed his brain almost immediately. He pulled her hand from his face and put his forehead to hers. "Be careful, please," is all he let himself say to her.

"I will, Jason," she replied with another kiss to his lips. "It's just business."

At the front door of his hotel, he gave her a grin and exited the limo. The young people she called her team greeted him, then climbed inside with her. His new bodyguards watched with him as the car pulled away. As it disappeared into Friday night traffic on the Las Vegas Strip, Jason pushed his hands inside his pockets again and strolled slowly toward the elevator with his new bodyguards behind him.

CHAPTER 38

From all the commotion at the front entrance, Michael knew the humans had arrived. As the young men entered, they were greeted by two escorts: one male, one female. Two young women entered with nervous smiles and trendy outfits. Michael found that today's twenty-somethings tried way too hard to draw attention to themselves. He was much more attracted to a woman with confidence in herself, not what she was wearing. Then she walked in.

At first, he thought everything he'd read about Alex Stone was right. She did seem arrogant. Her head held high, her walk confident. Then she smiled. Her warm, brown skin glowed under the moody lighting of the foyer. The black dress wrapped around her curves, stopping just above long legs that seemed to shine with direct light on them. Suddenly, Michael wondered what they'd feel like wrapped around him.

Easy, Mike, he thought. *She's not for you. Not that way.* He shook the thoughts of a more intimate meeting with her from his brain and moved into the shadows as they passed by him.

They were placed at a quiet table in the corner of the main dining room. The young vampire held her chair and whispered to her as he sat down next to her. She laughed and he looked pleased. As champagne and caviar were quickly placed on their table, they began to drink and talk and laugh with abandon.

He watched for about an hour. They had dinner with coffee after. They continued to laugh and enjoy each other's company. No one from Bianca's staff had approached them, other than waiters and the two escorts assigned to them for the night. If they weren't here for the real fun, then what were they doing here?

Michael took a deep breath to calm his nerves. He couldn't remember being this nervous about approaching a woman before. But this was different, wasn't it? She was work, not pleasure. When the others were led toward the Billiard Room, he straightened his tie, his posture and his focus. He could do this. No problem.

"I'll have what the lady's having," she heard him say in a rich tone, something akin to a Scotch brogue, but very much Americanized. Probably a couple of generations removed from home, this young man could go from a local accent back to his native tongue pretty easily, she figured.

Alex cut a glance at him, raised her glass, and then went back to the thoughts that kept her from being with her companions just a few feet away. Brice Campbell played into this somehow. His name had popped up twice now. That wasn't a coincidence, it was a solid lead.

On the barstool next to her, the young man

looked at her through the mirror behind the bar with a strange expression on his handsome face. It was familiar, but she really didn't have the inclination to try and figure out why. His icy blue-grey eyes sought acknowledgement of his gesture and his presence.

"Tell the Mistress I said thanks, but no thanks," she said to his reflection.

A sweet smile played at the edge of his well-formed mouth. He raised the martini glass to those lips, emptied the glass and tapped the bar for a refill. "Are you sure?"

Alex turned on the stool to face her drinking buddy as she emptied her glass as well. Crossing her legs, she was expecting him to do what most men did when faced with legs like hers. But his gaze stayed fixed on her face, his eyes clear and bright. "Yes, I'm sure."

"Well," he hummed as he took the fresh martini in long, manicured fingers. "I'm a good listener too." When the bartender placed a glass in front of Alex, he politely waited for her to pick it up.

"Once in a while chivalry rears its ugly head," Alex laughed to herself as she tapped his glass with hers. Just when she'd decided one vampire was enough right now, she trips over another in a brothel. He was much different than the pro athletes she'd hooked up with over the years. Where they were bulky muscles and not much else, he was lean, almost wiry. His polished appearance meant nothing really. He was paid to be whatever the Mistress told him to be. Groomed to please the client's every whim or request.

"Who says I need to talk?" Alex asked.

"I just thought, maybe," he replied. "Your friends don't really strike me as very good conversationalists."

"How would you know that?"

He smiled at her, chuckled. "Because they're in there and you're here alone."

"Maybe I'm not the good conversationalist. Ever thought about that?"

He gave her a thoughtful look. "I did."

"And?"

He turned on the stool, crossed his legs and brought them to a stop next to hers. Dropping his elbow on the bar, he continued to grin and drink. "And I think you have a lot on your mind. I'm just offering to listen, if you want."

Who comes to a whorehouse to talk? she thought to herself. Then again, this wasn't just any whorehouse, and they do whatever, whenever, so maybe it wasn't so farfetched. "That's okay," she replied. "I'm good."

He turned to the bartender, ordered two more drinks. Normally, she would have declined, but she found herself intrigued by this young vampire gigolo, or whatever you called a male version of a call girl. Sincere interest crept through her. Did the Mistress send him to seduce her or just listen? And what could she possibly tell him about herself that wouldn't be a breach of protocol or national security at this point?

"How about we move somewhere more comfortable and a little less public," he said, picking up both glasses with a nod toward the couch in a quiet corner of the room.

Alex didn't hesitate to follow her companion toward the dim corner. Again, he waited for her to sit. Once the drinks were safely on the low table in front of them, he unbuttoned his jacket, sat down at a comfortable angle on the couch and picked up the drinks again. Handing one to her, he stared into her eyes silently and somewhat sweetly.

"What do you expect me to say to a perfect stranger?" she asked.

"Whatever you want," he replied.

———————

So what if he actually talked to her. He wasn't told not to, right? Besides, she showed up here, not the other way around. He had tried to take the night off, in case someone missed that memo.

"I'm not sure where to start," she stated.

She let her shoes drop to the floor then curled her legs underneath her. Michael thought about doing the same, but didn't. She studied him closely as she sipped the drink. At first, she just looked him over; silently taking inventory, he guessed.

"Start anywhere you want," he answered. "I'm very interested in what you have to say."

That was the truth. He wasn't lying. But it would be easy to lie, wouldn't it? In every interaction with a human, Michael lied. He had to, didn't he? For his own safety and that of his kind.

"Are you?"

"Yes."

"Why?"

This was no place for the truth, he reminded himself. She thinks you work here. Go with it and you may find out something useful.

Michael placed his empty glass on the table, then took hers and placed it next to his. As he slipped out of his jacket, she eased back into the corner of the couch.

"I miss having conversations with people," he replied. "Talk to me, Miss . . ."

Well he hadn't expected to surprise her, but by the sound of her heartbeat, he had. It was thumping at a pretty good pace right now. Was it him or the invitation? Had no one actually talked to her before?

"Alex," she said, extending her hand to him.

Her grip was strong and warm, just like he'd expected it to be. "Michael."

Her brown eyes danced when she smiled. When he released her hand, he could still feel the warmth in his.

"How long have you been here, Michael?" she asked.

"Not long," he replied.

"And how do you like working for the Mistress?"

"It's interesting," he replied.

Her eyes narrowed as if she were seeing through his lie. Then she relaxed against the cushions again with a small grin.

"Yeah, interesting," she almost whispered. "But

why would she send you to me?"

"Who says she did?" he answered.

"You did."

"When did I say the Mistress sent me to you?"

"At the bar," she stated, then stretched her legs out in front of her and crossed one ankle over the other.

Michael figured she put the barrier between them, a way to keep him at a distance as she picked him apart. Instead of letting her have her way, he picked up her legs, moved closer and placed them in his lap.

"You assumed that," he replied. "I never said it."

She shrugged. "So why did you come over then?"

"Because I wanted to," he said as his hand slid slowly over her calf.

Her skin was smooth and soft—something she didn't appear to be. It surprised him that she let him touch her that way. But maybe that's what she expected from him. Wouldn't an employee make every effort to comfort his or her client before they got down to business? Wouldn't an employee touch, caress a client if they needed to?

"Lose a bet?" she asked, then his brain came back to her.

"No," he frowned. "Why would you say that?"

There was that childish shrug again. "First thing that popped into my head. Too many martinis, I guess."

"Then no more alcohol for you tonight," he chuckled.

She stared into his eyes and he swore he felt some presence inside his head for a second. Then it was gone when she lifted her legs to remove them from his lap. He grabbed them with one arm, holding them against his body. He wasn't sure why, but he didn't want to let her go.

"Closer," she whispered.

He did as he was told, as any good employee would do. When she was practically in his lap, he could smell her perfume and the martinis on her breath as she exhaled. His forearm rested across her knees as his hand lightly gripped her thigh. The strong muscle tightened under his grip as they stared at each other in silence. Then she surprised him.

Alex didn't know why she moved her lips inches from his, but they looked so inviting, she couldn't help herself. And she wanted to know why. Jason waited for her, would wait for her all night. This guy was paid to entice her, wasn't he? The ease at which he approached her, all polished and polite, that was his job though, right?

"Tell me the truth Michael," she whispered on his lips.

"Okay," he whispered back, then kissed her softly.

"Why did the Mistress send you to me? You're a vampire, right?"

"Yes," he answered with another soft kiss. "But she didn't send me to you, I swear."

Alex kissed him back this time, and when she

pulled at his bottom lip with her mouth he moaned. With his tie in her fist, she felt his hand slide down her thigh then pull her into his body. "Be careful, Michael, Bianca doesn't like freelancers, you know."

His body stiffened and the playful grin on his lips turned to a weird smirk as he eased away from her. He politely moved her legs from his lap and straightened his tie.

"I didn't mean to offend you, Ms. Stone," he said.

Alex folded her legs back underneath her butt and shook her head.

"You didn't, but I'm just letting you know how this game is played."

He chuckled and blushed. "Thanks."

"Relax," she laughed. "I enjoyed our talk, thanks."

Alex slid close to him again. As she slipped her feet back into her shoes, she placed a hand on his knee. "Maybe next time, we can do more than just talk," she grinned. "About me, I mean."

"Can I buy you a drink, sometime?" Michael said. "Outside this place, that is."

"I'm leaving in the morning," she replied.

"Too bad," he said as he helped her to her feet.

"I'll be back in a couple of weeks though. I don't see anything wrong with having a friendly drink."

"Sounds good," Michael smiled down at her as he held out a card with an embossed number on it. He nodded behind her as she took it. "I think the Mistress is ready for you."

As much as she wanted to, she didn't look back. As she made her way toward Mistress Bianca, she held tight to the stark white card, took a deep breath and smiled at her hostess.

CHAPTER 39

"Good to see you again, Alexa," she smiled as Alex placed a soft kiss on each of her cheeks.

As she turned, Alex followed the Mistress out the French doors that led to the gardens. When they reached a small table set for tea, Bianca waited for Alex to sit before she took her seat that faced the door.

"It appears you may have an enemy inside your organization," Mistress Bianca sighed as she poured two cups of tea with a delicate hand. The Mistress could report bad news as if reporting the weather.

"You mean traitor, don't you?" Alex said.

Mistress Bianca shook her head as she dropped one sugar cube in each dainty cup. "A traitor simply reports the news to bring about the destruction. An enemy will participate in it."

"Which one?" Alex asked. "It can't be the vampire. That would be too obviously easy to figure out."

Her laugh was quite elegant, Alex had always thought. She added a small bit of cream to her tea which Alex declined.

"You are nothing if not a keen observer of the obvious. He is not the threat, but I know I don't have to tell you to be careful around all of them."

Alex took a sip of the tea as Bianca watched. Then she did the same, only she held the pretty cup in her pale fingers instead of placing back on the saucer as Alex had.

"I haven't had to be this careful in a long time. It's pretty exhausting honestly."

"One of them is filled with rage," Bianca continued. "Like you were once. Only this rage is fueled by jealousy and hate. That's hard to reason with."

"I'm not in the mood to be reasonable," Alex answered. "Someone tried to shoot me and blow me up. Reason is in my rearview at this point."

When Mistress Bianca took Alex's hand, she felt the slight tremble. What little color she had drained away. Alex moved closer to her and look into her green eyes.

"Get out of this, Alexa," Bianca stated then released Alex's hand.

"I can't."

Her green eyes darkened to black at the answer. "Why not?"

"If I do this, if I go to this conference and track down this killer, I'm done. For good. The contract is fulfilled. I can't walk away from this now, Bianca."

Mistress Bianca straightened her posture again. She waved at the attendant at the door and he removed the tea service quickly and almost quietly. When they were alone again, Bianca lowered her gaze.

"At first I thought it was silly nonsense—Hellclaw returning to this century," she sighed with a shake of her head. "Now I'm afraid it's true."

Alex wanted to smile, to make her feel better. She wanted to Mistress Bianca's overactive imagination to be just that, her imagination.

"No one is left from that clan," Alex said. "I was there, remember?"

Mistress Bianca's eyes met hers. "Do you think I don't know about Tristan? He's been out for three years! What do you think he's been doing all this time, Alexa? Reading?"

"Three years is a long time, Mistress. If he were going to come after me, why wait?"

"Because he doesn't know it's you he's after," she shot back. "The only weapon that can kill someone as old as he is will be delivered to you in Texas in a few days," she said as she wiped her hands on the linen napkin from her lap. "Find him before he finds you, and this time, kill him!"

That was the end of the conversation as far as Mistress Bianca was concerned. She rose from her chair and left Alex alone on the patio.

Apparently his brothers had gone out without him. But Michael really wasn't in the mood for the *Brothers Gale do Vegas* anyway. He watched the television on mute. The strangeness from tonight still hung on for some reason. To see Alex Stone at Ashblood jarred him too. He expected her to be aloof and superficial, like most rich human women. Instead he was surprised at how ordinary she seemed to be. Now he tried to shake the feeling she left him with.

Stretched out on the couch, Michael let his mind drift. His father had always stressed the importance of guarding his thoughts in public settings, especially at Ashblood Manor. On the off chance there would be a telepath somewhere in the building, the secrets he kept would be safe. It would be rare to run into a telepath with the ability to read the pure, but it could happen. And tonight, he felt some sort of push at his barriers in Alex's presence. No one had mentioned her being a telepath before. Nothing in her biography suggested that ability either. So what did he feel from her?

Maybe he was just so relaxed that he had let his guard down too much. Or maybe the thoughts he heard weren't hers, but his own. Those thoughts told him to be cautious. Alex's secrets would come out eventually. They also told him that a threat existed that would challenge everything he believed about the human race. If the whispers in chambers were to be believed, the Romanian conference was only the beginning.

He shook his head and sighed. If he told his family his suspicions, they'd laugh and ask how much he had to drink tonight. Alex was human—nothing more. No way could she read minds, and even if she could, no human telepath possessed the power to read a pure blood vampire, as far as he knew.

When he heard a door open and close from above followed by light footfalls on the wooden stairs, he sat up and smiled when his father came into view.

"I thought that was you," Conner smiled back as he took a seat in the fluffy chair across from Michael. "How was your evening at Ashblood?"

"Good," Michael replied. "But you look beat, old man. What's wrong?"

"Long day," Conner answered. He crossed his legs and stared at Michael in an odd sort of way. When he raised an eyebrow at him, Michael chuckled.

"She asked after you," he said. "Hopes you're doing well."

Conner sighed. "I was more interested in Alex Stone's meeting with her, but I hope you gave her my best."

"I did, but I couldn't get close to that meeting," Michael answered. "And before you ask, Mistress Bianca didn't offer any information. She won't break her own rules about privacy, Con, not even for you."

Conner placed his hands in his lap as he continued to stare into Michael's eyes.

"She broke her rule of no business at the manor for her, didn't she?"

"Not really," Michael said matching Conner's posture. "It looked like a friendly conversation to me."

Conner appeared annoyed at that answer. Michael could tell he was suspicious of both the meeting and the Tracker team, but he couldn't prove anything right now. Maybe he shouldn't have let Conner know he had run into her there.

"And Ms. Stone," Conner picked the conversation up again. "Did she indulge herself in

Ashblood's many delights?"

Michael shook his head with an embarrassed smile. Conner looked disappointed.

"Were you expecting her to?"

"Maybe," Conner answered with a sigh. "She's too good to be true, don't you think?"

Michael stretched his arms over his head, then laced his fingers together behind it. "Maybe she is."

"What . . . too good?" Conner frowned.

"Would that be so strange?"

Conner laughed. "She's done bad things, very bad things in the name of national security," he said. "Some still whisper when they speak her name. I want to know why this fear still exists."

He'd never known his father to take this much interest in a human. Every time her name was mentioned, he bristled. Every report brought a frown to his face; every dead end, anger.

"What is it, Con?" Michael asked. "What do you want to know that hasn't been discovered? She was an active member of Night Command. She helped to bring Hellclaw down. You have to respect that."

Almost instantaneously, Conner's cool demeanor turned cold and hard. Michael could swear the temperature dropped a few degrees too.

"Where did she come from?" he growled. "Why are people so loyal to this woman? She has markers all over the country—maybe the world. Why? People who would rather go to their graves then be beholden to anyone, including me, are indebted to her. Someone like that demands attention. Someone like that shouldn't be dismissed because she's human."

Then he was calm again. Instead of pushing the subject, Michael kept quiet for a few seconds. "Maybe I can find out why," he finally said.

Conner's eyes narrowed on him. "How?"

Michael sat forward then placed his elbows on his knees. "I'm having dinner with her before they leave for Romania in a couple of weeks."

A small grin formed on Conner's lips. "How did you manage that?"

"Well," he grinned back. "We talked at the manor and I asked, so . . ."

The sound of his father's laughter eased the tension in the room. Conner mirrored Michael's posture on his chair. "She agreed to dinner with you?"

"Drinks, actually," Michael replied. "Don't sound so surprised. I do know how to talk to women, you know."

"You don't usually 'talk' at Bianca's, Michael," Conner continued to smile. "I'm surprised she didn't try to kill you or accuse me of having her followed."

Michael scratched at his head and squinted, "Yea . . . about that."

"What?"

"She thinks I work for Bianca," he replied. "At the manor."

To bring a smile to Conner's face made Michael happy. After weeks of dead ends and dead bodies, it felt good to see his father smile again.

"Just be careful," Conner said as he stood. "She won't be very happy when she finds out who you really are."

Michael rose and stepped into his father's arms. The vise-like embrace signaled his father's pride in a job well done. But at some point she would find out the truth, then he would be in real trouble.

CHAPTER 40

The hospital room was pretty much a walk-in freezer. Outside the airtight entrance was a black parka, hat, and gloves. She slipped the coat on, zipped it then pulled on the gloves and hat as the nurse placed her hand against the square bio-pad to open the door.

"Please keep this brief," she warned. "He's still very weak."

Alex nodded, stepping closer to the bed chamber. When the door closed, she heard the lock engage again to seal her in with Oren.

She could see her breath as she braced herself against the frigid cold. Glad for the thickness of the coat and hat, she would take the nurse's advice and be quick. He might not mind being a popsicle, but she did.

A whining noise that came from the floor got her attention. The big machine, flashing blue lights, pumped and cycled clean blood through his entire body. All the monitors tracked his heart rate and lung functions. They were both below human levels, which meant he was healing just fine.

As she stood next to the plastic chamber, she fixed her eyes on his face. Half of it was blistered, but healing slowly. The half that took most of the blast was missing whole chunks of skin. She could see his actual cheek bone, part of his nasal cavity and his lower jawbone clearly. It was hard to believe the sight but she couldn't turn away from it. His veins, muscles and tissue were repairing themselves with the help of the blood being pumped through his system. Her eyes moved down to the pink skin of his right shoulder. So smooth and slick, the skin blown off by the blast was growing back before her eyes. The skin on his right arm was cracked and dry from the process. Soon it would be as if nothing had ever happened.

His lower half was almost completely healed and covered by a paper thin sheet. There were patches of dry leathery skin on his stomach, but for the most part he was good.

When his fingers twitched, Alex looked at his face again.

"You'll forgive me if I don't get up," he croaked. He let out a long hard breath she assumed was an attempt at a chuckle. His lungs did a weird little dance and the beeps on the monitor freaked out too. Then he was still again.

"No problem," Alex replied. "I just have a few questions, if you're up for it."

His head nodded slowly. His eyes rolled in her direction when she stepped closer to the side of the chamber. She could see the bloodshot orbs through transparent eyelids. The lashes and brows were gone.

"You picked up a box before the explosion."

Oren's bright pink tongue darted out to lick at his cracked lips. "I got a phone call."

"From who?"

His head rolled left then right. His thin lipped mouth opened, but nothing came out.

Alex pushed her hands into the pockets of her coat and worked one from a glove, "From who?"

"Jason will kill me," Oren rasped and coughed.

"He's going to kill you anyway after he finds out you set him up," she stated.

His leathery face twisted as he rolled his eyes toward her again and hissed, "I . . . no set up!"

"Then what?"

"Ex-girlfriend."

"Yours?"

He tried to smile and the creases around his mouth opened and bled slightly. She could hear him pull in a sharp breath. "His."

She wanted to laugh, but it wasn't funny, not really. Jason kind of struck her as the kind of man who'd have psycho exes. "Name?"

His head rolled left to right again, only a little quicker. Again, his face contorted and his body shuddered at the pain.

The cold stung her skin as she pulled her ungloved hand from her pocket. Her fingers slid over the supple plastic tubing that hung over Oren's head and lead into his body. The clean human blood it carried to his heart and other organs was stopped when she pinched the tube between her thumb and index finger.

Oren's body bucked hard inside his plastic crate. He pleaded with his eyes for her to stop. She did and repeated, "Name?"

"You don't understand," he coughed. "I can't!" She stopped the flow again and he practically screamed. "Kit Blaze!!!"

CHAPTER 41

"So, we're all agreed then?" Alex asked softly as she pointed at the screen.

"She's the hooker, right?" Kai replied. "Why would she want to blow up Stavros?"

"Maybe he's a bad tipper," David laughed and the others joined in.

"We don't have time to figure it out," Sebastian replied. "We've got bigger problems, remember?"

Alex tapped the computer screen again. "He's right. If Coop's still alive, then so is Ben. His cabin may have been torched, but he wasn't in it." She looked up to see Creed headed in their direction. "Get back upstairs and make sure you're packed and ready to go. I'll see you in my room in one hour."

They passed Creed on their way out.

"Did I interrupt the Boy Scout meeting," he sneered as he sat down and gave the waitress his order: steak, rare, and runny eggs with a Bloody Mary.

"Did you find her?" Alex sneered back.

She hated to trust Creed with this, but he had the inside track in the world of paid escorts. And he'd done some work with her in the past that had turned out. According to Sebastian's contacts, Creed would throw clients her way when he was 'overbooked.' Alex shuddered at the thought, but he was their best shot to get Kit alone so that she could interrogate her.

Creed pressed his lips together, unfolded the linen napkin and placed it gently in his lap. "Not exactly," he replied as the waitress placed his drink in front of him. "But I'm close."

"Close," Alex giggled. "I'm close to dropping a dime on you and your creative bookkeeping."

"Oh, calm down. She's in the D.R. right now," Creed answered. "Some girlfriend experience for a private client. Just give me a week and I'll deliver her to you personally."

"One week," she said. "And don't tell her anything. Just make the appointment at the hotel I gave you and get lost."

"Alex, please give me some credit," he sighed. "I know how this works."

"Good," she replied as she packed her things. "I'd hate to have to refresh your memory the hard way."

"Yeah, I remember how you hate doing things the hard way," he chuckled with quick glance at her over the rim of his glass.

"Sorry I'm late," Jason said as he suddenly appeared at the table. "Meeting ran long. What'd I miss?"

Creed smiled when two plates appeared. Raw steaks and runny eggs ready to be devoured. "Not much. I was just explaining to the lovely Ms. Stone that my sources are a little reluctant to talk right now. But I'm confident I'll have something for her in a few more days."

"One week," Alex replied as she pulled the bag to her shoulder as she stood. Creed stood too as he smiled at Jason. "Don't play games with me, Mason. You won't win."

"And if I can't deliver what you want," Creed sneered down at her. "Are you going to spank me and send me to bed without supper?"

"If you don't," Alex whispered. "The next time you open your eyes you'll be on fire."

She kissed his cheek and disappeared through the doorway.

"Was it something I said?" Creed continued to grin at Jason.

"More like something you didn't," Jason replied as Creed took his seat again. "She doesn't like you very much. And I don't think I want to know why, but you need to get on the stick or I'll let her kill you."

"She won't kill me. Too much history, I'm afraid."

"Ancient history, Creed, and I wouldn't depend on anything that was said in the heat of the moment."

"She's not much of a talker," Creed smiled. "Not in the heat of the moment, that is."

Jason waved for another glass of champagne. "You would know wouldn't you?"

"I held the title until you came along."

"I'm not apologizing for taking your crown, so . . ."

"I wouldn't ask you to, Jason," he purred. "Although I was kinda getting used to being the only member in the Alex Stone Club."

Jason laughed with him and they toasted. "I don't think we'll be comparing notes."

"Then, why am I here?"

"To discuss one of your private clients," Jason replied.

Creed covered the plate with his napkin and stirred his drink watching the celery stick spin in the wake. "Which one? My calendar's pretty full right now, so you're gonna have to narrow that down for me." He adjusted his cufflinks then closed his mind as he felt Jason try to enter it like Alex had done a few nights ago and failed.

"Ms. Rose," Jason hummed.

"What about her?" Creed smiled.

"My sources say she's been on your calendar for quite some time now. Did you know about her connection to Alex before or after you decided to make her a private client?"

"After," Creed replied.

"And what does she know about your relationship with Alex?"

Creed stared at the glass next to his hand. "Nothing."

"You're lying."

"Then why ask?" Creed sneered at him. "So what if I knew about her connection to Alex before, why do you care?"

"Because I know you two are up to something," Jason growled then licked his lips. "And when I find out what that is, I'll ask again. Next time you should consider telling the truth or I'll let Alex ask the questions. We'll see if she can do it without drawing blood."

"This may be your town, for now, but things may change soon," Creed replied as he stood. "Be careful of the threats you make, Jason. They may come back to bite you."

Jason pushed the plate away and smiled at Creed. "I'll keep that in mind," he said as he stood, arms wide open.

When Creed stood he felt every muscle in Jason's body as they embraced—Jason's anger wrapping around him like bandages. They'd been friends, once, good friends. Jason's rise up the ranks required him to make different friends in different circles. Unless Creed decided to change his line of business, Jason had to keep his distance. But when he needed a favor that required Creed's abilities, he always called. He paid well, so Creed ignored the lack of respect he was shown in the interim. Until now.

"Make sure you're on the right side, Creed," Jason sighed in his ear. "Once the shooting starts, friend or not, if you betray us, I'll pull your heart out myself!"

Jason smoothed his tie as he backed away with a smile.

Creed sat back down and ordered another drink. This playing both sides against the middle was hard work. He smiled to himself as the thoughts of watching Tristan burn down the current regime played out in his head.

Chapter 42

Creed could hear the screams as he rolled up the driveway.

He'd never been able to hear from this far away before, but now he could hear everything, everywhere. Whatever this guy dosed them with, it was fantastic.

He rang the doorbell and waited for the tiny footfalls to reach him.

"Good evening, Mr. Creed," she smiled and bowed as he entered. "He's been waiting for you."

Creed followed the small woman down a long hall and she opened the door with another bow. It closed behind him and he heard her shuffle away as he descended the basement stairs.

Dark and dank, Sasha stood over a man tied to a steel chair in the center of the space. A small table in one corner and a bucket filled with water in the other, he rounded a worktable to see his new Sire sitting on a stool, drink in hand as he watched the show.

"Nice of you to join us," he said, still focused on the action in front of him.

"Sorry," Creed bowed, "I had another meeting."

"Mr. Stavros," he chuckled, "What did he want?"

Creed pulled a stool next to him and sat down. "Nothing really."

"It must have been important or you wouldn't

have been late."

"He knows about Ivy," Creed replied.

"So," Tristan chuckled. "Why would he care about a client of yours?"

Creed turned his attention back to Sasha with a shake of his head. "She's Alex Stone's partner, for one. If he gets too suspicious, he'll tell Alex and then we're all in trouble."

Tristan turned his head toward Creed. "Then you make sure he doesn't, Mason. I don't want her to know about Ms. Rose until it's necessary, do you understand me?"

Creed gave him a quick nod as Sasha landed a solid right cross to Ben's jaw. The sound of air as it left his lungs filled Creed's ears, and the smell of his blood filled the room. Then Ben spit on the floor with a laugh.

His face was all bruises and cuts because Sasha could hit him faster than he could heal.

And the sweet smell pushed the oxygen out of the space. Not that they needed much, but a little would have been better than the awful smell of melting candy.

"Tristan," Creed cleared his throat as it tingled. "Maybe we should pace ourselves. Give him time to heal and he might be more forthcoming with the information you need."

Tristan stood and his shadow covered Creed in cool darkness. His smile filled him with more darkness and fear.

"He can't take this forever," Tristan laughed. "Sasha doesn't tire, not easily anyway."

"I'm sure, but letting her turn his face to hamburger isn't really going to help either," Creed sighed.

"He's right," the voice echoed around them. Behind every tap of the cane was a muted grunt of pain as he took the stairs one at a time. Ben's senses may have been scrambled by the drugs and his missing more than one round of the supplement, but he could still smell Coop's awful cologne from a mile away.

Coop, with the dark wooden stick in hand, descended the stairs slowly. At the bottom, he hung it on the rail and stepped in front of Sasha before she could land another blow.

He bent at the waist, picked up Ben's head and wiped away the blood and sweat.

"Are you hungry? Thirsty?"

Ben's eyes fluttered open and he laughed again.

"I should have known. What'd you give up first, me or your soul?"

Coop laughed as he held the bottle to Ben's lips. He took two short sips and jerked his head out of Coop's grip. He spit on the floor again and winked at Sasha.

"Come on, Benny," he smiled and took the stool Sasha brought to him. "You don't wanna go out like this. If they don't kill you, Tristan's gonna let Sasha keep you as a pet! Just tell 'em."

Ben shook his head and could have sworn his brain moved.

"I've got nothing to say to you or them."

"You got a name. Just spit it out and you'll be back in your own bed when your eyes open again," Coop stated.

"They burned my bed! They burned my house," Ben growled.

"Oh, sorry," Coop replied with a chuckle. "But still, you'll get to live."

Ben dropped his head back and laughed.

"As what, a lap dog? No thanks."

Coop moved closer, leaned in and sighed.

"I can talk to Tristan, ask him to make you one of us."

"Ben the Bloodsucker," he laughed. "That does have a nice ring to it, but I'm gonna have to pass."

"If you don't give it up, they'll go after her," Coop hissed back. "You want that? Matt found out the hard way that staying loyal to her only gets you dead."

Ben pulled at the handcuffs, but he didn't have the strength to break them anymore.

"You miserable piece of shit. You're dead! If the Pack doesn't get you first, I'm gonna hand her your head!"

Coop stood tall and put his free hand in his pocket. Pushing the stool back, he stretched.

Although his body still ached from the process, he knew in a few hours he wouldn't feel it anymore. And after his first kill, he wouldn't feel human pain ever again.

"Don't be a hero, Colonel."

"Go ahead," Ben continued to laugh. "I dare

you to go after her." Coop turned and headed for the stairs again. "After she's done wiping the floor with these guys, she's gonna kill you slow! I'm gonna help," he yelled at Coop's back.

Coop turned and he saw Ben recoil at the sight.

The sharp teeth cut through his virgin gums for the first time. His vision changed almost as quickly as everything else.

Ben's strong, steady heartbeat and the sound of his blood as it rushed through his veins excited Coop. The heat of his body felt like being in a sauna.

"She's going to be my first," Coop growled. "And I'm gonna let you watch me bleed her dry! After I make her one of us, she's gonna devour you, Ben, at my command, her new Sire!"

Ben mustered a loud howl and tears fell from his puffy eyes. The salt stung as they rolled down his cheeks.

"You're a joke to them, Coop! You didn't have what it took to be one of us. You were a glorified errand boy for Dr. Carlisle! You played fetch for the program until they ran out of better recruits! You got lucky getting assigned to that team. My team! Tristan wants the identity of the Dagger, you idiot, not you!"

Sasha caught Coop before he slashed through Ben's neck with razor sharp nails.

Ben just laughed as she practically carried Coop upstairs and didn't stop until the roaring stopped and the door slammed shut.

Creed smiled down on him. Ben smiled back.

"You're really smarter than you look, Colonel,"

he said as he adjusted his cuffs.

"Too bad Coop's not, but I'm guessing that was what you were hoping for," Ben replied.

"Yes and we weren't disappointed."

"You didn't really think he could deliver the Dagger to you, did you?"

"No," Creed shook his head. "We wanted him to lead us to you and he did."

Ben tried to move away, but the syringe pricked his upper arm anyway.

Tristan's wavy image appeared next to Creed and the sound of the cuffs falling to the floor reached his ears as two men pulled him to his feet.

"One of you will tell us what the humans are hiding," Tristan said in a voice distorted by the drugs. "If I have to violate her in front of you to get that information, I will and I will enjoy it! What I won't enjoy is putting her and you to death. That weapon belongs to me for the pain and suffering I was subjected to over the last twenty years. Give me what I want and you'll live. Deny me, and a long, painful existence awaits you both!"

"Do you always talk like some cheesy comic book villain?" Ben coughed and laughed.

Tristan laughed with him as his hand locked around Ben's neck, cutting off his air. "I don't think you've quite grasped your situation, Colonel Palmer," he smiled as Ben's eyes closed. "But you will."

Ben felt weightless as cool fresh air hit his face and entered his lungs.

Back in his room, the air felt stale and heavy. They tossed him on the bed and left.

In the dark, he could hear voices all around him.

The first shot of pain came to his wrist, the other his neck, and the last, inside his right thigh. Their low moans left vibrations in the air as they fed from him like wild animals. He couldn't move and soon he was glad for the blackness when it came.

Tristan had memorized the stolen data over the three years he'd been free. This Dagger person was a born hybrid! Dr. Carlisle's experiments yielded a creature far superior to the soldiers of Night Command and later the Tracker program. The Dagger not only had strength almost equal to a born vampire, but was the catalyst for the supplements they still used today. There was no mention of a physical description of this person, but Jesse Cooper assured him Colonel Palmer and the woman, Alex Stone, knew the identity. If he was right, he'd be rewarded. If he was wrong, Tristan would drain him dry.

For their part in his captivity, both Benjamin and Alex would be subjected to some experiments too. Tristan's imagination could be very horrific and he was ready to try out some of those musings on human subjects. As for the Dagger: a weapon of that magnitude would come in handy when his war against the Council began. Once they were brought to their knees, the humans would fall easily.

CHAPTER 43

Sebastian held the door as Jason's people rolled their luggage outside. Everyone else waited for Alex to appear from her room. When she did, Kai took her suitcase and placed it on one of the carts. The silver case, the one she got from Lucas a few days ago, stayed with her.

"You guys follow the bags to the airport," Alex said to the twins, Erin, and Amy. "I need to talk with Xavier and Sebastian."

They did as they were told, but she could feel their collective suspicion. A strong vibe of fear came from Amy. After Alex had explained to her that part of her training would be done with the Warrens, she was understandably afraid.

"Did I do something wrong?" Amy sighed. "I can train harder. I mean, Sebastian has been working with me on my fighting stuff."

Alex stepped up to her, place her hand on her narrow shoulders. "You didn't do anything wrong. It's just that we may need your magic, so I just thought that maybe you'd like to learn from the best."

Amy's eyes lit up at that. If she was any kind of practitioner of magic, then she knew about Esmeralda and Morgan Warren. And everyone wanted to learn from the best, right?

"I do," she gushed. "I'm just sorta nervous. I've never been away from the team before."

"You'll be safe, I promise. Besides, you have a real gift. You have to learn to control it so you can use it whenever you need it. Esmeralda can teach you that."

She reluctantly agreed, but the entire team was afraid to let her go on her own. Alex remembered how it felt to be separated from her team too. But that had been different, hadn't it? She wasn't going away to learn some new skill, she was in a hospital suffering from a mental collapse and no one from her team had come to visit her there.

Once the others were on their way, Alex placed the silver case on the low coffee table and sat down on the floor. Xavier and Sebastian sat on the couch in front of her and the case. Slowly, her pulse obeyed her command to ease its rapid pace. She opened the case, took out a vial filled with a ruby red substance and a pure silver dagger. As soon as Sebastian saw the weapon, smelled the silver, he recoiled slightly. Instinctually, just the smell warned almost every vampire to beware. Although it would not kill them, silver and anything containing even trace amounts of it, could weaken a vampire. Alex knew silver poisoning would feel like a severe bout of flu. Nausea, vomiting, joint pain, headaches of migraine levels. She wouldn't wish that on anyone really, so when he pushed back from the table with a shiver, she understood completely.

"Relax," Alex said as she placed the dagger on the floor next to her. She closed the case and placed it on the other side of her. "I may have a way to find out what happened to Matt, maybe who attacked the compound. I'm not sure what will happen really, but . . ."

Xavier sat forward, narrowed his eyes as he stared at the glass vial with the black rubber cap. "Is that blood?"

"Yes," she replied. "Matt's blood."

Sebastian matched Xavier's posture and took a deep breath. Werewolf blood didn't exactly have a pleasing scent. That's how vampires could tell the difference between humans and Weres in a crowd. The sharpness of its scent was matched only by the pungent taste. A Werewolf diet consisted mostly of meat, and lots of it. So the smell had a strong animal odor and Sebastian found he didn't like it at all. Again, he pulled back and frowned.

"What are you going to do with it?" he asked.

Alex had stood and crossed to the bar. She came back with a bottle of Jack and three shot glasses. "I'm going to drink it," she announced.

"Whoa," Xavier squealed. "You can't drink blood straight like that Alex. It could kill you."

As she poured the whiskey, she grinned. "It goes in the whiskey."

It was Sebastian who picked up the vial, opened it and growled. Suddenly, the memory of the other night came back. Alex had been the cause of his collapse, not bad blood. His fangs dropped immediately at the thought. He placed the cap back on the tube and stared at her.

"You did that to me," he glared.

"Did what?" Xavier asked as he grabbed Sebastian's arm to keep him from jumping over the table at Alex. "What's going on?"

"What are you?" Sebastian growled. "Tell the truth or I'll do my best to rip you to shreds!"

She was calm when she took the shot of whiskey then poured herself another. Her hand came out and both Sebastian and Xavier jumped when the vial was pulled out of his fingers and floated to Alex.

Alex wrapped her fingers around the vial. If she couldn't trust them, who could she trust? They were the strongest of them all, natural leaders. And there really was only one way to find out if they were with her or against her—truth.

"I'm showing you this because I want you to trust me," she said in a low voice. After she twisted the cap off, she poured a small bit into the whiskey. Then the liquid began to move on its own. The alcohol turned a deep brown color as it mixed with the blood.

"What are you?" Xavier whispered fixed on the swirling liquid.

"Dhampire," Sebastian hissed before Alex could answer. His teeth retracted as he sat back against the cushions. Alex could see the relief wash over him as he did. "I thought those were just dumb stories—the offspring of a vampire and a human—fairy tales."

"Well," she grinned at him. "We used to think the same thing about vampires and stuff, but . . ."

"How?" Xavier continued to whisper. "Who . . . where . . . I . . ."

Alex waved his gaping mouth closed. "I'll explain it all later, but right now, I need to do this. I just need you guys to sit and watch. It might get a little messy, but don't let me leave this room and don't let me hurt you."

"Wait," Sebastian gasped before the glass reached her lips. "What's gonna happen? I mean are you going to turn into a Were or something? You're stronger than the both of us. What are we supposed to do if that happens?"

"Oh yeah," she grinned. She stood and disappeared inside the bedroom again. Returning with a gun, she handed it to Sebastian. "It's a tranquilizer gun. Just don't miss."

"So you are gonna turn," Xavier said, eyes wide with fear and amazement.

"No, but I'm going to experience whatever he did, so I might try to bolt."

"Oh," they said in unison.

"Alright boys, "Alex smiled as she raised the glass again. "Let's light this candle shall we?" She laughed, downed the shot, and then placed the glass on the table again.

———————————

At first she just sat there, staring at them and

then the ceiling. To Sebastian she looked like she needed to pee or something. Then she shrugged. Just as she began to reach for the bottle again, a thin stream of blood eased from her nose. The drops hit her white t-shirt and Sebastian could smell her blood mixed with whiskey and werewolf blood.

"Are you okay?" he asked.

Her mouth opened then closed as her face contorted and she doubled over with a weak moan. Both Sebastian and Xavier jumped to their feet. Her hand shot up, and they stopped in their tracks. Her eyes were solid black—no white at all. "Don't touch me," she said, her voice gravelly and not really hers anymore.

Sebastian wanted to help her, but he had no idea what to do. Maybe some vampires could do this, glean past events from a taste of a victim's blood, but she wasn't a vampire. Correction, she wasn't completely vampire. So maybe she could. He knew from the stories that if she had these abilities, psychokinesis, the ability to move objects with her mind and blood connection, her vampire parent could do the same.

Music suddenly filled the room. Sebastian and Xavier were startled as all the electronics in the entire suite came to life. Alex screamed as she slammed her foot down on the coffee table so hard it split into two even pieces. Then she spoke again.

"They came to the compound in combat gear," she croaked. "Masked and fully prepared."

Xavier cautiously knelt beside her, Sebastian stood behind her, ready to grab her if she made a move for him. "What else? Can you see Matt?"

"Yes," she whimpered like a dog. "He's fighting them, but there's too many!"

She fell on her back and screamed again. The music grew louder and Sebastian hoped no one would call the front desk. When the balcony doors blew open, a fierce wind filled the room. Papers and magazines scattered everywhere as Alex writhed in pain. Sebastian eased down on his knees near her head. As he reached for her, her eyes opened wide, still black as coal, and she shook her head at him with an expression that froze his blood. Then as if being lifted by invisible strings, her body rose from the floor. Xavier and Sebastian watched from their knees as she hovered in mid-air above them. Arms stretched away from her body, scratches appeared on her forearms, bright red with blood.

"Alex," Sebastian whispered. "Can you hear me?"

She was suspended in mid-air as the mysterious wind whipped her hair around her head.

"Alex! Can you hear me?" he screamed this time.

"So much pain," she moaned. "So much pain! They just kept hitting and hitting until he passed out. They killed everyone. Then they killed him!"

"Who? Who killed him," Xavier prodded. "Tell us who killed Matt!"

"I can't see," she whined as her body slowly descended again. When she was on the floor, the noise stopped abruptly, she rolled to her side and began to cry. "I couldn't see. The blood's too old now."

Sebastian helped her to her knees. Her head

bowed, they waited for the tears to stop before they asked if she needed anything.

"Hand me that trash can over there, please," she whispered.

Xavier slid it to her hand. For a few minutes, she just sat there, head bowed, face hidden by her tangled hair. Then her entire face covered the trash can. Sebastian held her hair as the whiskey and blood exited her body.

CHAPTER 44

It's true what they say about Vegas. What happened here over the last few days would stay here. No one talked much on the ride to the airport. Erin and David were glued to their laptops scanning evidence. Kai went over a composite diagram of the device from the box. If he could find something unique, maybe they could track down the architect. Amy had a special assignment. She was to learn two spells before she arrived at the Warren School in Salem later tonight.

Alex stared out the window, watching the traffic whiz by in silence. From the back of the SUV, the outside world looked tame. But she had always known that it wasn't. There was always something that waited in the dark and she thought she could feel it, even now.

Sebastian tapped her foot with his, "You okay?"

Alex gave him a nod, but she was far from okay. She wanted to believe both Ben and Coop were still alive, but probably not. If she appeared to worry, the team would worry and no one would be focused on the assignment. And if Jason died on this trip, so would they.

Sebastian put his magazine down between them. He stretched his arm over the back of her seat and leaned in close, "Talk to me."

"I'm just tired," she replied. "I've got a lot of work to do before Romania."

He exhaled long and hard, "But you have us now. And we are here every step of the way."

Xavier looked at her through the rearview, "Yeah. Where you go, we follow."

"We're a team. Your team," David added from the passenger seat.

Kai followed, "And we're the best there is!"

She leaned forward, "If we have any hope of getting through this in one piece, we have to stay focused. Amy will get her magic under control with the Warrens. When she's ready, they'll send her back. When the twins are done on the campaign stop with their Mother, we'll start our own planning. I have to teach you things you may not be ready to learn. I have to teach you to kill. That's not easy. I have to teach you to make people believe you will kill without hesitation, and that's even harder. You have to be ready to follow through when you have no other choice."

Erin cleared her throat, "What about Ben. Are we forgetting about him?"

"No," Alex replied. "But all of this is connected, I know it. We just have to figure out how. We do that, then we'll find Ben and Coop."

Just outside the departure gate, a group from TSA waited for them. Security was pretty accommodating for the world's most famous bodyguards. Alex appreciated not being stuck in line just to get through to their gates. They were immediately escorted to a private lounge, owned by Jason of course. Their bags were checked in front of them, then they were led to the lounge by a woman wearing the uniform of Jason's casino, along with two others in TSA uniforms.

Their escort made the walk to the lounge feel like an Epcot tour.

"To your right, FAO Schwarz. To your left are restrooms and courtesy phones. But the lounge has both and they're much nicer," she whispered that last part, then giggled.

They came upon a large space under renovation. The signs in both empty display windows read "Coming Soon." They could hear construction noise through the heavy plastic that hung in place of doors. Alex thought it was strange for this time of night, but then again, it was Vegas.

"This space is own by Mr. Wynn," their tour guide continued. "We've got a pool going as to what it might be."

Finally, the private lounge. The woman waved a key card over the electronic pad. A bright green light popped on and the pad buzzed. She pushed the door and allowed them to enter. Before saying her good-byes, she handed the card to Alex. It was the only card and if someone needed to leave the safety of this place, Jason thought it would be better to let Alex make the call. She waved again and left the lounge.

Inside the private space, Alex let out a long exhale. The entire room had a slightly musky smell.

Oversized furnishings covered in warm, rich earth tones gave it a homey feel. Sebastian bumped her as he passed by on his way to a fluffy armchair in the far corner. "Not bad, huh?"

"Perfect," Alex said, mostly to herself.

Erin and David settled at the round table, close to the outlets and the mini bar. Kai dropped his duffle next to one of the two large sofas, stretched out and asked not to be disturbed unless the airport caught fire or his flight was called, whichever came first. With Beats in place, he stuffed one of the pillows under his head, yawned and closed his eyes. Xavier and Amy settled on the floor in front of Sebastian. The three of them chatted quietly.

Alex settled on the small loveseat by the exit. If anyone wanted to leave, they'd have to go through her. Same with anyone who tried to gain entrance without a key card. Her laptop poised on her knees, right where it should be, and she got right to work. Her plan? To find a way to protect a vampire with celebrity status and find out what the hell was going on before anyone else died.

An hour later, their escort appeared again. This time to make sure Erin boarded her plane safely. She was headed to Atlanta for an early Thanksgiving with her parents. With the assignment so close to the holiday, they couldn't be sure they'd be home in time, so Erin asked if she could go home. Holidays were a big deal for her family and she didn't want to miss it.

"You sure this is okay, Alex?" she asked last

night. "I can tell my parents I'll have to miss it this year."

The look on her face told Alex she really didn't want to do that. And she saw no reason why she couldn't go home for a few days. She and Amy didn't really need to train like the guys did. They would be more in the background, as Alex discovered they always had been. No hand to hand and almost no weapons training for either of them. From the background information, both Erin and Amy participated in missions as tactical support. Which meant they didn't usually go into any dangerous situations at all.

Erin's biography stated that she was a genius, IQ almost 200. After graduating from high school at thirteen, she entered Yale on a full scholarship, though her commercial architect father and Fortune 500 CEO mother could afford any college in the world.

Computers were her forte. When Strategic went completely high tech, she was recruited to make sure all its information stayed safe and classified. Alex wasn't sure what all the techno babble about building firewalls and encryptions that were practically unbreakable actually meant, but if she knew her father, this girl was valuable, which made her important to him. He liked valuable things. Alex was valuable once.

As for Amy, she came from fairly comfortable surroundings as well. Her father was a doctor, pediatrics. Her mother, a housewife. She was not a genius, she graduated high school but no college. What she brought to Strategic was magic. Literal magic. How

414

she got started or discovered was sketchy. Alex's father had brought her in less than a year ago. There was no mention of why he wanted her in the program so badly, but she was here.

Their faces and biographies had sat on Alex's screen for so long, she got lost in their faces. Young, attractive, smart, strong—the team ran the gambit. When her father added a vampire into the mix of humans, he'd been criticized at first. It took two years for the DOD to agree to let him in. Probationary was stamped across the cover page of Sebastian's bio. He'd been probationary for a year and she wondered why.

It surprised her that the twins were brought into the program at all. Their mother was a U.S. Senator for God's sake. Why would she allow her children to be a part of something like this anyway? Then she read the part of the report where Senator Yun sat on the oversight committee that had held the purse strings in the beginning. When they were bought out to save a few million dollars a year on defense, the twins stayed with the program against her wishes.

Then there was Xavier. Xavier was on the fast track in the LAPD believe it or not. He was injured in the line of duty his first collar on the streets. Torn ACL would keep him out of SWAT and that was all he had ever wanted, according to an interview included in his biography. So it was pretty easy to see why he joined the program. That ACL thing was gone once the supplements kicked in. No surgery, no drugs, other than the supplement, and no pain, ever again.

Alex sat back and let the information embed itself in her brain. She may have to call on this information in a pinch in the near future. It had to be committed to memory now. She stretched and yawned. When she glanced at the screen, it was black. No activity for a while, Alex hadn't noticed that she hadn't touched the computer for quite some time.

"What's on your mind?" she heard Xavier ask as he stood, bent back slightly with a groan. "You zoned out there."

"Yeah," Alex shrugged. "I guess I did. Just tired I guess."

"Well," Amy said as she hopped to her feet," I'm gonna go to the toy store before my flight's called. My niece loves *Frozen*." She swung her purse over her shoulder, "Anyone wanna come with?"

Male mumbles rolled around the space. Heads shook quickly without making eye contact. Then she turned in Alex's direction. "Alex?"

The look on her face was too pathetic for Alex to say no. She slid her laptop back in her pack as she stood. The others stifled laughter as Alex followed Amy out the door. When she stuck her head back in, she frowned at the group. "I hate y'all and you owe me," she whispered. "Big time!"

She heard them howl with laughter as the door closed.

"Hey," Amy called from a short distance away. "You comin' or not?"

"I wish not," Alex mumbled as she walked toward her and the toy store.

"No fucking way," Kai laughed. "You can't fly!"

"I didn't say I could," Sebastian replied. "I said levitate."

"Whatever," he frowned. "You can't do that either."

Sebastian stood, pushed him to the side and kicked off his Vans. "Alex says I probably can."

"She may be right," David said and joined them in the center of the room. "If your sire could do it, you might have inherited that ability through her blood." He scratched at his chin as he circled Sebastian slowly.

Xavier stretched out on the couch to watch. "What are you doing," he chuckled. "Looking for wires?"

"Try it," David said as he waved Xavier off. "Focus on lifting your body off the floor."

Xavier joined the others in the center of room. Sebastian hoped it was to help them catch him if he fell, but he was pretty sure it was to laugh when he did. He closed his eyes, then pushed out a hard breath. Not that he needed the air in his lungs, but kept some there, just in case sometimes.

With the thought of lifting his own body from the floor, Sebastian raised his arms for some reason. He opened his eyes to see his friends as they stared with bored expressions.

"Dude," Kai huffed. "I swear if you start flapping your arms, I'm gonna shoot you."

"Shut up," Sebastian huffed back. "Gimme a second."

David pushed his brother back. "Remember what it feels like to float on water?" Sebastian nodded. "Same thing, only you're floating on air. Relax your body, think weightless."

They all stepped back and Sebastian tried to imagine being weightless. What it felt like to float on the water after a long day of surfing. At first, he didn't feel anything. Then, a slight tingle ran up his spine. His eyes popped open to see his friends, their eyes wide as they stared at the floor then back up at him.

"Holy shit," Sebastian whispered to the group. "You see this! I'm floating!"

"Can you go higher?" Xavier whispered too.

Before he could will his body up, he dropped to the floor again. "Dammit!"

"Sweet," Kai chirped. "Do it again!"

"Alright," he smiled big. "Gimme some room boys."

He rolled his head right to left, closed his eyes and wished. But no tingle. The more he thought about it, the more lightheaded he became. His eyes opened and his friends sighed.

"Oh well," David said with a pat to his shoulder. "It was a nice try. You need more practice."

Sebastian felt good about his first try at levitation. He'd be sure to tell Alex and Amy when they returned, maybe rest and try it again when they got back. Suddenly, he realized how long they'd been gone.

She'd left Amy on the stuffed animal aisle to explore this place on her own. It would give her time to think without Amy's constant, "What about this one?" every five seconds.

As she browsed through what they called vintage toys, Alex couldn't remember ever having played with a toy. Her first memory of any sort of game was poker. Ben taught her when she first arrived at 51. He said it would be a way for her to fit in with the team—build trust.

"I mean, you're a girl and these guys are kinda skeptical about this whole setup," he'd said as he shuffled the deck. "If they could just get to know you over a friendly game of Hold 'em, then you're in."

"What's that got to do with my skills," she replied.

"If you cheat at poker," Ben frowned. "You can't be trusted with anything."

Alex laughed at that memory. He looked so serious. But he was right in his own dumb-ass way. She was a quick study and won after a few hands. So every free night they had, the card game moved from room to room. And the more they respected her card game, the more they respected her.

An anxious feeling moved through her out of nowhere—that feeling of being watched. Heading back to where she'd left Amy, Alex scanned every row. At the end of an aisle filled with movie characters, she saw Amy. A young woman, about her age, tugged at her arm with a frantic look on her ruddy face. Clearly, something was wrong.

Her cheeks flushed red as tears rolled down them, her olive skin slick with them, but Alex didn't get the feeling those tears were from fear. Amy followed the young woman toward the front of the store, with Alex trailing after them.

When she reached the main concourse, Alex saw the young woman take Amy's hand as she pointed down the tiled path that led back to the lounge.

"I just turned my back for a second," the young woman, who had told Amy her name was Sasha, cried.

"Maybe she just got turned around in the store," Amy offered, as she tried to keep her calm. "What makes you think she came out here?"

She didn't want to spook Sasha any more than she already was, but Amy felt a twinge of fear about what could happen to a little girl alone in a big place like this. She'd seen the horrible news items every time a child went missing. The poor mother, frantic and guilt-ridden, pleaded at the camera for her child's safe return. She didn't want that for this mother, or any, for that matter.

"I told her not to move," Sasha sniffed, then wiped her nose on her already damp sleeve. "She's only six!"

Amy let her lead them closer to the space that was under construction. Maybe her daughter had wandered in there by mistake, she'd said. As they passed through the heavy plastic sheets that hung in place of real doors, the young woman stopped her tears and began to laugh.

"Everybody's a sucker for a lost kid," she continued to laugh.

"I don't understand," Amy replied. But when Sasha smiled, long white fangs descended. Her laugher bounced off the sheetrock walls. Her pink tongue slid across those sharp teeth as she smiled at Amy.

"Well," she pouted with devilish grin. "I'm hungry and you're gonna die. That clear enough for ya?"

Out of fear, Amy tried to focus her power on the danger in front of her. Instead of sending Sasha into the air and running, the big green trash bin behind her shot out its contents like a cannon. Soda cans and assorted trash rained down around the bin and Amy felt her heart sink with disappointment.

Sasha laughed, shaking her head as she approached. "You need more practice, witch! Too bad you won't get the chance to visit Eastwick for those lessons."

No matter how hard Amy tried, her target laughed as everything around them exploded in a fury of debris. Pretty soon she had nowhere to go.

The dusty sheetrock wall Amy found herself pinned to wouldn't budge. She pulled at the cold hard hand that wrapped around her neck to no avail. When her feet left the floor, all hope left her body. She really was going to die, wasn't she?

Good news. She could still breathe. Bad news. She couldn't scream for help. Amy figured that was the point, right? Keep her alive while she fed. From everything she'd learned, mostly from Sebastian, the victim should be alive in order to benefit from the taking of blood.

Human blood contained all kinds of tasty vitamins and minerals that did a vampire body good. And when adrenaline was thrown into the mix, Sebastian said that concoction was like no other drug he'd ever taken when he was human. In that moment, Amy wondered what her fear would taste like.

The low rumble of noise drew Alex to the construction area. She eased between the plastic sheets and tried not to trip on anything as her eyes adjusted to the dim lighting.

From where she stood, she could see Amy try and fail to zap her assailant successfully. She could smell Amy's fear and her attacker's desire mixed in the air. That triggered an excitement in her she hadn't let out in a long time. A clean kill was coming and she wanted it. Of course, she'd save Amy's life in the process, but the kill called her name now and she'd answer that call with pleasure.

On her approach, Alex picked up a stray piece

of rebar. It had a sharp edge at one end so she flipped it over in her hand, held it like a spear. The soon to be dust vampire kept up an irritating laugh at Amy's failed efforts to get away. Not that it would have really hurt to be zapped, but it may have given Amy a chance to run, had she hit her mark at all.

"What are you grinning at?" Alex heard the girl growl. "You're about to die!"

Amy winked at her, or maybe that was meant for Alex. The she eeked out a meek retort, "So are you."

Amy thought she was seeing things. Just a trick of her brain because she had very little oxygen available to hold on to reality and her breath too. And she wasn't even aware of the smile on her face until Vampira mentioned it. She relaxed her grip just enough for Amy to reply.

The smug look on her face disappeared as Sasha turned her head and Alex's fist rearranged it slightly. Amy's feet hit the ground as she coughed and gasped for air. Sasha was doing the same, slumped against the wall. Blood poured from her busted nose, much to Amy's delight.

Alex jerked her forward, then pushed her behind her back toward the exit. "Go!"

"But," Amy stumbled back as Alex slapped the key card in her hand.

"NOW!"

Alex barely got that order out before she was

blindsided by another vampire, fangs bared as they tumbled across the trash strewn around them. All Amy glimpsed over her shoulder as she ran was tangled bodies.

Almost taking out the cleaning cart in her path, Amy ran at top speed or what passed as top speed in a pair of Doc Martens anyway. She slid to a stop at the door, practically tore out her pocket for the key card and forced the door open when the lock beeped. Sebastian was three feet in the air when she entered the room with the others cheering him to go higher.

"Alex! Trouble," Amy puffed and waved her hands at them.

Sebastian's focus disappeared as a mental picture of Alex being killed popped into his head. He fell like a stone only to be saved from a face-plant by Kai and Xavier.

"What?" David grunted as he tried to stop her from leaving the room.

Amy took a deep breath, jerked free and ran as she let out a loud, "Come on! We've got trouble!"

Sebastian forced his feet back into his shoes and brought up the rear. He saw Amy and then the others jump through the plastic covers over the doorway of the empty space. When he reached the entrance, he could smell ash, lots of ash and blood.

Alex was faced off with a giant. Way bigger than her, or any of them for that matter. All shoulders and back muscles, she dodged his punches and landed a few kicks to his massive chest with no real effect. He laughed and spit in her direction.

There were three men and a young woman watching the show. The young woman seemed the most engaged in the action.

"Kick her ass, Jolly," she yelled with hunger in her voice. "That bitch broke my nose!"

"And she killed two of our brothers, Sasha," Jolly barked back.

"Yea, I did," Alex baited him. "And you're next, Jollytime!"

The group laughed as Jolly growled at her again. When Kai kicked a glass bottle, all the action stopped. All eyes moved in the direction of the sound.

"You started without us?" David chuckled in their direction.

"Well there's plenty more," Alex replied, then took a back hand to the face from Jolly. It spun her into the wall with a thud. She shook her head like a dog to steady her brain. "Take your pick, please!"

Xavier cracked his knuckles as he stepped forward. The first thing Sebastian noticed about the vampire was his shockingly blonde hair. Against the dark chocolate of his skin, it was practically white. He flared his nostrils, then spit on the floor. Xavier smiled.

"Well, I guess I get you Billy Idol," he said. "Nice tan by the way."

"Ello, was that a joke?" he smiled at Xavier.

His cockney accent was thick and boorish.

However, his roundhouse was powerful and quick and sent Xavier through two partial walls in the distance.

Kai took one step in Xavier's direction, but found it blocked by a creature the size of a chubby little kid. He did a little jig and a cartwheel then clapped his stubby hands together like a wind-up toy. Sebastian felt a tingle crawl up his spine at the sound of the trollish man's high-pitched giggle.

Kai laughed as he looked down on his opponent. "Really, dude? You're like three feet tall!"

The troll laughed again, only the tone had dropped to a deep timber. "Don't let my height fool ya, boy!" From across the space, he smiled at Kai, raised his tiny hand and a flash of blue light shot out, then lifted Kai off his feet and into the side of a metal bin with a loud bang.

As Amy raced to his aid, David took a right hook from the most normal looking of the bunch. His nerdy demeanor enhanced by the horn-rimmed glasses he wore. There was no evil smile, no witty reply. One punch after another landed where he threw them and David was on his ass before long.

Sebastian realized he would get the girl fairly quickly, and not in a good way.

"Well," she giggled as she pulled her long stringy hair into a ponytail. "I get the traitor! How fun!"

That insult stung him deep. He'd never been called a traitor before. Then again, he'd never faced off against his own kind either. You couldn't count the turf wars he'd participated in when he was still working for his sire. That was expected and for a good cause. Taking up with humans against your own was not expected or appreciated.

"I'm not a traitor," he sniffed at her.

"You work with these filthy humans, fight by their side against your own! That makes you a traitor in my book!"

Her long leg shot out before he knew it. It felt like being hit by an iron post; it rattled his teeth and sent him to his back, hard. He rolled over in one smooth move and was on his feet. Because she was already hurt, he'd have to use that to his advantage if he wanted to win this fight.

His first punch landed squarely on her nose. Blood splashed down the front of her shirt and mixed with the dust on the floor. It turned a rosy color with the consistency of clay as it dried at their feet. She howled in pain mixed with laughter. A roundhouse sent her head over heels across the floor. One side of her face was powdered with the rose colored dust. Before she could recover, Sebastian grabbed her by the messy ponytail at the base of her long neck.

He swung her into the side of the metal bin and kept bouncing her head off it until she passed out. That side of her face was a bloody mess of dust and green paint flecks. Unfortunately, she wouldn't be out long. Once her body started to repair itself, she'd come back with everything she had.

Alex felt her teeth rattle when he threw her into the wall. Her body left an impression in the sheetrock as she landed on her feet, then rolled to her left right before Jolly's foot drilled through the sheetrock and got stuck there instead of her stomach.

As he struggled to free his leg, Alex forced her elbow into his spine. A low pop and he collapsed like a rag doll. The spine would mend in a few minutes, but that was all she needed to finish him off. She rolled across the floor, taking out a glass bottle in the process, and grabbed a piece of two-by-four. When she tried to stand, her right leg buckled under her weight. On her way down, she threw the makeshift stake as hard as she could at Jolly. As he began to rise, the stake entered his back and part of it came out of his chest. She knew she'd hit his heart when his flesh began to crack and glow orange as the tiny cinders burned him from the inside out. His body disintegrated to ash after a couple of seconds.

Her leg was on fire with pain. She tightened her grip around her thigh as Xavier brought down his opponent by using a shovel as a sword. Billy's head separated from his body, rolled over to where Alex sat and glowed orange then turned to grey ash as well. His body did the same. She dropped back on her elbow as Xavier stomped through the mess to help her.

"Here, let me," he said as he removed his belt and wrapped it around her thigh. "You ready?" She nodded and before she was done, he'd ripped the shard of glass from her leg.

"Thanks," she grunted, taking his hand and letting him drag her to her feet again.

"You good?" he asked.

"I'll live," she tried to smile, but she knew it looked like a grimace instead.

Xavier took her under the arm, then helped her toward Sebastian and the young woman lying on the floor. He looked up with a satisfied look on his face. "She'll be awake soon. What do you want to do with her?"

The three of them stood over the body as it twitched and jerked to repair itself. The flash of blue lightening and the sound of odd words in some language Alex had never heard before turned them away from the unconscious young woman for now. Xavier stayed with the girl as Alex and Sebastian went toward the blue light.

To both their surprise, Amy held the troll at bay with a magical force field. His fireballs bounced off one by one as he cursed. Kai, David and Amy were safe behind the sheet of energy, but Alex could see she couldn't hold it for long. A thin stream of blood slid from her nose, over her red lips and down her chin. She was about to lose the battle and they'd all be deep fried together.

Alex reached down, plucked an unopened can of bright white paint from the ground. She steadied herself on her good leg and flung it like a bowling ball. It struck the troll in the back of his bald, round head, which sent the fireball way off its flight path. He landed on his face with a witchy scream of pain. Amy dropped the field of light and Kai caught her before she did the same.

"Nice shot," Sebastian laughed.

Taking a weak Amy from Kai, he and David headed for the troll.

"Leave him," Alex stated. "He's nothing. The girl was leading these idiots. David, call Jason and tell him we need some help down here, now."

Chapter 45

"Like hell this isn't my concern," Alex snapped at Adam. "They tried to kill us!"

They stood outside the private lounge a few steps from the door that was now guarded by two of Jason's best, according to Adam anyway. The prisoner was being readied for transport somewhere Alex couldn't follow.

After the EMT patched up her leg, which was just a scratch by the time they arrived, she and the team were kicked out of the lounge when the interrogation of the young woman they had captured began. Over Adam's shoulder, she could see her team as they sat against the wall like children at the Principal's office door. Their bags on a cart next to them.

"We'll take it from here," Adam replied.

He was so relaxed and smug it drove Alex crazy. She'd never seen him without a suit this whole weekend. Now he looked like they'd pulled him off the golf course. Pristine grey polo shirt and black pants with black leather shoes to match. If it hadn't been for the fact that it was nighttime, she would have thought he'd just finished a round and probably won.

"I want to be there too," she continued. "I want to know where she came from, who she works for."

"And we'll let you know as soon as we find out,"

his hissed down on her. "But you are expected back in Texas. If you deviate from the plan, whoever hired her will get suspicious. Jason's jet is waiting. Get on it. I do agree, delivering the others to their final destinations is a good idea, though."

She wanted to slap that condescending grin off his thousand-year-old face. Another quick glance at the team and Sebastian stood, followed by Xavier. She shook them off and turned her attention to Adam again.

"Where are you taking her?" Alex asked.

"Don't worry," Adam answered with a pat to her shoulder. "She'll tell us what she knows."

"And if she doesn't?"

"She will. I've been doing this a lot longer than you, child! Run along. Let the professional handle this one." His smartphone buzzed in his pocket. He threw his finger up when she opened her mouth. She wasn't sure what she was going to yell at him, but all she could think to say brought a smile to his face as he looked at the screen.

"Bite me, Adam," Alex growled.

"The Secret Service will meet the twins in San Francisco," Adam went on as if she hadn't said a word. "The Senator insisted."

"Great," she said.

"I understand Mr. Rayne and Mr. Ramos have insisted on returning to Texas with you," he sighed with bored look on his chiseled face. His phone buzzed again. "Ms. Sinclair is safe, I just received confirmation."

Alex opened her mouth, but he'd already walked away. He spoke to the guards at the door in a hushed tone. Her head hurt too bad to try to hear the conversation. They both nodded as they all looked in her direction.

Adam said his good-byes to the team then stepped in Alex's personal space.

"Don't do anything stupid. They have very specific instructions," he grinned. "And the next time you make an offer like that to a vampire as old as I am, be prepared to follow through."

He nodded and walked away with two more guards in tow.

Jason's leg shook because the ride to where the young woman would be interrogated seemed to be taking forever. He checked his phone every few seconds even though he would have felt it vibrate and hear it ring if Alex called. Why hadn't she called?

Adam ordered him to go to the safe house instead of the airport. He felt Jason's presence there would muddy the water too much. He didn't think Jason could exert enough power over her to tell her she couldn't be involved in the interrogation. Like he didn't have the strength to tell her no or that she wouldn't listen anyway. The very thought made his blood boil, but he did as he was told.

His hand began to itch again and he absently scratched at the bandage. As if defying his effort to stifle the irritating itch, it began to throb.

"Screw this," he hissed.

Snatching at the tape, Jason unwrapped his hand expecting to find torn red flesh and blood. But, what he saw took his shallow breath away. His skin was intact and perfect. After only a few days too. He'd never healed from silver burns that fast before. Only once had he had a silver burn and it had taken at least two weeks to heal and it hadn't even been as bad as this one.

He turned his hand over and back again with amazement in his eyes. With his hand close to his face, he sniffed it, examined it with the same results. It was completely healed. No trace of silver on his skin.

"What the hell?" he asked out loud.

She was glad for the silence of a private ride back home, compliments of Jason Stavros. All around her, the team slept. As she scrolled through the messages on her phone absently, she thought about Jason for the first time tonight. Where was he? Why wasn't he there to take her side? Too busy with other business, Adam announced when he arrived without him.

Adam was on her list of vampires she'd like to kill now. Back to her messages, she saw that Ivy would pick her up at the airport. *Won't she be surprised when Sebastian and Xavier get off the plane too?* She smiled at that thought. The photos were ready to be reviewed. And Leland Ramsey had called. That made her stomach turn.

"Leland Ramsey, please," she sighed into the receiver. "It's Alex Stone, returning his call."

The most awful hold music blared through the tiny speaker as she waited. Whatever he wanted, Alex hoped it would be quick. He probably wanted to bust her chops for saving Jason's life. Or maybe he wanted to gloat about forcing her to take this job in the first place.

"Alex," his voice oozed condescension. "I was beginning to worry."

"Why?"

He laughed, then dropped the timbre of his voice slightly. She took that to mean he wasn't alone. Good. This would be a quick conversation then. "I heard about the attack," he sighed. "Mr. Craig was kind enough to call."

"I'm sure he was," she replied. "Is that why you called?"

She heard him clear his throat. "Of course. I just wanted to be sure you were in one piece. And to remind you of your mission."

"I don't need you to remind me of my mission. I know what I need to do. Anything else?"

Alex felt the plane rumble; turbulence. She felt a gradual ascension and then the pilot came on to report a storm just ahead. They were going above it, but it might be a little bumpy. Salem had just received snow, so she wasn't surprised they'd run into some weather on their way back to Texas. The guys didn't wake at the announcement. She buckled up.

"When you return, we'll talk more," Leland replied. "Have a safe trip."

He was gone before she could respond. A sharp pain sliced though her head. And a sick feeling overtook her body. She reached into her bag and pulled out the pain pills she always kept for these types of headaches. They came more frequently now—just like trouble.

Once she was eased back in the leather seat and felt the pills kick in, Alex lost the desire to worry about what was coming next. All she really knew for sure was that she wouldn't be alone. How much she trusted her new team was irrelevant. What she wanted most was peace. And even if it was just for now, on this flight home, she would have it.

ABOUT THE AUTHOR

Being an introvert doesn't mean you have no voice. It just means you have the ability to communicate in different ways. For author and champion introvert, Janice Jones, that way is writing. She began by reading anything she could get her hands on, but after college, she found herself in roles that required more business-focused writing than fiction. This didn't stop her—she continued to create her own stories to feed her passion for the written word.

Honing her skills as a paralegal for several years, Janice continued to feed the beast by spending every spare minute she could creating the world of her first fictional character, Alexa Stone. The idea for In Her Blood came during a rough time in Janice's life. Overcoming loss can be tough for anyone, and for Janice, writing helped her focus and heal. As a tribute to her late sister, she had the opportunity to release a short story entitled "Dancing on a Sunday Afternoon" in 2009. Receiving positive feedback, she continued to write and focus on improving every way she could. Earning a Master's in Creative Writing from Southern New Hampshire University, Janice was encouraged to finish the *Dagger Chronicles* series.

ACKNOWLEDGEMENTS

Mom and Dad, thank you doesn't feel big enough, but I'm saying it anyway. Bo, I couldn't be prouder of everything you've accomplished and I can't imagine not having you in my life. Madison, you are filled with a joy that is infectious—don't ever change. Myles, my movie buddy, I see your Mother in you and I know you will do great things. Nickolas, keep drawing kid, one day we'll do a comic book together. And, Serena. How do I thank you for never letting me fall? To the biggest and best family ever, I feel the love! And finally, to the most amazing friends anyone could ask for and Kayla R., Dayna and the Amberjack Publishing Team: "Y'ALL ROCK!"

CPSIA information can be obtained
at www.ICGtesting.com
Printed in the USA
LVOW01s1059130416
483361LV00001B/1/P